THE AGE OF THE AVIATOR

JAMES CRAWFORD

ISBN 978-1-4116-9809-3

To my two grandfathers,
NORMAN TOPSHE & J. H. CRAWFORD,
whose idea of heaven was
"the rush of the wind against the goggles,
the roar of the engine in the open air."

The Age of the Aviator

CONTENTS

CHAPTER 1

The Boy from Woodvale

IN ORDER TO STAY in the place that he loved, Dr. Milton Harrison had years ago given up any hope of becoming wealthy. Most people in his part of rural Georgia had no money to give him, so they instead bartered whatever they had in their possession in exchange for his medical attention: food, livestock, cookware, tools, and even jewelry. Some were unable to do even that. They were the ones who ran up large debts to him and promised to pay him back whenever they could—which, of course, would be never.

It was always a pleasant surprise whenever a patient offered him some stray cash from under a mattress or some coins from a Mason jar in a hidden corner of the pantry. At such times the doctor felt compelled to do two things: one, to hold the money up to the light of the nearest window to make sure it wasn't counterfeit; and, two, to look forward to that glorious future time when he would finally accumulate enough of such currency to buy something valuable and finally decide what it would be.

That time came at the end of 1908, when Henry Ford's company began selling Model T's for $825. No one in his village yet owned an automobile, but Dr. Harrison felt his children would benefit from having one now. His two daughters, Kate, aged 16, and Ellen, aged 20, needed to be introduced to eligible bachelors in distant places. And his son, 12-year-old Raymond Milton Jr., needed to start going with him on house calls to learn about the harsh realities of disease and sickness in the world. Milton Sr. was worried that young Milt's boundless imagination was getting the better of him. The doctor had endured enough of poverty and frustration after his own childhood habit of daydreaming to know that it wasn't a likely precedent for happiness in life.

The first time Dr. Harrison or his son ever saw an automobile in person was when they met the Atlanta train at the Toccoa depot in April of 1909, and several railroad workers maneuvered their newly-purchased 1200-pound buggy down a wooden ramp off of one of the rear railcars.

"Need any help getting this home, sir," one of the men asked Dr.

Harrison after the Model T had been put to rest in the gravel by the tracks. "Ever drive a motorcar before?"

"Never in my life. Have you?"

"No, sir, I haven't."

"Don't worry about it, gentlemen," the doctor's son proudly announced. "*I* can drive it!"

"You can do *what?*" asked one of the men.

"Drive it. I've read about flivvers in newspapers. Anybody can run one."

"You gotta be kidding me, boy. No way your daddy'd let you wreck this fancy piece of machinery. Ain't that right, Doc?"

Dr. Harrison wished his son would keep quiet and not embarrass him during this otherwise special occasion.

"Oh, of course I know better than that," he scoffed. "It's all a matter of common sense."

"Show us how it's done, Doc," said another man. "Just get on in and drive away while we stay here and watch. She's gassed up already."

Milton Sr. tipped his gray cap at all the railroad workers and went to position himself in the driver's seat of the Model T while the men looked on with close interest. His son seated himself on the passenger side.

"Daddy, what are you doin'?" Milt asked him under his breath once he had shut the door of the car.

"What do you *think* I'm doin', boy?" snapped his father. "I'm gittin' ready to drive us home in our new automobile!"

"First you gotta turn the crank in the front."

"Oh, of course," said Milton Sr. "I forgot all about that."

“Be careful,” said the boy, “or it'll snap your arm off. There's a lever on the steering column to control the spark. I'll adjust it for you.”

The doctor left his seat and went to crank the lever in front of the chassis of the Model T. Having been forewarned by his son about the dangers of getting his arm broken by the spinning crank, he turned it very tentatively at first, and not until his fifth try did the Tin Lizzie fire up.

"Wonderful sound, isn't it, boys?" Dr. Harrison said to the men who were watching his every move. He pulled a clean white handkerchief from the breast pocket of his coat and wiped the perspiration off his forehead with it before returning to the driver's seat. His son remained unimpressed. He exuded skepticism like sweat as he sat with crossed arms in the right seat of the Model T.

"Milt," said the doctor, "I know I'm 52 years of age, but I haven't outlived my usefulness. Your daddy might be gittin' a little old, but he's not dead yet. Remember that, now. Just when you start to count a fellow out, that's the time when he usually jumps up and surprises you."

Milton Sr. experimented for awhile with the three floor pedals and the throttle on the steering column. Once or twice the boy might have sworn before the Lord Almighty that his papa was trying to make the flivver go forward and it wasn't going anywhere, but he had learned his lesson—at least for the time being. His moral duty at this moment was to try to keep his mouth shut in order to respect his elder. Maybe now was the time when his father would finally jump up and surprise him.

Just then there was a sudden movement. The Model T bolted forward and surged down the railroad embankment into a ditch, where it stalled by a newly sprouted green field of oats. Two nights earlier there had been a torrential downpour, and the rear wheels of the flivver plowed into several inches of soft wet mud. Dr. Harrison was hurled from his seat and landed in his son's lap.

"Daddy," said the irritated youth, "please get off. You're heavy."

The railroad men rushed in a group over to the edge of the embankment.

"Y'all all right?" one of them called out.

Milt rolled down his window and yelled: "We're really in a mess now! I don't know how we'll ever get this thing out of the mud!"

Red-faced and doused with perspiration, Milton Sr. removed himself from the car and went to examine its rear wheels. They were embedded in the slick muck nearly up to the rims of their tires. His son quickly leaped out to join him in evaluating their difficult predicament.

"What a hell of a note," said the doctor. "A brand new automobile, and we're stuck in the worst damn quagmire I ever saw in my life."

"It wouldn't have happened if I'd been driving," Milt said defiantly.

Dr. Harrison looked as though he wanted to belt the boy with a horsewhip, but he held back. What bothered him more than anything was that he was afraid his son was probably right.

"Since you seem to know all the answers," he told the young braggart, "I'll let you take over. You get that thing up and running, boy, and you'll make a true believer out of me."

The doctor took off his cap and coat and went to sit leisurely in the shade of a nearby tree.

"You couldn't have made it any tougher on me, could you, Daddy?"

"Dammit!" he swore at his boy, "quit sassing me back and get moving. *You* drive it, then!"

The 12-year-old bit his lip and thought for awhile about what his next move should be. He knew he needed to get the tires out of the mud in some way and put something under them to give them traction. When he saw all the railroad men looking down on him from the embankment he was struck with an idea.

He went to get a coal shovel off of one of the stationary railcars and then pulled a two-by-four wooden board from a stack of lumber which had just been unloaded. As the railroad workers and his skeptical father continued watching him, young Milt proceeded to open the trunk of the Model T and pulled out the tire-changing jack. He placed the wooden board underneath the car just in front of the left rear tire and mounted the jack on top of it. Now the jack would stay above the mud while it hoisted the weight of the Tin Lizzie. He turned the lever of the jack several times until the adjacent tire had been lifted out of the muck.

"Here's where the shovel comes in, gentlemen," he explained to his audience.

Milton Jr. took the shovel over to the railroad bed and filled it with loose gravel, which he returned to disperse strategically under the car's elevated wheel. After two more shovelfuls of gravel, he lowered the jack, moved the board to the opposite side and jacked up the right wheel. Underneath it, too, he put several shovelfuls of gravel before he lowered the jack again and placed it back in the trunk.

"See what I'm onto, fellas?" he asked all the adult men. "It's the only possible way to get an automobile out of the mud—unless you've got some horses or another car to tow it out with a chain."

He hopped into the driver's seat while all the spectators, foremost among them his father, grew nervous. Could the kid really pull this off?

"Daddy, crank ‘er started again up front, then get behind and push with all your might while I twirl the wheels."

The doctor did as his son instructed, and like a seasoned mechanic the 12-year-old boy put the vehicle in gear, spun the wheels around until they vaulted the Model T out of the ditch and maneuvered the throttle on the steering column so that the car was idle.

"Come on, Daddy! Let's take 'er home!"

The mechanical prodigy gestured for his father to get into the car on the passenger side, which he did. Gently the new toy rolled across the farmer's field and onto the dirt carriage road beyond it. The spectators at the depot applauded in amazement while Dr. Harrison and his son, turning around to wave at them, sputtered away.

"Well, boy," said the doctor, "now you've done it! You've made your daddy a true-blue believer! Of course you made me look like a damn fool to those guys, too, but something tells me that won't be the last time you ever turn one of your doubters into a fool."

Half an hour later, the muddy road had led them past the wooden sign that the railroad company had put up in 1893 to identify their little settlement to the rest of creation. It said: WOODVALE POP. 187.

FOR SEVERAL DAYS AFTER the doctor brought home the Model T, he and his family had little rest. At all wakeful hours a passerby was apt to knock on the door of 125 Oak Street and ask for a demonstration of the modern miracle. Dr. Harrison started telling everyone that his son would be available to demonstrate it on the following Sunday afternoon after services at the First Baptist Church of Woodvale. It dawned on him that he was unfortunately obligating himself to attend those services for the first time in years, but by then it was too late to change his plan. Every member of the congregation was now expecting Dr. Harrison to be uncustomarily present this Sunday, and he knew Reverend Andrew Gray would make some mention of his absence in his sermon if he failed to come.

Rev. Gray, the only man in Woodvale who might be called prosperous, never failed to give his listeners what they wanted to hear. Tall, silver-haired, fat, with steely blue eyes that scoured his congregation hawk-like for any stray nappers, he had a booming voice that could rattle the windows of the church house if he brought it to its highest volume. That Sunday he was in vintage form.

"It's the will of Our Lord that Woodvale should move forward into the modern age!" he thundered. "Why, I understand our doctor's invited us all to ride in his brand new Model T with him this very afternoon! That's typical of him to share all that he has with us, and expect nothing in return."

All 187 living Woodvaleans clustered around Oak Street later that day to watch Milton Jr. drive his father back and forth, up to the railroad tracks on Main Street and back. The two thirds who were white were gathered on the opposite side of the road from the one third who were black. But respect knew no boundaries or barriers. The Reverend Jeremiah Patterson of the First AME Church of Woodvale was one of Dr. Harrison's biggest admirers and he stood among the front ranks on the black side. If ever there was a true man of God, Rev. Patterson would tell his parishioners, it was this seemingly unanointed man who felt all the world's wrongs as if they were his own.

"My son hasn't taught me to drive it yet," Dr. Harrison stood and addressed the crowd, "so I want all y'all to ride with my boy. I don't think there's a rule about who can and who can't drive one of these things yet, so Milt, even though he's twelve years old, is the best we've got."

Rev. Gray made sure to be the first to ride and the rest of the townspeople deferred to him. Dr. Harrison sat in the back and the minister cautiously edged his way into the front passenger seat.

"You didn't have to butter me up that way in church today, Andy," the doctor kidded his lifelong friend. "You know I'd have let you ride anyway."

"Oh, that wasn't butter, Milton. That was lard. I was just greasing the pan so you'll taste better when they roast you over the fires down under."

They both chuckled while Milton Jr. quietly put the car in motion and glided up to Main Street.

"This boy's a marvel," said Gray. "Son, you ought to teach your pa how to drive."

"I will, Reverend Gray. I'll do anything for my daddy."

The minister leaned over and tapped the youngster on the hand.

"Nice boy. You take care of you pa, now, son. He's a dreamer and he tries to do too much. I don't know why he never left this place. Why *did* you stay here, Milton?"

"I'm the same as you, Andy. This is home. I can't make any other place my home."

AFTER DR. HARRISON FINALLY learned how to drive his new motorcar he felt a new sense of power and confidence. His domain of potential patients increased from a few neighborhoods in and around a one-horse town to two or three entire counties. Inevitably, his name became known outside his immediate circle of friends and, with some encouragement from his enthusiastic new patients, he began making preparations to seek political office, which had been his secret aspiration for years.

When friends and neighbors heard that Dr. Harrison would be campaigning in the Democratic Party primary against Bill Carlyle, the six-term incumbent U.S. Congressman from their district, they were giddy with the same far-fetched hopes that affected their candidate. Carlyle had established a foothold in several important committees in Washington, was a well-known and well-connected lawyer in Jackson County, and had a seasoned corps of vote-grabbing lieutenants in all the district's major polling precincts. It was a running joke in courthouses throughout the region that every election day with Carlyle on the ballot was Good Friday because so many people mysteriously rose from the dead on that day to vote for him.

During the spring and early summer of 1910 Milton Sr. drove his Model T strategically over the rutted dirt roads of northeast Georgia into the town squares of all the county seats. There he would typically hold an impromptu rally during lunch hour when several dozen people were available to hear him. He struck on a theme that he knew would be popular among the common folk and would strike the big-money Carlyle in a vulnerable spot. Because Carlyle had figured that most people in his district had no money and envied anyone who did, he had gone on record as supporting the establishment of a federal income tax.

But Milton Harrison believed that the voters, all of them men in those days and many of them property owners, would resent any increase in taxation of any kind. So he would always give a stump speech accusing

Carlyle of "hobnobbing with lawyers and corporations who are trying to turn this country into another Russia with a handful of Czars in Washington telling you what you can and can't do with your own enterprise."Reelecting Carlyle, he would tell his listeners, would be "Reconstruction all over again, with tax agents coming to take away your farms and houses." The campaign slogan was simple, and Dr. Harrison would pay farmers to paint it on the tin roofs of their barns and town shopkeepers to post it on their windows: SAVE OUR FREEDOM. VOTE M HARRISON FOR U.S. CONGRESS.

When Carlyle read a newspaper article in his Washington office claiming that the upstart Harrison led him in a straw poll, he summoned one of his pages.

"I never thought a little ole country doctor with barely a pot to pee in could raise such a ruckus," he told the assistant. "I'll give the man some credit for thinking he could be another Icarus and fly to the sun on wings held together by spit and sealing wax. . . . Say, I just thought of something. That used to be one of my favorite analogies when I was District Attorney and a rival lawyer would get a little too big for his britches."

"What do you mean by that, Congressman?" the page asked him. "I don't understand."

"You ever learn about Greek mythology at Princeton between frat parties, son? Icarus. His daddy gave him a set of feather wings bound with wax and he flew so close to the sun the wax melted and he came crashing down to earth."

"Yes, sir, I remember now. Sure. But what's that got to do with shutting up this Dr. Harrison down in your district?"

"That story is more than just a myth nowadays."

BACK IN GEORGIA, DR. HARRISON could feel a groundswell of momentum building for his makeshift brand of populism. On July 4, 1910 what would have once been regarded as a miraculous upset seemed all but inevitable in the primary election two weeks later. And once the Democratic primary had been won, election in November was a certainty, since no Republican even bothered to run in that district any more. Milton Sr. had still not gotten any public response from the arrogant incumbent. The doctor had been designated grand marshal of the Independence Day parade in Toccoa, where convivial crowds of people were gathered to celebrate the holiday.

When the parade reached an end at the town square, the front-running challenger stepped atop a podium to address the few hundred people there to listen to him and, of even more importance, reporters from six different small-town newspapers from surrounding counties. He was preparing to give another variation of the same speech he had used repeatedly to such brilliant effect throughout the three previous months.

But just as Dr. Harrison was about to speak and the crowd had quieted, everyone became conscious of a low rumble originating from somewhere in the distance. It was a sound totally unlike what anyone there had ever heard before. Several hundred heads now turned upward and caught sight of a wispy winged creature flying low above the distant treetops, drifting in their direction.

It was *a flying machine!* Or so many in the crowd thought, though no one among them had ever actually seen one. A gentleman was sitting in the front of the apparatus with a wheel in his hand, nakedly out in the open as though his body were no more than an extension of two loose fabric-coated wooden wings, a few crossing wires with turnbuckles, a roaring motor and a propellor twirling furiously behind him. In a matter of seconds the machine was directly overhead, a mere one hundred fifty feet above the town, and a white canvas banner tied to its tail was plainly visible to everyone below. In big red letters the message on the banner read: GO HIGHER AND FURTHER: RE-ELECT CARLYLE JULY 18.

Soon the airplane was past the town, headed straight for the hills that hugged the northern edge of the village. Just as it seemed to be on the verge of crashing into a mountainside, its nose shot up and it disappeared over the horizon, leaving the crowd in a dead hush. The challenger would never be able to upstage his absent opponent on this day, no matter what he put in his oration; that much was apparent. Many in the crowd could not read, but those who could quickly spread the news of what the banner had said.

"Carlyle, you bastard!" Dr. Harrison groaned to himself, though grudgingly impressed by what he had just seen.

For his son, it was another matter.

"WOW!" the boy whispered to himself as the plane disappeared over the horizon. *"I always thought they flapped their wings like birds!"*

CHAPTER 2

A Daredevil's Advice

THE NATURAL ORDER OF politics fell into place on July 18th. Dr. Harrison won only two counties: Franklin, the one of his birth, and Stephens, and the one of his current residence. The other fifteen were devoured by Carlyle, sometimes by as much as a three-to-one margin. For the sake of appearance, the incumbent did actually ride the train home to Georgia for Election Day—to vote for himself, pose for a few cameras and convince the common folk all was right with the world.

Perhaps the crude polling that had been done during the summer by some of the local newspapers had been wrong. Or perhaps news of the airplane reminded voters that Carlyle the Great really could move heaven and earth. But, most likely of all, Good Friday once again was moved to the third Tuesday in July, and all manner of ghostly happenings usually confined to the Holy Scriptures mysteriously affected polling precincts all over northeast Georgia on that steamy summer day in 1910.

When the final manual tally of votes was posted on Wednesday morning, Dr. Harrison, trying his level best to keep a stiff upper lip, left the Masonic lodge in Toccoa where an assortment of friends had gathered to pretend to be in suspense about the outcome, and drove somberly home. He could see the future clearly now. There would be sleepless nights. There would also be nightmares about his current and apparently permanent lot in the world: a man usually too late to save the lives of screaming children with rabies or the gangrenous limbs of farm laborers. What had he accomplished in his life that was really worthwhile? His old doubts would surely revisit him.

At home the doctor found Kate and Ellen, his two daughters, in tears, and his wife trying to console them. Milt was frowning silently in a hidden corner of the parlor, feeling sorry for his daddy. Kate, aged 22, was now engaged to Graham Johnson, and Ellen, 18, had her heart set on one of the Carruthers boys; so as Milt saw it he was soon to be all alone with his parents, and he was very confused about what the future held. He wished the girls would quit sobbing in front of their father and act more dignified, but he said nothing.

"That Carlyle cheated, Daddy," Ellen cried, daubing her eyes with a handkerchief. "No way he would've won fair and square."

"Don't talk that way," said Mrs. Margaret Harrison. "That's bein' a sore loser. What happened was part of the Lord's plan."

"Mama," Kate replied, "if you're rich and know the right people in this world you get whatever you want. Is that God's way?"

"No," said her mother, "but God don't need riches or power. Why do we? If your daddy'd gotten more votes would that have made us any better people?"

"Daddy would've made a great Congressman. He would've helped people better themselves."

"How do we know your father won't help more people by staying here? Maybe all kinds of good things will happen now that wouldn't have happened without us here."

"Girls, Madge," Dr. Harrison interrupted, "let's don't talk about this right now. I lost and that's all there is to it. Let's don't work any Divine Providence into it. It's just an election, and I lost it. I accept it, and I'm sure the sun will rise and set tomorrow just like always and a year or two down the road nobody'll even care what happened."

The only son in the family stood up from his pouting session and went to hug his father.

"You'll always care about it, Daddy, and so will I. I won't forget about it, and I'll even the score some day."

Conventional wisdom told the doctor that he should scold his son for being defiant and vengeful, but at that moment those words were just what he wanted to hear. They were a tonic for his soul.

"Thanks, boy," he hugged his younger namesake. "And I know you mean it, too."

LATER ON THAT EVENING, when the three children of the family had scattered to their separate spheres of interest, Milton cuddled up next to his wife Margaret and confided in her.

"Thanks for trying, darlin', but you can't fool 'em."

"What do you mean by that?"

"What I mean is our kids know all this is eating away at me. What's left for me to do now? I've let my children down and shamed my family."

Madge, ever the pragmatist, tried to console the incurable dreamer she had loved since age sixteen.

"Maybe you didn't do what you wanted, but you came close. You might not've climbed up on the roof yourself, but you set a ladder out—you put the steps in front of 'em. All they need to do is climb what you built. That's more than your daddy left you."

"Papa left a good example for me. He fought honorably against Yankee aggression. But he lost. All my honorable fights I've lost too. So how am I different?"

"Part of your papa's honorable fight was to keep slavery in place, and you've spent most of your life tryin' to give everybody a fair shake. That's how you're different."

"My daddy wasn't fighting for slavery. He didn't own slaves. He was fighting off a ruthless invader."

"But slavery was still a part of it, and what you've done for your kids that your daddy never did for you is leave 'em with no reason to doubt any cause you've ever fought for."

"Is that good enough? Is that all you ever expect me to do in this world?"

Madge gave him a motherly peck on the cheek. Though thirteen years younger than her husband, she sometimes thought of him as her mischievous boy. She sighed with the seriousness and resignation of someone used to a life of hardship and unfulfilled wishes.

"Milton, we're just clay stepping stones on the road to something better. We're servin' our purpose—we don't know how, but we're servin' our purpose."

JUST AS HE FEARED, the doctor's old bouts with depression returned to him in the months after his failed political campaign. He had a few placid months in 1911 after his eldest daughter married the son of the Woodvale General Store's proprietor and moved into a little house on the opposite end of the village. And in 1912, when Carlyle was actually defeated by another upstart challenger, he felt a vicarious sense of accomplishment, as though he had set a successful precedent for attacking the fat cat. Then in 1913 he felt proud again when he gave his younger daughter away to a prosperous farmer's son who lived on some rich bottomland between Woodvale and Lavonia. But any real sense of serenity was short-lived during the next few years.

He kept hearing his teenage son, now his only child left at home, talk about airplanes. At first Milton Sr. dismissed his son's dreaming as just another of his adolescent obsessions. He asked Joe Freeman, the village blacksmith, to take his son under his guardianship and dissipate some of the boy's restless energy by teaching him how to forge metal and iron into tools. But then gradually, the more he thought about it, the more the doctor became interested in airplanes as well. It didn't matter that an airplane had helped to turn the tide in favor of Carlyle, he thought to himself. Carlyle would have beaten him no matter what. He simply was unsuited for politics, and now he realized it. But what *was* he suited for, other than country doctoring? His conclusion was that, at this stage of his life, his purpose was to join in and foster the boundless fantasies of Raymond Milton Jr. It was his last, best hope for the future.

One day in early June of 1914, as the starry-eyed physician combed through the family's Sunday edition of *The Atlanta Georgian*, he saw the following advertisement in a prominent location on the second page of the front section:

LIFFEY-BARRETT
Competing for the
CHAMPIONSHIP OF THE UNIVERSE
LOOPING LOOP &
FLYING UPSIDE DOWN

Come see Mr. Stratton Liffey,
The World's Greatest Aviator,
& Mr. Owen Barrett,
The World's Greatest Automobile Racer
Engage in Feats of Speed and Daring

ATLANTA SPEEDWAY RACETRACK Sat. June 20 1pm
Rain, Shine or Cyclone
Admission 50¢, 25¢ children

"June 20, that's next Saturday, Milt," the doctor said, showing the ad to his then 17-year-old son. "We've gotta be there—we *can't* miss that."

They immediately made plans to take the train to Atlanta on the morning of the 20th to be in attendance. That year a pair of daredevils named Stratton Liffey, a 28-year-old Texan who had begun flying hot-air balloons in 1905 then graduated to outrageous upside-down maneuvers in airplanes, and Owen Barrett, a well-known car racer, were touring dirt racing tracks throughout the United States in a series of mock races meant entirely for entertainment. Barrett would rush around oval tracks with his 100-horsepower Fiat motorcar while Liffey would roar above him in his Curtiss Special pusher biplane, invert his plane in midair and plunge down menacingly close to the grandstands while his adversary raised a tornado-like cloud of dust in his wake. The exhibitions were generating wealth and fame for the two performers, and their audiences had spread the sensational news of their exploits by word of mouth.

The Harrison boy barely got any sleep the night of the 19th in a feverish anticipation of the air show. Every time he closed his eyes he saw Liffey in his Curtiss pusher plane gliding over fields, skimming water, ducking under telephone wires, doing loops and spins and climbing arcs. A mostly female audience was cooing with every flourish of the biplane, and red roses were being strewn at Liffey's feet after he skidded to a halt in a field and leaped down from his perch. Or was it Liffey? By early morning, when the teenager had finally fallen into actual sleep and was really dreaming, he might have sworn the man climbing out of the seat was himself, only ten years older.

When morning finally did come, father and son made the nine-mile trek to the Toccoa train station in their Model T and boarded the train to Atlanta, about two hours away. The younger Harrison had never been on so long a journey—had never been more than twenty miles away from the house in which he had been born and lived ever since. And he certainly had never been in a big city, where rich people had electricity and running water and there were no outhouses chock full of dried corncobs to help their users with life's unpleasant necessities. But was it also true that neighbors didn't talk to one another down there, nor did passing strangers greet? He had heard rumors about it.

At the Terminal Station in downtown Atlanta, the Harrisons transferred to a different line that led to a sleepy little village called Hapeville about eight miles to the south. Hapeville lay on the edge of one of the largest expanses of level ground in the Piedmont, a four-thousand-acre tract of mostly pastureland that was owned by the Candler family, one of Atlanta's wealthiest, who had a primary stake in a new local soft drink called Coca-Cola.

In the midst of this vast clearing sat a two-mile long egg-oval dirt track where automobile racers had been having contests for several years and where Stratton Liffey himself had appeared in exhibitions as long ago as 1909, five years previously. Beside this track a wooden grandstand seating 3000 people had been erected to create commercial opportunities for the Candlers. Dr. Harrison and Milt, after a mile and a half walk from the Hapeville depot, arrived at the grandstand, bought two tickets from an old man at a wooden kiosk, and went through the gates into their seats. At 11:30, they were among the first spectators.

By 12:45 a collection of perfumed ladies in all their Sunday finery, scruffy kids, city gentlemen in Panama hats and caps, and freshly scrubbed farm families newly train-delivered from the boondocks packed the grandstand. Some of the young women were ready to scream themselves dizzy. Rarely did anything in the lives of rural Georgia girls lend itself to such rapturous excitement as this spectacle seemed to promise. The youthful and handsome Liffey's reputation for daring heroics had lured many of the region's most beautiful lasses into attendance.

At exactly 1 o'clock a man walked out to a parked car positioned in the middle of the racetrack, put on a red helmet, waved to the audience, and cranked his 100hp Fiat started. It made an ungodly clamor and when the wheels began spinning they churned up a whirlwind of dust. Soon Owen Barrett had reached a furious speed of well over a mile a minute, faster than anyone there had ever seen a vehicle move, and he was rushing around the oval with flamboyant recklessness, skidding and sliding around the turns and raising a monstrous cloud behind him that rivaled in impressiveness the cumulus clouds of vapor in the sky.

Near the completion of Barrett's second lap another and even louder rumble began to envelop the racetrack. This was an ear-splitting roar that intermittently slowed to a sputter before resuming its roar again. Suddenly, just as the Fiat was passing in front of the gallery for the second time, a massive winged creature swooped down from over the eaves of the grandstand and seemed to be headed nose down onto the car like a hawk onto a field mouse. The crowd screamed, but the biplane just as suddenly nosed upward, shot into the sky, turned upside down, flipped over again, and dove toward the ground. When the plane completed its loop, its operator, the great Stratton Liffey, dressed neatly in a double-breasted gray pinstripe suit and tie with his characteristic golfing cap turned backward, flung his arms wide apart to thrill the audience.

Again the spectators shouted with excitement, and now the car and the biplane, each traveling at about the same speed and making earth-shattering noise, went racing neck and neck around the track, alternating narrow leads and reckless stunts, with the car swerving and skidding and the plane swooping, spinning and flying upside down. After several laps a man ran onto the track and began waving a white flag, seeming to signal a final and decisive lap. Barrett and Liffey then abandoned their stunts and went at top speed, the aviator hovering 50 feet above the track and the car driver hugging the track's inside edge with the dust spewing behind him. They stayed almost exactly astride each other until they rounded the final corner and the determined Liffey lunged ahead by a few feet. Barrett began gaining on him until, by the time they crossed the man waving the checkered flag, they seemed to have come to a draw.

When Liffey landed his plane and Barrett slid to a stop both claimed victory. It was then necessary to do it over again, of course, to remove all doubt. But the uncertainty would continue when the second contest also, coincidentally, produced a draw. In this manner the two competitors, who were in fact business partners, kept their spectacle going long enough to give the public its money's worth.

After the conclusion of the exhibition, the gallery cheered and whistled, and many of the younger girls went wild. This was liberation, this was ecstasy. They *had* to meet these men, especially the flyer, who was so dashingly handsome, brave and debonair! Hundreds of heretofore sheltered ingénues were now prepared to pepper Liffey with their virginity as though it were nothing more than a business card. There was a mad rush down to the bottom railing of the grandstand, and several policemen on horseback, who had been deployed by the city of Atlanta at Liffey's request, emerged from behind the seating area to contain the fervent mob. Barrett and Liffey removed their headgear and waved from a safe distance away down on the track.

Milt leaned against his father and said in his ear, almost in a shout to rise above the surrounding noise:

"Daddy, I gotta meet Stratton Liffey. I can't let him leave without talking to him."

"It can't be done right now, boy," said Dr. Harrison, though he had devised a plan well in advance for achieving the goal he knew his son would have. "These fools are about to trample the man."

"Can't we do anything?"

"Why, of course we can, son. Have I ever let you down before?"

Milt's father turned and winked at him. He pointed to the man who had been waving the flags for the racers during their competition. This man now leaned inconspicuously against the bottom railing at the far corner of the grandstand, while the crowd continued its screaming applause for Liffey and Barrett.

"Nobody's paying any attention at all to that flag-bearer. Let's go talk to him."

The two of them weaved their way across the grandstand down to ground level until they were just above the flag man.

"Excuse me, mister," Dr. Harrison called out. "May I ask a favor of you?"

The man turned around and looked upward with a mild air of annoyance. Dr. Harrison, whose right hand had been clenched in the pocket of his trousers, offered it to the man to be shaken, clasping something in his palm with his thumb. When the man shook his hand, Milton Sr. pressed the folded up piece of paper he had been hiding under his fingers into the flag-waver's palm.

"I'm Doctor Milton Harrison, from Woodvale, Georgia. Pleased to meet you."

"Hey, what's this?" the man asked, looking down into his hand and seeing a twenty-dollar bill.

"My boy wants to meet Stratton Liffey. Here he is, a fine-looking young gentleman, as you can see. He don't mean any harm. He just wants to talk to him, and I'm sure you can work something out for us, can't you, mister?"

The flag-waver's grin was as wide as a crescent moon.

"You don't leave nothin' to chance, do you, doctor? Well, if I was your boy I'd be in the lobby of the Piedmont Hotel tonight at seven o'clock sharp. I don't know how or why, but it's possible Mr. Liffey just might be there lookin' for a young feller named . . . say, what's your boy named, sir?"

"Milt Harrison, same as mine."

"You ain't the same Harrison who ran for Congress against Bill Carlyle a few years ago, are you, Doctor?"

"Yes, sir, I am. How'd you remember that?"

"Well, I hate to tell you this, but . . . *Carlyle paid Liffey $1000 to carry his banner for him that year."*

The doctor's heart sank inside of him, twinging with a mixture of pain and embarrassment. But his son tapped him on the back, and he was quickly reminded that he loved his son more than he loved himself.

"No, I didn't know that," Milton Sr. said with a straight face, revealing none of his true emotion. "Well, let's let bygones be bygones. It's about time I proved I'm smarter than Carlyle. He got Liffey for a thousand, now I'm gettin' him for twenty."

BY SIX-THIRTY THAT NIGHT the Harrisons were downtown at the Piedmont Hotel, a 10-story edifice that had been built eleven years earlier and was now considered the prima donna of Atlanta's hostelries, referred to by the proud citizenry as "our New York hotel." Celebrities of Liffey's stature always stayed there when in town, and now a nervous young country boy, whose mind was still reeling from the amazement of the race and seeing skyscrapers and streetcars and a city for the first time, sat quietly waiting in the plush interior of the lobby. His father had taken leave of him to go watch the bustle of city life on the sidewalk by the front entrance. Milton Jr. was thus all alone to face a legend who would, he was told, come looking for him on his own.

Just as had been promised, at exactly seven o'clock a tall thin man with neatly coiffed and slicked brown hair and blue eyes emerged from the elevator. A rich man whose company was now netting $250,000 a year, he was dressed impeccably and carried himself with a swagger. Though the lobby was well-peopled, no one there recognized the boyish and handsome young aviator—not even the youngster who was seated and waiting for him. He had looked a great deal older and more authoritative in his plane. In this setting amid the cream of established society he seemed a mere fledgling, a fresh-faced and innocent boy in his own right. At about the same time as the aviator greeted him, his admirer realized who he was.

"Are you Milt?" asked Liffey.

The boy gulped awkwardly and nodded his head. He rose from his seat to shake the aviator's hand.

"You really came, Mr. Liffey. I can't tell you how much this means to me."

"I guess you may have some hard feelings 'cause I loaned myself out to your dad's opponent in that race for Congress. Well, I'm sorry about that. Back then I had to scrape for money and I wasn't so well off as I am now."

"I don't have no hard feelin's for you, sir. If I did, they'd be gone now because you went to all this trouble to meet me."

"It's no trouble at all to me. . . . Did you, uh, have anything in particular you wanted to talk to me about?"

"I just wanted to tell you, sir, that I wish I could do just what you're doin' now—flying them machines and going where no one's ever gone before."

"Well, I'm flattered you think that. It's not quite as easy as I make it look, though. Sometimes it still scares me to death. You know, Milt, if no one's ever done something before there's no guarantee it *can* be done."

"You mean you're actually *scared,* Mr. Liffey?"

The aviator held his index finger up to his lips.

"SHHHH, don't let anybody hear that. It's true, though. Fear's my constant companion. But the way I look at it, if you're not scared you're not going far enough, you're not pushing yourself hard enough."

"I can push myself that far, but if I've gotta make a livin' at it I don't know if I can. My family's not so well off, sir. We're country folk and I'm workin' in a blacksmith shop."

Liffey paused to reflect on what advice he should give the boy. It was a serious matter—one literally of life and death—and he knew he needed to choose his words carefully.

"Don't do it for money. I'm not an example to follow there, Milt. I just happened to get lucky and make a fortune out of it. And don't do it for *them."* Here Liffey waved his hand in the direction of the garish parade of society that was mingling in the hotel lobby. "They just want to see me dead. Don't do it for any other reason except the love of it. If you were all alone and nobody was watching you, you'd still do it. Or if God Almighty tapped you on the shoulder and said, 'Next time you try that, son, you're dead,' you'd still do it even then. Do it because, if you didn't do it and you lived like everybody else, you'd *rather* be dead. *Do it because you can't live any other way."*

Milt almost felt he was listening to the words of a deity and not a man. He offered his hand to the aviator.

"Thanks, sir. Thanks for the advice. I guess you have to go now, don't you? Well, I hope I'll see you again."

Liffey hesitated and seemed interested in continuing the conversation, but gave up the effort. His humanitarian deed for the day had been done; his conscience, guilty for having once sold itself out to a political fat cat, put at ease.

"I hope so, too, Milt. I'll remember you. Whatever you do, boy, don't get too high and don't get too low. Either way lies trouble. The secret to beating the odds is always knowing you can, while at the same time always fearing you won't."

The aviator waved and headed toward the front entrance, where a gorgeous young woman with creamy buxom flesh had just arrived and appeared to be waiting for him.

"Good-bye," the visitor called out when his hero had taken the woman under his arm. The aviator and his companion turned to acknowledge the boy. The woman smiled at him tantalizingly, sloe-eyed and with her head slightly ajar.

"So long," said Liffey.

After the aviator and his amour had gone through the spinning glass door leading to the outside, Milt wanted to follow them, to spy on them, even to cling to them. They were a part of a world that fascinated him—a world of beauty, pleasure, riches, glamour and danger.

MILT'S MASTER AT THE blacksmith's shop in Woodvale, Joe Freeman, had a distant cousin in Columbia, South Carolina named Mack Storms. Mr. Storms owned a fledgling car dealership and was also just then beginning to sell kits for airplanes that ran on Model T engines. Storms Flying Flivvers, as the monoplanes were called, could be shipped by train almost anywhere and assembled by a mechanic on site. They did come with a hefty price tag, however: $1000. Within a week after his meeting with Liffey the aspiring aviator decided that he needed to ask his dad's help in this matter. The two of them were rocking on their back porch one steamy night in late June, hearing the rhythmic sizzle of the cicadas in the surrounding woods, when Milt made mention of it.

"Dad, I need to borrow a few hundred dollars."

His father almost fell off his chair.

"You need WHAT?"

"I want to build me an aeroplane of some kind, and fly it around here."

"Impossible. You gotta be out of your mind, boy. You can't just build a plane and fly it."

"Why not, Daddy? Somebody else did it, why can't I?"

The elder man stopped rocking in his chair and stared quietly for a moment into the sultry twilight beyond the treetops. *Somebody else.* These were words he had heard too often in his life. It was always somebody else who did something. Somebody else had beaten Carlyle, too. His own last chance to be that somebody else himself had now passed him by. Was it worth certain bankruptcy to give the next great chance to his son?

"Milt, I don't mind if you try anything you want, but we don't have that much money."

"Well, uh, Daddy," the boy hesitated, trying to be as diplomatic as possible, "even if you don't have that much, can't you contribute just a little?"

Dr. Harrison took a deep breath.

"Oh, I don't know. . . . You think, uh, *nine hundred fifty dollars* would set me up pretty well in this thing?"

"You gotta be kidding me!" his son said in shock. "Gee, I'll never be able to pay you back for that!"

"That's all right. If you default on your loan I can take possession of the plane back and use it to . . . well, I guess I can always rent it out to some poor feller who's trying to get elected to office, can't I?"

The youth sprang up from his chair excitedly.

"You're the best dad in the whole world!"

They now hugged, father and son, and for the first time in years the elder man felt a sense of total satisfaction. But he was also well aware that his wife would need a great deal more convincing than he had. Later that night after his son had gone to sleep he called his wife out of the sweltering house to the cool night air of the porch to revisit an old subject. When he explained to her that he had committed $950 of their total remaining lifetime savings of $983 to their son's bold project he set off an argument.

"Milton, you're spoiling that boy to death!" Madge chided him, "and you're bringin' us right down with him. And for what? It's nothing but a dangerous toy. Our son'll end up dead, and we'll be in the poorhouse."

"This kid Stratton Liffey's done pretty well, Madge. I sure wish we lived in the same poorhouse he does."

"Aw, *Liffey.* He's a freak of nature, about like Houdini. You expect to turn our boy into a freak? There won't ever be another feller who strikes it rich off this fad like Liffey did."

"You don't know that, darlin'. That's what they were saying about Tom Edison when I was coming along. I heard people say it was a miracle a tinkerer went so far in this world. Now look at all the tinkerers. Look at Henry Ford and Alexander Bell and the Wright brothers. You think their daddies ever said to them 'I'm sorry, boys, I won't support your wild ideas'?"

"They were inventors and businessmen," his wife countered."I don't see how throwin' away our life's savings is gonna help turn our son into either one of those. That Liffey's a circus performer. Here you are, a doctor, and you want to train your only son for the circus."

"This is what he wants to do, Madge. He doesn't want to be a doctor or a businessman. He wants to fly aeroplanes. Maybe he'll get rich doing it, maybe he won't. Maybe he'll die right away, maybe he'll figure out how to survive. That's beside the point. Whether we like it or not, that's what he wants and that's what he's gonna do."

"We need to send him off to college so he can be around educated people."

"I agree he needs to be in college, but we can't force that on him. This boy's got a mind of his own and he likes to teach himself how to do everything. Sure, I'll admit it's a long shot this'll be a good thing. I'm like you: I can't see where all this is leading. He can't, either. But I've got confidence in him, and I believe he'll do the right thing."

"I wish you'd teach me some of that confidence, Milton. I just don't understand why we're doing this."

"You told me you wanted me to be a ladder for our kids. Well, I'm just giving support. I don't want our boy starting at ground level when I'm here to give him a boost."

There was a period of silence, Madge half-heartedly considering her husband's point. The two of them rocked quietly in their separate chairs as the summer trees sizzled into the night. Mrs. Harrison then stood up without turning to face her husband.

"You had your say, Milton, but it all comes down to this. I don't want our son dying young, and that's always what happens to daredevils, and always for no good reason."

He realized it was pointless to carry on the discussion any further, so he said nothing else to her and let her go into the house and on to bed by herself. Now he understood the full scope of his risk. In the event that his son's dangerous pastime did prove catastrophic, the remainder of his life would be unceasing misery, void of affection at home and peace within. It mattered not. He could see the truth now. *This was what his son was meant to do*. And he had faith in the Lord, even if most people didn't see that faith outwardly. Years earlier he had privately asked—not prayed, but asked—God or whoever dwelt in the next world to take care of his children, and so far the request had been honored. He believed that his son would live long, no matter the danger; that some unseen and unknowable force would spare him for the greater good.

That was his religion.

CHAPTER 3

The Flying Flivver

MACK STORMS HAD NEVER sold an airplane kit to anyone before he received a telegram from Dr. Harrison requesting one for $950 up front, plus $50 to be paid in four monthly installments of $12.50. He breathed a sigh of relief that someone was actually interested in buying one from him. He regarded that phase of his business as highly experimental in nature and unlikely to be profitable. His original goal was to become a pioneer distributor of private aircraft in the South, but so far the market for his idea had been dead. At least up until July of 1914, when he heard from his cousin Joe Freeman's friend in Woodvale, Georgia.

"HOLD THE 4 PAYMENTS," Storms answered in his telegram back to Dr. Harrison. "JUST SEND THE $950 & CALL IT A DEAL."

Milt and Joe Freeman spent about a week designing and building a special flatbed trailer that would hook onto the back of the Model T and support the two large crates in which the airplane frame and its engine would be shipped. They had special oak planks cut up at the sawmill in the neighboring town of Avalon, bolted together a steel frame mounted atop four hard wooden wheels, and fitted the oak planks within the frame.

When the airplane arrived at the train station in Toccoa at the end of July, the aspiring aviator brought along four of his good friends and former schoolmates, Ezekiel Blaylock, Curtis Clifford, Aubrey Blackwell and Johnny Adams. Of course, the boys all went by different names than the ones they were given. Ezekiel was always Zeke, Curtis was Cliff, Aubrey was called Blackie, and Johnny Adams, due to his awkwardly large nose, had from earliest boyhood been pegged by his unmerciful friends as Shnook.

This motley assortment of raging hormones proved fit for the task of unloading the large cargo off of the train, and as Zeke, Shnook and Blackie rode on the flatbed to steady the load, Milt carefully and ploddingly drove the Model T along the rough dirt road back to Woodvale with Cliff at his side for conversation. Cliff never was much good for anything except talking, but he was the first to notice an alarming sight when the boys turned the corner onto Oak Street.

"Jesus!" he cried. "The whole damn town showed up!"

It was no exaggeration. Now the booming Woodvale numbered 194 people, and they were all assembled along Oak Street to witness the Harrison boy's latest undertaking, all the whites on the even-numbered address side and all the blacks on the odd side; people with nothing more urgent to attend to on this night than the arrival of two nondescript wooden crates at an ordinary house a block off Main Street.

"What the hell are these folks here for?" Milt asked his friend. "I haven't even put it together yet."

"Aw, Milt," said Cliff, "they just came to see history made. It ain't every day a feller brings home an aeroplane."

"It ain't no aeroplane yet, Cliff. It's just parts."

"To *them* it is."

When the car and the tow pulled into the dirt driveway in front of the house, the crowd surged into the street and like a swollen river spilled onto the Harrison yard. Milt jumped out of the car and stepped up onto the flatbed to address the crowd. He glanced at the front windows of his house and noticed his father peering through the windows at him. He knew he had to say something to satisfy the townspeople, but what?

"Folks, please folks," he lifted his hands to hold them back, "calm down now. I'm glad all y'all came, but we still need to do some work on this. It'll take a while before we really have an aeroplane. When it's ready I'll let everybody know, and I'll let y'all see me fly it. So just go on home now, and everybody get some rest."

The crowd retreated momentarily, and then the Rev. Jeremiah Patterson of the First African Methodist Episcopal Church cried out in a thunderous voice: "Our boy brought home his dream, Lord—HE BROUGHT HOME HIS DREAM!"

WHILE EVERYONE ELSE IN WOODVALE speculated about his activities, the young Harrison boy worked secretly to assemble his new toy during the course of the next three weeks. He could be seen from Oak Street furtively darting back and forth behind his garage, banging a hammer against something back there from time to time, lugging his father's tool bag with him wherever he went. Joe Freeman would let him out of the shop early each day to go home to continue his project, hoping eventually to receive an invitation to go with his apprentice. But it never came.

Quietly and steadily the doctor's son pored over the blueprints for his project at night under kerosene lamps, then gave those plans material form during the day. The bare framework of a monoplane began protruding up above the tin roof of the garage one afternoon. By nightfall the unholy foursome of Zeke, Cliff, Blackie and Shnook were summoned to help hoist the Model T engine into the front compartment of the fuselage with a pulley and chains on loan from the blacksmith. Other than Dr. Harrison and his reluctant wife, these boys were the first to see in close detail the handiwork of the mysterious craftsman. When the engine was in place they all began stretching the precut fabric around the bare ribs of the evolving machine. For the first time in the process the unmistakable form of an airplane now occupied the bare clay behind the house on Oak Street.

During the next three days Milt daubed a doping chemical on the fabric with a paintbrush to cause the covering to shrink and tighten. Then after it dried and cured a few days later, he invited the rough-and-tumble entourage of boys back again for the final, ceremonial act of construction. With his dad's handy set of wrenches the would-be aviator bolted the propellor into place while his buddies held it steady.

"What day's tomorrow, Shnook?" Milt asked Johnny Adams.

"Tuesday, boy. Why you askin'?"

"Tomorrow's the day. Sure wish I could get a dry run in, though."

"For what?" wondered Cliff. "It ain't no contest. Nobody gives a damn how you do it, just as long as you try it.

"For *me,* Cliff. Once I get in the air I don't know how I'll get down."

"You ain't scared, are you, chief?" asked Blackie.

"Shoot no," answered Milt. But he was. "I . . . well, it ain't something anybody ever gave me lessons in."

"That ain't never stopped you before, cap'n," said Zeke. "Nobody ever taught you anything, but you got this far, didn't you?"

"Sure," said Milt, trying to seem cavalier. "I just like to do things right the first time, that's all."

"Other people done it right their first time," said Cliff, "so why not you?"

ON TUESDAY EVENING, August 8, 1914, all 194 Woodvaleans then in existence were gathered to witness an historic event. In a fallow field adjacent to the village, about 700 more people from the surrounding territory had joined the natives to form an audience for Woodvale's favorite son. The main object of attention, the just-assembled Storms Flying Flivver, had been pushed by several of the boy's assistants from 125 Oak Street a quarter mile away to the present site. It now rested peacefully in the coarse stubble, awaiting the stroke of life, as its beaming young owner leaned against it.

"Ladies and gentlemen," he announced to the crowd, pointing at his pride and joy with a sweep of his cap, "now *this* is an aeroplane!"

The crowd hooted and whistled, as though Milt had just proclaimed the relocation of a glittering celebrity to their midst.

"Zeke, pour the gas in the tank," the 18-year-old daredevil instructed one of his helpers, trying to be as calm as possible. His heart was banging inside him like a drum with fear, tension, passion and excitement. This was where his life had led him. Now was the time to prove that he really could conquer the air. Might he change his mind now and just start the engine and taxi harmlessly about the field, claiming the machine didn't work properly so the people would go away? It was too late for that. Normal life would now be too dull for him if he ever tried to return to it. He could only live one way after this, and that was with his heart banging like a jackhammer against his ribs.

He waved to the people and grabbed ahold of one blade of the propellor. In the distance he recognized his mother and father, who were at the front of the line of people that had formed in ranks of four and five deep at roadside. His parents were together in physical proximity only. A gulf as wide as the heavens above separated them spiritually. The mother knew only anger, fear and confusion; the father only pride, enthusiasm and confidence.

To prime the engine in his machine the young experimenter spun his propellor around a few times with his ignition switch off, then climbed up on the footrest of the wing and leaped into the cramped open cubbyhole behind the propellor and engine. He now motioned for his friend Blackie to take position by the propellor and flipped on the startup switch on his simple instrument panel. Blackie then furiously hurled the propellor into motion while Zeke and Shnook stood by to pull back the logs that were chocking the front wheels to keep the plane stationary. The propellor grumbled for a few seconds, hesitated and then finally roared into full motion. Shouts of exhilaration rang from the crowd while Zeke and Shnook unchocked the wheels and the machine began lumbering forward. The crude plane had no controls other than a stick and throttle, no instruments besides a compass and an altimeter, and no way of braking itself except for a steel skid under the rear of the fuselage.

The sound was deafening, just as Milt had heard it at the Atlanta Racetrack four months earlier, and the propellor blast buffeted his face. He tossed his cap over to Shnook and, minus any goggles or headgear, he squinted into the afternoon summer sun. He maneuvered the ailerons and rudder with the control stick and observed how the plane veered to either side in accordance with his movements of the stick. The machine almost seemed to have a will of its own, moving so fast toward the woods on the edge of the field that he thought he would need to shut the engine off to avoid going in there.

He steeled his nerves and felt the machine surge ahead like an angry bull. Nudging the control stick gently forward and then back to observe how the plane moved, he decided that in a quick double motion he would nose the machine down a bit to get the skid off the ground and then pull back slightly to lift everything into the air. He saw the trees on the other side of the field getting treacherously close to him, so he applied his forward and back motion on the stick and felt himself thrust into the air.

When he realized that he was off the ground and clear of the trees he felt dizzy. Everything was moving so quickly and there was such tremendous clamor from the propellor and engine that he found it impossible to relax in his flying seat. Oil was being splattered all over him, the wind was pelting him in the face, and when he looked over the side of his fuselage he saw the earth passing beneath him with alarming speed and he wondered what would happen if he just kept going and never turned to go back. His senses throbbed with the beauty, excitement and the raw terror of the experience of operating a machine in flight. He guided the stick slightly off to one side, tilting the plane and beginning to turn it back toward the other direction from which he had come. Below him lay a patchwork quilt of fields and a distant gathering of people clad mostly in bright colors on the edge of one of the clearings. He knew that had to be the field from which he had taken off. Why else would that many people have gathered so far out in the country, except to watch a boy try to kill himself?

With heavy perspiration and an unsteady hand, he lowered his wing flaps and began a careful descent to the field. The plane drifted smoothly during its downward glide, and Milt almost felt as if he were in another body watching himself as his Flying Flivver struck the ground and swerved and skidded to a stop. He shut the engine off and the propellor spun itself to a halt.

When he realized that his trip was over and he had successfully flown a plane that he had put together himself without any instruction from anyone, his dominant feeling was not exuberance or even self-satisfaction, but a much more humble one: RELIEF.

Now the people who had held themselves back on the edge of the field spilled out and came forward in a wave to greet their hero. His flight had taken four minutes, but a lifetime of varied emotions had been compressed within it, both for him and the people who had witnessed it. The tide of humanity stopped when it had formed a tight circle around the plane. He was glad to be back on earth again and it was comforting for him to feel loved by so many people.

"Great job, chief," Blackie congratulated him from behind and then shook his hand. Milt's ears still rang loudly and he was disoriented and drenched with sweat. "When you takin' it up again?"

"I don't know, Blackie," said Milt. "It was a pretty grueling experience. I might need some time to recover from it."

"Damn, boy," said Zeke, "you mean you might need about thirty minutes, then you'll be right back up again.

Dr. Harrison now pushed his way through the ranks and hugged Milt tightly.

"You showed 'em the way, son," he said with tears in his eyes. "You took me up with you."

"Where's Mama?"

Dr. Harrison gestured for Madge to come and embrace her boy. The crowd quieted and the timid woman wrapped her arms around the strong young daredevil. Hers was the face of a woman who had just been to a funeral and had seen the coffin open and the deceased leap out and do a cartwheel.

"See, Mama, I told you I could do it."

"Don't try that again," said his mother, still trembling. "Please, Milt. There's only been one person who ever rose from the dead, and his mama had a lot better connections than I do."

CHAPTER 4

In Search of a Doctor

FOR THE NEXT TWO MONTHS, Milt continued to experiment with his flying crate, and his reputation spread throughout several counties. People from miles around were coming to watch the boy when he rolled out his plane every weekend and flew it.

Milton Sr. and his wife remained in complete disagreement on the subject of their son's interest in airplanes. The quarrel was exacting a heavy toll on them both. The doctor was feeling like a stranger in his own home, constantly tired and under tension.

Woodvale's black and white pulpits thundered with the praises of the Harrison boy every Sunday and Wednesday, and the doctor was reluctantly attending services at the First Baptist, as much to keep an eye on the newly-intrigued girls who were trying to entrap his son in their romantic webs as to field compliments for his boy from the admiring congregation. After services on Wednesday, October 21, the doctor developed an upset stomach. He thought maybe all the hullabaloo surrounding his son's airplane adventures had caused him to overeat.

He avoided mentioning his discomfort to his wife, who was rarely talking to him nowadays. But when he was absent from bed at a quarter past midnight, Madge awoke and went out the bedroom door to the parlor, where she found her husband quietly reading a newspaper with the palm of his right hand pressed against his navel.

"What's wrong? Why aren't you in bed?"

The doctor took a deep breath and, with his face twisted in a look of distress, tossed his newspaper off to the side.

"I'm really sick to my stomach, Madge. The last several hours I've felt a little bloated, but now it's an awful pain."

"Did you take sodium bicarbonate already?"

"Darlin', I'm afraid this is more than just indigestion."

She came across the room in her white lace nightgown, and sat worriedly down on the sofa next to him, stroking his cheek with the fingers of her hand.

"What is it, Milton? Tell me now. I'm sure you know what it is."

He continued nervously rubbing his midsection.

"I don't know anything yet. I can speculate, but right now that doesn't serve me any purpose. There's nothing I or anybody else can do about it right now."

She stood up and with a frightened expression covered most of her face with her hands.

"What do you mean? *You tell me now!"*

He rose to his feet and put his arm around her shoulder.

"I told you everything I know. Let's go to bed and after I get some sleep I'll evaluate my symptoms in the morning."

"Are you sure you're doing the right thing, Dr. Harrison?"

It had been twenty years since she had addressed him in such a way, and as he studied her face now he felt mildly amused at this uncertain moment.

"Who else can I call on for medical advice? I don't know of anyone better around here, do you?"

They held hands and went into the bedroom together, for the first time in many months. Like two newlyweds they cradled one another that night, though he never even came close to getting any sleep. About two hours into the attempt he realized what was happening to him, but he knew he was powerless to take any action until sunrise. He sweated in miserable uncertainty until the songbirds began to chirp at the imminent arrival of dawn. How happy a sound, he thought, for so unhappy a feeling. Oh, to be a bird or any other creature without the knowledge of mortality!

Madge was awake at the crack of dawn, and as soon as Milton Sr. felt her stirring he pretended to rouse himself from sleep as well. After they kissed she asked him how he was feeling and he abandoned any attempt to seem upbeat.

"Darlin', the later it gets the worse I feel the nausea, the chills, the fever. But the telltale sign is this pain I keep having in my lower right abdomen. . . . I've come down with appendicitis, and we're gonna need a doctor in here today to do an appendectomy."

"Lord help us!" she cried, "we'll never find anybody!"

He clenched his hand on his now throbbing abdomen.

"Sam Kelvey's the only one I know who can get here in time. I can't take the train all the way to Atlanta in this condition, so it's got to be done here."

"Sam Kelvey's a butcher and everybody knows it! There's no way I'll let him cut on you!"

"This isn't the time to be particular, Mrs. Harrison. There's no other surgeon around here who's trained to do an appendectomy, and I've got to have one, and fast, or I'm done for this world."

He curled up on the bed spasmodically, then put a handkerchief to his mouth and retched up some bile into it.

"Call our son, now!" he whispered.

MADGE WENT UPSTAIRS and shook her son out of his sleep.

"Milt, your father's got appendicitis! Quick, you got to fetch Doctor Kelvey in Toccoa and bring him back here to do an operation, or your father won't make it! . . ."

The rudest awakening of his life stung the younger Milton out of his sound sleep like a wasp bite.

"Where's my daddy now, Mama?"

"He's in bed."

The son quickly threw on his clothes and scurried down the stairs into his father's bedroom. When he pushed the door open he smelled a musty, damp closeness in the room and saw his father curled up on the bed like a terminal invalid. The two minutes he had endured from being shaken awake to now being confronted with this jolting sight were as traumatic an experience as he had ever had up till then. He was literally brought to his knees at his father's bedside.

"*My God, Daddy, what's happened?"*

His father, keeping a fresh handkerchief pressed to his mouth, gestured for Milt to get off his knees and stand up straight.

"My appendix ruptured, boy. Now let's don't waste time talkin'. Go jump in the Model T and round up a surgeon. I know you won't let me down. You never did before."

The young son grabbed ahold of his father's hand and kissed it.

"Daddy, I'll try as hard as I can."

"Well, that's as hard as anybody can," said his father.

For the next seven hours the boy combed the countryside in a desperate search for a doctor, any doctor, to come and administer to his ailing daddy. Dr. Samuel Kelvey, admired by many of the common folk for his charming bedside manner, but cursed by many others for his questionable surgical proficiency and out-of-date techniques at his advanced age of 71, was away from his Toccoa home. Insofar as he was the only physician in that part of Georgia other than Dr. Harrison who was known to have successfully done an appendectomy, Milt had no choice but to spend the day trying to hunt him down.

He went next to the home of some family named Bagley who lived out in the country near Eastanollee, but they told him the doctor had treated their little Silas's whooping cough already and was now on his way to see Elizabeth Worley, who had pneumonia and was on her deathbed. Milt caught up with Dr. Kelvey at the home of Elizabeth Worley in town, but the physician informed him that he was committed to staying with the dying girl for another hour, and then he had to set the broken arm of a train engineer who had tripped and fallen off the platform of one of his railcars. How long would all this take? No telling—maybe till late afternoon. So Milt then went straight to the Stephens County Courthouse and asked the sheriff if he knew of any medical practitioner anywhere who could help him immediately. The sheriff sent a telegraph to Westview Hospital in Atlanta, where Dr. Harrison's good friend Benjamin Parkhurst, one of the most highly acclaimed surgeons in Georgia, was summoned. Forty-five minutes later a telegraph came back saying that Dr. Parkhurst would be on the next train to Toccoa but he wasn't sure how long it would be before he made it.

With so little assurance of any other help, Milt returned to Kelvey's home and waited anxiously for him to complete his rounds. Finally, at around three o'clock, the slow-paced physician eased his Packard up to the curb and sauntered over to the front porch where his visitor was waiting.

"Dr. Kelvey, are you ready now?"

The white-haired old medicine man doffed his big black top hat, cleared his throat into a handkerchief embroidered with his initials, and pulled a gold watch dangling on the end of a chain from his breast pocket to glance at the time.

"As ready as I'll every be, kid. Let me get some instruments out of my house, and I'll follow you down there."

For what seemed an eternity, though it was actually only ten minutes, the physician was heard shuffling back and forth inside his house, then he emerged with two large black bags and gestured for his visitor to go ahead of him.

"Oh, by the way," Kelvey inquired as Milt was getting into the Model T and preparing to return home with the doctor's vehicle trailing him, *"what did you say your daddy had, boy?"*

Milt squinted at him in disbelief.

"Appendicitis."

"Appendicitis! That can be serious."

"It's *always* serious, doc," said Milt, "if you're the one who's got it."

THE DAY HAD NEARLY SPENT itself by the time the wandering son came home with a surgeon on his heels. There was a peculiar odor in Dr.

Harrison's bedroom and he was pale and motionless. A gathering of concerned citizens held vigil outside on the front lawn. Suddenly Dr. Kelvey remembered something else.

"I'll need somebody to assist me. Know of any nurses in this town?"

Madge and her son, along with Kate and Ellen, who had come to be with their father, went out on their porch and inquired if anyone knew of a person in Woodvale who might act as a nurse. Josiah Martin, one of the black men who was watching from out by the street, spoke up loudly.

"Rev. Patterson's daughter Ruth. She went to school on nursin'."

"Go get her then, Josiah," said Milt. "Tell her a man's life depends on her."

When the family went back in the house and informed Dr. Kelvey that they were calling for a colored woman to come help, he scoffed.

"No, I meant a *white* nurse," he said. "A Negro won't be of any use to me at all."

Milt felt a strong impulse to grab the old man by the neck and choke him. Instead he leered at him and said:

"She's all we've got, Dr. Kelvey. So unless you want me to help you, you'll take what we're giving you."

Kelvey sensed the anger of his fellow doctor's son and the desperation of the situation, so he backed down, though not without snickering.

"Fair enough. I've heard all my life that beggars can't be choosers."

The crusty doctor then turned to his patient, whom he had known from the time when Milton Sr. was a boy.

"Sorry to see you like this, Milton," he offered Dr. Harrison his hand. "I don't want to alarm you, but you're quite a bit worse off than what I was inclined to believe. Your boy described it right, but—well, usually loved ones will exaggerate. I'm sorry I didn't make it earlier. I should have."

Milton Sr. now struggled to speak, but his words still came out clearly.

"Doc, can you save me? I'm pretty far gone already."

"I'm worried about peritonitis. It may have already set in, and once it does it usually means we can't control the spread of infection."

The dreaded word, the one that as a doctor he suspected the most but tried the hardest not to think about, had just been uttered by his fellow physician. *Peritonitis.* The ailing patient, his arm draped limply across his midriff, stared fatalistically through the casement window at the bright sunshine outside.

"Do what you can. There's not much daylight left."

Dr. Kelvey removed his coat and washed his hands in a large pewter bowl that had just been filled with well water. He removed several sharp instruments from his bag and set two small basins on the nightstand by the bed. He put a thick cotton mask over his mouth and pulled a bottle of chloroform out to examine it. He went and hoisted the casement window open and poured a small quantity of the chloroform into one of the basins. He knew his patient needed no instructions about what to do next, so as Dr. Harrison held the basin up to his mouth and nostrils and breathed in slowly and deeply, Dr. Kelvey went out of the room to ask for help. He gestured for the doctor's son.

"Your dad'll be out cold in a few minutes, but when I go back in I'll pass out myself unless we circulate the fumes out the window. If that colored nurse don't get here in time, you take a straw fan and paddle like crazy toward the open window."

Just as the doctor spoke a young black woman of about thirty knocked on the back door of the house, as nervous and confused as anyone there. Mrs. Harrison escorted Mrs. Ruth Bonniwell, who had received two years of nurse's training at the Tuskegee Institute before she left school to get married, into the room. Ruth was well-bred and even-tempered in the same way as her father, Rev. Patterson. She had known the Harrison family for years and as a teenager had worked as Madge's kitchen helper for 25¢ a day. She was tall, statuesque, had perfect white teeth, light brown skin, beautiful feminine features, a soft voice, and felt perfectly at ease in white society. But like everyone else in Woodvale, she was perplexed by what had happened to Dr. Harrison and worried about what she was about to endure. In her family Dr. Kelvey had the reputation of being a racist, and she dreaded having to work with him.

"You my nurse?" Kelvey grumbled.

"Yes, sir," answered Ruth.

"You really a nurse, or you just claiming to be one?"

"Sir, I'm not claimin' anything. They wanted somebody who had nurse's training, and that's me. But no, I'm not a nurse."

Kelvey's expression brightened somewhat.

"That's a good answer, lady. I like honesty. Excuse me, will you step inside here with me?"

He opened the door to the bedroom and allowed her to precede him, then closed it behind them. He looked earnestly through his spectacles at her, his aging blue eyes probing her bashful brown ones. He then continued speaking, in a low voice, so that no one on the other side of the door could hear the words, though Dr. Harrison could.

"Can you stand the sight of blood and the smell of rotten flesh in this room? Can you watch a man get cut up before your eyes and not faint?"

Ruth looked down at the bedridden man and felt a twinge of pain and gratitude in her soul.

"I have two children, sir, and that man came to deliver 'em both. If he could do that for me, then I can do this for him. Yes, I do have the strength to do whatever he needs me to do."

"I expected you to say something different," said Kelvey. "You're not—well, you've taken me by surprise, ma'am."

She extended her hand out to him, sensing that he had probably never held a colored lady's hand with any type of affection before and that at this moment he wanted to hold hers. After a little hesitation he clasped ahold of her hand and she put her other hand on top of his so that she was cradling it.

"We're all God's children," she said. "Don't be afraid of me."

The doctor proceeded to perform the incision as soon as Milton Sr. had grown unconscious. Ruth held a kerosene lantern up over the patient with one hand and fanned the chloroform fumes with the other as Kelvey, with tired and shaky hand, extracted the appendix and stitched up the incision with a needle and catgut thread. Ruth periodically had to administer more chloroform to keep the patient unconscious, as the anesthetic usually wore off every fifteen minutes. It was a bloody and messy operation, and a horrendous experience for Ruth, who watched the surgeon's hands wobble throughout the procedure. After about two hours, well after nightfall, Dr. Kelvey finished his work and took his leave, refusing any payment, perhaps guilty about what had happened that day and unsure about the patient's prospects. The Harrison family then had no money anyway, so Kelvey would have gotten only barter for his services, but he wanted none of it. In his heart he knew what he didn't dare to tell the family: the patient should have taken action a lot sooner and done everything possible to have a more skilled doctor in Atlanta treat him.

WHEN DR. HARRISON REGAINED consciousness he was in miserable pain that he recognized instantly as peritonitis, an inflammation of the abdominal walls that was a reaction to the ruptured appendix. He crossed his hands and placidly laid them across his stomach. He realized he had an infection that would be fatal to him, and he now tried to reflect on his life, to wonder what else he could have done, and to prepare himself to meet his Maker.

He had never been conventionally religious in his life, but he somehow felt at peace in these final hours, unafraid of what lay ahead. His somber family attended to him at his bedside and Ruth, along with most of Woodvale's other townspeople, partook of an all-night prayer vigil in the yard, conducted by her father Rev. Patterson and also Rev. Gray. From time to time dear friends would be ushered in to have audience with the dying man, then ushered out in grief.

Milt and the others had to cover their noses because of the unbearable odor from the fetid blood-soaked sheets and contagion-filled air of the room. He was feeling many emotions: anger, frustration, sadness, uncertainty, even betrayal at the hands of an uncaring deity. But his father assured him all would be well. This was as much a part of life as birth. He needed to take care of his mother and sisters. He needed to be careful in what he did so young in life, for the rest of his time on earth might be ruined by a bad decision now. And one other thing . . . There was now another visitor, this one a doctor from Atlanta.

Ben Parkhurst, who had gone to medical school with Dr. Harrison in Augusta almost forty years earlier, had come to see his dear friend. He had boarded the mid afternoon train in Atlanta and arrived in Toccoa by 6PM. The Stephens County sheriff had driven him from Toccoa to Woodvale, where he hoped he might be in time to do some good for the ailing man.

When Dr. Parkhurst was shown into Milton's room he was shocked to see his friend on his deathbed. As many times in his career as he had seen people on the verge of death, this still caught him off guard. He was appalled something so readily treatable had turned into this, but it was too late now to correct that problem. This was a time to soothe the sufferer, not to try to reverse what fate had already written. Ben leaned down to embrace his fellow doctor and then knelt at his bedside.

"I'm sorry about this, Milton. I couldn't get here any sooner."

The dying man still spoke clearly, though with considerable effort and deliberation.

"I should've come to you in Atlanta. No way this would've happened to me if I'd been there. . . ."

Dr. Harrison clenched his eyes shut and for the first time a tear trickled out of one corner of one of them. His visitor began quietly weeping as well.

"I always thought I'd make it to my full allotment of years," the ailing man continued. "What does the Bible say? Threescore years and ten? I won't even get to the threescore."

"It's not how long you live that matters,"said Ben. "It's what you do in that little bit of time you have. You could've gone off and lived somewhere else—maybe had an easier life. But all those people wouldn't be out there on your doorstep if you'd done that. Even if you'd made Congress, the people out there now wouldn't have had the respect for you they do now."

"You flatter me too much."

"Not at all. I hope you believe me, but I wouldn't mind going where you're going now and doing what you've done. When I go, Milton, there won't be five people sorry for me."

———

LATER THAT NIGHT, when Dr. Harrison had gotten still worse, he wanted to speak to his son in private, and Madge ushered their boy into the room. The dying man looked at his own flesh and blood and saw in the boy a reflection of himself from forty years earlier. If only he could convey to him how lucky he was to be young and with his full life ahead of him . . . but that was impossible. Only the passing of time could do that. The last thing the doctor wanted now was to scare his namesake out of living his beautiful life with the exquisite richness and fullness his restless spirit craved.

"Son," he said, "thank everybody who tried to save me. All the townsfolk who are praying outside. Thank all of them for me."

The boy leaned down into the atrocious miasma of infection and decay that soaked the air about his father, hugged him and kissed him on the cheek. Then he wept like a child as his father calmly continued addressing him.

"I'm going to meet Jesus now, boy. I didn't pay Him enough mind down here, but I'm still expecting to meet Him. I hope you stay down here a long time, but don't be scared of dying. I want you to keep flying aeroplanes. That's what you love to do the most and this life's too short to be wasted doing what other people think you oughtta be doing. *No matter what anybody else says,* when you come to talk to me next time I want you to tell me you listened to your own conscience and not somebody else's."

CHAPTER 5

Kid

MILTON HARRISON DIED PEACEFULLY the following afternoon, not even two full days after he had realized anything at all was wrong with him, and less than one full day after an unsteady surgeon's ill-fated attempt to save him.

His dying hours were free of soul-searching or regret, and there was no pining in him for what might have been. He had lived fifty-eight years, from 1856 to 1914, most of them productive. He had saved many lives in his time, and touched many of the ones he had not been able to save. He left behind three beautiful children, two comfortably married and the other with the potential to conquer the world if he desired to. The doctor trusted that the townspeople of Woodvale would look after his wife and keep her company; he knew them that well. Now was the time to reap the rewards of a lifetime of loyalty to a community. His wife would have almost 200 dear friends, an extended family of sorts, to help her endure his absence.

Foremost among his curiosities as the infection wore him down—and no amount of speculation could satisfy him on this account—was the future of his son. He would never live to see what would happen to the boy. He would never know if the airplane, like the train and the automobile before it, would prove to be a passing fancy in the boy's mechanically adventurous mind and would yield to an even more sensational interest later. Or, if this proved not to be the case, just where the airplane might lead him some day, how he would survive the danger and uncertainty of it, and what he would prove by his efforts. Perhaps death might have been less disagreeable to one who had seen everything he cared to see and had no consuming interest left in any other worldly thing. But one hope still dominated this particular man's vision, and the prospect of not being able to follow that hope to its fit resolution was what made the gradual drowning out of his senses painful to him.

On the following Sunday, Woodvale responded to the unexpectedly sudden death of one of its most prominent citizens with an elaborate open air funeral attended by several hundred mourners from throughout the region. With all the pomp and ceremony due a deceased dignitary, the body lay in state at the First Baptist Church, and a long procession of mourners formed outside the portico to pay final respects. Incognito among the mourners was a rotund gentleman from Jackson County, formerly of Washington, D.C., a man who had returned to law practice after a stint in the U.S. Congress: one William Carlyle, who took pains that no one recognize him there. And the current U.S. Representative from the district, Walter Stanstead, who took pains that everyone recognize him, came as well.

A donation was taken to provide financial help to the widow, who was left with nothing but a $2000 life insurance policy. In little time an additional $1200 was raised as grateful mourners, remembering all the times in life when they had paid the deceased man nothing, repaid his heiress in whatever way they could after his death. It lifted Mrs. Harrison at least for the time being out of poverty, but she would need a benefactor of some kind in the future, or a profession of her own, to stay out of it permanently.

When the ceremony reached an end, the casket was taken by a shiny new Duesenberg motorcar belonging to the Sunny Meadows Funeral Home of Toccoa to the family cemetery by Ford's Creek Baptist Church three miles away in a remote part of Franklin County. There, a few hundred yards from the site of the antebellum farm where he had been given life, the doctor was interred in his final resting place.

HIS FATHER'S DEATH TOOK a heavy toll on Milt. He felt a void in his life that no one could fill, and he quickly turned introspective and irreligious. A god who would strike his father down in such a way was not a god he wanted in his life. The notion that his father might now be luxuriating in the bliss of Heaven was little consolation to him. He ached for his father to be with him in the here and now, offering him guidance and support, but his solitary trips to the tombstone by Ford's Creek produced only haunting silence. His mother, accepting her theology's teaching that death was a blessing, was less aggrieved. Since this life had so little left to offer her, she started looking forward to the time when she herself would be similarly welcomed by the singing angels into the bosom of Paradise.

It was many months before the boy ceased to be haunted by his father's memory at unguarded moments. He had a dream once, not long after Milton Sr. had passed away. In the dream his father's corpse lay on the couch in the parlor room of the family's house. Suddenly the body moved and stood up and the dead man was alive again, in the exact same form as when he had been healthy, speaking the same way and acting as if nothing had happened. The boy wanted to shout out the news to all the village that his father had been given life again and all would be well—life would go on indefinitely and the bitter pain of separation would disappear. He asked his father how long he would remain with him and he said: "I might even last another year. I've gotta die sometime." Then Milton Sr. shrugged and grinned at his son, as though the length of his return were of no importance to him. At this confusing point in the dream it ended and the boy awoke to harsh reality again. Not only would his father not be alive another year, but he would never be alive—not for a second, not for eternity.

Day by day he struggled with the constant pain of losing his father, and each night he hoped that maybe by tomorrow there would be some relief, some new emotion in the world to blot out his sorrow. He sought in vain for spiritual help; he sought in vain for the comfort of friendship. His only outlet for escaping was his airplane. Up there in the sky, the great beyond, he still felt near his father. There and there alone he felt at peace. In an airplane, all things were possible. Some day, if he flew long enough and diligently enough, he felt his father would be with him again, to congratulate him for his worthiness, to thank him for making him proud again. Gradually, he grew to accept the pain, to learn to carry on in the world, and if not to prosper in his father's extinction, then at least to transform himself by it, to learn from it, to steel himself with fearless intensity and single-mindedness of purpose. Some day, if he ever became perfect, if he advanced the name he bore with honor, he would see his father again and all would be well. This was the hope that sustained him in his darkest moments, when despair seemed on the verge of overwhelming him.

LIFE AROUND WOODVALE eventually returned to normal and everyone's attention became fixed on the deceased man's namesake. Milton Jr. resumed flying his home-built airplane that November, despite fears that a second tragedy hovered about him every time he took his machine up. To support himself he quit his apprenticeship in the blacksmith's shop and took a job at a cotton mill in the nearby town of Lavonia, where he spent twelve hours a day six days a week loading cotton bales into a massive gin. It was grueling drudgery, paying only three dollars a day, and he soon grew tired of it. He began wishing he had heeded his father's advice and had gotten some type of college education. Yet all would not be lost if he followed his dreams. His father had guaranteed him that. He experimented with the Flying Flivver for several hours every Sunday afternoon before appreciative crowds if the weather permitted, taking off and landing perhaps a half dozen times each session and becoming steadily more confident and proficient each time he tried.

His father's dying advice, unlike some of his earlier advice to his son, had been heeded. No matter what anybody was saying, no matter what jeopardy he may have faced, the boy from Woodvale was still going to fly airplanes.

When he realized that all the crowds watching him would probably have paid money to see the spectacle if he hadn't spoiled them by showing it to them for free so often, he began thinking about leaving Woodvale and going somewhere else where nobody would know him. Working in a cotton mill was no way to get ahead; that much was obvious. But how else could he earn a living and what else could he do? He wasn't sure, but it would almost certainly not be a profession available to him if he stayed around Woodvale. Besides, he was having trouble living in the same house as his mother. He was tired of arguing with her about the alleged foolishness of his airplane-flying. He wanted to be among people who saw things his way, had his interests and agreed with him. Most of all he wanted some semblance of the happiness he had enjoyed while his best friend, his father, had been with him. His life, as he now led it, held only tedium and unhappiness for him except during the hours when he flew his plane.

HIS DIFFERENCES WITH HIS MOTHER came to a head in February of 1915. She had scolded him repeatedly about his scruffy collection of friends who traipsed in and out of her house every Sunday when they came to work on the Flying Flivver and push it to its takeoff spot a few blocks away. Since the fallow field that Milt had been using for his plane had just been planted by Bobby Williams with this year's corn crop, he had decided to appropriate Main Street itself, a flat hard dirt straightaway that the state called Highway 17, as his landing strip. His mother was up in arms. Why, this was downright *illegal*, using a state right of way reserved for carriages and vehicles as a place to operate a flying machine! Her son begged to differ with her. He only needed Main Street for a few minutes, just to taxi, takeoff and land, and he wouldn't be disrupting any traffic because there never was any. Nobody wanted to go where that road led, in either direction, because it led to nowhere. But finally Mrs. Harrison had found something substantial to bolster her case. It was an article on the front page of the Monday, February 22 edition of *The Athens Daily Gazette,* which Emily Johnson had brought over earlier that afternoon and called to her neighbor's attention.

"Now, now," said Madge to her son when he came home that night from the cotton mill, "you read this and tell me what you think."

Her son took the paper in hand and noticed the headline she pointed to about halfway down the page:

LIFFEY KILLED IN AIR CRASH
Falls 4000 Feet When Wings Collapse

Stratton Liffey had been performing at the Texas Winter Air Exposition in his native Galveston on the previous afternoon. Local boosters, in order to advertise south Texas's mild winter climate and Galveston's rapid recovery from a devastating hurricane in 1900, had offered Liffey $30,000 to appear in their air show. In a new monoplane that he had designed himself Liffey had been trying to execute a vertical S, the most difficult of stunts then known to aviators. A crowd of 50,000 spectators had gathered by the waters of Galveston Bay to watch the daring native son attempt to master the dizzying heights of the sky and the laws of gravity with an 80-horsepower Gnôme engine. He had risen to 6000 feet and pulled off the first loop of the S to perfection. But he had picked up too much speed for the design of his plane, soaring to nearly two hundred miles per hour before the rear spars of his wings gave way in the final loop of the S. The plane had plunged immediately and violently into the choppy water and exploded in a burst of flames.

As Liffey's young admirer and recent confidant from Woodvale ran his eyes back and forth across the page he showed little emotion, and when he finished he put the paper down on the table beside him and said nothing. His mother sensed that was a concession of sorts, so she kept on confronting him.

"There goes your hero. A lot of good he did, throwin' his life away like that. What was he, twenty-eight? You'll be lucky you even reach that age if you keep flying that thing."

Her son glared at her as though she had just uttered blasphemy.

"Mama, that man died doing what he loved to do. And when I die I hope I'm doing what I love to do, too."

"Enough of that foolishness. What's it gonna take to scare you out of this? You watched your daddy die in front of you, and you still don't have any respect for life."

"I'm doin' what my daddy wanted me to do. If I quit now, what would I do the rest of my life, bale cotton? You oughtta be encouraging me to keep it up. It's my ticket out of this sorry place."

"If you think this place is so sorry, why don't you leave now, then? Go fend for yourself and die on your own, if you think that's such a wonderful thing to do."

"I didn't say dying was wonderful, Mama. *Living's* wonderful—if you love what you're doing with your life. Right now I don't."

The teen's mother, usually matronly and soft-spoken, pouted in a self-pitying sort of way and raised her voice louder than was her custom.

"You don't show any love at all for your mama! Your daddy'd be ashamed if he saw you now!"

He went over to the staircase which led to his room in the attic loft, then turned to face her again.

"My daddy was never ashamed of anything I did—let's get that straight. The problem's with you, not me. Everybody else in this town admires aeroplanes except you, my own mother. When I leave here, there won't be a damn thing left to excite people in this place."

"That's what you think. The world begins and ends with you. But you're the one who needs to understand me, not the other way around. You don't know how I suffer every time you go off in that terrible machine and I worry I may lose my son right after I just lost my husband. Why can't you understand what I'm feelin'?"

He paused to consider the question with his tall strong frame leaning against the stair railing.

"Because I'm not a woman. I never had children or got married or did much of anything. So don't expect me to understand. I need to *do* something first, then I'll finally *understand* something."

ONE MORNING THREE WEEKS LATER, at the crack of dawn, Milt packed a few small personal items and some garments into a knapsack and scrawled out a note in pencil on an envelope which he left on the dining table for his mother to read:

> Mama,
>
> I've decided it's time for me to get out on my own. So today I'm quitting my job and taking the train to Atlanta. I'll leave the car here even though I know you won't drive it. But some of my friends will push my aeroplane over to Joe Freeman's barn and store it in there while I'm gone. I don't know when I'm coming back or where I'll be staying. I might just live outside and sleep in the grass for awhile.
>
> Milt.

Shnook Adams rode with his friend in the Model T to the milling factory in Lavonia, where Milt told his supervisor he was leaving the job and asked to be paid the balance of his salary, a total of $8, which he got in cash. Then the boys drove over to the train station in Toccoa, and Woodvale's favorite son bought a one-way ticket to Atlanta and points beyond for 85¢. He told Shnook he wanted the car driven back home to his mother, and bid him farewell. Shnook felt glum when he saw the train pull away. Now he would be forced to convey the news to a still-proud little Woodvale that it was suddenly no better off than any other one-horse town; that with the senior and junior Harrisons gone life would be stale and uneventful again, and time frozen into the ruts of the past.

The aviator's destination now was not Atlanta at all, but Mecca to the aerial dreamers of the South, the sleepy village of Hapeville, eight miles past the capital city. He didn't know why, but he had a powerful instinct that was pulling him toward the Atlanta Racetrack where he had seen Liffey perform nine months earlier. The idea of being by himself, on an adventure of his own making, without responsibilities or rules or regulations, without anyone knowing who he was or prying into what he was doing excited him. He knew almost as soon as he hopped off the train at the Hapeville depot that this was the most satisfying decision he had ever made.

Though the weather that late winter day was unseasonably dismal and chilly, the newcomer felt a burst of sunshine pouring into his soul. He was impoverished, fatherless and without a home, but he was finally where he wanted to be. Before he left the train station he thought he needed at least a minimum of guidance, so he went over to the ticket booth, where a man sat whittling on a piece of wood with a pocketknife inside a small kiosk.

"Excuse me, sir, you know anybody in this town who flies aeroplanes over by the racetrack?"

The blue-eyed old man, his thick white mustache hanging down over his mouth like the whiskers of a walrus, smiled as he made an extra long and hard stroke with his knife.

"Oh, yeah," he said. "We got a couple boys over there about your age. I think they're squatters. I don't know their names. You go on over there, and I'm sure you'll see 'em. They're always there."

Milt began walking down the sleepy byway called Virginia Avenue toward the large open field he saw ahead about one mile in the distance. The road was deserted and the fickle March winds swirled around him as he drew excitedly near the clearing. He finally reached the barbed wire fence encircling the area, climbed through it, and recognized the silhouettes of several flying machines clustered around what seemed to be a small warehouse about 300 yards away. The wooden grandstands and the egg-oval track itself were still further away, totally unattended. As he drew nearer to the planes, he saw the very two people the man at the depot had promised him would be there, pushing one of the planes toward the track.

One of the boys in the distance was named Dawes and one was named Brackens. Both had been born and bred in small white cottages within a loud yell of the Atlanta Racetrack, and neither had yet reached his twenty-first birthday. They had been boyhood friends, had attended events at the track together from earliest memory, and had developed a mutual fascination for flying machines at about the same time as the approaching stranger. Now they were two of the only people in the area who knew how to fly those machines, had a reputation for skill at it, and even a storied mystique about them in the minds of their fellow Hapevillians.

It was Chester Dawes who had been squatting on the grounds of the racetrack eking out a meager living as the caretaker of the facility while he had thrown up the makeshift storage shed to stash away his pride and joy: a powerful Deperdussin racing monoplane he had salvaged from a wreck at the track during an exhibition in 1913. And it was Robert Brackens who had converted one entire section of the racetrack grounds into an airplane exhibit, with a half dozen machines rope-tied to iron stakes he had driven into the ground himself with a sledgehammer. Though both hailed from poor families, they were beneficiaries of the local philanthropist who owned the vast property, Asa Candler, the first owner of the Coca-Cola Company, who was known to bless the boys with his financial favor in matters pertaining to the maintenance and acquisition of airplanes.

Now the stranger had come within shouting range of Brackens and Dawes, and he called out:

“Say, fellas, y’all know how to fly that plane?”

Dawes, a tall, pleasant-faced man, stopped pushing the plane and turned to face the visitor.

"Course we can fly it, boy. Who are you?"

"Nobody you ever heard of, but I can fly planes too. I built one myself and flew it myself."

Brackens, who was gruff and coarse in comparison to the gentlemanly demeanor of his friend, stopped what he had been doing and squinted at the intruder.

“Fat chance of that, kid-o. I believe that like I believe in Santa Claus. What you doin' on this property? You get permission to come out here from the Candlers?”

"No, I didn't. And who the hell are the Candlers?"

Dawes smiled and walked over to the visitor, whose naïveté amused him.

"The Candlers are the people who own all this. Matter of fact, we call this spread you're lookin' at Candler Field."

The visitor surveyed the magnificent expanse of open land around him.

"Sure is beautiful. Now this is where a man oughtta fly a plane. We got nothing like this back where I come from."

"You're right, it is beautiful," said Dawes. "There's a fortune waiting to be made out here. Gimme fifty good flying men in fifty planes, and I'll find all fifty of 'em a good place to land out here at once."

"I ain't concerned about fifty," said Milt. "I'll settle for one."

Brackens came around from the other side of his plane and walked up to the visitor so that they were practically cheek-by-jowl.

"You still ain't answered my question, kid-o. What are you doin' out here?"

"I came out here to see if y'all can help a fellow down on his luck make some real money flyin' aeroplanes."

"Hah," scoffed Brackens, "you came to *us* to learn how to make money? That's like askin' a couple of monks how to pick up whores."

The large plug of tobacco in Brackens' cheeks bobbed up and down as he chortled, and a long black stream of juice spurted from his mouth into the grass a few feet away.

"I apologize on behalf of my rude friend," said Dawes, offering Milt his hand. "He don't know no better. He's just a born savage."

They shook hands.

"Hi, I'm Chet Dawes. And this here's Bobby Brackens."

Milt shook hands with both of them.

"What'd you say your name was, kid-o?" asked Brackens.

"Milt Harrison."

"'Milt Harrison'," continued Brackens. "Has a nice ring to it. Sounds like a man who'd enjoy an eighty-mile-an-hour breeze in his face, with his arms and legs cooped up in a little box, and oil getting splattered all over 'im, and a motor bangin' away in his ears like all hell broke loose!"

"'Bobby Brackens'," retorted Milt. "I like how that sounds, too. Sounds like a man who can eat crow with the best of 'em."

"Hold on there, guys," said Dawes, "let's not get into a pissing contest. Bobby, this feller says he can fly an aeroplane. Why don't you take him up in that two-seater over there and see if he can back up his talk? It's got dual controls so you can take over if the kid's a dud."

Chet pointed to one of the planes from their collection, an Avro 504, another salvage from a wreck at the racetrack. This was a 1913 British-designed trainer biplane thirty feet long and with wings spanning thirty-six feet.

"That's fine by me," answered Bobby. "Whattya say, boy? You won't back down now, will you?"

The country boy looked in awe at the gleaming plane, his heart once again banging like a jackhammer against his ribs.

"I ain't about to back down, Bobby. That's why I just ran away from home today and came all this way on the train."

The three of them worked to unfasten the Avro from the iron stakes in the ground, and they rolled it several hundred feet over to the oval racetrack. The thrill of being on the very same track as Liffey and a few other aerial heroes was beyond the young visitor's imagining. So far his plans seemed to be working to perfection. Bobby and Chet dumped the contents of three cans of gasoline into the Avro's tank, and Bobby put on his helmet and goggles.

"Sure you know what you're gettin' into, boy?" Brackens asked Milt. "You can turn back now and go back to Boondocksville on the train if you want and we won't have no hard feelin's. Hell, we all done bragged about stuff we never did before."

The visitor bristled at the notion.

"Course I know what I'm getting into, Bobby. First I'm getting into the seat of the plane. Then I'm getting into the air with it. Then I'm getting into different parts of the world with it."

"Ah, confidence!" Brackens cried. "Well, it don't always work that way, boy. That thing may decide to run for you or it may decide not to. And if it ain't gonna run, you ain't gonna fly."

"I've got a feelin' it'll run when I'm in it, man, if you don't mind me saying so."

Chester Dawes began laughing.

"Tell you what, Bobby, this guy's spunk beats all. I'll say this for you, Milt. It's a good thing you're an optimist. You've got to think God's on your side to thrive in this line of work."

"I know he's on my side, Chet, I don't just think it. I got over thirty hours in my home-built plane, so I ain't scared of *nothin'!"*

Dawes smirked and tossed aviator goggles and a leather helmet in the direction of his bold visitor.

"Put these over that great big head of yours—if they fit—and you and Bobby hop in while I spin the propellor."

The upstart from the country mounted the footrest on the bottom wing of the biplane and hopped into the front cockpit while Robert Brackens got into the rear. Dawes then walked over to the propellor and spun it into motion. The Avro roared like a tornado, and the excited visitor opened the throttle gapingly wide so that the plane shot with a bullet's speed by the grandstands. A rebel yell pealed from the lungs of the brash outsider. He pushed the stick forward and maneuvered the rudder bar perfectly during takeoff, lifting the plane rapidly aloft as the wind pelted him in the face. Now Milton Jr. wasn't the only youth with a pounding heart. Brackens began shaking nervously and his bladder emptied into his trousers like a full bathtub with a jerked-out drainplug.

It was ecstasy for the country boy as he saw the glorious breadth of God's earth below him and the splendor of man's handiwork on the horizon as the spires of Atlanta lurked in the distance. The raw speed, the ear-shattering noise, the freedom from rules and limitations of any kind—all quickly mingled together into an intoxicating stew inside the boy's mind. He now had an almost drunken sense of invincibility. He had never done a full loop before, but his masculine energy and adolescent pride took possession of him. With his backseat rider quaking like an aspen leaf he leaned over his shoulder and yelled:

"Got your seatbelt on, buddy? Let's loop the loop!"

He spun the Avro up to a high arc about 3000 feet above the ground, and went upside down with smoke spewing from his engine and drawing a curving line across the upper reaches of the atmosphere. Then he yelled again, with a furious and almost insane joy:

"Yeeeeeeeeeeee-haaaaaaaaaaah!"

Brackens threw up miserably while the Avro was inverted, and by this point he was a urine-drenched and vomit-soaked abomination hanging on to alertness by the slenderest of threads. But the pride of Woodvale was only warming up. Now he nosed down into a dive, studying the horizon carefully until, a mere 800 feet above the racetrack, he leveled the plane again with a smooth maneuver of the stick. The Harrison boy looked back at his now wretched comrade.

"Want some more, Brackens? Let's head downtown, buddy."

Milt turned the Avro northward toward the steel towers of downtown Atlanta, where he intended to duplicate his loop a few thousand feet over Peachtree Street in front of what he suspected would be many hundreds of spectators. In about ten minutes the Avro was poised over the Flatiron Building, Atlanta's tallest skyscraper, in the heart of the bustling city. Once again the intrepid teenager shot his plane high up into the heavens, inverted it just below the cloud cover, flipped it over, and began a perilous dive down to the ground where he hoped he would frighten at least a few people into thinking he was about to crash into them. But a thousand feet above the city he righted his plane again and darted away to the south back toward Hapeville. The mission was accomplished, the point driven home. He had done two perfect loops completely unrehearsed, and in a plane with which he had been unfamiliar. He spotted U.S. 29 from above and followed it back to Candler Field, then landed gently back on the dirt track and skidded to a stop.

"I ain't ready to join you yet, Daddy," he mumbled to himself as he shut the engine off. "There's still more work for me to do down here."

Robert Brackens was as limp as a soggy dishrag, soaked with regurgitations of various kinds, and as grateful to be back on the ground as he was worshipful of the young maverick who had just put him through all that.

"Now I know where the expression of havin' the piss scared out of you come from," he said, "because I done it. Boy, I hope you're proud of what you done: you got me soakin' in a lake of piss."

"Glad I could help out that way," said Milt from the front seat.

"God dammit, boy," Brackens swore."What the hell is your *real* name? You ain't Stratton Liffey's brother, are you?"

"Nope, Bobby, I told you who I am."

Chester Dawes anxiously jogged over to the stationary plane, worried about the condition of the young country boy.

"You OK, Milt?"

"Course I am. Why shouldn't I be?"

"I didn't know Bobby had it in him to put you through that. Brackens, why the hell'd you never tell me you could fly like that?"

"*Holy shit, Chet!*" his friend cried. "He's the one who flew like that, not me. This here fellow must've invented the goddamn aeroplane—and the sky with it, the way he was carryin' on."

"You some famous guy tryin' to sucker us, mister?" Dawes asked the visitor.

"No way," said Milt. "I ain't nobody. My daddy died last fall and before he left he told me to throw caution to the winds, so that's what I'm doin'."

"What a discovery we done made today, Chet!"sighed Bobby. "It came at the expense of a whole lotta upchuckin' from me, but, lordy, that's a small price to pay for what we got here."

The drenched Brackens jumped down from his cubbyhole and wiped his mouth with the back of his hand. Dawes handed him a rag that he'd been carrying in his hip pocket, then he looked back at the upstart aviator.

"He's right, Milt. You made us look silly. You wouldn't mind stayin' around here for awhile, would ya? You got anywhere else to go?"

"I'd love to stay, but I got a grand total of seven dollars and fifteen cents in my pocket, so I don't know how I'd pay for anything."

"We'll figure something out. You're welcome to stay with us until you're up on your feet."

The boys were pleased to hear that Milt's stunt over downtown Atlanta was mentioned in all three of the city's major newspapers the following day. However, at this point, attention was less important to any of them than money. Though Chet and Bobby were not well off themselves, they had been helped by the Candler fortune to amass a noteworthy collection of planes that were actually able to fly. They also had friends in Hapeville from whom they could borrow a little money from time to time in order to finance some of their projects. They shared a small apartment on Virginia Avenue which they now opened up to the newcomer, allowing him to sleep on the sofa in the main room while they occupied a bunk bed in the bedroom. At sunrise they would all walk back to Candler Field, play with their flying machines the whole day, and return home exhausted every night.

———

THE PAIR OF HAPEVILLE FRIENDS were both good aviators, but not close to the skill of their third partner. They quickly latched on to the potential of their new acquaintance, and also recognized a way to exploit his naïveté. The three of them struck a deal amongst themselves. They would enter a race or an exhibition of some kind and split whatever proceeds any of them won equally amongst the trio. This seemed fair to the Harrison boy. But it never occurred to him that his shrewd pals weren't expecting him to share in their success anywhere near as often as they were expecting to share in his. Only a few days after they had begun making plans together Bobby saw an especially interesting notice in the classified section of *The Atlanta Constitution*:

AIR DERBY
SAT APR 3, 1915 12N
CICERO FLYING FIELD, CHICAGO, ILL.
A race from Cicero Field to Speedway Field, Minneapolis
FIRST PRIZE $5,000
Contestants Enter in Person
Sponsored by *The Chicago Tribune* & Sears, Roebuck & Co.

"Boys, I think we finally found us a meal ticket," said Brackens after he read the notice. "I just don't know how we'd get the money to ship all our stuff up there."

In order to transport three airplanes in a commercial railcar to Chicago, plus themselves, the boys figured they would be spending about $400, almost four times as much as Chet and Bobby could possibly cull from their personal savings plus those of their friends and relatives. Since it soon became obvious that they only had enough money for one to enter, the choice about which one to send was an easy one.

"Boy," Chester Dawes said to Milt, "you think you can fly the Deperdussin in the cold weather and at least get us our money back?"

"Sure, Chet. I'll just wear an extra coat and set of earmuffs."

"It might take more than that," cautioned Bobby. "Hell, you might need two or three coats."

"Have you ever flown in really cold weather before?" asked Dawes. "I mean, not just chilly but *ice-box* cold?"

"Come on, fellers," said the country boy. "It'll be *April*, for God's sake. How cold can it be in April?"

Bobby and Chet looked quizzically at each other.

"Let me ask you something, kid-o," said Brackens. "What's the furthest north you ever been?"

Milt shrugged casually, as if the question were completely beside the point.

"The town square in Toccoa, about nine miles from where I was born. What's that got to do with anything?"

"Well, nothing except this," said Dawes. "The further north you go, the colder it usually gets."

"Hell, I knew that, Chet. What do you think I am, a moron?"

"Aw, no," said Brackens, "we know you got a brain. We just don't know if you got a track record for usin' it if it's frozen."

"I ain't got a track record for anything. I'm makin' it up as I go along."

Robert Brackens, with the ever-present tobacco chaw in his jaw, leaned over and spat into the brass cuspidor that he dragged with him wherever he went throughout the apartment.

"Chet, there ain't no point in questionin' this man. He's got a pair of cast iron balls that ain't like anything we ever seen before."

"I just wanted to warn him, Bobby, that's all."

Brackens stood up and went to wrap his arm around the shoulder of Woodvale's favorite son.

"You can't warn this fool. Ain't you learned that yet? You can't warn him about *nothin'.*"

FOR SEVERAL DAYS THE young aviator, encouraged by his two friends, practiced flying Bobby's precious racing monoplane, the Deperdussin, a simple, sleek model that on a good day could approach 90mph. The word about the aerial wunderkind from the back roads of northeast Georgia spread quickly throughout Hapeville, and soon several townspeople began a daily gathering around the edge of Candler Field to watch him fly.

Reporters from the nearby metropolis, intrigued by the impromptu stunt flight over their city that they had featured in their newspapers, were soon hot on his scent as well. Their editors began dispatching them to the sleepy settlement to the south, and the modest Hapeville depot became a daily stomping ground for the local press. The reporters were also noticing this Chester Dawes fellow and this Robert Brackens—they were almost as equally colorful bums as the country boy. Their comrade's fearlessness had rubbed off on them, and now they had been emboldened to do loops and stunts in his rambunctious style. So every day there was now a free spectacle of flight on display in the air above the racetrack, with three boys trying to outdo each other in their various machines as one of them prepared to enter a race.

"Say, what's that kid Harrison's given name?" one of the reporters asked a colleague sitting on the top row of the grandstand.

"Who knows? Why does he need one?"

"We owe it to the boy to get his name right, don't we?"

"Why don't we just call him what he is? A kid. 'Kid Harrison', that's his name. At least now it is."

In a matter of only a few days fantastical stories abounded about Kid Harrison, the self-taught aviator from the Georgia backwater; Bobby Brackens, the crude tobacco-chewing teenage plane collector; and Chet Dawes, a self-promoting tale-telling prodigy who had taught Brackens to fly and allegedly talked Coca-Cola magnate Asa Candler into letting his property be used as a public landing field. On April 1 it was reported Brackens gave Kid a backhanded sendoff at the Hapeville train station, calling him "the fool of all April fools" for entering a plane race in the still-cold Midwest when he had never even been as far north as Tennessee. The reality was somewhat coarser.

"Whatever you do, don't freeze your ass off," Bobby told him under his breath, safely out of earshot of the three reporters that were there. "You do that, Kid, and you got just as good a chance of winnin' as any of them goddamn Yankees."

Chet was somewhat less acerbic in his assessment. He shook the aviator's hand and patted him on the back.

"We got the public on our side now, Junior. You ain't just a boy from Woodvale any more. Now you got thousands in back of you instead of hundreds. Just study the landmarks and keep the ground in sight so you don't spin out, and you can bring us home a big payday."

CHAPTER 6

Snow Derby

WHEN MILT STEPPED OFF the train in central Chicago to transfer to the line to Cicero, a suburb a short ride to the southwest, he was spanked in the face by the brisk outside temperature and an icy wind from off of Lake Michigan. He had heard it would be cold in Chicago in early April but hadn't taken the warning seriously. And eighteen hours in a heated train had done nothing to prepare him for the weather he would be facing on Saturday.

After only a few minutes of waiting to transfer to another line his eyes were teary, his lips chapped and his cheeks numb. The thought that only two days later he would be facing these same elements in an open-air cockpit traveling with the blast of wind magnified at least to 85 mph would have been daunting to someone older than 18 and prone to normal human circumspection. But the boy from Woodvale had been cut from coarser fabric than soft city slickers; born into a place without running water, electricity, paved roads and even telephones, and tempered by the searing heat of a blacksmith shop and a boiling cotton gin; and to him the cold was refreshing. He was thinking it would be fun to try this little game.

The train deposited him and his Deperdussin monoplane at the Cicero Flying Field later that afternoon. A collection of about two dozen flying machines of various makes and sizes huddled around a small hangar. Milt wheeled his plane's fuselage across the stubble to join in the group and then went back to the train landing to drag his wings to his plane. He pulled out his tool bag, the one his father had used for his medical instruments, and with all the precision of a surgeon he mounted and reattached his wings and tuned up his rotary engine. Other aviators, many regulars at the Cicero Flying Field, had been observing the kid from afar as he went about his work, wondering where this stranger came from and what on earth possessed him to think he could compete against these seasoned veterans. One of them who said his name was Arch Hoxsey came to talk to the boy before he finished, curious to know his story.

"What'd you say your name was, mister?" Hoxsey was asking.

"My real name's Raymond Milton Harrison, Jr. But reporters back in Georgia the last couple of weeks have been callin' me Kid Harrison."

"That sounds catchy, boy. Got a postcard yet?"

"Whattya mean?"

"Kid, every flyer with any reputation's got his picture on a postcard, so people can admire him. Here's mine."

Hoxsey handed a card with a painting of himself in front of a backdrop of a gossamer Curtiss pusher plane soaring to the heavens. The characters on the ceiling of the Sistine Chapel scarcely looked so glorified or so otherworldly as the homely Hoxsey did in this work of imaginary excess.

"Durn, Mr. Hoxsey," said Milt, "if somebody as ugly as you can look that great on a card, I guess I should get one for me too. I bet they can turn me into a matinee idol, 'specially after I win this race."

Hoxsey laughed and shook the Southerner's hand.

"You're a swell guy, Kid. Too big for your britches, but we'll humble you on Saturday."

Milt rode the train back to downtown Chicago, stayed in the LaSalle Hotel, a luxurious 23-story red brick establishment on Michigan Avenue, and returned to Cicero the next day. It was a fact almost lost to the teen by this point that the temperature always seemed to be near freezing and the winds were often akin to the gusts that explorers had reported encountering in the polar regions. Acclimatization had taken the boy all of twenty minutes, and now he deemed himself as fit as anyone who would be entering the race to brave the elements.

AT THE FIELD ON THE DAY before the air derby he met most of his competitors. They were a formidable lot of the pioneers of aviation at that time, many with pasts as rough and colorful as his own, their names a roster of American adventurism: Bud Mars, "Uncle" Tom Baldwin, Farnum Fish, Silas Christofferson, Earle Ovington, Fred Hoover and two women, Matilde Moisant and Katherine Stinson.

Later on, outside his hotel, he went for a brisk walk in the freezing evening breezes of the Windy City. The novelty of his hotel room had by then worn off: of running water in a faucet, a bathtub that could fill itself up, an electric light that magically went on and off at the flick of a switch, a balcony that looked straight down on a city that was crowded with spires like a thousand needles on a pincushion. He strolled along Lakeshore Drive with the bleak whiteness and lonely grandeur of Lake Michigan keeping him company. He noticed the temperature dropping considerably and the clouds rolling in from the west, but the weather had yet to faze him. After all: it *was* April. In the hotel that night he had a long and peaceful night of sleep.

His first act the next morning was to draw open the curtains and look again through his hotel window. The sky was a sickly shade of pale gray, the streets at the bottom of the narrow canyons of steel on this Saturday morning were deserted, and tiny ice pellets were being whipped through the air by a howling wind. Lake Michigan looked the color of dirty snow and the puddles on the pavement down below had turned to solid ice. Milt put on three layers of undergarments, two of his coats and two of his scarves, and checked out of the hotel. It was 27ºF outside, and he was far from the most warmly dressed passenger on the train to Cicero, though he yawned in indifference as the rails clicked by beneath him.

After the train let him off at the Cicero depot, Milt trudged along the sidewalks to the airport's canteen, crunching ice under his rubber boots as he walked. A doughty waitress was all alone in the snack bar and she accepted Kid's payment of 20¢ for four roast beef sandwiches and another nickel for enough coffee to fill up the thermos he had brought from home. He wrapped these tightly in a blanket and tucked it behind the flying seat of his plane next to other essentials: a collection of maps, a hatchet and two pairs of gloves. He was proud of his brand new silver flying suit, borrowed from Bobby Brackens, but it was buried from view underneath his bulky scarves and coats.

When Kid returned outside to the cold he was somewhat startled to see the silhouettes of twenty flying machines on the hard flat field—twice as many as had been there on the previous afternoon. The planes were all similar to his Deperdussin in size, though the majority were biplanes. There were such models as the Thomas D-2, the Sloane H-1, Martins and Wright-Martins, Easterns, Standard H-3's and several Curtiss Model D's—all alike in their crudeness and unsuitability to brave any but the most benevolent of meteorological elements. But none of the aviators seemed to care much about the weather. Among them, fear was a distant second in prominence to enthusiasm.

A large kerosene heater with an open flue on one end was being shared by the various competitors and rolled under each plane's engine to heat it so it would start more easily in the cold. At 11:50 AM a portly man wearing a heavy black trench coat, a tall black top hat and sporting a thick brown waxed handlebar mustache asked each flyer to sign an official entry form for the contest. When all the signatures were collected he gestured for the aviators to gather around him.

His name was Joshua Reed of the Sears and Roebuck Company, and he was one of the sponsors of this race. He was hoping all of them had taken the necessary precautions to tolerate the weather, which was, he noted, expected to get worse. Every landing field between Cicero Field and

Minneapolis was well-equipped with fuel, supplies and telegraph lines, so in an emergency they would all have some recourse. The first aviator among them who was able to land his plane at Speedway Field would receive, in Mr. Reed's handwriting, courtesy of the Sears and Roebuck Company and *The Chicago Tribune*, a check for $5000. When he gave the signal they were all to start their machines.

A few moments later Mr. Reed waved a white handkerchief and in a burst of noise and upheaval twenty aviators then swung their propellors into furious motion. And then twenty flimsy airplanes, among them the Deperdussin flown by the boy from Georgia, began lumbering forward on the frozen ground. Earle Ovington's Curtiss Model D was first to the runway and he took off swiftly, as did the next seven planes until Kid's turn in line finally came. He looked behind him one last time through his thick goggles, glanced heavenward at the distant outlines of a pair of the buzzing machines that had risen aloft ahead of him, and opened his plane's throttle, asking silently for assistance from his late great father in the next world.

THE YOUNG AVIATOR'S EARS were stuffed full of cotton underneath his helmet to muffle the roar from the engine, and the sputtering machine, continually threatening to stall in midair, succeeded in climbing steadily into the frosty overcast. It was only by studying the patterns of roads and railroad tracks down below on the prairie that an aerial navigator might tell exactly where he was going. His compass only served as a general guide. Absent a fixed landmark, he was as apt to land in the wrong state in a landscape of such monotony as he was to reach his intended target. Young Milt soon became oblivious to the raucous noise, the bone-chilling cold, the cramped quarters in the cockpit, the 90 MPH rush of icy wind in his face at all times. His attention was fixed instead on the constant need to survey the countryside below for open empty fields where he might be forced to land on the shortest notice if, at any moment, the plane's engine failed, its wings collapsed or its fabric caught fire.

Only a few minutes after takeoff at Cicero, Kid was sucked into a blinding snowstorm that forced him to descend to the treetops just to see the ground. He had maps and a notebook with him, but even the quickest of glances at anything except the panorama outside of his plane carried the risk of an immediate spinout. He lost track of where he was flying as the whole territory beneath him was bombarded by ice and wind. By accident, he was flying well off the course that all the other planes, guided by flyers determined to stay true to their compasses, had taken. A straight-line route from Chicago to Minneapolis that day led directly into the teeth of a raging blizzard, though the best weather reports prior to the race had predicted that the storm would strike further north. However, a route due west out of

Cicero across Illinois, where Milt was flying, just happened to bypass the worst conditions.

Ice began glazing the wings and even the right side of Kid's helmet and goggles as his monoplane teetered between one and two hundred feet off the ground, at times barely clearing the leafless branches of windbreak lines of trees. A northwest wind blew him steadily off his course to the south. In the meantime, unbeknownst to him, a thick crust of ice was building up on the propellor shaft, the wires and turnbuckles, the wing tips and ailerons, and even the tires. Eventually, unless it was scraped away, this buildup of ice along the leading edges of the Deperdussin's wings and framework would spoil the machine's aerodynamics and cause it to spin out of control.

Kid kept looking at his watch to gauge how much fuel he might have left. After an hour and a half he decided he would land at the next recognizable settlement of any kind. Fortunately for him, the storm did let up a few minutes later and by leaning over the side of the cockpit Milt could discern a few distant features on the ground such as grain silos and windmills. However, for as far as his eyes could see, he found only rural prairie lands and no sign of a town.

His nerves had been deadened by the cold, and his face, ears, toes and fingers were entering the first stage of frostbite, which he had never before experienced. He continued to try to dismiss any discomfort as an unavoidable byproduct of the fight to survive and triumph: the stuff that might wither an accountant or a newspaper reporter, but not so tough and determined an adventurer as himself. It just wasn't *manly* to notice pain, and so he *didn't*. Almost to the point of insanity, he was refusing to acknowledge the faintest urges for self-preservation. He was beginning to lose sensation in much of his body.

He began to shake his head back and forth, trying to rouse himself from his frozen stupor. Through his blurred goggles his dizzy eyes looked down over the side of the cockpit, seeking any welcoming community down below. If he landed in too isolated a spot he knew he might freeze to death, and so he fought doggedly on, waging his one-man battle against gravity, the sky, the land and the cold. He figured his plane might run out of gas at any minute, and his worries about what he would do next started nagging at his already disoriented mind. Just when it seemed he would freeze to death, or pass out from exhaustion and crash in oblivion, he saw a narrow black ribbon parting the horizon through his clouded goggles. Like other pioneers in generations before him he was rejuvenated by the blood of the land's main artery.

"*The Mississippi*!" he cried. "I'll just follow it north till I see some life!"

Kid continued tilting his head back and forth in an effort to tease sensation back into his face. He had every reason to expect his engine to quit on him soon with an empty gas tank, and he was pondering how he would glide into a snow bank with a dead engine. And yet the main artery of the land was leading him north to salvation. In a few minutes he recognized the outskirts of Dubuque, as well as an airstrip to the south of it.The snow and the wind had almost stopped completely by the time he lowered his flaps, and the pride of Woodvale had used just about every drop of fuel in his tank when he slid to a stop in the snow on the edge of the landing field.

"I sure am glad it's April," he sighed when he cut his engine off. "If they hold it in January next year they can count me out."

He pulled his goggles up off his eyes and lifted himself up out of his cramped perch with his arms. When he leaped down from the airplane into the snow his sore legs buckled under him and he landed flat on his face. He staggered back up to his feet and surveyed the deserted snow-covered landscape around him. Somebody emerged from a small shed about 200 yards distant and began waving his arms and gesturing for the aviator to come in his direction. Kid took a few halting steps through the snow, fell down again, and then crawled briefly on his arms and legs. He went a few feet until even crawling was too strenuous an activity for him, then he collapsed face down in the snow. When the caretaker of the little terminal finally came to his aid, Milt turned himself over and extended his arm out to be helped to his feet.

"You hurt, mister?" asked the caretaker, Mr. Jaworski, pulling the ice-encrusted teenager to his feet.

"No, just hungry and out of gas. I'm trying to get to Minneapolis before anybody else does."

"The other flyers in the race got into even worse trouble than you. I read over the wires a couple of 'em might be gone already. You ain't planning on going up again, are you?"

"What, and not win the race? You got a truck and a plow to clear the runway, don't you?"

"Of course."

"And you got gas in those barrels over there, don't you?"

"Yes, sir. We stay equipped in Dubuque even in a blizzard."

"Then I'm going back up just as soon as I eat a couple of sandwiches, drink a little coffee and start feeling my fingers and toes again."

Jaworski, a burly strong man of about forty, led Milt into his little shed where the teenager made himself comfortable in a wicker chair that he positioned by a glowing radiator. He devoured two of the nearly-frozen roast beef sandwiches that he pulled from his bag and engulfed several cups of the still-warm black coffee from his thermos. Jaworski looked on with a mixture of admiration and envy.

"So, young man, where you from down South?"

"A little two-bit town called Woodvale, Georgia. Ever hear of it?"

"No, I haven't. Is it a famous place?"

"Hell no. Ain't a damn thing ever happened in that town except the Civil War. People still talk about that like it happened yesterday and they're still fighting it."

"I bet they'll finally quit talking about it soon, 'cause you're wrong. There's something else going on down there now."

The country boy snickered and took down one last huge gulp of coffee.

"Guess you're right. Now two big things have happened down there: the Civil War and me."

Kid offered Jaworski $5 to help him refuel the airplane, scrape the ice off of it, and clear the runway of snow with his truck and snowplow. In another half an hour the aviator was revived and ready to withstand more abuse. The snow and the wind by then had stopped completely, and he was poised by the propellor of his plane to start it.

"There's another storm up north of here," said Jaworski. "Sure I can't talk you into staying here? It's just a race."

"No, thanks," said Kid, "I'll be fine."

The propellor roared into motion and the flyer climbed back into his perch. His new friend leaned down to pull back the chocks from behind the wheels underneath the engine.

"So long, Kid," he shouted above the din to the boy in the cockpit. "I hope you win the race."

With a wave back at the man who had helped him, Milt raced his machine across the landing strip between the high banks of cleared snow, gathered speed and soared aloft again.

"No way I'd be going back up again if that were me," Jaworski muttered to himself as he saw the little machine drift away like a buzzing insect. "But I guess we're lucky we got kids like that nowadays."

CHAPTER 7

Barn Burning

THE MAN FROM DUBUQUE proved to be correct, and less than an hour north of town was another blizzard just as stormy in its wrath as the previous one over Illinois had been. By now, the weary teen's stamina was far less than it had been earlier in the afternoon, and for the first time since he had taken off from Cicero he was considering giving up his quest and conceding the air derby to some other superhuman fool.

It was after three o'clock, and the constant difficulty of making out the simplest features on the ground from his frigid cockpit seat again began to take its toll on Kid. He was being buffeted by the wind and ice, his helmet and goggles were grimed with oil and sludge, his nose was raw, his lungs and throat were inflamed and swollen, and he felt the preliminary agonies of frostbite. He began noticing another damaging accumulation of ice on his wings and resigned himself to having to land again in the first flat open field he could find to try to scrape the ice off before he lost his aerodynamics and spun out. But the storm raged on and on, and he couldn't see well enough to land safely for another hour.

Finally, this latest outbreak of bad weather dissipated and the snowy prairie began glowing under the boy and his plane in the bright afternoon sunshine. After a few minutes of drifting over the hill country of northeast Iowa he recognized flat land again and he was encouraged to continue in the race and not give up hope. Moreover, he was struck with an idea when he saw a collapsed wooden barn on the edge of a modest farmstead. He aimed his plane directly at the collapsed barn, throttled down his engine and lowered the elevators with his stick. The Deperdussin drifted down into a wide flat field that would be full of corn four months later but that now was a half foot deep in snow. The plane swerved as its skid plowed up a heavy wake of snow, but it came to rest remarkably close to its intended target of the fallen barn.

It was quiet now, the wind was still, and Kid was all alone in a strange snow-covered territory. He climbed down from his cockpit and began trudging through the snow toward the only residence he saw, a cozy red farmhouse on a ridge a quarter of a mile distant. Though he stumbled and fell in exhaustion twice on the way there, he was buoyed by the thought that his plan, if successful, would enable him to fly on to Minneapolis without any further stops and reach the end of the race before nightfall. He thought it was possible that all of his competitors, facing the same weather that had dogged him for the entire afternoon, were having similar problems keeping their machines airworthy. The key to success would be removing the ice completely from the plane's fabric, and he felt confident he had a workable plan for doing that.

Kid went around to the leeward side of the red farmhouse where the snow hadn't piled up against the door and gave three firm raps. A shuffle of footsteps came from within, a curtain parted behind a nearby window and a pair of eyes stole a skeptical glance at the stranger in the unfamiliar garb. A moment later the door opened and a man of about fifty in a green plaid shirt, denim overalls and a grey mustache appeared, frowning and hesitant.

"Good evening. What can I do for ya?"

"I, uh, wanted to ask a favor of you, sir."

"Who are ya, young fellow, and what brings you this way on a day like this?"

"The papers back where I come from call me Kid. Kid Harrison."

The farmer squinted at his visitor.

"What papers? Why would papers be interested in you, boy?"

"'Cause I fly aeroplanes. I got one with me now. You wanna see it?"

Milt gestured toward his plane with a sweeping gesture of his hand. The farmer held his storm door slightly ajar and leaned out to look in that direction. Just as the stranger had claimed, a beautiful flying machine was resting peacefully in the snow on the farmer's own property. Never before had he set eyes on an airplane.

"I was wondering," the boy continued, as the elder man stared at the machine in amazement, "if you had any use for the wood in that caved-in barn you got over there. I'd like to start me a fire near my plane so I can thaw out the ice on it."

The farmer's mouth dropped half-open as he heard the plan. This seemed like something out of a dream to him—a swarthy youth in a heavy brown coat, boots, and a leather aviator helmet and goggles suddenly dropping down from the heavens on a snowy afternoon and appearing on his doorstep.

"Why, certainly, Mr. Kid, certainly. I was gonna burn that old barn anyway—you'd be doing me a favor. . . . Now, you come on in here out of the cold and we'll talk about it."

The farmer's hesitation had caused Kid to doubt whether the man trusted him, and he let out a sigh of relief when he saw that he did. He entered through the door as the farmer held it open for him. As soon as the door shut behind him he was soothed by the crackle of a fire in the next room and by the warm glow of light against the homey furniture and wooden wallboards.

"My name's Tom Larson, pleased to meet you," said the farmer, shaking hands with Milt. A middle-aged woman now leaned into the tiny foyer from what appeared to be the main parlor, holding knitting needles in her hands.

"Mary Ann, we've got ourselves a visitor. This young feller's a flying man and his aeroplane got caught in the storm."

"You don't say! I never even saw an aeroplane before!"

"Neither have I, but let's get him out of that polar bear suit and sit him down before we bother him with questions."

"No, please," said Kid, "don't make a fuss over me. I need to have my plane back up and runnin' as soon as I can."

"Aren't you hungry?" asked Mrs. Larson. "Surely you can spare a few minutes to sit at our dinner table, can't you?"

The visitor looked at the farm couple and realized that he couldn't possibly ask for something from them without giving them something else in return, and what they wanted from him was not money but time. He had none of either to spare, but, having been bred in a place where rudeness was an unforgivable sin, he had no choice but to be at the mercy of his hosts now.

"Well, I'll stay, but I won't have you cook for me."

"*Cook?* You think that's anything special, and you fly planes? Why of course we're cookin'. Where's Mabel? *MAY-BULLLL!"*

"Mabel's our older daughter," Mr. Larson told Milt.

A little 7-year-old girl in sandy-colored ponytails peeked through the doorway bashfully at the stranger in the unusual outfit.

"Lilly, say hello to our guest," said her mother, "and tell your sister to come out of her room this instant."

"Hello!" little Lilly said demurely.

"Never mind," said Mr. Larson, "I'll go and dig Mabel out of her room. Kids!" He glanced at the visitor and threw his hands up.

No one had yet invited the Georgia boy into the main sitting room or offered him a place to hang his grimy coat, goggles and helmet, so he stood uncomfortably by the door, the snow and ice on his clothing melting and dripping onto the floor. Mr. Larson, meanwhile, was knocking on a door at the other end of the house.

"Mabel, we need you out here. There's someone I want you to meet."

"Not right now, Daddy. I'm too sleepy."

Her father opened the door to her room, went inside it, and shut the door behind him.

"You don't understand, young lady," he explained to her in a firm but muffled voice. "I'm not asking you, I'm telling you. Get out there now, before I get angry."

Mr. Larson pointed with his finger for her to leave her room. Her eyes clouded up with moist tears and she stood up reluctantly. She was sixteen and fully developed, with thick brown hair and hazel eyes, and at that stage when nothing her elders ever did or said to her was worth listening to.

"The things I do for this family," she growled sassily. "It's just one old fuddy-duddy after another, and I'm always the one who has to keep him occupied."

Mr. Larson chuckled to himself.

"Poor little girl. You've gotten to where you know everything about everything."

Mabel lurched through the two rooms between hers and the front door like a prisoner marching to the gallows. Her mother snatched ahold of her just before she passed through the entryway to the foyer and whispered:

"Behave yourself and be nice. Help him off with his coat and sit him down!"

She was so upset she wanted to scream, but her mother nudged her gently out into the foyer and she was then confronted by the sight of the visitor for the first time. She didn't want to scream any more.

"Well, hello!" she stuttered, having never seen so handsome and rugged a creature before in all her existence.

"Hi there," said Milt, grinning wryly. "I'm Mr. Fuddy-duddy!"

She laughed hard and gave a prissy little curtsy.

"I'm Mabel."

"Sorry to interrupt what you were doing, Mabel, but my aeroplane iced up over your farm and—well, I didn't want to keep goin' and crash when I could just stop here and meet you."

The girl began blushing while she stared at him.

"That was good thinking," she replied. "You look so tired and uncomfortable in all that stuff you got on. Here, lemme help you take your clothes off—oh, I mean—"

Mabel bit her tongue and both she and the visitor laughed.

"It's all right, Mabel, I know what you mean."

"I'm so terrible. I didn't mean for it to come out like that, I really didn't."

"I know. It ain't too often a stranger comes dressed like this."

"But I wasn't even *thinking* that, mister."

"I bet you were. Come on, admit it now. I won't be here long enough for you to be coy. Come on, now."

Mabel's face again turned noticeably red.

"Do I really have to?" she grinned.

"No, I'll keep it a secret. Just between us."

"You won't tell your girl back home?"

"I don't have any girls back home, darlin'. Right now I'm too poor."

He removed his coat, helmet and boots and she went to hang them on the rack by the door. She then escorted him into the parlor and sat next to him on the sofa. In the meantime Mrs. Larson had retreated to the kitchen to prepare the guest a plate of the biscuits and honey that had just come out of the oven in preparation for her family's dinner.

"I'm much obliged to you, ma'am," he told Mrs. Larson somewhat hurriedly at the kitchen table after several minutes of small talk and the wolfing down of three biscuits and a pot of tea. "How much do I owe y'all for all this?"

"Why, we wouldn't consider taking anything from you," said Mabel. "Just make us a promise. When it warms up we want you to come back and see us when you're not in a race. Promise?"

"Anything's possible. If I can just hurry up and get up there to Minnesota before anybody else I'll have lots of money and I'll be able to do what I want."

He stood up abruptly from the table, wiping his mouth with his cloth napkin, and glanced down at his watch.

"Four-thirty. Durn, I gotta be running. It'll take an hour for me to burn the ice off and clear the field."

The guest offered a handshake to Mr. Larson, as if to take his sudden leave. All four of the Larsons then stood up from the table.

"Hold on," said the father. "You need a snow shovel and some matches and fuel, don't you, for what you're planning on doing? I want to go out there and help you."

"I can't impose on you like that, Mr. Larson."

"It's not imposing on me. My daughter wants me to do it, and I'll work and sweat all day for my daughter. Any father would."

Any father would. Kid glanced at Mabel, her smile at him full of curiosity.

"If you say so, sir," he answered, after a pause. "I'm sorry to be pushy, but it's time for us to get moving, then, if you wanna help."

THE ENTIRE FAMILY VENTURED out to the airplane along with the aviator, and the farmer dragged along a large old quilt, some matches and a jug of kerosene over to the dilapidated shed the Georgia boy was proposing to burn. Kid held his finger up to the wind to determine its direction and speed (from the northwest at about five knots with gusts to ten, he figured), taking care to position his site downwind from the plane. He pulled a sharp ax with a long handle out of his plane's cockpit and he knocked several planks loose from the pile of aged wood that had given way to the storm winds. The teenage girl watched him ardently, pleased by his strength and dexterity, as he lugged several of the drier pieces to his chosen spot in the snow by the Deperdussin's fuselage and began forming them into a pile.

"I want everybody to stand way back, 'cause this might cause an explosion," he told the family. "If this fire gets one inch too close to the plane I might get blasted to Kingdom Come."

The others moved about a hundred feet back, and a few minutes later the youth doused the woodpile with kerosene and ignited it. Soon there was a roaring blaze just far enough from the plane to keep from burning its cloth skin and wooden frame and igniting its highly explosive reservoir of fuel, but just close enough to melt the glaze of ice off of it. From time to time Kid would lift the plane's skid and turn it on its wheels so a different part of it would be facing the hottest part of the fire.

He took the stained and moth-eaten quilt the farmer had given him and began waving it at the fire from a safe distance to fan the flames and dry out the moist wood that was still crackling. Then with furious exertion he hacked several dozen more planks loose from the fallen barn and tossed them to the top of what was rapidly becoming an inferno. Now the fire was so hot that he couldn't tolerate standing within a few steps of it, so he dropped his hatchet, took one of the two snow shovels in hand, and, with Mr. Larson's help, he began clearing a path in the four-inch-deep snowpack for his plane's taxi and takeoff. They cleared snow away from an area about 100 yards long and six feet wide, just enough to allow free movement for the plane's wheels. The snowbanks on either side of the path were no impediment for the high-winged monoplane, and the men completed the job in forty-five minutes.

By this point all the ice on the plane and on the ground within several steps of it had melted completely. Kid went to put his hand on the blades of his plane's propellor and found them as warm as a newly baked loaf of bread. Then he glanced at his watch to gauge how time, his chief enemy, had been moving against him. It read ten minutes till six.

"Well, I hate to be so short here," he called out to the Larsons, "but I've done everything I needed to do. How can I ever thank y'all for everything y'all did for me here?"

"Come back some day, Kid," Mabel answered, throwing her arms around him and giving him a hug. "Here." She took a few steps with him to the other side of his plane out of earshot of her parents and handed him a strip of paper on which she had scrawled her address in pencil. "Just so you don't forget."

Mabel Larson, Route 24 Box 9, Jackson Junction, Iowa

"I wish I could take you with me, darlin'," he told her sincerely under his breath.

"And I wish I could go," she whispered. "You don't know how much I wish someone would take me away from here."

The aviator went to bid farewell to the rest of Mabel's family, then chocked one of the Deperdussin's wheels with two large rocks that he pulled up from the snow in the adjacent field. He whirled his propellor around and on the first try it caught and began roaring as if on a hot summer's day. The farm family beheld the scene in astonishment. So this was how a flying machine looked and sounded! Kid jumped into his cubbyhole and gestured for Mr. Larson to pull the rocks from under his wheel. The petrified farmer crouched down low and obliged him, then the plane surged forward, gathered speed under its open throttle, and rumbled into the firmament.

The awestruck observers held their places for awhile, until the voyager and his mechanized bird were a tiny speck on the horizon. Only once in their lives would a man come down from the sky to call on them, and that time had been now.

NATURE HAD FINALLY CALMED by now, and though the rush of cold wind in the cramped cockpit was still fierce, no more did the heavens pour out their icy wrath on the solitary aviator and no more did the horizon drift in and out of fog and sleet underneath him. He could see forever now, and the hilly bluffs that shouldered the continent's great artery soon gave way to the neat geometry of the prairie, the checkerboard pattern of ice-covered roads, telephone wires and railroad tracks basking silently in the fading sunlight beneath him. He needed no compass, for the river led him north all the way to his destination.

He wondered whether he was deluding himself, whether instead of finishing first in the race he might actually finish last. Seven and a half hours had elapsed since his takeoff from Cicero Field—not much less time than a train trip from Chicago to the Twin Cities and far more than the six and a half hours the route had been traveled before by airplane. But today was different, surely. No aviator had ever flown through conditions like these. Still, there was a possibility of disappointment. He needed to steel himself for failure, so if it hit him the shock would be less jolting. It was no shame to lose. He had competed, at least. He would finish the race. And he would prove that he belonged among the very best of his peers, all of whom were older and more experienced than he was. And, if nothing else, he had made new friends and managed to get himself north of Stephens County for the first time in his life.

At last the sprawling twin metropolises of Minneapolis and St. Paul appeared on the horizon, and the slithering black Mississippi River led the aviator to Speedway Field. Down went his elevators and flaps, and down went the Deperdussin, gliding without fanfare to a swerve and a stop on the landing strip just as its engine sucked out the last trickle of gasoline from its tank. Now what? The absence of any activity here was a big letdown. Apparently everyone had already landed and left and he was so far off the pace as to be of no consequence. But at least he had finished. No one could take that accomplishment away from him.

As the boy from Woodvale took his helmet and goggles off, he saw two men in hats and business suits running in his direction. This worried him. What had he done wrong? The men were by his side in seconds, and both removed their hats in unison.

"Well, I'll be damned," cried one, "it's Kid Harrison! He did it!"

He offered Milt his hand, which the weary teenager shook in complete confusion.

"Everybody thought you'd crashed and killed yourself," said the other, *"but you made it!"*

"Yes, sir," the Georgia boy said with the emotion of a corpse, which his deflated hopes made him resemble. "I made it."

"All the other flyers hit the storm and turned around and went back," said the first man. "But not this boy. Like a damned fool he went though it and he survived!"

"Sure enough, mister," Milt said blandly. "I survived."

"You don't understand, Kid," proclaimed the second man. "*You won the race! Nobody else even came close!* Two dozen planes will be landing here after dark, and a crazy rookie who flew through a blizzard beat 'em all!"

CHAPTER 8

Flying Miss Peace

WHEN THE SHOCK OF HEARING that he really had won the air derby set in, the boy from Woodvale pumped his fist, tossed his helmet and goggles into the air, and shouted for joy, with the exhilaration of a schoolboy, which he almost was:

"Yaaaaaaaaaaaaaa-hoooooooooooooo!"

"Kid, come on down out of your perch," said one of the officials who had broken the good news to him, "and let everybody congratulate you. Some people in the hangar are anxious to see you."

He jumped down from his cockpit, fell exhaustedly to his knees in the light dusting of snow, and staggered back up to his feet. The two officials in Panama hats assisted him as he limped across the field toward a tiny shed. Just now he noticed that a bevy of photographers had crawled out from their hiding places and were popping their flashbulbs at him. Several had in fact been at work for awhile now, having captured his landing for hundreds of thousands of adventure-starved newspaper readers all across the land. Now Kid was being told what had happened. A pair of previously unheard of flyers named Alistair Norton and Franklin Bessemer had been lost in the storm, now given up for dead and their whereabouts unknown. Every other competitor, including all the ones of renown, had abandoned the effort to fight the storm as hopeless and had landed at various locations to let the teeth of the blizzard pass by before attempting to continue.

But despite having deviated from a straight-line course, Kid alone had reached his destination. Almost immediately after takeoff he had ignored his instruments in the rough weather and had flown simply on the basis of what he could see, and this haphazard method of flying toward the brightest part of the horizon had gotten him away from the heaviest winds and ice pellets. Also, he had accidentally stumbled upon what proved to be his greatest advantage. While the other planes were encrusted in ice and unable to fly, Tom Larson's fallen barn had given Kid the fuel to burn the ice off of his machine and restore its aerodynamics.

A number of newspaper reporters were assembled inside the tiny hangar to report and, if necessary, embellish the exploits of the latest hero in the fledgling science of aviation. Some of these journalists had impressive piles of bric-a-brac inside their imaginations from which they drew tidbits to describe the derby winner. It turned out now that Raymond Milton Harrison had been born in a log cabin that had formerly housed slaves; that "Kid" had been his father's pet nickname for him from the cradle; that the frustrated physician had taken his own life by shotgun after suffering mental depression following a political defeat; that Woodvale was a collection of four moonshine stills, six Negro shanties, and Kid's log cabin; that Kid had driven the state of Georgia's first automobile at age eight; that Kid had met the late great Stratton Liffey at an air meet and had wooed away Liffey's mistress in an Atlanta hotel lobby after besting him in a violent fistfight. No account of the wunderkind from the boondocks was too improbable for these reporters, even though the bald facts were interesting enough to stand by themselves.

A check for $5000 was presented to the new celebrity, and he was taken to an upscale Minneapolis hotel and given royal treatment. Everywhere he went people were giving him things for free. His hotel room was free, his taxi rides were free, his sumptuous meals were free, and his adolescent imagination concluded that several of the women who were hanging about his coattails were to be had for free too. It all seemed surreal to the country boy. He barely had room to express thoughts of his own while being escorted from one gray-headed official to another and being told all manner of high-flown bluster about what he had done and what he had meant to the world. The main point of satisfaction for him was the prize money. He hated having to share it with Brackens and Dawes, but even a one-third share was enough to guarantee that he wouldn't be sleeping next to Bobby's spittoon in their Hapeville dustbin any more, nor in the tall grass at Candler Field, nor in his mother's house, but instead in a place of his own.

The next morning he received a gold medallion on the end of a red, white and blue ribbon proclaiming him the winner of the Chicago-Minneapolis Air Derby of 1915. He posed for several more newspaper photographers throughout the morning and continued to give interviews in which he occasionally contradicted some of his own earlier exaggerations. Nobody minded. No two newspaper accounts of him or his accomplishment were alike, and a reader in one city was apt to think of him as a totally different character than a reader somewhere else, swayed by a differently colored version of his story.

He was being treated so well that he had an inclination to stay in Minneapolis for several days to bask in the steady attention he was receiving. But by Monday morning the reporters were gone and the workaday world already seemed to have passed him by. Such was fame. He

He didn't even have enough money in his pocket to pay his train fare home, so he had to wait in front of the doors of a bank across the street from his hotel until opening time at 9AM, then endorse his prizewinning check in exchange for $5000 in cash. Now he suddenly became desperate to go home. With more money on his hands than he had ever even seen in his life he felt like a marked man, and every set of footsteps behind him for the rest of the day became a cause for suspicion.

THE TRAIN RIDE HOME gave the aviator many hours of idle time to think. Being rich really wasn't all that satisfying, as he now considered it. Too many people out there were after your money if you were rich. Being famous wasn't so wonderful either, because now that he had been famous today he would feel disappointed unless he were equally famous tomorrow, and almost nobody ever was. That's what he didn't like about all this. It had been more satisfying for him to look forward to winning than it was to win. Now he started resenting Bobby and Chet because he was bound to give them $3333.33 of *his* money, and he would probably never have that much money again in his life. His sudden acquisition of modest wealth had transformed his friends into his enemies. And his accomplishment of only two days ago was now drowned out by another headline screaming from the front of that afternoon's *Minneapolis Star-Tribune*, which was being read by a fellow passenger aboard the train:

War in Europe Spreads Across the Continent

"What are they fighting about over there?" Milt asked the man across the aisle from him.

The bespectacled newspaper reader, who wore a mustache and a long gray coat, shrugged as he turned the page.

"Some archduke got assassinated and now all those little countries over there are attacking each other, trying to get revenge. Germany's the main one in it now, I think."

He folded up his paper and yawned.

"Germany's awful powerful," he continued matter-of-factly. "We better be careful or they might come after us."

"Well, I hope they *do* come after us," said Milt. "I guarantee you it won't last long if they try it."

The man chuckled, removed his spectacles, and rubbed his eyes.

"They're way ahead of us now, son. They got tanks and submarines and they're about to use aeroplanes for combat. Just think of it: a fleet of German boats barricading the East Coast, and a whole squadron of aeroplanes taking off from ships and coming to drop bombs on our cities, and we'll be caught flat-footed because our government hasn't funded any air defense."

The man said it casually, as though it would be happening far away from him and would affect only a younger generation of people. But his listener was provoked.

"Trust me, sir," said Kid, "that won't happen."

"How do you know it won't happen?"

Milt began to pout, as though he hadn't thought the matter out very fully. But just as his listener picked his newspaper up to resume reading it, thinking he would never get an answer, Kid shot back:

"'Cause we ain't France, that's why!"

BY THE TIME MILT'S TRAIN chugged into the Hapeville depot late Tuesday afternoon, a gang of Atlanta reporters and Hapeville locals, among them Chester Dawes and Robert Brackens, were on hand to toast him. Despite all the hoopla about how wonderful he was, Kid tried not to lose sight of the fact that he had only been as good as his plane, which belonged to his two friends, and that at a time when many planes at exhibitions either didn't fly at all or crashed and burned in midair, his machine had been completely sound and had functioned perfectly. And when he greeted his two friends he remembered another thing: a month ago he had been a penniless bumpkin of no distinction and still would have been that today without them. Instead, he was the great Kid Harrison, an instant legend, a sudden sensation in national headlines.

"Ain't nothin' to it, huh, Kid?" asked Brackens when Milt came down the steps of the train. "It was never in doubt was it?"

"The Almighty wrote it in stone at the beginning of time," answered the returning hero, shaking hands with his two colleagues.

"You done us proud, boy," said Dawes. "We couldn't have done it better ourselves."

"You know that ain't true, fellers," said Kid. "It's the plane that did it and not me. Either one of y'all would have brought the prize home if you'd been there."

"I ain't so sure about that," said Brackens. "The two of us got more goddamn common sense than to set a bonfire off within ten feet of a gas-filled firetrap like you done. You really do got Jehovah in your hip pocket, man. You do the dumbest damn things anybody ever tried, but for you they always work."

"I gotta agree with Bobby on that one," said Chet. "Putting a fire next to a plane's like putting a fox in a chicken pen."

An assortment of local functionaries from the worlds of commerce and politics had assembled on the landing down below. The most persistent of these people was a young thin clerk with hair parted neatly in the middle of his scalp and dark brown hair and a navy blue double-breasted suit. He had been grilling both Chet and Bobby for the last hour about their friend as he awaited the arrival of the train, and now no sooner had Kid weighed in with his buddies than the clerk tapped him on the shoulder and said, with the most honeyed of Southern drawls:

"Kid, my name's George Grantland. I'm a clerk in one of the major downtown law firms, and I just wanted you to autograph this copy of the headline on the *Constitution* for me. Will you do that?"

The law clerk handed Kid a fountain pen, and the aviator signed his nickname to the front page of the Sunday *Atlanta Constitution* which carried the news of his victory: "To Mr Grantland, Thanks for your support. Kid Harrison." Then he gave the paper back to the clerk and shook his hand.

"Young man," said Grantland, "you got a glorious future ahead of you. You keep it up now, you hear? I wish I had the bravery to operate an aeroplane, but I don't. I'm like a lot of people: I've got to live my dreams through people like you. You're doing all of us a wonderful service, and people are gonna remember you a long, long time."

"I appreciate hearing that, Mr. Grantland," Kid replied, "but I don't think it'll happen that way. A week from now, nobody'll remember what I did—unless I do something even better this week."

The reporters and their associates laughed a bit, and the conference ended a few minutes later. After the Deperdussin had been wheeled off the train, the three aviators reattached its wings and pushed it down Virginia Avenue toward Candler Field. Several dozen Hapevillians buzzed around them like a swarm of bees. All traffic came to a standstill as the sacrosanct airplane and its attendant tide of human suitors marched up the thoroughfare toward its customary resting place. When it had finally reached the edge of the vast pasture, the boys chained it to a tree and the parade of glad-handers then followed them to their tiny apartment. People kept asking them what they would do next.

"Well, folks, we finally got us some money," said Chet, "but we could always use more. Don't be surprised if we have us a fly-in exhibition right here at the track this summer."

MILT HAD NO DESIRE to hear Brackens' snore that night, so he asked someone in the crowd for a ride to Atlanta, and he went and made a $20 down payment for a nice apartment on Ponce de Leon Avenue for $40 a month. He had already given his two chums their exact share of $3,333.33

from his derby winnings, but that still left him with more cash than anyone in his circle of acquaintances had ever possessed. He had absolutely no furniture whatsoever, so that night he slept on the bare floor of his apartment. The next morning it dawned on him that he needed a woman's touch to furnish his home and the only woman who might do it, his mother, was a three-hour train ride away in Woodvale. He would be headed home much sooner than he had ever expected, and in much better condition. He had been away from home only three weeks, but nothing would ever again be quite the same as it had been.

When the prodigal native son made his unnanounced return to the hinterlands of northeast Georgia, he paid for a taxicab to take him the nine miles from the Toccoa train station to Woodvale. Madge gave him a warm hug and pulled him into the house. "You home for good now, son?" she asked him. "You done with aeroplanes yet?"

"Mama, didn't you hear what I did?"

"Of course I did, son, and we're all proud of you, but you don't ever expect to do something like that again, do you?"

"It'll be even bigger next time, Mama. I hear the Germans are about to attack us and I'll have to go over there and fight 'em to keep us safe."

"Oh, son, you hush up. Germans. My family were Germans and they ain't about to attack."

He took off his coat and laid it on the kitchen table, pulling a large stuffed envelope from its inner pocket.

"Lookee here. I got enough to pay you back. Daddy gave me $950 for the Flying Flivver, and this here's over $1600. Ever think you'd see this much money in your life?"

Her eyes widened with astonishment.

"You sure you didn't break the law to get all that money?"

"I won it fair and square. I'm a regular celebrity now, and the reporters even gave me a new name. They call me Kid now."

"Well, that's a good name for you, 'cause that's what you are."

Milt began counting out $100 bills with his hands, and gave his mother nine of them, plus one fifty.

"Here, take it. All I want's for you to ride to Atlanta with me and help me pick out furniture. Also, I want you to let me have the Model T. You never use it, and it sure would come in handy for me down in the big city."

Margaret stared guiltily down at her son's cash-filled hand and hesitated.

"Go on," he continued, "take it, and let's get out of here."

"But, Milt, we can't just leave. We got to let all the townfolk see ya. They've just been bustin' at the seams waiting for you to come back."

"So I was right, wasn't I, Mama?"

"Right about what?"

"I was right when I said this town wouldn't have anything else to keep it goin' except me."

WORD SPREAD QUICKLY that the pride of Woodvale had returned from his journey to the ends of the earth and would now be staying permanently in his native village to exhibit the aerial prowess that had wowed a nation. Or would he? No one could gauge for certain, so a crowd soon gathered outside the house on Oak Street to cut off the beloved adventurer in the event he tried to make a secret getaway without briefing them. He quickly realized from inside the house that he would never get off the premises without conversing with the townfolk, so he went out on the front lawn, accepted hugs and backslaps from Zeke, Shnook and many other friends and neighbors, and began digesting the events that he had missed—all two of them. Arch Williams had finally died of consumption, and Ruth, that colored girl who helped nurse his daddy—what was her married name?—oh, Mrs. Bonniwell—why, her husband was on Army duty in the Panama Canal Zone and he'd come down with malaria and died, leaving her all alone with an 8 and 10 year-old.

Milt looked past the several dozen white people who were surrounding him on his front lawn and noticed a gathering of blacks humbly watching him from across the street, trained by the rigid customs of the day to stay on that side of the street unless invited to do otherwise. He spotted Rev. Patterson and broke free of his racial peers to visit the far side of Oak Street.

"How you doin', boy?" Rev. Patterson asked excitedly, smiling and patting the youngster on the shoulder. "So they callin' you *Kid* now, huh? Well, it's about time the world woke up."

Woodvale's Negro community now embraced its hero in its own way, with handshakes and friendly chatter.

"Reverend, I was sorry to hear about Ruth's husband," he consoled his listener, as the people around them grew quiet.

"Thanks, son. I know you mean it. The Lord is guidin' us through. Day by day, step by step, we're divinin' the true meaning of suffering. But for every heartache, there's a joy. We have a limb of our family severed, but then we see our Woodvale boy go out to conquer the world. Ruth, come on over here."

Mrs. Bonniwell had been quietly standing on the fringe of her group, shy and inconspicuous, but she now emerged from hiding and went and hugged Milt. The crowds on both sides of the street drew gravely quiet when she boldly kissed him on the cheek.

"The pain will never go away," she told him, whisking away a tear. "I'll never get back what I had. But, you—oh, child, you've had it too with your daddy, you've had somethin' stolen from you that you can't ever get back."

She took two steps back and held both of his hands in hers.

"You're wonderful," she said. "Lemme hear the sound of your voice. Your voice is the most soothing sound in the world to me, now that so many other sounds I loved are gone."

"What can I say, ma'am? I feel a little uncomfortable right now."

She pressed her lips together, grinned, and closed her eyes briefly.

"I don't care what you say. Anything. I just wanted to hear you speak."

He paused awkwardly.

"Thank you, Mrs. Bonniwell. I—I'm not much for talkin' at a time like this."

"You're still just a boy now. When you're a man, that'll be the time for talk. And I will be there to listen to you, sugar. Always."

AT SUNRISE OF THE FOLLOWING morning Milt and his mother began the long trek to Atlanta in the old Model T on the rough country roads that then constituted the main vehicular arteries of northeast Georgia. When Margaret Harrison was turned loose in three downtown Atlanta furniture stores with her son's money it began dwindling at an alarming rate. Eventually, a mountain range of furnishings began forming in his apartment's main room as waves of delivery men surged through his front door. Milt was overwhelmed. He found that he needed some time to himself, to consider the sheer scope of the material acquisitions his mother had made on his behalf. He therefore drove his mother without delay to the Terminal Station downtown, put her on the afternoon express locomotive back to northeast Georgia, gave her cash enough to hire a cabdriver to get her from Toccoa to Woodvale, and waved good-bye to her.

Kid was in Hapeville before too much longer, at the racetrack, entreating Brackens and Dawes for help.

"Y'all got all the money now, I've just about pissed all mine away. Can we strike while the iron's hot and do some type of air meet here while people are still interested in me? Pretty soon I'll be back where I started, without five cents to my name."

Brackens guffawed and put his oil-stained paw around his friend's back.

"It's women, ain't it, Kid? Don't lie about it now."

The country boy blushed a bit, as much out of anger as embarrassment.

"Hell no, Bobby, it ain't women. It's *woman.* Just one. My mama. She turned my room into the Waldorf-Astoria."

Robert Brackens frowned and removed his arm from his friend's shoulder.

"Don't bullshit me like that, Milton Harrison. It ain't no shame to admit to a weakness for the ladies."

Now Milt was downright infuriated, because he was reminded that despite having youth, good looks, and a measure of fame and money to commend him, his only date so far had been with his mother.

"Shut up, Brackens," he growled angrily. "I don't want to hear this from you."

"Leave him alone, Bobby," said Dawes. "We cleaned up off this man, so we better do what we can to keep him happy."

Robert Brackens walked over to his latest passion, a Blériot XI monoplane that he was just now on the verge of getting into flyable condition again with the new infusion of cash he had gleaned from Kid's prize money. He put his right hand lovingly on the wing and stroked its fabric.

"Chet, we oughtta tell this man about the girl Georgie Grantland brought over here this morning. The painter."

"Good idea," answered Dawes. "She's the one who can do his postcards for him. He'll need that for our air shows."

"What the hell are y'all talking about?" wondered Milt.

"Mr. George Grantland," said Brackens, "that highfalutin' law clerk who showed up to meet you at the depot the other day. The guy can't get enough of our aeroplanes. So this morning he comes over here with the most beautiful woman I ever saw in my life, a black-haired love kitten, and he says he wants her to paint some of our planes and would that be allright with us. Hell, Chet and I 'bout come out of our drawers."

"We sure did, Kid," added Dawes. "And this lady was sorry you weren't around. She kept askin' about you."

Milt tingled a bit with anticipation. This time he knew the two of them were serious.

"Really? Who was this woman?"

"A college girl at Agnes Scott," said Chet. "Says she's an art student over there. She's about our age or maybe a little older—must be about 21, 22 years old."

"Think I should meet her?"

"You bet, buddy," Bobby snorted. "I wouldn't wait five seconds to meet her if I was you and I ever got a chance. They ain't a man on the face of the earth that wouldn't do backflips for that gal."

"Well, what's this girl's name?"

"She never said what her name was," said Brackens. "But Mr. Grantland kept calling her Miss Peace. That don't sound like the right name for that gal. I'd've called her 'Miss War', 'cause the whole damn time she was around I had a war goin' on down in my trousers."

"Trust me," Chet assured him, "you won't care what her name is. Just take our advice and relax, Kid. George said he'd bring her back here on Sunday morning to meet you. By Sunday you better tear down that brick wall you built around your heart to keep the gals out, or you'll be really sorry."

KID NEEDED VERY LITTLE further persuasion. He was anxious to see whether this Miss Peace would be Miss War for him too, just as she was for Bobby. The plan was set for her to be brought back out to the field on Sunday. She and George Grantland had met a few weeks earlier at Piedmont Park in Atlanta. At the time she was peddling her watercolors by Lake Clara Meer one morning, and he had stopped by and bought two. He returned again the next week, bought another, and appointed himself her Platonic mentor. They derived mutual benefit from the arrangement: he, the staidly married man, got to enjoy looking at her; and she, the temptingly single vixen, got to enjoy earning a little money from selling her artwork to somebody who either thought it was good or was willing to pay for it to give her some reason to spend time with him.

The unholy threesome of Kid, Chet and Bobby were primed and ready when George brought her to the field again. As they sat in the deserted grandstands a black Oldsmobile sedan, churning up a dustcloud, turned off Virginia Avenue and parked on the roadside shoulder about a quarter mile away. Two people emerged from the car: George and a girl wearing a skimpy white outfit of dimensions seldom seen in that time outside establishments of ill-repute. She was, indeed, a stunningly beautiful creature. Her thick black hair hung down to her shoulders in soft waves, her large green eyes glimmered within long thick lashes, her skin was as smooth and unblemished as pure cream, her thick full lips framed a perfect set of straight white teeth, and her figure seemed to have been duplicated from the prized statuary of antiquity.

"Kid," drawled George Grantland when he and the girl had drawn near, "I brought an artist to paint you and your surroundings today. This young lady is named Jasmine Peace. Jasmine, I'd like you to meet Mr. Milton Harrison."

"Pleased to meet you, ma'am," he mumbled, taking her hand limply into his. She laughed coquettishly and winked at him.

"The pleasure's all mine, darling."

Miss Peace had a charcoal pencil and a sheaf of papers, and she asked the ruggedly handsome Mr. Harrison to sit on one of his plane's lower wings while she made a sketch of him. She completed her rendition in about five minutes while Chester Dawes peered over her shoulder.

"Say, George," he called out, "come over here and look at what this lady done."

The thin clerk walked out to them, examined Jasmine's sketch, then glanced approvingly at her through his spectacles.

"I think you've found your specialty. Marvelous work, dear, just exceptional."

Kid took a deep breath and put his goggles over his eyes.

"Well, ma'am, you done your part, now here's mine. Stand back and don't get scared."

"What are you doing, Mr. Harrison?" she asked, as if he had done something to hurt her feelings.

"Why, ma'am, I'm about to show you what I can do. You showed me your stuff, now it's my turn."

"You mean you're planning to take that aeroplane up and not ask me to go with you? Shame on you. Whatever became of chivalry? What *is* the world coming to?"

Milt pulled off his goggles, squinted, looked at his friends who seemed just as confused as he was, and threw up his hands.

"Say what? Talk American, miss. Remember, I'm just a dumb gorilla from the sticks."

They all laughed aloud now, despite her nervous doubts about what she was trying to force herself to do. She wanted to do whatever this fellow did—to follow him and live in his world.

"I want to be next, Mr. Harrison," Jasmine told him.

"Come on, now, miss. You don't understand."

"Yes, I do understand. I want to be the first *passenger* who ever rode in an aeroplane. I mean, the first person who couldn't actually fly it herself, but just wanted to do it for the fun of it."

"I don't think I oughtta do that ma'am," said Kid. "I don't want to scare you to death."

"Why not? Why can't I be the first?"

"Go on, Kid," said George, "go on and let her be the first."

"*I'll* take you up," said Bobby. "You don't want to go up with this fool, believe me. He'll turn your stomach inside out, this boy will, and I learned that that hard way."

"No, no," said Jasmine. "I want Kid Harrison to take me up with him. I want him to show me the joy of flight."

"You can't go up in an aeroplane dressed like that, Miss Peace," said Chester Dawes. "It just won't work."

"It *will* work," she persisted. "Go get me one of those coats you fellows wear, and I'll put it on."

Milt thought about the matter for a few seconds before a gleam came to his eye. He took off his coat, helmet and goggles then tossed them over to her.

The three other men went to stand back in the distance while Kid helped Jasmine into the front seat of the Avro 504. He removed his pocketknife and cut loose the ropes that held the biplane to its moorings. She was absolutely dreading every second of the experience, and it was obvious to all four of the men watching her that she would have preferred to be just about anywhere else than where she now was.

"You don't have to do this if you don't want, ma'am," Milt tried to reassure her. "Ain't nobody forcing this on you, now."

"I'll never understand anything unless I do it," she responded with a quivering lip. "I want to know firsthand how it feels to fly above the earth."

"Have it your way, then, miss. That's just what I thought the first time I ever tried it."

"And how long ago was that?"

Kid scratched his head and stepped down from the perch beside her, now that she was securely belted into her seat.

"Oh, I guess about . . . *eight months ago*."

"My God!" she swore. "And who taught you?"

"*I* did," he beamed proudly. "I taught myself."

"Really? And you weren't scared?"

"Why should I have been? It's just a life. There's a billion more even if I lose mine. This world sure don't begin and end with a little ole poor boy from Woodvale, Georgia, you know."

Now her skin turned pasty white and was covered with goosebumps. She tried to swallow, but her mouth and throat were dry. She barely heard him as he cackled with delight and spun the whirligig in the front of the strange machine, and now her senses were flooded with noise and vibration and her heart had beaten itself into her mouth. The man jumped into his cubbyhole behind her and the machine shot ahead with breakneck speed. When the plane lifted itself up into the air, the world had never looked so frighteningly beautiful to her, and it seemed to her to be ages before they turned around and started their descent. . . .

The first flight ever to carry a lay passenger at the old Candler racetrack departed at 12:17 PM Sunday April 11, 1915 and arrived several minutes ahead of schedule at 12:51 PM on the same day. It was conducted under windless conditions and unlimited visibility, and its course was forty-one miles in a circuitous route over the red-clay piedmont of three counties.

The passenger, a 22-year-old college student, reported no ill effects from the journey and reached her destination, which just happened to coincide with her starting point, in perfect safety.

CHAPTER 9

Crashing and Courting

THAT SUMMER OF 1915 the skies above Hapeville hummed with activity, as aviators from around the nation came to display their hard-won talents at the invitation of the three boys who held dominion over the kingdom of empty space above the old racetrack.

An aviation meet of that day consisted of a series of races, takeoffs, landings, and attempts at altitude records, evaluated by a panel of judges whose credentials never really mattered but whose opinions always seemed to match the prevailing sentiments of the audience. The vagabond airmen of the day, select in number, tended to make their rounds along the seasonal circuit of exhibitions from town to town, sometimes to crash and burn along the way, sometimes to lose their lives in their pursuits, sometimes never even to get off the ground in their fickle machines.

American aviators had been known to embarrass themselves in the early teens at European aviation meets through the sheer flightlessness of their machines. But in many cases at exhibitions at Los Angeles, San Francisco, Chicago and a handful of other places they had held their own. And at Hapeville . . . well, the word was now spreading that three of the best airmen in the world now inhabited Candler Field, and they began demonstrating their skills before large audiences that year. Of greatest note was the one they called Kid, the one who was featured in the most ornate postcards and placards and whose handsome profile wooed many a sheltered lass into the hot and dusty grandstands by the egg-oval track.

Colorful paintings of aerial machines in various stages of flight adorned notices that appeared on posters and in newspapers throughout the area: ATLANTA INTERNATIONAL AVIATION MEET. JUNE 5-13, 1915 AT CANDLER FIELD. FEATURING KID HARRISON, CHET DAWES AND BOBBY BRACKENS. Miss Peace adorned her pictures with fashionable faces in florid attire looking awestruck at pusher biplanes and monoplanes, dirigibles and hot air balloons. And somewhere in all of her posters lurked the visage of the Kid, the overnight sensation who had learned to fly only eleven months earlier but who now, courtesy of the myth-makers in the press, seemed to have been born with a set of his own wings.

She of course had great influence in building up his image, as did news reporters and local boosters like George Grantland. Attendance at Kid's exhibition was almost mandatory to anyone who considered himself an aviator of importance. The atmosphere about the field for those glorious nine days was electric and contagious, as vendors hawked 25¢ programs and popcorn, motorcars jammed Virginia Avenue, and 50,000 spectators tried to outdress each other in their finery. Hot air balloons floated above like painted clouds, dirigibles buzzed about, and every size and shape of airplane was on display as the Harrison boy wowed the crowds.

His first daring feat was an altitude flight, in which he soared over two miles above the racetrack in a Curtiss biplane before running out of fuel and then gliding to a landing. He won several competitions for spot landing on various points along the racetrack, and established a new thirty-mile distance record of only nineteen minutes. And of course he looped and dodged his way about the field with the nimbleness of an eagle. In addition, Brackens and Dawes demonstrated their flying skills as a sort of complement to the flamboyant gyrations of their colleague. But it really did seem as though this aviation business belonged to the Kid.

All the success and adulation began to affect Milt like a powerful drug, and his head started drifting even further up into the clouds than his planes. At the end of each day's exhibition the cream of parasol-twirling society collected around the attractive young daredevil to bathe him with smiles, handshakes, expressions of gratitude and stares of love. He felt too dignified to spend his nights in a mere apartment on Ponce de Leon Avenue, so he lavished more of his money on a penthouse suite in downtown Atlanta at the Piedmont Hotel, awaiting the arrival of hordes of mistresses. But they never came. He expected to open his door at any hour of the day or night and to drag them in like fish out of a troll net, but life was never so easy. His sheltered background had given him little preparation for the wily ways of the world, and the mere fact that he could operate an airplane with masterful skill did not erase his social awkwardness or lack of years. In truth, he preferred being alone in a plane to anything else, for then he could dream anything he desired about his life on the land below and not worry that it be grounded in any type of reality down there.

It was during such a moment of detachment on the next to the last day of the air meet, a Saturday, that the pains of the earthbound world invaded Kid's private perch in the sky. While trying for yet another altitude record in the Avro that afternoon he became aware of a loud hissing noise coming from his engine. The Avro sputtered and coughed, and Milt leaned his head over the side of the cockpit to find a stream of oil spewing out from the engine into the open air. His plane's oil line had ruptured completely 6500 feet above the racetrack, and now he realized his entire life depended on his ability to improvise.

The plane suddenly lost all its power and began to spin out. Kid quickly shut off his engine completely and tried to level his machine so it would glide safely down to the track. But the spinning only increased and he grew dizzy and disoriented. About a thousand feet above the ground, he straightened his plane and calmly nosed it toward the ground. However, he was too dizzy to keep his fuselage level during his landing and his plane crashed nose-first into the track, flopped over on its side, and collapsed. The engine never exploded nor did the plane catch fire, but Milt was thrown from his seat, pinned under the wreckage, and knocked unconscious, the femur bone in his right leg broken like a twig.

A black ambulance drove onto the track to the victim's side, and he was gently lifted into the rear compartment by Bobby, Chet and two other aviators. The crowd in the grandstand screamed at the moment of the crash and then grew gravely quiet as the ambulance bore away the aerial miracle worker. Yet the show had to go on, with or without him, and it resumed just after the debris from his accident had been cleared from the track.

MILT WAS TAKEN TO WESTVIEW Hospital in Atlanta, where his broken leg was set in a plaster cast. He was placed in a quiet private room several stories above the bustling city, and left alone to consider his future. Two reporters came to bother him that night, and the following day, after the aviation meet concluded without him, the inseparable duo of Brackens and Dawes paid a visit. With them were Mr. Grantland and Jasmine Peace, who was dressed as provocatively as a courtesan. She was carrying a small brown package of some kind, clutching it protectively in her hands at all times. Chet went over to his friend and shook hands with him.

"How you doin', Kid?"

"I'm alive. That's all that matters, I guess."

"We sure missed you today, Junior," said Bobby. "All the excitement was gone from the crowd."

"I guess so," said Milt. "They were hopin' I'd be dead by now and couldn't stand thinking they paid a buck apiece for a wreck that didn't kill me."

The men all chatted amongst themselves for awhile as Jasmine stood patiently and quietly off to the side. When the other three finally left the room and she was alone with Milt she put her package down on the nightstand by his bedside.

"Why won't you come meet my parents?" she asked him.

"I've said it before and I'll say it again. I won't stand for being made to feel like a second-class citizen. I can hear 'em now, them blue bloods. Your dad'll say, 'So, what do you do, boy?', and I'll say, 'Fly aeroplanes, Mr. Peace,' and he'll say, 'No, I meant what do you *really* do?' and I'll say, 'That's it,' and then he won't say another damn thing, just look at me with this mean know-it-all stare that just screams out: 'Don't you dare rub your filthy paws all over my little girl, you greasy bum!' If you think I'm gonna put myself through that, you're crazy."

"You're a famous figure now and everybody in Atlanta wants to meet you. My parents wouldn't grill you like that."

"No matter what, Jasmine, it would come down to one thing. They wouldn't want you to be mixed up with a bum like me. And you know why, sweetie? Because they'd know I ain't your kind. The only reason you're with me is you like to rebel against them, that's all."

"And what's wrong with that? A little rebellion every now and then is a good thing, don't you think?"

"Not when you're old like they are. Old people don't like rebellion—especially if it's their own children doing it."

Jasmine took a step back from his bed and crossed her arms. She seemed to hesitate a bit before handing him a slip of paper. "Suit yourself, then, Mr. Rebel. I want you to come dine with me at this address, just as soon as you're able to walk. Don't worry, it's not my parents' house. It's my little cottage over in Decatur, where I live alone. I promise, my folks won't be there."

"And what if I say no?"

"You can't. I'm exquisitely beautiful. I'm brilliant. I'm a tease. And you won't stop thinking of me until you've proved your manhood to me."

"I *am* saying no, and right now. This whole thing is a trap. I've heard about women like you all my life, and I don't want to get mixed up with one."

Jasmine took the package she had brought off his bedside table and handed it to him.

"I think it only fair that you should see the merchandise before you turn it down. That's why I want you to look at the photos inside of this packet. You need to be taught a few things."

She gave him a dry peck on the cheek and abruptly stole out of the hospital room. He kept wondering why if she considered him such a simple-minded bumpkin she was so interested in him, but then again he had so little experience in such matters that he actually believed that everything a woman said was to be taken at face value. He unfastened the string binding around the package, tore off several layers of wrapping paper, and saw a handwritten note on top of what appeared to be a stack of photographs:

I posed in class for some girls to practice sketching, and one of them also took these lovely photos.

Jasmine.

The first photograph in the black-and-white stack of eight-by-tens was a delightful shock to the teenage boy. A young woman of classical dimensions and perfect shape was in a nude pose before a dark gray backdrop. The boy saw the body first and then the face, which belonged to Miss Peace. He had never seen an unclothed woman in his life, and though this was only an image on a flat page it elicited a three-dimensional response, just the one she had intended.

"Good God!" cried Kid, "this gal's plumb crazy—she could go to jail for this!"

But he decided to wait awhile before he called in the authorities. For the overall good of society, he felt obligated to appoint himself chief examiner of the criminal evidence. There were more pictures that he forced himself to look at, all of them nudes, all of Jasmine. Rather than pornographic, the poses were of an artistic nature that sculptors and painters had been studying and rendering for several thousand years in other parts of the world, but that were a revelation in this time and place to this man. He examined every one of them with pure hunger, one after another, then he repeated the examination of every stimulating detail until he was worked into a frenzy.

"If this is what I get for crashing, Lord, please let me crash every week!"

Milt would have gone straight to the address she had given him that night if he had been able to walk, but he stayed in the hospital two more weeks, until the doctors told him he was safe to walk short distances on crutches. By that point, airplanes were the furthest thing from his mind. He wanted one thing: women.

When he returned to his apartment, hobbling on crutches and still in a cast, he was subjected to one of the most miserable periods of his life. He felt like a eunuch, unable to shake off his virginity, unable to fly his beloved airplanes, to drive his Model T about the city, to do any but the most sedentary of activities. He wasted away in sweaty idleness, trying to read books and magazines, looking through his high window at the beautiful summertime as it peaked into glory outside. The worst time was at night as he tried to sleep after having done nothing for an entire day. Every time he shut his eyes he imagined a naked female underneath him, then he would feel the bulky plaster cast on his right leg and realize he was dreaming again and would have been unable to turn over even if the seductress had actually been there with him. It was even worse whenever Jasmine came to visit.

Inflamed by the recurring images of her naked photos which danced around in his head, he wanted to jerk himself out of his cast and pounce on her. But instead he had to suffer her teases and promises of glory once his leg healed. He was expecting her to be a woman of her word.

BY JANUARY OF THE FOLLOWING year Kid had regained his strength and felt the time ripe to take Miss Peace up on her longstanding offer. Arrangements were made for him to dine with her at her address, 49 West College Avenue, Decatur, the next Saturday at 7PM.

He had never been too particular about grooming, spent little time in front of a mirror, shaved only occasionally, and usually wore baggy woolen trousers, soiled caps, and unironed cotton shirts with the top several buttons undone, his sleeves rolled up to the elbows, and no undershirt. His shoes were always cuffed and nicked, his hair nearly always uncombed and sticking up on all the points on his scalp that had cowlicks. Before his outing with Jasmine, however, he bought a fine new gray pin-stripe suit, a pair of black alligator shoes and added a matching Panama hat. Then he washed himself completely, shaved, combed his hair neatly just the way Ruth had shown him years ago back when she worked as his mother's kitchen helper, and slicked it back with pomade. He looked carefully at his wardrobe mirror that his mother had bought him, tied his tie with tailor-like precision, and made sure to be completely civilized for one of the few times in his life.

He had a half hour's drive to Decatur in his Model T, and on Ponce De Leon Avenue, just a few blocks from Jasmine's house, he saw a flower girl hawking colorful bouquets in the raw wintry air on the side of the road. He pulled over, gave her a dollar, and was handed the showiest bunch of flowers in her basket.

It was now pitch dark. Jasmine's neighborhood consisted of several small, neatly maintained houses, many of which were being rented by the lady students of the nearby all-female college. When Milt arrived at a burnt red wooden cottage with the number 49 illuminated above its front door, he was surprised to find four other automobiles parked in the driveway. He had nowhere else to park except along the street in front.

As he emerged from his car into the cold January night he heard music and the rattle of laughter from within. He hesitantly made his way over the stepping stones to the front door, bouquet in hand. The front window to the left of the door had its curtains drawn open, plainly revealing the brightly lit room inside, as well as its objects and occupants. Kid wanted to study this scene a little more carefully before he ventured into it, so he stooped down into the camellia shrubs under the window and began spying through the glass.

He saw Jasmine in a white silk gown, elegantly jeweled and leaning against a large cabinet, on top of which a phonograph was playing a jazz record. Three other girls were there, pretty in their own right but not so striking as Jasmine, and four collegiate boys. The room itself was plushly furnished with a chandelier, an antique table and set of chairs, and two Oriental rugs. There was so much laughter from inside that Milt began to suspect that they had seen him duck into the bushes and were really laughing at him. That wasn't the case, but with every new outburst of merriment Kid grew more resentful. Inside, four joyous young men were completely ignoring the three other girls and were practically drooling over Jasmine's beauty, each trying to upstage the other by being the biggest smart aleck. The teenager outside glanced down at his watch, just to make sure he hadn't misread it, but it now read seven o'clock sharp.

Just now he saw her coming to the window, and he ducked further into the camellias while she peered curiously outside. In a moment she was gone, and he heard more riotous partying coming from another part of the room. He kept himself hidden under the bushes and continued spying on them from outside, muttering under his breath: "And I was fool enough to come to this circus!"

They were now all holding glasses inside and drinking rum from them. A half-drunken sophomore groped at Jasmine's breasts, and she giggled as about half the contents of her glass spilled onto the sleeve of his coat. When she retreated to the record-player on the cabinet, Kid stood up, brushed off the sleeves of his coat, and adjusted his necktie. "I think I've seen all I care to see," he grumbled to himself as he stepped carefully out from the bushes and began trotting back to his car under the shadow of darkness. "I guess the girl just can't get it through her thick skull just what I want. Alone, the two of us, one man and one woman. *Nobody treats Milt Harrison this way. Nobody!"*

When he was about halfway back to his Model T, Kid angrily flung his bouquet of flowers into the grass, but he paused two steps later and reconsidered.

"She might find it there later on and keep it. I wouldn't want that. That would be the biggest waste of flowers in history!"

His mouth curled up wryly and he leaned down, tucked the bouquet under his arm, and placed it inside the car. Then he cranked the Model T and drove off, just as Jasmine came to look through her window again to see if he had arrived yet. Offhand, Kid had trouble deciding what he should do with the flowers or where he should go in his perfectly tailored outfit. It brought to mind the cliché about being all dressed up with nowhere to go. The problem of the flowers was solved when he saw the flower girl again on the way back to his apartment. He stopped at curbside in front of her, snatched the flowers in his hand and jumped out of his driver's seat. The woman recognized him and was expecting another sale, but when he offered the flowers back to her she looked confused.

"Miss, I can't find any other girl worth givin' these to, so I want you to have 'em." He doffed his hat and kissed her on the cheek. "My compliments."

Milt tore up Jasmine's risqué photos the morning after she played her little trick on him, and never missed looking at them. She appeared unannounced at his apartment a few days later and asked him why he had never come to her little party, but he told her he owed her no explanation and wanted nothing to do with her. He was a proud youth who never would stand in line to get anyone's attention. He had been brought up to excel in the world and he had no room for anyone who took him for granted. Jasmine had made the great and tragic mistake of her life, the full effect of which she would not realize until many years later.

CHAPTER 10

Private Harrison

BY SPRINGTIME YOUNG MILTON Harrison's leg had healed, and he was back where he most longed to be: at the Candler racetrack, cursing with his rough pals and indulging in the spectacular horseplay that American aviation was at that time.

When the racing season began again at the track, Kid was there in his Curtiss Model D, emulating the late great Liffey, racing the newest auto speed champion of the day, an Illinois man by the name of Jonathan Albritton. Britt, as everyone called the racer, took an immediate liking to Kid, who was five years younger. When the race cars were brought in before the first outing of the season, the renowned driver made a point of going out to Chester's small hangar to introduce himself to the boy-wonder of the biplane.

"I wish I could fly one of those machines," said Britt. "You think it's too late for an old man like me to try one?"

"Mr. Albritton," Milt answered him, "I don't mean to slight aeroplanes, but, really, what would a rich guy like you be messin' with these deathtraps for? Aeroplane-flying leads straight to two things: poverty and broken bones."

"You mean to tell me you don't have any money, after all you've done? I can't believe that."

"I might have $400 to my name, that's all."

"Don't worry," said Albritton, "that'll change. You stick with me, and I'll see you get what you're worth."

"We'll make a deal then. I'll teach you to fly if you teach me how to get rich."

"It's a deal. I promise you I'd give you every penny to my name just to operate an aeroplane the way you do."

"I don't believe you," said Milt, "but that's the best compliment anybody ever gave me."

The next day Johnny Albritton proved a formidable competitor against the young airplane-flyer in the exhibition race. An intense, quiet man, the 25-year-old racer seemed more intent on winning than he did on entertaining, and he didn't brook any nonsense in his singular effort to best Kid's Curtiss Model D. He won four of the seven races against the plane, and was cheered just as loudly as the hometown hero at the end of the day. Britt preferred straight auto racing and never competed against an airplane again, but he was gratified to have met the youngster who had brought such fame to this humble little racetrack and he genuinely hoped that some day their paths would cross again. By hook or by crook he would learn to operate a plane himself one day, and privately his goal was to be able to outfly Kid Harrison at some point in the future. He hated nothing more than being number two to anybody.

CHESTER DAWES HAD SUCCESSFULLY persuaded entrepreneurs in other cities that were having aviation meets that summer to pay hefty sums for the three Georgia boys to come and participate in their events. Such a drawing card had the trio become that financiers were willing to give the boys an upfront outlay of five hundred dollars just to have the names of Harrison, Brackens and Dawes on their billings. The biggest name belonged to Kid, and, just as Johnny Albritton had foreseen earlier in the year, money began pouring in to him.

Restaurants, clothiers and department stores in various northern cities began offering Kid money to say he frequented their businesses, which, just to maintain some semblance of integrity, he always tried to do. Consequently, all his meals on the road were free, hotels never asked him to pay, car dealerships were offering him free automobiles if he would allow his image to be used in their advertisements, and the harsh realities of poverty became more and more a distant memory.

Several women tried to seduce him that summer, and a few were successful. He lost his virginity to a 35-year-old twice-divorced society belle named Rosemary Wetherington in Richmond, Virginia who offered him a multitude of helpful hints as she joyously broke him in. Then the act unfortunately became an addiction to him, and Miss Wetherington's tried-and-true techniques were put to regular practice from town to town and girl to girl.

He could now do everything the great Liffey had done. He could loop and figure-eight a plane until an audience grew dizzy; he could fly with impossible speed and quick movement; he could knock a head off a cow with a landing and slice off a single leaf of a tree with a takeoff. He could do almost everything that anyone else had ever done in airplane, only he was a mere 19 years old.

That year he made almost $20,000, about twenty times the average yearly wage of a worker of that time. Chester and Robert made a fine living themselves, though not so ample as that of the boy from Woodvale. In the winter of that year Milt bought himself a mansion in the north Atlanta suburb of Ansley Park for $10,000, and accepted two expensive cars, a Packard and a Duesenberg, as gifts from appreciative dealerships in exchange for endorsement. Then he called his mother in to do what she did best, lavish enormous amounts of money at department stores to set up his house.

The nation was fascinated by airplanes because airplanes were becoming a prominent part of the major event of the era, the most horrific war the world had yet seen, the war that would soon end the glorious yearlong orgy of the handsome youth from Woodvale.

Ever since May of 1915, when a German submarine had attacked and sunk the Lusitania, a British vessel carrying munitions and passengers from New York to Liverpool, American public opinion had been strongly against Germany. Nearly two thousand civilians had been sent cruelly to their deaths, and neutrality for the United States was nearly impossible from then on. The soldiers of the Teutonic nation quickly became demonized in the popular lingo as "Huns", a cruel subspecies of humanity, caricatured in newspaper cartoons and vilified by politicians as heartless predators and killers. In March of 1917 German submarines attacked and capsized three American merchant ships, prompting President Wilson and the Congress to declare war on Germany early the following month and institute a national military draft.

Pandemonium followed. Millions of young males, terrified at the prospect of being conscripted to a foreign land, poisoned with mustard gas and buried in trench warfare, now lay vulnerable to the distant upheaval. A new expression entered the English language when hundreds of the most determined pacifists in Woodvale and many other communities in all corners of the nation began removing their shoes with a shotgun in hand and blowing off their toes to avoid eligibility for Wilson's draft: "shooting themselves in the feet" to create a lame limp on an otherwise perfectly healthy body. Milt's own friend Shnook Adams did it, as did Rev. Gray's son with his father's approval.

For these acts of self-mutilation for the sake of self-preservation Milt had nothing but contempt. He could scarcely imagine ever speaking to the Adams boy again after he heard Shnook had joined the mob and shot himself in the foot, and it was with great difficulty that he occupied the same room as the Reverend or his son for the next several years. Ever the contrarian, Kid was trying to do the exact opposite of untold numbers of boys his own age;

he really did have a handicap in his bad leg and he wanted to conceal it so he *would* be allowed to serve. In Hapeville Chet and Bobby, neither of whom would have a significant military career, thought him out of his mind for his desire to join in the European war. And in Woodvale, though most villagers admired his courage for wanting to go, the one closest to him did not. When he went home to explain himself to his mother, she begged him on her knees not to go.

"I just knew them planes would kill you!" Madge cried hysterically. "You gotta do what you can to stay over here. . . . I can't lose my son! If you'd just listened to me and gotten married everything would've been fine!"

"Mama, it's time for me to prove my superiority. I'm the best aeroplane flyer in the world and it's time for me to save America from them evil Huns."

"You hush up with that juvenile claptrap, you hear me? This world don't need some piddling little boy to save it—you save yourself first, you hear me?"

"My grandpa fought them evil Yankees, so it's time for me to fight evil in my time."

"You crazy fool, you don't know anything! It's the same evil Yankees in Washington that your grandpa fought that're tryin' to steal you away from me now. It's their war, not ours! They invaded us and took our land and property just so they could steal our boys away from us in the future and force 'em to fight their silly wars."

"Nothin's gonna happen to me, Mama. I'll be safe. I can do anything in an aeroplane."

WHEN HIS FANCY MOTORCAR had brought him back to Atlanta, Milton Jr. forgot about all his mother's arguments. Experienced in love but still naïve in war, he had trouble keeping still at night while worrying that his injured leg might disqualify him from being a bombing aviator over the Western front. He needed to find a physician somewhere who might pass him, and quickly, before the conscripts established seniority and position over him. Maybe he could lie and say nothing had ever been wrong with him—but fame had its price. It was likely most military officials had heard of him and knew he had snapped his leg in two the year before last. But wouldn't the Army be craving the great Kid in its air war in Europe, since very few others knew how to fly? The suspense grew unbearable to the boy from Woodvale, so he went across town to Fort McPherson in mid April, one week after the official war declaration, to enlist.

"I want to sign up for service today," he told the officer behind the desk at the headquarters building. "I want to put my talents to use for my country."

During the past year he had rehabilitated his leg thoroughly by riding a bicycle up and down city streets for an average of two hours each day when he wasn't flying. Army doctors passed him without hesitation, though had Milt been so inclined he might easily have persuaded any number of his father's old acquaintances, including Dr. Parkhurst or even Dr. Kelvey, to declare him unfit to serve on the very real basis of his serious recent injury. But his heart was set on serving his country and the Army was in no mood to quibble with someone of his renowned talents and his ripe age.

"You'll start off at the bottom," said Colonel McIntyre Olsen at Ft. Mac's company headquarters after the enlistment paperwork had been signed and approved. "You'll be just like everybody else, and go through drills just like any other enlistee. Think you can handle that?"

"You ain't plannin' on turning me into an infantryman, are you? I wanna be flying planes, because that's what I do best."

"We'll decide that. Remember, from now on, you do everything through the chain of command. We're not here for you, you're here for us. If I pointed over there and told you to die for that man, could you do it? That's what the Army's about. He'll die for you and you'll die for him, if necessary."

"I'll die for what I believe in. That's the way I was raised by my mama and daddy."

"In that case, you're a good fit."

COLONEL OLSEN DISPATCHED KID to Fort Benning, an unpleasant training ground near Columbus, Georgia, and instructed Sergeant Ronald Gilmore by telegraph to ride hard on the rich, cocksure young recruit during basic training. "Humble the boy, bring that inflated head down to fighting-man status," the missive read. "Bring him to his knees so he'll die for the man in the adjoining bunk if he has to."

When the young aviator arrived within the spartan gates of Fort Benning Sgt. Gilmore was primed and ready for him. Milt was promptly assigned the duty of mopping floors at the mess hall and the latrine, then ordered to appear before company command along with his comrades at sunrise of the following day. The reveille awakened all the men at 5:30 the next morning and Milt neatly made his bunk, donned his new uniform, and marched out to the quadrangle along with his mates. A line of stern-faced officers, wearing their hats and full insignia, stood placidly waiting for them as Sgt. Gilmore paced in front of them. The sergeant made his way up and down the ranks, examining the new enlistees closely, looking at the face of each man. Kid was already in a nervous sweat by the time Gilmore came to him, and the sergeant singled him out immediately.

"And just who might you be, young man?" asked Gilmore, breathing down the aviator's neck.

"Private Harrison reporting for duty, sir," he called out mechanically, and gave a salute.

Gilmore clasped his hands together behind his back, squinted at the famous enlistee and stepped slowly in front of Milt, glaring at him the whole time as he proceeded. The sergeant's black boots shimmered as if they had been buffed with paraffin wax, his belt buckle was burnished like a newly minted ingot of gold, his gray trousers were so stiffly ironed and creased that they barely bent at the knees while he walked. He was tall enough to be nearly nose to nose with the youth, and Kid felt the warm breath from his nostrils on his cheek as he stood straight up and stared ahead.

"I don't think we shaved today, did we, Private Harrison?" Sgt. Gilmore said defiantly.

"Yes, sir, I did shave."

"I see little hairs on your chin, Private," the sergeant breathed into his ear. "No, you didn't shave, did you?"

A bead of sweat emerged from under Milt's hat and rolled down his forehead. He kept staring ahead without looking at his superior.

"I asked you a question," the sergeant persisted, and then he nearly blew the poor boy's ear out when he thundered: "DID YOU SHAVE TODAY, PRIVATE HARRISON?"

"No, sir," the boy lied worriedly, hoping he was making inroads at comprehending military-speak, "No, sir, Sergeant Gilmore, I didn't shave today."

"Go then, Private, and shave so we can get on with our business. You've got ten minutes."

The country boy rushed back into the now-deserted barracks with his heart fluttering like hummingbird wings. He lathered his face with a brush, grabbed a razor, and scalped his cheeks and neck so hard that they nicked and bled in several spots. He tried to blot them with a towel, but by then his ten minutes were nearly up, so he rushed out to the quadrangle with blood oozing out of his skin, hoping that Sgt. Gilmore would accept blood as surefire evidence that he really had shaved. The poker-faced Gilmore squinted at him again when he returned, nodded ever so subtly, and turned his attention to the new recruit's black shoes, which shined like glass.

"We haven't polished our shoes yet today, have we, Private Harrison?" Gilmore taunted the boy, nose to nose with him again as several trickles of blood rolled down his neck onto his collar. The sergeant lifted the sole of his boot and scraped it against the side of one of Milt's shoes, creating a long scuff mark.

"No, sir, Sergeant Gilmore," said the indoctrinated boy. "We didn't polish our shoes today."

"Let's do that in the next ten minutes, young man," said the sergeant, "and again report for duty."

The green recruit again rushed back to his barracks, pulled out a can of black shoe polish from his personal kit, daubed some of it onto the scuff mark of his shoe with a handkerchief, rubbed it in, then drizzled some water on it, brushed it hard and buffed it to a sheen. He was back again before the sergeant only seven minutes after he had been sent away.

"I notice we're making some progress," said Gilmore. "But a soldier gets a haircut every now and then. Private, if that hair gets any longer it'll look like a horse's tail."

"I'll go cut it then, Sergeant," said Milt, giving a salute. His freshly-barbered head was as trimly coiffed as that of the sergeant or any colonel, major, brigadier general or general in the whole Army, and he was at a loss as to what he would do to satisfy his superior this time. "How much time do I have to get a haircut, sir?"

"The whole goddamn day's about to go to waste because of your sloppiness, Private," answered Gilmore. "You've got ten minutes to trim that long hair."

Milt ran to the barracks again in a panic, not knowing how he would fix this imaginary problem. His previous occupation, however, had already prepared him for quick thinking in times of critical importance, and he realized at once that the only haircut indisputably shorter than the one he already had would be a bald scalp. He pulled his pocketknife from his trousers, cut the longer hair on his head as close to his scalp as he could with the small blade, mixed up some shaving lather in a wash basin, and rubbed the same razor that had nicked his cheeks over the stubble on his scalp. Blood and cuts were all over his head now; he was bald and disfigured, and as ugly as a buzzard in his way of thinking; but he daubed his bleeding scalp with a towel, put his hat back on his head, and rushed out to his superiors on the quadrangle.

For the first time the faintest traces of a grin now appeared on Sgt. Gilmore's face when he observed the new enlistee on his return a full twenty-four seconds within his allotted time. Blood was all over his face now, dripping from under his hat. The other recruits held deathly silent and at attention all the while.

"Remove your hat, Pvt. Harrison," ordered Gilmore, "and keep it in your hand down by the side of your waist."

Off came the hat in accordance with the command, and the ivory white shaven scalp, flecked with a few splotches of stubbled hair that he had missed, now lay naked to inspection. Gilmore turned to his fellow officers, winked at them with his back to the new recruit, and turned back around to face his subject. He nodded subtly and went nose to nose with Milt again.

"Now I can see the makings of a soldier, Private Harrison. Now you're finally ready for duty. In the future let's take care of all this before we report. I'd suggest waking up a half-hour earlier next time."

"Yes, sir, Sergeant Gilmore," barked the country boy, giving a salute with his free right hand while he held his hat at his side with his left. "My apologies to you and the other officers, sir."

The officers next determined to test the boy's physical mettle, and they made him run laps around the bull ring before throwing him back in with the others in normal training procedures. He slogged through mud and climbed walls with the best of them, shot more accurately with a rifle than anyone there after years of hunting wild game around Woodvale, had the endurance and foot speed of a conditioned athlete, and was universally liked by the other young trainees. Ambition motivated him in everything he did. He knew the straighter and narrower a path he walked, the faster he would get promoted to do the thing he most wanted to do. Gilmore and the other officers marveled at the gem they had discovered. Though there were no airplanes or flight courses at Fort Benning and they never actually saw him fly a plane while there, his reputation suggested that would come as second nature to him. Within a month they realized that Fort Benning was a waste on this particular boy—he belonged in Europe among the Allied majordomos, leading others by example against the dreaded Huns.

Sgt. Gilmore telegrammed Col. Olsen in May of 1917: "TAKE BACK PVT HARRISON AND SEND HIM TO GET LICENSED FOR FLIGHT X HE IS AS READY TO FIGHT NOW AS YOU OR I X I HAVE NEVER SEEN ANYONE STAND UP SO FIRMLY AGAINST HUMILIATION."

At the end of May Kid was back in Atlanta again, seated before Colonel Olsen at Fort McPherson company headquarters. Due to his exceptional discipline at Fort Benning, he was now promoted to Second Lieutenant in the United States Flying Service and was being sent up north to the Rhinebeck Aerodrome in upstate New York on the edge of the Catskills. There he would get licensed to be what was called, in a previously nautical term now being made popular for aviation by the European war, a "pilot". If he continued along his present course it was not unlikely that he would be in Europe by the middle of the summer, as casualties on the Allied side were now creating a desperate shortage of skilled manpower.

———

PASSENGER TRAINS WERE NOW a pipeline clogged with hundreds of thousands of military personnel being transported to all points on the compass to serve the war effort. Kid was being shipped on the rails himself, north along the eastern seaboard to New York City, then north out of Grand Central Station to the central Hudson River Valley. As he did during his trip to Cicero Field, the Harrison boy felt alone and unknown, as if all that had gone before had been erased and nothing mattered except the present.

An aerodrome of that day consisted of a large flat field, flanked by three or four large hangars filled with several dozen airplanes, and a constant hubbub of activity as instructors took off and landed to demonstrate flight for their unsteady beginners. The trainer planes that filled the field at the Rhinebeck Aerodrome were all Curtiss JN-4's or JN4-D's, "Jennies", as they were popularly called: American-made models that never saw combat or supported machine guns, but that served as a mass instructional tool for acclimating the military youth of America to the sensation of flight. Major Laurence Simoneau, one of the certified instructors, was in the awkward position of having to evaluate Kid Harrison's airworthiness—an ironic twist, given that he had been a cheering member of Kid's audience himself the previous summer at the Newark Aviation Meet, where Milt had been a featured performer.

"Let's make it short and sweet, Lt. Harrison," said Maj. Simoneau, handing him a helmet and goggles and gesturing for him to hop into the flying seat of a Jenny. "I've seen you fly, and you know all the maneuvers I'm trying to teach these other fellows. You show me what you know, and all you know, and I'll go ahead and give you certification."

"Sure you want me to show you everything, Major? I'll just show you the basic stuff if you want."

"Show me everything, Lieutenant."

"So you want me to give you the Bobby Brackens tour of the sky, Major? That's the tour that may cause you to lose some of your lunch."

Maj. Simoneau hesitated, as though he had gone too far out on a limb but was too proud to ask for a helping hand to be pulled back to safety. He couldn't very well go back on what he had ordered now and still hold credibility to his lieutenant.

"Yes, sir, you heard me correctly. Everything."

"Sure you won't court-martial me?" Kid winked at him.

"Not unless you crash, Lieutenant. If you do that I'll ask St. Peter to court-martial you in heaven."

Major Simoneau assumed Kid was familiar with how to operate a parachute, which he was not, but when the two of them put on parachute packs the Georgia boy only inquired about the location of the rip-cord and hoped his book-learning would be enough to teach him the technique of buffering a fall. He thought it unlikely that would matter anyway, since the

Army kept its training fleet in tip-top operating conditions and the weather that summer day was perfect. Milt hopped into the front cockpit and the Major into the aft one, and two other instructors combined to spin the Jenny's propellor started and pull back the chocks from its wheels.

Word quickly spread around the field at the Rhinebeck Aerodrome that the 20-year-old flying prodigy, the great Kid Harrison, was about to take the Major for a ride. Virtually all other commotion ceased, and the Army forces fast turned into a summer crowd at an air exhibition. Unfortunately for Maj. Simoneau, he was forced by duty to be a participant in the display himself, and he had an ever-mounting suspicion that the ride wouldn't exactly rival that of a Ferris wheel for ease and enjoyment.

With breathtaking speed and precision, the masterful aviator shot the Jenny up to its top-out altitude of 3000 feet, gently swayed back and forth in a perfect figure-8, and nosed the plane down into a dive. The Major's heart leaped up into his throat as the plane plunged toward the earth, and he grabbed ahold of his dual-controlling stick and straightened the machine out. Kid threw his hands up in the air unhappily and looked over his shoulder behind him. He clutched the stick tightly, determined to resist any effort from behind him to alter his intended path for the Jenny, and went into a dizzying loop that churned the Major's stomach and made him silently beg for heavenly intervention. Accompanying the furious upside-down flip was the boy's ear-piercing yell: "*Yaaaaaaaaaa-hoooooo!*"

Milt completed the loop and turned the plane upright about 500 feet above the ground, to the uproarious cheers of all the soldiers watching down below. He next nosed the Jenny slightly down and aimed it directly at the tin roof of one of the aerodrome's hangars as though he intended to crash into it, but he pulled up within inches of the roof, lifted the machine up again, and swooped down on the next hangar several hundred yards away. He repeated the near-miss, pulled up within inches of clipping tin, and flirted with the two other hangars at the aerodrome in the exact same way, barely missing the buildings with his wheels and skid.

The mass of soldiers on the ground cringed when they saw the plane nearly strike the first of the four hangars, but once they recognized the trickster's intent they burst into applause at his other near-misses. Soon the plane had risen to 2000 feet above the field, and the aviator dove again, swayed, flipped the Jenny back around, and made it ripple and sway like a gray kite in the breeze. Without warning he brought the machine down toward a squadron of five parked Jennies on the grass, coasting smoothly to a landing a few feet away from the nearest plane. The lieutenant shut off his plane's engine, and the awed group of enlistees rained loud cheers on their bold comrade.

Major Simoneau's flesh was as clammy as soup, he was covered by goose bumps and sweat, and his stomach was agitated and queasy. He could do each of the stunts of his alleged pupil, but with nowhere near the speed, exactness or flamboyance. Never had he spun around and soared and plunged in a plane like that. To his mind, what he had just experienced had defied gravity and physics.

"Lieutenant Harrison," Simoneau groaned, "congratulations. *You're certified.* How does the rank of captain sound to you?"

He offered the youngster his hand, as much to keep himself from keeling over as for a handshake. Raymond Milton Harrison, Jr., with no previous military background and no powerful friends or relatives to nudge him up the hierarchy, had thus gone from a private to a captain in the U.S. Army in little over two months, during a period of revolutionary upheaval and desperate demand for skill at the front lines of combat.

Soon he would be shipped to France, at the edge of the Western Front, the battle line between the Central Powers and the Allies. His overseers there would be no mere sergeants or even colonels but the very generals who were running the great "war to end all wars." And his skill at flying, which had been incubated in a home-built experiment that was useful in impressing girls and getting bird's-eye views of cotton fields, would now become an instrument of force, espionage and death.

CHAPTER 11

The War to End War

CAPTAIN HARRISON WAS SOON on a ship out of New York's harbor, nearly alone among his countrymen in being sent abroad at so early a period of U.S. involvement in the Great War. He was going now because the Washington government was under pressure from its Allies to contribute quickly to their losing efforts, and he was among the few considered to be capable of making an immediate mark on the fighting without an extensive period of training. Not until almost a full year later, the spring of 1918, would hundreds of thousands of other Americans be bound for the continent of their ancestry—mostly young, unsuspecting boys who had never been more than a few miles from their homes and had no inkling of any of the political ramifications of the conflict; boys for whom the task had been simplified as making the world "safe for democracy."

Milt was more worldly than most of them by now, though he had been born less so. As the landmass of America slowly drifted away from him on the horizon as the ship went ever-further asea, he had a foreboding that he would never see it again and he regretted that he had failed to bid his mother and his nearest of friends a satisfying farewell. His pride seemed of little consequence now to him. Instead, he began feeling an almost biblical sense of responsibility. He remembered Rev. Gray's frequent quotations of Luke 12:48: "For unto whomsoever much is given, of him shall be much required: and to whom men have committed much, of him they will ask the more."

Now the expectation was that in an insane conflict pitting the might of the industrial giants of the world he, a mere 20-year-old, would somehow help to sway the odds in favor of one of the giants. And in order for him to succeed, he knew, he would need to kill any number of similarly innocuous boys his own age for no other reason than that they happened to occupy another giant's sphere of influence.

His own thoughts would be reproduced countless times, in the minds of many of the boys who were exported with him. It was only natural for them to have a certain amount of fear, uncertainty and hesitation pulsing through their veins. But they would also share a vision that theirs was the right side in the conflict; that if they failed then some of the values they had been taught would die with them; that without their spilled blood the great ideal of liberty and justice for all, no matter how far from reality in the present day, would be annihilated from the face of the earth and not even be aspired to by any future worlds.

MILT'S SHIP DOCKED AT Le Havre, France on July 8, 1917. There he was met gladly by French and British officers of the French Air Service and the Royal Flying Corps, who sent him by train to Paris and on to Nancy, in the east central part of the country on the edge of the German lines.

"Welcome to the front, Captain Harrison," Major Harold Lofton of the Royal Flying Corps saluted him at the Nancy train station. Lofton was the British commander of the Argonne Escadrille, to which the American flying prodigy had been assigned. "I understand you've been sent to become a member of our squadron."

"Thank you, sir. Mind if I ask where I'm going next?"

"Just follow me," Lofton instructed him.

The Georgia boy's mind still reeled from the novelty of being in a foreign land. He had been expecting to find a territory completely devastated by war, and yet his train out of Le Havre had passed through one medieval village after another where life had seemed to be standing still. Paris seemed self-delusional to him, full of eager girls and fat old men in bowler hats who behaved as if nothing out of line were happening anywhere in the world. It was only as he approached Nancy that he began to see recurring signs of devastation, in the form of bombed out factories and warehouses, torched villages and shell batteries. Yet it seemed less terrible than his imagination had led him to think it would be, and the fear of what he could not see was stronger than any emotion he felt over what he actually had seen.

"Major Lofton," he asked, "is this war really all that bad? I can't see many signs that there even is a war around here."

"That's because you haven't entered the combat zone yet. Once you do, you'll be amazed you ever wondered if this war was bad or not."

"I wasn't tryin' to make light of it, sir. I was just telling you what I've noticed."

"I know that. You've never been in a war, and we've got to get you ready for one. You won't live long unless you always expect the worst. Just remember that, now. The minute you let your guard down and assume you're safe will be the minute your enemy's lying in wait to strafe you into oblivion."

Major Lofton took a liking to Kid and attempted to assimilate him into the ranks of the other members of the Argonne Escadrille, who were stationed at the aerodrome at Souilly, a tiny village a few kilometers southwest of Verdun in the rolling wooded hills of Argonne. It was mostly a futile effort on the part of the major. As the lone American in a group of entirely British and French aviators, Milt was already at a social disadvantage when he arrived there. The other thirty men there spoke English and French interchangeably, were college graduates, of aristocratic rank, and of longstanding military pedigree. The Frenchmen there wouldn't deign to speak to him in his language, and the Englishmen, mostly Oxford or Cambridge-educated, considered him a bumpkin and a Johnny-come-lately, unfit to occupy their company.

The squadron had only in the last week been assembled of the best known Allied flying men, designed to combat the aggressive German sorties due west toward Paris that were making inroads on the French capital. Every one of the soldiers there had been fully trained for combat, except for the newcomer. After two lonely days of schooling, any sense of vanity or smugness in the American had been humbled out of him by his being ignored. Now Lofton, the commanding officer, pronounced them ready to fly, and Capt. Harrison was prepared to show the other pompous lads that he belonged among them. The Major advised them that he wanted to lead a flight across the German lines on the following morning to show them the war.

"Captain Harrison," said Lofton, "I want you and Captain Lee to go with me. Let's start at 9:30."

There was a buzz amongst the other squadron members, and Capt. Colin Lee of the Royal Flying Corps was congratulated by his comrades, who advised him that they would be sure to forward his belongings to his family estate in Gloucestershire if the Huns shot him down and see that he got a proper burial. The American hick they considered to be a sacrificial lamb. They were sorry he had to be taught the harsh lessons of warfare so soon after arriving on the scene, but—well, such things happened.

Capt. Lee was awake early the next morning, urging his mechanics to ready the three planes that were to be taken over enemy territory. The fleet of the Argonne Escadrille consisted entirely of French Nieuport 17 biplanes with rotary engines, and three were fueled and running at 9:25 when the American finally emerged from the barracks to meet Lee and Maj. Lofton. The other lads all gathered around them, partly relieved not to be going with them but partly envious of their dangerous adventure.

"Remember, men," said the major, "stay near me at all times and keep in formation."

Lofton sped his Nieuport across the aerodrome grass and soared heavenward, followed closely by Lee. Now Milton Jr. finally sat on the brink of warfare. His machine guns were ready and armed, and all the hours he had spent perfecting the dangerous art of acrobatics in a flying machine gave him confidence. Up he soared into the perilous sky, casting a parting glance at the haven of relative safety that existed on the field. He quickly caught up with the two other planes, followed their slips, rolls and turns, and maintained a position within a few hundred feet of both of them all the way up to 10,000 feet. The ferocious subfreezing blasts of air at that altitude numbed his senses, but he kept in perfect control of his machine.

Soon they were over the plains of Champagne, and for the first time the American beheld the full scope of the devastation of modern warfare below him. For two years the fighting militia had been digging trenches into the earth and battering their enemies with shells. Practically the whole landscape of that region, for as far as he could see, was an ugly mud pit of trenches and shell holes. While Kid looked in dismay at the labyrinth of trenches down below he heard a violent explosion that seemed to be right on his very tail, and his plane began rolling and swaying. He shook while several more went off, each one blasting his ears and rattling his plane. *POW! POW-POW! POW-POW-POW!*

He had been briefed about the shooting battery the Germans had entrenched near Reims, and how it fired eighteen-pound shells of shrapnel. The battery was plainly visible along the banks of the Vesle River, and there was little doubt that its men had spotted the three enemy Allied planes. Again the rumble of fire shook him to the bone. *POW-POW! POW-POW-POW!* This time he felt a few particles of shrapnel hitting his machine and he realized it had been pierced with at least a few holes. Apparently Major Lofton had also been hit, and he swung his plane around to head in the opposite direction, followed closely by his two apprentices.

When they turned to seek safe territory Kid spotted three red planes of unfamiliar model flying in ranks directly at them no more than a mile distant. The Major put his Nieuport into a dive, followed closely by Lee and Milt. But the trio of German Albatros D.III biplanes bore down on them with ferocity, and now the Allied men knew they had gotten themselves into a gun battle on their first expedition across enemy lines. Kid tried to keep the Major's advice in mind and stick with his ranks, but it occurred to him that the closer they all stayed together the easier it would be for their attackers to mow them down with a minimum of shots. In his opinion, he owed just about all of his success in the world so far to unorthodox and unconventional thinking, so why with his life now on the line should he change? His intuition took over and he broke ranks, swerved to the south over the antique architecture of Reims, and tried to egg on one of the three Albatroses to try to outmaneuver him.

The ploy worked. One of the pursuing fighters, seeing the Nieuport turn to the south, opened its throttle and tried to bear down hard on its tail.

As soon as Kid saw his opponent trailing him he knew this would be a battle decided in one or two ways: either he would be losing his life or the other man would be losing his, and he had no intention of taking any trick to his grave with him.

It was a competitive and deadly sport, this combat flying, involving brute violence and deception; a serious version of the game of football that college boys his age were playing back home. He used to frolic with the pigskin himself in the Woodvale schoolyard with his friends, tackling and running until his body was bruised and sore. When being pursued by a tackler he remembered that any sudden shift in direction or change in speed by the ballcarrier usually caused the tackler to overpursue his mark. Hearing the gunner firing at him from a distance, he imagined himself being overpursued by an angry tackler and he throttled his engine so that his plane suddenly lost speed. The shots had led him and his plane never reached the point of the gunner's aim. The Albatros's pilot realized too late that his target had slowed and before he fired again Kid flipped his Nieuport over, waited momentarily, then revved his engine at full power again just as he expected the German to be slowing down to try to match his previous move. By this method, the boy from Woodvale had tricked his opponent into entirely predictable behavior. The Albatros would do whatever he had seen Kid's plane do, only three seconds later.

When the German flipped over to try to match him, Milt was upright again, on top of his prey, his machine guns poised to shoot his enemy down. He cut his throttle again, waited for the Albatros to get as close as possible, and opened fire. The bullets riddled their target, a line of fire ran from the Albatros's tail to its cockpit, and the machine swerved under the random guidance of the dead hand at its controls. Kid watched in relief as the plane crashed into the ground and exploded. He had scored his first victory, and his principal emotion was gratitude that he was still alive.

Having broken free of enemy pursuit, the American turned back toward Allied territory, rushing for it furiously with throttle fully out, trying to trace the course of his two colleagues. Within ten minutes he caught sight of four planes doing battle almost directly over the front, and with nervous intensity he drove his machine directly at one of the enemy aviators who, completely engaged in his battle with Capt. Lee, was blindsided by Kid's pursuit. Again the American pulled his trigger, again he riddled the fuselage of his target, and again it spun out on its plunge to oblivion.

Lee's plane was punctured with holes, but he glided safely across the front to friendly territory. Still remaining was the third Albatros, which was now engaged with Major Lofton. The last remaining German pilot had noticed the Allied plane's blindsided assault of his comrade, and he began firing away at Kid furiously, almost insanely and from too great a distance to have any hope of connecting. When the American noticed how wildly his

German pursuer was shooting he decided he would just duck and dodge for a few minutes, diverting the enemy from his pursuit of Maj. Lofton so the latter would have an easy shot at him. But there was now a lull in the Albatros's gunfire and Milt heard his enemy pull away. Aviators of the Fatherland never pulled away, as far as he knew. For all their dastardly deeds, one had to give the Huns credit: they never backed down from any fight; their mean streak of determination was burned into their beings like a brand onto the hide of a calf. Kid thought it quite obvious this overzealous predator had exhausted all his ammunition after his wild shooting and was now hoping to lure his American adversary further into German territory.

Milt bore down on him and within a minute was nipping at the tail of the unarmed opponent. His thirst for blood had created an insane if temporary sort of fever. He had killed two already and now this boy would make an easy three. The Albatros's depleted ammunition belt flapped like a flag in the wind, and the German now stood up impassively, threw off his helmet and glasses, held his arms behind his back, and turned around to look defiantly at his pursuer, as if to urge Kid to blow him away. The blond man looked almost like a baby, so slight of build and frail he was, and in a momentary twinge of conscience his adversary took pity on him and held his fire. But mercy had no place in warfare. Kid opened fire on him, riddled his flailing body with bullets, and watched the downward plunge of his plane over Allied lines during the course of the next few seconds, not without feelings of uneasiness and remorse.

With three confirmed victories on his first combat mission, Capt. Raymond Milton Harrison was now a World War hero in his own right, and telegraph lines carried the news of his exploits to far-off lands. Congratulations came pouring in from many quarters. The last two Germans shot down by Capt. Harrison came to rest in the wreckage of their planes in Allied territory near Reims. Along with a commendatory Maj. Lofton, Milt rode out to the site from the Souilly aerodrome later that afternoon to examine the mangled corpses of the two boys. He was fortunate it had been they rather than he who had been so destroyed, and yet the sight of their lifeless bodies with torn flesh and shattered bones and teeth made him sick to his stomach. He had never felt so distressed over doing something that everyone else thought was so praiseworthy.

Suddenly the members of the Argonne Escadrille had a different opinion about the American in their midst. He wasn't a simple bumpkin any more. He was a valiant warrior, and they all wanted to be like him and fawned over him as if he had turned into a prince.

He dutifully filled out the official Combat Reports verifying his triumphs, but in time he would grow tired of the procedures. He never sought to prove he had downed an enemy plane again, though he would be credited officially with seventeen more kills, and would actually down far more than that. The idea of keeping score for that always seemed morbid to him.

CHAPTER 12

Ace

THE ARGONNE ESCADRILLE CONTINUED their training maneuvers after their newest member had brought them fame and glory, but the commanders safely kept their boys within Allied lines for several days after the squadron's first brush with danger. The American fellow seemed to be going about his business somewhat glumly, though the other boys hovered around him with admiration. The Frenchmen were speaking his language nowadays. In a light moment he had even taught them the word "y'all", one of the foremost staples of Georgia conversation. *"Non, non, y'all,"* he would brush them off politely whenever he wanted to be by himself, and they understood and gave him his privacy.

Major Lofton noticed the American boy's newly solemn attitude, and speculated he knew the reason behind it. He wired the Lorraine Aerodrome near the tiny village of Étain, where he had heard an American colonel was staying, to send a compatriot, someone who might perhaps be able to boost morale in the boy. Colonel Paul Percival, a young brash man still in his thirties who had been promoted to an officer's rank when barely past his childhood, was summoned to meet with the new war hero.

When Maj. Lofton summoned Kid from his barracks to his office and introduced him to Col. Percival, the latter congratulated him on his brilliantly orchestrated air victories. He also mentioned that the two of them had something in common, for his own father had once tried unsuccessfully to run for the U.S. Congress in Michigan. This helped to relax the nervous young pilot, and the British commander left the quiet room to the two of them.

"I understand you're a bit remorseful about the dead Huns," Percival addressed Kid on the subject of greatest concern to him. "It's only natural, I guess. But you want me to tell you something maybe you hadn't thought about, Captain?"

"Yes, Colonel. Yes, sir."

"If we weren't here fighting, nothing except the Atlantic Ocean, which the Kaiser's ships have already shown they can easily get across, would stand between the Huns and the Statue of Liberty. They'd roll right through France and Britain, put their air fleet on naval carriers, and the next thing you know they'd be on our shores, coming to terrorize our cities with their bombing submarines and aeroplanes, murdering our women and children. I'm sure you'd rather see a few dead Hun soldiers over here than to go home and find your neighborhood wiped out and your yard littered with the mangled bodies of your sweetheart and your neighbors, wouldn't you?"

"I sure would, Colonel. But you really think it would come to that if we didn't stop 'em over here?"

"Captain, you and I know what aeroplanes can do, how they can be an instrument of force the likes of which the world has never seen. It's the politicians in Washington who don't understand it yet. We won't have a fair chance until we bring two million infantrymen over here and equip a whole armada of machine-gunning aeroplanes to blow these ruthless invaders to the hell where they belong."

The colonel's listener was now positively swayed by his rhetoric. George Washington himself, if had had still been alive and kicking, couldn't have been any more persuasive, Milt was thinking. At least for the time being, the boy from Woodvale had forgotten how mentally exhausting it was to be constantly forced to riddle other pilots with bullets in order to escape the same fate himself.

"Thanks a lot for puttin' it like that, sir. That really makes me feel better."

Percival patted his countryman on the shoulder.

"That's my job—to keep your morale up. Just remember one thing, my man . . ."

"Yes, Colonel?"

"The best way to bring about peace in the world is to give the troublemakers one of two choices: behave, or be killed."

THE YOUNG AVIATOR WAS rejuvenated, at least for the next several days, by Colonel Percival's pep talk, and went about his business thereafter with an unfettered conscience. Ironically, he would soon lose the luxury of having any spare time to consider questions of right or wrong in a frenzy of combat. The disadvantage of being the escadrille's top fighter was that he quickly became a marked man to both his friends and enemies. By his friends he was singled out to go on dangerous solitary missions that no one else was deemed capable of surviving. By his enemies he was declared a primary military target, a scourge on the Fatherland whose demise would entitle its author to an immediate elevation in rank and eminence. One way or another he seemed doomed, as Percival had privately foreseen, to suffer in a horrendous way: either a violent death in combat, or, if taken alive by his antagonists, heinous torture in a war prison.

Yet the colonel's words had inspired his young blood and appealed to his natural vanity. Freedom itself, and the aspirations of an entire way of life, depended on him—or so he had been led to believe. Before he gave his life, if he had to, he wanted to engage in the battle of his dreams: an all-out shootout between his plane and the most feared one on the other side, the one rumored to have a large white skull and crossbones painted on the side of its fuselage so it would be easily recognized, flown by the aviator the Britons were calling the *Rittmeister,* "The Riding Master."

He never had a fully restful night again at the Souilly barracks, since sleep seemed so wasteful to him when he might otherwise be putting that idle time to good use in planning and invention. Many a sleepless night would produce an idea or a strategy to outfox his cunning adversaries, a new concept to be shared with his colleagues during the next late night hour. Captain Lee and Lieutentant Wesley Denning, the two Cambridge men who had become apostles of the unlettered country boy from across the sea, often listened to his theories on the edges of their bunks and vowed to incorporate his suggested tricks on their next sorties into battle. When Major Lofton informed him he would be venturing out on his own for his second mission, he decided he would do so in a way that would take the Germans by surprise.

"Fellas, I'm taking off before daylight tomorrow," Kid told his colleagues, "while the Huns are still asleep. If I go up high and out of sight I'll catch 'em off guard when they come out for morning reconnaissance."

Only five days after his first brush with death in the sky, Milt took off in his Nieuport in the dead of night. Up he soared to the frigid altitude of 8000 feet, where he hovered above friendly lines and the sylvan beauty of the Argonne while lying in wait to shoot down his next victims. The crystal clear sky seemed ideal for aerial photography to him. He speculated the Germans would be up with the sun in such favorable weather to try to trump what they assumed were their lazy sleeping foes. Back and forth he flew in the stupefying cold that few other human beings had ever experienced. Perhaps two dozen times he redoubled his path over the Meuse and Moselle River valleys between Nancy and Verdun. He grew atrociously cold and hungry, and the thought of the warm mess hall at the Souilly barracks tantalized him. He was burning his limited supply of fuel in wasteful amounts. His watch told him he had but an hour of such jockeying left before he would be compelled by his Nieuport's exhausted gas tank to return to his base.

In frustration he decided to seek activity on the enemy side of the front. As the sun's preliminary rays warmed France for the first time that day he rose to 10,000 feet and crossed over the lines to Thionville, still with no signs of activity below. He figured that the sound of his motor must be audible to the German batteries below him, though at that height it would be difficult for anyone on the ground to see him. Since an enemy aerodrome was situated near Thionville, Kid throttled his engine to be as inconspicuous as possible and glided nimbly in almost silent circles around the battlements and trenches underneath him. His eyes were fixed on the aerodrome, and he soon saw just what he had been waiting to see. He noticed a German Albatros biplane lifting itself off the green earth, followed quickly in succession by three other Albatrosses. Their course was straight for the Allied lines, and when the last of them had his tail to the secret predator high above, Capt. Harrison put his plane in a descent and quickly began closing the gap between them.

When Kid slowed his descent to try to allow the four German fighters passage over the front, hoping to trap them like quail for the easy shot of Allied gunners on the ground, he forgot that at his present location he had become such an easy target himself for the German batteries. Three deafening explosions that shook his plane roused him from his daydreaming. In the nervous hope that he would escape being hit by any of the upcoming shells Kid put his Nieuport into a dive, trying to nip at the heels of the rearmost of the Albatrosses and convince the enemy battery man that if he were to fire in the direction of the lone American plane he might well endanger four planes from his own side.

One more blast shook the earth, and now a plume of black smoke became clearly visible in the sky ahead of all of them. The American had saved himself from a direct hit, but he quickly realized that the last shell had been meant as a warning signal to the German pilots, for they could see the black smoke clearly and they certainly knew it meant for them to look around them for danger. They had still been unaware of the attacker at their rear, but now they began diving in tandem to try to avoid his assault.

By the time the squadron had realized it was being chased, Kid was within half a mile of the nearest German plane, and he bore down on his quarry with furious speed, perhaps 180 miles per hour. Soon Kid was on the very heels of the fleeing Albatros, and he fired his guns fiercely for several seconds, until he saw the telltale streaks of orange fire across the fuselage and through the cockpit seat—and the flailing head of the dead pilot—that signified another deadly conquest. He continued plunging headlong with dangerous speed and dispatched another round of fire at his second victim. His bullets pierced the fuel tank, the second plane exploded in a burst of white hot fury, and the vaporized atoms of an airplane rained down in sparks over the morning fields of France.

But no sooner had Milt dispatched two of his enemies than he realized two others would surely be aiming at his tail by this point. Turning his head and catching them on his periphery, he pulled his joystick back and rose abruptly to try to flee their charge. Two of them were now concentrating totally on him, and he knew that either of the pair was probably more skilled than any pilot he had ever seen in America. Almost as soon as he began his climb, Kid heard a terrible ripping sound and he looked up to find the fabric covering of his right wing sheared off and the wing on that side flattened against the side of the fuselage. The Nieuport's entire cloth skin peeled off of it and plunged into the depths of empty space, and Capt. Harrison, now flying a mere skeleton of a plane, felt a sudden upward jerk at his tail.

Absent one of its wings and all of its covering, the Nieuport was diving like a lame pigeon, spinning into oblivion, its pilot seemingly powerless to avoid the violent fireball of death that would consume him when his machine hit the ground. No matter how he maneuvered the controls, his plane continued its spinout as he looked upward into the blue heavens to see two gloating silhouettes of enemy fighter planes bearing down on him as he helplessly struggled to right his course.

To dive out of his spasmodic machine now and attempt escape by parachute was out of the question. Both of his pursuers would riddle his drifting body like a dummy at target practice if he did that. Even in the miraculous event that they misfired, he would land in enemy territory and be brutalized by his merciless captors, and such was even worse than a sudden death. The two German fighters swooped upon the falling plane and riddled it with bullets, then soared away, figuring any further attack would be a waste of ammunition. Kid curled up into a fetal ball, felt the line of bullets skim over the rim of his pilot's seat, and sat up again with the feeble relief a few extra seconds gave him to try to stay his own execution.

His mangled plane continued plummeting toward the wooded hills above the right bank of the Meuse, no longer pursued by any enemy planes. He considered the possibility that his craft might collapse in on itself completely and leave him with no choice but to pull his parachute cord and hope nobody on the ground shot at him. There was a chance his chute might hit the tree line and get hung up in the treetops, and that he would survive only temporarily with a crushed body of broken bones, to be tracked down and finished off by his captors.

At the imminent approach of death his life passed before him as it had never before while he occupied the seat of an airplane. His mother, who had pleaded with him on her knees, begging him not to fight in this horrible war; who dreaded every trip he ever took in a plane, terrified that it would turn the little baby she had nurtured into a disfigured corpse—how would she absorb her life's latest tragedy? His father, who had died encouraging him to continue wooing the dangerous mistress of the air—could he see his son's life ending now, could he lean on the shoulder of the Lord above and ask for divine help to snatch his son away from the jaws of death? And Woodvale—would it die too, with nothing to excite it, nothing to inspire it except the prospect of redemption in another world?

Milt furiously tugged and swung at his joystick, threw his weight from side to side in his cramped seat to try to counteract the spinning downward motion of his machine. His screaming engine announced its trouble to the world below with a desperate wail, and the aviator could see a line of happy vultures leaning against their tanks along the military supply road, dressed in the regalia of the Kaiser's army, awaiting his fall to the ground a mere 2000 feet below. How perverted would their celebration be as they ripped away commemorative chunks of his body and his machine!

The thought of it was more than Capt. Harrison could take. He yanked out his throttle and with a terminal burst of energy his engine roared at full blast and jerked him out of his tailspin. He pulled his rudder hard to one side to compensate for his absent wing and he began flying ahead! The Allied lines were only a few thousand feet ahead of him and if he could keep his plane up until then he might survive! He tried lifting the mutilated machine's nose, but without success. It would only fly one way, straight ahead, and not horizontally but with a slightly downward tilt. No matter. He might pull out, if only . . . if only—

The familiar dread sound shook him to the bone. *POW! POW-POW! POW-POW-POW!* The Hun battery men were aware that the American hero had righted his plane and they were aiming to end his flirtation with salvation. The ear-shattering booms of shells shook him back and forth, but the target was too far away from the gunnery men to be reached with accuracy. The German infantrymen on the ground, complacently sure they had been about to receive a fallen hero gift-wrapped in wreckage, scrambled to arm their machine guns and kill the enemy before he got away, but they were too late as well.

Kid had succeeded at keeping his capsizing plane aloft long enough to cross over the front and by various maneuvers with an engine running at full blast he brought it down over his home base at Souilly, leaping out of it a few hundred feet before impact, opening up his parachute, and hitting the ground safely a few seconds after his plane flattened itself on the grass field. Later the two dead bodies of his latest victims, whose machines had drifted over Allied territory after being shot on the other side of the front, were salvaged in the Argonne woods by some French soldiers.

Though he cared little at that point about being credited with additional kills, relieved as he was still to have his life, Capt. Harrison was thus verified to have two more victories, bringing his total to five, the number required to be declared an ace. He quickly came to the attention of the German high command, who put a bounty on his head.

With such notoriety came the knowledge that many other battles remained to be fought, danger would always be near at hand, and escaping death for the full term of the conflict would require manifold occurrences of superhuman escape. In time, elation would be an alien feeling to him. Instead, with each day done and another victim shot away, he would view his plight with the detachment of a student reading a history book, as though the latest reprieve was but a prelude to something else, probably worse, that had already been written and remained only to be carried out. The hand of the Lord may have been extended to him, but for what reason and for what end he could not know. Nor did any abstract concept of liberty seem to be promoted by anything he did—at least for awhile, until he had gotten away from there and considered the scope of his accomplishments. The present was consumed by the dichotomous constant of two goals: kill today, and live tomorrow.

CHAPTER 13

The Attitude of a Hero

THE BOY FROM WOODVALE was struggling with the apparent futility of the Allied mission. Though he himself had had uncanny success, the Allied side in general had so far been beaten soundly in the Great War. Were the Germans simply superior, or was it a lack of manpower that was creating ever-increasing losses? The autumn gave way to the winter, and the American ace, though outwardly heroic and imperturbable, had a tight knot in the pit of his stomach that relaxed only slightly with the survival of each day, then constricted again with the return to battle on the following morning.

All his friends, it seemed, were being killed just as soon as he made their acquaintance. First a chap named Moresby, and then Captain Lee and even Major Lofton had fallen in battle. A new crop of boys seemed to be sown at the barracks at Souilly each week, only to be harvested by the scythe of the Grim Reaper within a matter of days. Milt felt as if he had to be the father, the mentor and the protector of them all, even though he was but 21 years old himself and hailed from a quiet corner of a foreign land. He began writing his mother once a week during these bleak times, instead of his customary interval of one letter per month.

December 13, 1917

Mama,

I hope everybody's still doing fine in Woodvale. Over here the weather's terrible—cold and rainy every day. This week I shot down three Hun dirigibles. I flew battle planes on those three days over Verdun, and Capt. Rampal, a Frenchman, sat in the front seat and dropped torpedoes on the air ships. We sliced them up like cucumbers. They used up several rounds of ammo trying to shoot us down, but we destroyed them instead, then we blew up our ground targets. There's nothing so amazing as an explosion of an airship. It would make the best fireworks display known to man if it didn't kill people.

The Huns are ganging up on me now. Every day I see about three or four of their planes hovering over the front, waiting to take me out. My plane's painted just like all the others and except for the American flag I taped to the side of my fuselage for good luck, they can't tell which one is me, but they know my aerodrome and they expect to catch me some day. I guess it's a good thing they're wasting so many of their planes on me instead of blowing up military targets and killing other boys. Just in case they get me soon, remember I wrote my will out before I left and all my possessions go to you. My savings and my final papers are in safe deposit at the Trust Company Bank in Atlanta.

By the way, am I still famous over there? It don't matter a lick now, but it sure would be nice in the future if people remembered me like they remember Daddy. I know it'll always be that way in Woodvale. If I don't make it back, be proud of me and don't be sorry I loved aeroplanes. I trust that God wanted me to live this way and if He says it's time for me to go, then it's time and I've served my purpose. That's how I look at it.

I figure I've shot down at least 35 or 40 planes by now but I've quit trying to confirm my victories, to heck with what my commanding officers say. Officially it's 11, and that's fine by me. The more notches the Huns think I've got on my belt, the more of them will be trying to come after me. Instead of four or five, the Kaiser would send about twenty of his men to shadow me if he knew the whole truth. I care more about staying alive than about getting credit for things. So don't brag too much, and maybe I'll make it out alive yet.

Time to go, I've used up 4 pages. God willing, I'll write next week.

Love, Milt.

As a Christmas gift that year, Kid received a commendation from General William Stanton, one of the main overseers of the American forces in Europe. Though there were almost no such forces there as of yet, Stanton was attempting to create them from nothing and Capt. Harrison represented to him a very promising example of the potential of the American fighting man. The problem, however, was that Kid had been fighting for the *Allies* for the five months that he had been in combat over France, not for the

United States. His ultimate superior had been Marshal Pierre Lefors, the commander of the French and British forces along that part of the front. Lefors' intention was to assimilate all the other Americans, when they finally did arrive, under his all-encompassing rule. Stanton, however, was under different orders from the government in Washington. His mission was to forge a distinct unit of American troops, cooperative with the Allies but independent of them.

The first pawn in the struggle for power between Lefors and Stanton proved to be the unsuspecting Capt. Harrison. On the morning of December 25 he was summoned to appear before the two of them as well as Colonel Percival at the offices of the Lorraine aerodrome near Étain, a few kilometers east of Souilly. There he stood solemnly at attention, nervously wondering what he had done wrong but relieved to be getting a temporary respite from shells and machine-gun fire.

"I want you to know, Captain," Stanton addressed Milt, "that your bravery and devotion haven't gone unnoticed back home. As a matter of fact, Uncle Sam is giving you a special present on this Christmas holiday."

The general pulled out a navy blue box around which was wrapped a golden ribbon.

"Open it. It's from our Commander in Chief."

Stanton rose from his high-backed chair, his steely blue eyes and craggy gray-headed visage fixed on Milt. He was nearly sixty years of age, a career military man, strong-willed and rigidly disciplined. The slightest rudiments of a grin appeared under his thick gray mustache as the corners of his lips curled up ever so slightly, and at this faint nuance the young ace relaxed. He knew all would be well now. The chief liked him. Within seconds a wide smile overtook the general's face, and he was paternally patting the youngster on the back. Capt. Harrison was being awarded the Distinguished Service Cross, the second highest Army decoration after the Medal of Honor.

Stanton shook Milt's hand, and was seconded by Marshal Lefors and Colonel Percival. Lefors, a dyed-in-the-wool Frenchman in his late sixties, had a long white sweeping broom mustache and wore the flat-topped cap of the French militia with its frilly garlands embroidered in a band around the side. The upper left lapel of his thick double breasted tunic was draped with his many decorations, which almost rattled when he walked.

"We all thank you, son," he addressed the young American in a thick French accent, but clearly. He patted Milt affectionately on the back of the elbow. "We know these are desperate times, but always maintain the faith. We are assigning you the *drachens* next. Only the bravest are fit for the *drachens.*"

No sooner did he have possession of one of the most esteemed of military honors than the young aviator realized the steep price at which it had been purchased. Because of his seeming indestructibility he would now be assigned the most dreaded of aerial targets: the 200-foot-long hydrogen-filled balloons that the Germans had placed at strategic points along the front for observation of Allied movements and positions. These balloons, or *drachens*, were attached to 2000-foot cables that were operated from trucks by winches on the ground. They were guarded to the teeth by surrounding patrols of Fokker planes and on the ground by antiaircraft batteries and machine guns. Enemy planes had to stay low in order to strike the *drachens*, concentrate bullet fire into a small area to blow open a large enough hole to set off a hydrogen explosion, and evade the gauntlet of shell and gunfire from above and below.

"Thank you, Major Lefors and General Stanton," Milt saluted them unsteadily, not knowing whether he had been attending his christening or his last rites. "I really don't know what to say, it's taken me so much by surprise."

When he examined the expressions on the faces of the two of them he recognized at once whose decision it had been to send him to death's doorstep. It was Lefors—he was the one in charge here. Gen. Stanton disliked having to yield to the marshal on this point—that was obvious. Why then should the young aviator be a volley ball, to be bounced back from one side to the other? And who would stand up for him? Did his deeds and his Distinguished Service Cross not count for anything? But then he remembered. Woodvale. The words of the minister back home. Unto whomsoever much is given, of him shall be much required. Duty. He glanced at Colonel Percival, who seemed unusually formal.

"Congratulations, Captain," the colonel offered Milt his hand. "And good luck."

"I appreciate it, sir. And I'll be happy to do whatever I'm told to do. I don't doubt God's on my side, and whatever happens will be what's meant to happen."

Lefors, his wide broom mustache curling heavenward, chortled pleasantly.

"Indeed, this is the attitude of a hero."

LET OFF FOR THE HOLIDAY honoring the Lord's birth, Kid was up and out of the Souilly mess before sunrise of the next day. He quickly donned his flying suit, his helmet and goggles, then whirled his propellor into motion and flew away without dwelling too much on the precariousness of his mission. He was flying France's new gift to aviation, the Spad S.XIII, a graceful biplane armed with two Vickers .303 machine guns. Late on Christmas night, Milt had made sure the magazines in his guns were loaded with incendiary bullets that would be sure to ignite the combustible gases of the interior of the balloons he would be attacking.

Several of his mates were put on the alert to man the Allied batteries and give him assistance by firing artillery at any of his pursuers within their range. Ever mindful of filching the smallest advantage from favorable circumstances, the American ace was hoping the Germans had allowed Christmas celebrations to become excessive and had come down with 24-hour hangovers, little expecting an assault so soon after their merriment. In moonlight, *drachens* formed vast silhouettes against the starry sky, easy to spot from afar, whereas the little Spad might buzz invisibly through the darkness like a gnat and alight on one of the enormous floating hot dogs without being suspected. Night flying was always perilous, however, because of the lack of internal illumination in the airplanes of that era and the ineffectiveness of the airfield lights on the ground, which were nothing more than flares that burned for only a few minutes at a time.

The bitter cold of a winter morning in solitary dangerous flight high above the snow-covered Western Front was a perverse sort of stimulation to the decorated war hero from across the sea. If death came today, then these extremes of sensation—of motion, whiteness, blackness, frigidity, rushing wind, noise and angst—were to be savored as the final delicacies of a life devoted to adventure. But he was determined that this would not be his final act. Evil would not prevail, not today and not ever, not while he lived; and he would not give up his life without a raging fight.

Balloons were being used by both sides, spaced every fifteen to twenty miles along the front and positioned about two miles behind the trenches. From the observation seats hanging below the balloons, spies might easily view all significant details of enemy movements within a ten-mile radius. Using telescopes and telephone receivers to communicate with their colleagues in the trucks down below, the spies might inform their forces about the success or failure of battery fire, the availability of certain roads, and the imminence of squadron attacks. So used, the balloons were of inestimable military importance and those that were shot down were always quickly replaced. Not without considerable cost, of course, and therein lay the goal: to exhaust the enemy's resources and materiel in any way possible.

The deceptively easy lure of these large stationary airborne targets had swallowed up many unwary aviators in deadly traps. For their very vulnerability made them the objects of ferocious ranks of encircling anti-aircraft batteries and planes trying to ward off their attackers. How to rupture them while avoiding their hostile chaperons—that was the challenge facing anyone assigned to the balloon-chasing circuit.

During the previous nearly sleepless night at the Souilly barracks, Kid had developed a plan that he thought would enable him to surmount the many obstacles that were sure to face him and stand a reasonably good chance of hitting his targets and coming out of the enterprise alive. That was to strike early, in the predawn when the approach of a predator could not be precisely detected by the batteries; to come in low to the ground so that the surrounding squadron of planes would have difficulty seeing him and firing at him; to stay low so if the truck winch began lowering the balloon he would still be on its same level and able to fire straight at it; and, most importantly, to fly at top speed, get done quickly, and dart away before the enemy had time to react.

The batteries surrounding the balloons were likely to be firing bullets upward in such heavy quantities that trying to fly a plane through their columns of grapeshot would be almost suicidal. Survival would only be possible if one were absolutely certain about all possible sources of gunfire. Kid had become so familiar with the territory around that part of the front that he thought he could pinpoint, even in near darkness, the location of the batteries on the ground and weave his Spad around them while shooting at and then fleeing the balloons.

He was soaring high above Metz, surveying the horizon to ensure that there were no gun flashes of any kind within sight. He was in luck; it was now at that very hour of the night when the fighters on both sides, lulled into carelessness by several hours of inactivity, tended to let their guards down and take a catnap or two. At 7000 feet of altitude he cut off his motor and glided silently over the front. Three large floating cigars were visible, and all looked ripe for bursting. If he hit the first one he calculated that he would be within striking range of the second within five minutes, if his Spad reached its top-out speed of 130 mph; and perhaps reach the third balloon five to ten minutes after that. Imagine the joy and the nerve! Three exploding *drachens*, all reddening the dawn sky at once over eastern France, all the work of one lone American warrior! That was his mission now. If he died in the pursuit—well, he would be going out with the proverbial bang.

He glided steadily down in the direction of his first target, drifting over the dark woods hugging both hilly sides of the valley of the Moselle River. All was silent and breezy and he fixed his sights squarely on the black Maltese Cross that was painted in the very middle of the nearest *drachen*, a tempting bull's eye that seemed to bait him like a chunk of cheese in the middle of a mousetrap. The apparent ease with which he was bearing down on his target was, however, illusory. Notwithstanding the relative quiet of his approach, the Germans were aware he was in their midst. Suddenly there was an outburst of fiery bullets coming up from the ground, and Kid knew the time was now short. He opened his throttle wide, fired his engine up and raced at the balloon, side slipping the column of battery fire. Once inside the battery line he raced to within 150 yards of his target. Pulling both of his triggers with a steady aim, he watched as six fiery streaks of flame traced a course straight for the balloon, pierced a gaping hole in its side, and set off an explosion of such violent pyrotechnics that the burst of fire nearly consumed his own plane.

Time was now extremely short. He knew the Fokkers would be gunning for him from this point onward and by the time he reached the next balloon he would be in the midst of a hailstorm of bullets. But fear was no part of him. The Allies had their own batteries in the area and he felt confident they would be coming to his aid if he needed them. In a complete trance of concentration, he dodged the next battery column, tore through the several miles of open air to the next balloon, and repeated the process. Again the trigger pulls, again the fiery streaks, again the black cross of the Fatherland up in brilliant flames. A Fokker pulled behind him in pursuit, but the explosion knocked it off its course and an Allied battery shot pierced the German plane's fuselage and spun it out.

Everything around Captain Harrison was moving at warp speed. Another *drachen*, the third, was soon within his sights. More hostile fire from the Germans, more bullets. All of no consequence. A Fokker was pouncing down upon him. No matter. Again the pulls of both triggers, the fiery streaks, the pierced German cross. This time the conflagration actually consumed the plane that had been chasing him. The first two explosions had demonstrated the wind direction and the pattern of fire-burst, and this time Kid, taking advantage of recent experience, maneuvered his plane so the explosion would engulf the German enemy in his wake.

Word had spread that the American ace was on his way. The mother truck had been attempting to pull this last balloon in with its winches, but Kid was low enough to intercept it anyway. The German soldier who had been occupying the observation deck leaped from his seat at this latest attack, pulled at his parachute cord and drifted down. Kid made out the terrified expression on his face, but showed him mercy. There had been enough killing for one morning, so he held his fire and let the man float away. Time was of the essence now. He needed to head for friendly territory posthaste. There were a few more battery explosions, which he craftily avoided, but Milt was soon back among his friends. The sneak attack had worked with devastating, humiliating, and deadly effectiveness.

Finally the news was good in the training camps back home for the American boys preparing for the military mission that in over 100,000 cases would prove fatal to them. The newspapers proclaimed Capt. Kid Harrison's exploits vividly for all to see. One man, one plane, three German targets up in flames. Allied photographers had captured the dramatic explosions in pictures which now decorated the broadsheets of the world with powerful imagery. With one good fighter in one good aeroplane, the Allies had landed a heavy blow on their adversaries.

———

ROMANCE, ABSENT FROM THE poor men who fought in the trenches and breathed poison gas and contracted influenza in the decisive ground battles of the great conflict, belonged to the aviators. It was they who, free from mortal bounds of mud and ditches, soared like gods above the stationary massed armies, flaunting their daring for all the other warriors to admire: their scarves flapping in the breeze, their machines flipping and twirling in acrobatic dances of death, their nerves steeled against sudden violent destruction by fervent devotion to cause and duty.

It was they, the modern knights, who fought with chivalry and grace, in spectacular jousts of fire and bullets, man-to-man, with none but themselves or their own machines to blame if they should fall. The value of their efforts was measurable not in territory lost or gained, casualties accounted for, or important targets destroyed, but in the far more important effect they had on the minds of humanity. Cool and detached knights, they fought on the highest stage, before an audience of God and the makers of myth.

Marshal Lefors, General Stanton and Colonel Percival again summoned the boy from Woodvale back to their offices after his latest extraordinary feat. Stanton, amazed at the thoroughness and effectiveness of the captain's attack, was beaming with pride and admiration.

"I'm at a loss for praise, young man. If you keep on at this rate we'll be running out of medals to give you in another month or two. I hereby recommend you for the rank of major, but after this, what more?"

Milt grinned, saluted his commander and shook the general's hand.

"I know only one way to fly and fight, general. And the main thing I want now is for us to win this war so I can go home. I'm tired of killing people and thinking every day's gonna be my last. Get me some American troops over here, so we can wipe these people out and be done with it all."

Colonel Percival nodded.

"Patience, my boy. Just hold out and keep faith, and when it's over the world will always remember you."

In the meantime, the generals on the opposite side in Hamburg were incensed that the American ace had caught them napping yet again. This type of incident could not be repeated without serious damage to the Fatherland's cause. The balloons could be and already had been replaced, true. The damage was more *psychological* than anything else. Up to now, the army of the Kaiser had seemed invincible, at least to the Allies. Moreover, the propaganda war had been decisively one-sided. The German *Feldfliegartruppen* had complete superiority in the air, so common wisdom went: superiority in skill, equipment, training, morale, purpose. One could not allow the enemies, especially the sleeping Americans, to entertain the idea that they might challenge that supremacy. Once they became imbued with that notion it might become a self-fulfilling prophecy of sorts, the sleeping giant might awake, the fearless cowboys from the wild frontier of America might gain confidence, pluck, determination.

For this challenge only the most highly skilled aviator of the Fatherland was fit. He was the greatest myth of all. It was he who had the nickname, the trappings of glory, the redoubtable reputation, and the talent to match. The lead aviator of the Jagdstaffel 7, the Rittmeister, Hans Eichhorn, was summoned at the Longwy Aerodrome and given his curt command. Defeat the American Satan. Take him out before he reproduces a thousandfold and turns into a Juggernaut. Take to the skies about Verdun and Metz, find the wild cowboy, and send him to his end.

Within days the German aerodrome at Thionville had a new pilot, its most famous addition as of yet: the Rittmeister, whose expressed mission it was to track down the American ace in the territory he was known to frequent, to wage battle against him, and to end his life and remove his menacing presence from the theater of the war. Of course Hans would be assisted in this by the fellow pilots of that squadron who had previously been given a similar charge but had yet to complete it. This time, under the skill and daring lead of Herr Eichhorn, the expectation was for immediate success and a return to the German domination of the air war that had existed prior to Kid's arrival at the front.

DECEMBER YIELDED TO JANUARY. Snow, ice and fog plagued the shell-ravaged landscape around Verdun; and the miserable fighting men on both sides, bogged down in muddy pits, fought horrendously deadly battles on the ground with frequently no more than a few feet of advance gained on either side. Major Harrison, an extra stripe newly added to his epaulette when his higher commission officially arrived a few days into 1918, was primed for a showdown. The three best Englishmen of the Argonne Escadrille, Lts. Briggs, Foskey and Gardner, along with the two best surviving airmen of France, Leroux and Beaufort, now accompanied him on all of his missions, flying in ranks to be ready to back up Kid when the Germans finally decided the time was ripe for attack.

It came in February, on a windless sunny day. Each side had been shooting down its enemy's balloons, studying its enemy's movements of men and materiel from hostile air space above its lines, dodging battery fire from the ground, and preparing for the happy convergence of time, luck and circumstance when it would occupy a common point in the air with its rival squadron. The perfectly clear sky on the fifth day of that month provided such an occasion. Both the Allies and the Axis sent their squadrons up early that morning to gain strategic advantage. When the men from each side espied each other on the horizon, the red of the German Fokkers from the east and the olive green of Kid and the Allies from the west, they all prayed for some sort of divine guidance through the valley of the shadow of death. And when the flyers of the Argonne Escadrille saw the dreaded white skull and crossbones on the fuselage of one of the red planes, an extra measure of tension was added to the mission.

"You want me, Hank?" Kid shouted to himself. "Let's go at it, pal!"

All the red planes, having the advantage of altitude, tried a diving attack on the Spads at the end of the formation, but Leroux and Beaufort were true with the aims of their machine guns. Their bullets pierced the tails of two of the Fokkers, and two red planes were quickly sent spiraling downward. Eichhorn, with nerveless precision, strafed Foskey from close range, riddled the unfortunate pilot with bullets, and watched as his Spad dove out of the sky with a balletic death spin. Kid decided now was the time to provoke the German ace. He turned his plane to the west, hoping to outrace the Rittmeister to the front, to drag him all the way back to Souilly and there to shoot him down before an appreciative audience of messmates.

When Hans noticed his opponent making so frenzied a retreat toward France he was surprised. He had heard it said before that Americans, like the French and unlike the dutiful English, were weak-willed and afraid to fight, but surely this American was not that way. This was the pride of his nation, the chosen fighter for their version of freedom. It was impossible that any consideration other than the purely practical was compelling him to retreat in such a way. Might this be a ruse of some kind? If not, why did he find it necessary to go off in such a way? Why not fight a straight duel, shot for shot, and let the better man fly away? Under normal conditions, Hans had no doubt his rival would have welcomed such a duel. *The American ace was running out of fuel.* That was the only explanation plausible to Hans. *He was nearly out of fuel and due to his own carelessness and bad strategy he knew his dead-engined machine would soon be strafed out of the sky.* Glory to the Fatherland. The Rittmeister pulled out his Fokker's throttle and aimed for the Kid's tail. Sweet retribution was soon to be his.

The boy from Woodvale was pleased to see his adversary coming after him. The blue-green Moselle River, glistening in the frosty winter air between snow-dusted bluffs, was now beneath them. To the left was Metz and twenty minutes away was Souilly. Milt glanced at his watch and did a quick calculation. The time and the circumstances were nearly right for a surprise turnaround, if only the German ace would keep following. When Milt spotted Souilly below him he suddenly flipped his plane in the opposite direction and began flying straight toward the very plane whose pursuit he had been fleeing only a moment before.

By Kid's reckoning he had no more than three seconds to get close enough to his enemy to have a reasonable chance of striking. He raced forward, pulled on both triggers furiously with every bit of ammunition left in his belts, some fifteen rounds, and pelted the red plane with holes. The terrified German curled up in his flying seat while the bullets devoured his plane.

A lesser aviator would have perished under the circumstances, but the Rittmeister was no ordinary man. Somehow he managed to guide his damaged bullet-riddled wreck of a plane to a safe landing place in friendly territory, in a pasture east of the front. When his plane hit the ground his head was dashed against the side of the fuselage and he hurled his shaken body from the wreckage before his machine caught fire. His loud groans for help were answered a few minutes later when he was rescued by an infantry division and sent by ambulance to a nearby infirmary. He had sustained no broken bones and no debilitating bruises or lacerations.

In flesh he had survived to fight again, but in spirit he was a beaten man. Doctors guided him back to some semblance of health again in the next several days, but the gold-tinted mirror in which he and much of the rest of the world had viewed his reflection had now been shattered. Kid was disappointed to hear of Eichhorn's miraculous survival. Not because of hatefulness or bloodlust, but because of the merely practical consideration that if the Rittmeister still lived then Milt would probably be forced to fight him again, and to best him two times seemed to defy all normal odds of probability.

There was never any guarantee that one would live long enough to fight again, that one's good fortune would outlast a seemingly interminable war.

CHAPTER 14

The Women of France

IN MID FEBRUARY OF 1918 Major Harrison, the Flight Commander of any squadron to which he happened to be assigned, whether of British or French domain, was sent by Marshal Lefors to assist the RFC 137th squadron in the deadly battles over the valley of the Meuse.

The conditions there were exceptionally miserable. New pilots had an average lifespan of eleven days. They were now being required to fly four missions a day, with accommodations in flimsy tents without hot water, and assigned the perilous task of strafing ground forces and killing them on the attack. In addition, a deadly influenza epidemic was afoot in the filthy, unsanitary conditions. By war's end this epidemic would claim far more American lives than the actual fighting.

Since Kid continued to be shadowed by enemy planes on each mission he was under particularly intense pressure. He began longing for a few days away from the firing line, a few days of tranquility somewhere, somehow. He longed in vain. Only an injury exempted any pilot from active missions during these critical times, and he remained perfectly healthy. Oh, for a return to peace, when flying had been fun! He had been so long in harm's way—a full seven months when the average career of a combat pilot was less than two weeks—that he had nearly forgotten the sensation of taking up a plane for the sheer love of it, absent any mission to kill or destroy or danger of being pelted by harsh bullet fire from a man he didn't know for a reason he couldn't comprehend.

Day after day the pride of Woodvale witnessed fresh-faced boys his age and younger, boys with a life full of promise ahead of them, taking up planes they had no more qualifications to fly under these conditions than a first-semester medical student did to perform surgery. And one after another of them was sent away soon, his mutilated body lying limply on the cold muddy ground like that of a stuffed scarecrow tumbled over in a windstorm, his flying machine smashed into fragments.

The collection of tents in the northern part of the Argonne was called Buzancy, and there the 137th bivouacked during the cold and dreary battles of February. A new and very dangerous model was now being used to fend off the Germans: the Sopwith Camel F1, a machine that may have eliminated as many Allies as it did enemies because its speed exceeded the handling abilities of many of its pilots. Kid did much of his best maneuvering in the Camels during the offensive, and he kept urging his men to stay alert and follow his leads.

"I know y'all are tired of all this fighting without rest or sleep," he repeated morning after morning, "and I sure as hell am. But the Heinies are in even worse shape than we are. They ain't had a rest in four years. Let's whup 'em today, men. Let's whup 'em so we can go home."

And so the day would begin, usually with some degree of forced optimism, and after knocking out one or two German planes, dodging the fire of a half dozen others, spinning like a dervish and darting hither and yon like a bat, occasionally curling up to avoid the flurry of bullets that strafed his plane then straightening up again and bringing his damaged machine to a forced landing, Major Harrison would defy death yet again, unlike several greenhorns who had forced themselves to take that morning's pep talk to heart. Hans Eichhorn's Jagdstaffel 7 and the 137th went at each other relentlessly, but neither the Rittmeister nor the Kid was able to isolate his archrival during the battles of the early part of that month.

THOUGH THE RATE OF fatalities among Milt's comrades was deplorable, a few were able to endure with him and inflict great damage on the enemy. One such flyer was Carson Everett, a Canadian who combined extraordinary skill and experience with a tragic frailty of nerve and delicacy of temperament. After a particularly bloody day in which Everett and Harrison had shot down three attacking Fokkers, helped to stymie a ground assault of Allied trenches near Verdun, and torpedoed a zeppelin that had been spotted returning to its base near Longwy, Everett appeared to have a nervous breakdown in the tent at Buzancy. Lts. Anderson and Capshaw called for Maj. Harrison to help the bedraggled pilot.

Now in the twilight there seemed to be an interlude in the fighting. A thick fog hung over the Argonne, and a cold drizzle cascaded from the gray sky above the denuded landscape of mud and chopped up trees around the front. Milt entered the tent to find the young man from Ottawa prostrate on his cot, a kerosene lantern flickering on a small table next to him. He went and sat down beside him, holding his hand like a concerned brother.

"Carson, you hurt?"

"I don't have any wounds, Kid," said Lt. Everett, "if that's what you mean. Physical wounds."

"You tired of this business?"

"There's no pleasure or satisfaction in killing people. It's a job and I'll do what I'm told, but—ever wish we could just *fly?*"

"Don't we all? I used to think there was glory in the war over here. Well, Carson—I guess you could say we all been forced to grow up over here."

The two young men continued holding hands, and to them and the several other soldiers around them it seemed a perfectly natural thing for them to do. Lt. Everett was weeping like a schoolboy, his nose was running, his eyes were drawn and bloodshot. His ulcerated stomach had prevented him from a normal diet, he had grown emaciated, and the hair on his 24-year-old head was falling out and graying.

"I don't know if I even want to live after all this, Kid. It'll take a miracle for us to survive this, and even if we do, how can we forget—how can we ever go back to normal?"

"I thought that way when my father died. I didn't think I could ever go back to normal, but I did. We've just gotta keep trying to do something nobody ever did before, keep discovering new things. It may be terrible or it may be beautiful, but somehow there's a plan and a reason for us and it's never easy."

Everett wiped his teary eyes and his runny nose on the sleeve of his uniform and smeared his face in his hand again.

"You might think that way, but I don't. Not any more. There's no purpose for any of it. I don't think there's a superior being who cares. Can't be. No way a god of mercy would allow this to happen to his children. No matter what else happens, there won't be a happy ending to all this."

Milt squeezed the lieutenant's hand more tightly, as if to transfer more of his boundless energy and faith to his downtrodden friend.

"How do we know? Carson, I won't speak for you, 'cause I can't get inside your head, but I know what works for me. I feel there's always a way to come back, no matter how bad life seems. We're only given one life, and we know it won't last long, so let's make the best of it and do what we can to leave things better than they were when we found 'em. That's how I feel, my friend. I feel there's a force that can guide us through."

Everett sat up and placed his feet on the ground below his cot.

"I wish you'd teach me to feel that way. It seems so awful to me, all these dead bodies, all this waste—and I'm a part of it—and my body'll probably be there next. . . ."

"If it is, there's still gonna be somebody left who remembers what you did. And if there's not—if every damn human being on the face of the earth gets annihilated—then we'll make the buzzards happy. They never had so much good meat."

The Canadian smirked and gave a subtle nod at his commander. He broke loose from the grip of Milt's hand and propped his elbows on his lap.

"I remember when my parents spent $500 to send me to flight school in Toronto," Everett said, "and the instructors made me sign papers promising my family wouldn't sue them if I crashed or killed myself. Can you believe that?"

Lt. Everett grinned at the recollection, and Kid stood and gave his comrade a salute.

"Why should we be scared of dying, Carson? We've seen things that nobody ever saw before or will again. I've gotten more joy out of revvin' a single seater firetrap over Candler Field or the boondocks in Iowa or 15,000 feet over France than most people get in a whole lifetime. We may not be livin' long, but we're still livin' high. I met Stratton Liffey back in '15 and he said to me: 'Don't fly if you can live any other way.' Well, I can't live any other way, can you?"

The war ace from Canada rose to his feet, looked up into the eyes of the much taller man and saluted Major Harrison.

"No sir, Major. *I can't live any other way.*"

"That's what I like to hear. Now let's get back to doing what we love."

EARLY THE NEXT MONTH, Major Raymond Milton Harrison Jr. received a telegram at Buzancy from a familiar source.

2MAR1918

CONGRATS MAJ HARRISON X ENEMY ACTIVITY IN YOUR PART OF THE THEATER APPEARS NEUTRALIZED X YOU ARE HEREBY ORDERED TO COME AT ONCE TO MY HQ AT ÉTAIN X WE HAVE AMERICANS HERE NOW AND THEY ARE READYING FOR BATTLE X MANY DESIRE TO SEE YOU X WE SHALL DISCUSS A WELLDESERVED LEAVE FOR YOU UPON YOUR ARRIVAL

COL PAUL PERCIVAL

The next morning a staff sergeant drove him by truck to Étain, more than an hour's ride to the southeast. When he entered Colonel Percival's office at the Lorraine Aerodrome, there stood General Stanton and another familiar face—a dapper, youthful, upbeat American face that he had encountered before by the dusty racetrack at Candler Field.

"*Britt!* What are you doin' here, man?"

Johnny Albritton, the famed driver who had once raced against Kid's plane, nearly came out of his shoes with laughter and a smile. His complexion turned ruddy and cheerful; he shook Milt's hand, slapped him on the shoulder, and the two of them hugged.

"I didn't want you to grab *all* the headlines, Kid. It's about time for the rest of us to prove we know a thing or two about fighting, too. I'll win if it kills me, I will."

"How'd you get here?"

"I read in the papers back home General Stanton was a big fan of auto racing, so I sent him a picture of me in the Indy 500 and I asked him a favor. I says, 'Let me be in the Air Service. I want to do what Kid Harrison's doing—I bet I'll do it even better.' So here I am."

"You learn how to fly yet?"

"Durn, boy. Wasn't nothin' to it."

The second pleasant surprise of the morning came when Colonel Percival informed Kid that due to Percival's own intercession he had been granted two weeks furlough for rest and relaxation. Marshal Lefors had been against the idea, taskmaster that he was. Lefors said the time for rest was in peace, the fight would intensify as the weather grew warm, the enemy was now controllable since American muscle power had been brought to the front, this was not the time to relent by letting the best warriors soften themselves in the lap of luxury. The hell it was, Percival had scoffed. This boy had been in harm's way at every turn, never once complaining or shirking duty, never once receiving a scratch in some of the fiercest fighting in the history of warfare. The hell it was.

Stanton had tried to curb Col. Percival's hot temper and his insubordinate attitude, but the plain fact was that the Colonel was right. This boy was no pack animal, a beast of burden to be ridden and spurred and whipped and lashed until he was foaming at the mouth. Every soldier had the right to occasional leaves for his own personal pleasure. It was about time Lefors realized he wasn't running America's war. The orders from the President were explicit. In Europe it was the American generals who had command over American forces, not Lefors or any vague consortium of European potentates. The Huns might be running their men into the ground, but these were Americans, they made the conditions of their union with the Alliance, and Stanton, at the request of Col. Percival, had made his final decision. Two weeks of furlough were hereby granted. Lefors, given no choice, had to agree. Perhaps the other Americans there would take up the slack in Kid's absence. A new American aviator who had just been taught to fly while in France was showing great promise: this *Albritton.*

KID NEARLY WANTED TO shout for joy when he heard the news that he would finally be allowed some time away from the front. Two weeks of freedom to him seemed like ten years to a civilian. The one consuming thought on his mind as soon as he heard he was at liberty was not war or peace, but something oddly in between: WOMEN.

Other than the occasional fly-by-night encounter with a French peasant girl, Milt had lived in an all-male world for nearly a year. He had two thousand francs in a safe he kept under his cot at Souilly, his salary and some of what he had brought from home. At this point he craved two things more than any other: girls and sunshine.

The train from Verdun led south to Nice, Monaco and Monte Carlo, the *Côte d'Azur,* where wartime Europe was congregating to warm its sorrows in Mediterranean decadence. Even with the clacking of the rails underneath the railcar, he had a steady ringing in his ears, a dizzy blur around the corners of his eyes whenever he opened them, and an ineradicable impulse to turn and look about him in all directions when he heard an unfamiliar sound within the confines of his train compartment, just to be certain no one was pursuing him. Thus he learned firsthand the meaning of the term "shellshock". Even on the ground and within the relative safety of a locomotive coach car, his system was still permeated by the violence and obsessive caution in which it had been steeped almost continuously since the previous autumn.

WHILE AT THE CASINOS of Monaco, surrounded by smartly-dressed women, the aviator was recognized and welcomed whenever people in his presence were informed of his identity. It was true, they all said in their various tongues. The American ace was indeed a Hercules from the frontier. However, he proved all too human at the gaming tables and in the perfumed ambience of the hotel *boudoirs.* After eight days amid the Mediterranean gaming traps and fast women of his dreams, he had squandered most of his money and was as impotent as a limp dishrag. Too much variety and richness of cuisine at the restaurants, and noise and commotion in the gaming salons, and mirthful interaction with lascivious Continental damsels had rendered him as feeble as many of the invalids at the infirmaries along the front. He began to fear that maybe he had contracted a dreaded disease from one of his girls. A handful of spectacularly beautiful women had done what a well-oiled war machine of men trained in death and destruction had been unable to do: they had used up the boy from Woodvale and driven him to his knees. They were almost conspiratorial in their effectiveness.

If only Lefors had been there to witness it all—Lefors who had been so adamantly opposed to letting the Kid withdraw from his ruthlessly successful regime in the first place—then there would have been an overbearing display of French pride before the American generals, a taunting "I told you so" air of superiority. This was his country, and the marshal knew the many dangers that lurked about it far better than any American outsiders. How could they know as well as the marshal what a deadly weapon the women of France might be to a young American boy with fame, medals and good-looks? One could not have lived so long as Lefors without learning a great many things about the world, even that portion of the world outside the military.

Milt was reeling in illness and solitude in his hotel room by his ninth day along the *Côte d'Azur*, imagining in his confused hallucinations that the grizzled marshal hovered above him, wiggling a knowing finger at him and shaking his head. All the free world had been let down by his excesses, the wizened Frenchman would be reprimanding him. Then his father would appear, maybe from his place in heaven. His father didn't want him to go out this way. His father still wanted him to go out in an airplane.

In frustration young Maj. Harrison scrawled out a note to his mother, hoping that it might in some way help him. But if he had syphilis . . . well, the fact was that he knew nothing whatsoever about it, nothing about its symptoms or effects except that if you got it you were more or less a walking corpse. His mother too would be chiding him and scolding him and reminding him she'd warned him, but he had to tell somebody something, even if what he revealed to her was nowhere near the whole truth.

March 14, 1918

Mama,

Monaco's a beautiful place and I've been sampling a little bit of everything since I got here. The roulette wheels and card tables in the casinos have been eating some of my money, but that's fine, I still have more of it. I think some day I might get good at blackjack and poker—too bad I just learned how to play them. I know you'll be proud I haven't had a taste of liquor or wine since I left home, even though everybody drinks that stuff all the time over here.

All this free time is starting to wear on me. I hate to say it, but I'd rather be in a plane trying to kill somebody. That's how you feel after awhile. You get so used to it you really have to keep doing it in order to feel comfortable. At first you hate a war, then it becomes a regular part of your life. That's how it is with me, I guess. When I got my furlough I thought it was the best thing in the world. Now I can't wait to get back to the front, where I have orders and rules and important missions to do and where I can fly.

You probably can't understand it, because you're a woman and my mother. I've just gotten so used to discipline and orders that when I don't have them I go crazy. Freedom's hard on people, because if you're free to do what you want it's easier to do something stupid than something smart. Pretty soon, when I get back to fighting, I won't have any choice about whether to do the right or the wrong thing. I'll either do it right or I'll be dead. I'm just trying to tell you the truth.

It's terrible I've fought so hard for freedom, then when I get it I waste it. I hope other people aren't like me, or we'll be in real trouble if we ever win this war.

Love, Milt

After four days of bed rest in his curtain-darkened hotel room in Monaco, Kid began to regain at least some of his customary vigor. Maybe it was just a standard cold, brought on by exhaustion, noise, and overindulgent debauchery. Maybe it wasn't actually the dreaded syphilis, which would have scarred the rest of his life. Never, never again would he do this, he kept repeating to himself while he recuperated. Never, never again. At least until the next time he got the urge. Fair enough. He would never, ever allow himself to be eaten alive by women—until the time came when he had totally forgotten about this experience, and then he would do it again, and with completely intemperate gusto.

When he reported promptly for duty at Souilly at 9AM on the morning of the eighteenth, Kid appeared to have lost as much vitality as everyone who had seen him off had expected him to have gained by then. The word soon spread to Stanton and Lefors that the Great Ace, back from the south of France, had burned himself to the nub while away from the war. The French marshal angrily summoned Colonel Percival to his quarters, determined to let him know who had been right all along.

"Have you seen him, Colonel?" the Allied mastermind asked Percival.

"Yes, sir, Marshal. I've seen him, and he'll be fine."

"On the contrary," said Lefors, "I hear he is pale and fatigued."

"Of course the boy's fatigued. He made off with half the dames in France, so what do you expect?"

Lefors, though puzzled by the defiant colonel's phraseology, gathered the meaning of his words.

"Lust has killed far more men than bullets."

"And complacency has killed far more men than either," said Percival. "He'll see the campaign with different eyes now. He won't rely on the same tired old vision he used last month and the month before that. He's had some time away, and now that God-given talent will shine all the more brightly since it went down over the horizon and came up again."

"He was in the middle of the stream of the war," countered Lefors, "and then he left it. He had grown used to the cold water and the violence of movement. Now the water will feel too cold for him and the current more than he can withstand. He was doing the impossible, not knowing it was impossible. Now he knows he shall never make it across if he goes out into the middle again."

The mature French commander, born into a long-vanished world and steeped in the philosophy of another century, looked at the young American colonel like Moses upon an untested Joshua. He seemed contented that his latest pronouncement had put an end to the argument, that Percival had nothing else to do but concede the wrong-headedness of his views.

"To us, Marshal, nothing is impossible," the colonel answered. "That's why we'll win you this war. And you're wrong. That boy never did anything in his life without being a hundred percent sure he'd do it right. Maybe it didn't happen the way he wanted—but all along he *thought* it would. He still thinks that way, and he always will."

"We shall see, Colonel," said Lefors, with wrinkled brow. "What's past is past. One cannot erase what has already been done. We shall see."

CHAPTER 15

Slaying the Riding Master

KID WAS SLOW TO return to his old form, despite Percival's confidence. No longer was he the lone eagle in the skies above the front. Albritton and others were swift in their training, and by the end of March the first aerial kills made by American-trained aviators flying for the United States were recorded. A sense of relief settled over Milt when he realized that a whole nation was *not* perched on his wings any more; that others who had been inspired by his example and who shared his boundless, irrational love of flight had volunteered to serve in the most dangerous military capacity ever devised by man.

Major Harrison began devoting as much time to the training of young recruits as he did in strict combat missions. But he never shrank from the most dangerous patrols, nor did he ask any of his men to do that which he was unwilling to do himself. As a matter of fact, he made sure to log more combat hours than any of the pilots who had been under his instruction, and he frequently went out on his own at night, already exhausted from daylight skirmishes. The morale of his squadron, despite its frequent casualties, thus remained high. From the sound principle that example leads better than instruction, the squadron commander of the Argonne Escadrille eventually generated an unflinching loyalty and a selfless commitment among his understudies. In this way the blueprint for his talent was passed on to others and soon permeated the Air Service. But first there was the problem of breaking the new boys in, and that wore Kid down during the first few weeks of their deployment.

One of the most promising newcomers in the squadron, though also certainly the biggest braggart, was a 20-year-old lieutenant named Robert Francis Lattimore, son of a cattle rancher from the remote outpost of DeQueen, Arkansas. Sandy-haired, blue-eyed, of nondescript appearance, "Arky", as everyone called him, never tired of exaggerating his own exploits or of vowing to kill an inordinate number of Huns. Though he lionized Kid, he pretended to be nonchalant about his trainer and commander. He seemed an apt enough pupil, learned acrobatic maneuvers quickly, and showed no unwillingness to strike out on his own. But invariably when he came back he would claim to have shot down a German plane, despite never having any witnesses. After awhile, Milt grew tired of Lattimore and others like him. Though he had been relieved at first to have American boys along with him, he wanted no part of their faintly-disguised jealousies and attempts to upstage him. He spoke with Stanton about the dilemma and was given permission to go back to the valley of the Meuse for a few days so the green rookies would learn not to take him for granted.

"Arky," he addressed his squadron's young braggart one day in mid March, "I think it's about time I turned this joint over to you and the other lieutenants. I ain't doin' you a damn bit of good. You know enough already about this business, don't you?"

"Thanks, Major," Lattimore smiled with pride. "'Preciate hearin' that."

"That's why I felt comfortable about puttin' in for a transfer. I want to go back and help the 137th a little north of here. You and the boys can take care of things around here, Arky—you, Britt, Castleberry, Cameron, Williams, Singleton and the rest."

The young Arkansan's heart seemed to fall to his feet.

"W-why you wanna do that, Kid? Why don't you stay here?"

"I've got some unfinished business up there, Lieutenant. Ever since I had my little holiday, I've had something stickin' in my craw. Stanton and Colonel Percival already said they'd let me go back up to Buzancy."

"Buzancy? What the hell's up there?"

"The Rittmeister's aerodrome's in that area. He still rules the roost up there, and I better get my ass up there and kill him before he goes on another one of his rampages and wipes out half a squadron."

THERE HAD BEEN REPORTS of renewed German aggression by the Jagdstaffel 7 near Longwy, with extensive casualties. The close proximity of several Allied aerodromes to that region made it particularly vulnerable to the Kaiser's militia. If the *Feldfliegartruppen* were so inclined, it might easily launch a preemptive strike on the Argonne from that location, minimize resistance for the German infantry to seize a few more miles of precious territory, and put a stranglehold on France before the American troops could be fully deployed. Now was the critical moment in the brutal conflict. The Rittmeister and his flying entourage were being told to strike now, strike for the death, strike for the Fatherland, or perish in the attempt.

Milt kept thinking of the nobility of Lt. Everett, currently the best fighting man in that part of the military theater. It was now rare to find an aviator who had survived as many hours of aerial conflict as Everett, though that survival had exacted a heavy toll on his nerves. More than any gas or bullets, it was a persistent anguish of mind that was threatening to kill the

Canadian pilot, and Milt wanted to be with him to help him overcome his traumas.

On March 27th the boy from Woodvale was back in the Spartan tents of Buzancy. Col. Percival had utmost confidence that the Rittmeister would be given his death blow after his next encounter with the American ace; that the ultimate coup in propaganda would follow from their second meeting; that the doughboys would charge the trenches with the inspiration of mystics when they heard the latest exploits of their famed boy-wonder of the biplane. As he and Stanton saw it, the war was all about morale at this point, for the tactical and logistical might the Allies had assembled along the front was superior to that of Germany and the Axis. "Go on, Kid," Percival had urged him, "and bring back the trophy." After the ace's pathetic holiday in the south of France, his anxieties about combat had lessened considerably.

When Milt arrived at the grim bivouac at Buzancy he found conditions even more distressing than they had been on his previous term there. The men had taken to drowning their fears in bottles of scotch before each dawn patrol. From one mouth to another the brown bottle would pass, each man taking a hearty swig, until the vessel was drained of its last drop. Then another poor boy would pull out another bottle from his satchel, the men would drink communally from it again, and repeat their ceremonial rite until their systems were all adrift in that nebulous border zone between sobriety and intoxication.

On the morning of March 29 a cold heavy fog hemmed in the valley of the Meuse, and the Allied men sat bored and restless in their tents waiting for the fog to lift. Maj. Harrison moved furtively from one tent to another, treading softly over the wet mud, trying to keep the other boys alert and ready. At Carson Everett's tent he caught his comrades by surprise, coming through the flaps just as one of the men was craning his neck back to suck the last bit of scotch out of the bottle with the others huddled around him.

"Hey, what the hell are y'all doin'?" Kid asked them. "Cut that bullshit out now, you hear me?"

Lt. Sheppard, the Australian who had been the provender of the booze and the orchestrator of the drinking binges, tossed the bottle he had just drunk dry to the floor of the tent. Then he turned and gave a salute to Kid.

"We're done with it now, mate. It won't do us a bit of good now."

"That stuff never done anybody a bit of good," said Kid. "It'll just get us all dead quicker. Is that what you want, Lieutenant?"

"I'll bet you the Heinies are doing the same thing in their tents. This'll only make it even."

"Like hell it will," said Kid. "Whatever they're doin' is the opposite of what we need to do, 'cause they're about to get their tails blown off. They're a beaten bunch, and they know it."

"We got Lt. Taylor, a rookie, here," said a pale and sickly-looking chap named Alderson. "What's wrong with a fellow relaxing his nerves a little, before he gets baptized by bullets for the first time?"

Milt looked at the baby-faced Scotsman by Everett's side, Alexander "Lex" Taylor, who was visibly trembling.

"The best way to fly is stone cold sober, boys," said Kid. "If flyin' an aeroplane through the sky and goin' wing to wing with an opponent makes you chicken, then you shouldn't be here. You oughtta be home selling war bonds, or driving an ambulance for the Red Cross if that's how you feel."

The beleaguered men hung their heads. The boy from Woodvale, who had trouble understanding why what came so easy to him was difficult to others, stepped over to Lt. Everett and put an arm over his shoulders.

"Carson, I'm telling the mechanics to have our Camels up and running in twenty minutes. You tell these guys they can keep right on drinkin' and die today, or they can put away the whiskey and do something worthwhile. Who knows if today won't be the day the Kaiser gets a stake driven through his heart?"

Half an hour later every pilot in the squadron was in the flying seat of his machine, wondering if the return of their side's great ace would indeed prove decisive on this otherwise miserable day and this otherwise hopeless time. Kid was just as willing to fight as anyone there and he would be leading the patrol. But he was guaranteeing them that *he* would not die today, and if they followed him then they surely would not die either.

At the same time 70 kilometers to the east the ragged men of Jagdstaffel 7, Eichhorn's flying circus, were readying for another mission and having similar anticipatory visions of success. Rittmeister Hans had promised them the American ace would be destroyed today. The future of the Fatherland, like a winter rosebud, was about to burst into bloom with the coming of spring warmth. Their success in battle, at least when the renegade American had participated, had not been entirely satisfactory. Yet he was just one man, this remarkable American from the wild frontier, and he was not immortal. The fame of the Great War had at its center one man, the Riding Master, and he had already survived an encounter with the best that the rest of the world had to offer. It was obvious, Eichhorn insisted to his men, that the renegade's luck had reached its end and today would be snuffed out.

Hans stressed this to his comrades, but deep within himself he had doubts. Upon reflection, he did not think he was a particularly gifted pilot. A marksman, yes. A hunter, certainly. But he privately held the conviction that his archrival really was the most skilled and calculating operator of the flying machine that the world had yet produced. By his way of reckoning the American had probably downed far more enemy aircraft than he had—

though, as the story went, the American refused to accept credit for his kills and had been officially granted only a handful.

If in fact this man were back at Buzancy—as German intelligence gathered he would be—and if in fact he happened to be flying today, the Rittmeister knew the odds would be greatly in favor of his archrival. For Eichhorn was tired, feeble, weary; the injuries he had sustained from his last battle with the Kid were not yet healed; and, worst of all by far, he could not muster the passionate hatred of his archrival that the Fatherland demanded of its *Kampfliegers*. Not only did he not dislike the man who was hellbent on killing him, but he actually admired him. He considered himself to be a prized stag upon whom the most gallant hunter of a tribe of warriors was bearing down. It was no shame to be so pursued. In truth, it was an indication of how well Hans had served his country and how skillfully his reputation had been embellished for the world at large. If peace ever did return to the world again, Hans wanted to meet the man named Milton Harrison, to shake his hand, to invite him to his ancestral Bavarian estate and go on a wild boar hunt with him. They would be brothers in peace and ambassadors for aviation.

WITH THESE CONTRADICTORY emotions swirling within them, the men from both sides left their respective aerodromes around 9:15 that morning. Within an hour, the red German Fokker Dr. I triplanes had engaged the olive green Camel F1's of the 137th squadron, and their special guest, Maj. Raymond Milton "Kid" Harrison, Jr. All of the Jasta 7's men flew similar-looking planes, but only Eichhorn had the skull and crossbones painted on the side of his fuselage. It therefore quickly became obvious to the Allied men that the Rittmeister himself was a part of this battle. The Germans, on the other hand, were uncertain about which plane was being flown by the Kid. Like an elusive ghost he hovered about the skirmishes, catching his hapless victims by surprise when he made his acrobatic turns and dives and revealing himself to be the greatest of the great only when he pummeled their planes with showers of lead and they saw the small American flag taped below his flying seat.

The warring squadrons, combining single-seat combat planes and two-seat bombers, went at each other with abandon in the skies directly over the Meuse River. Two Fokkers came at Kid, but he dove in the direction of the Allied lines and an Australian batteryman took one of the triplanes out with a shell. The pilot of the other Fokker grew skittish when he realized he was so low to the ground above enemy territory and he hesitated for about theee seconds. In the meantime, Milt swung around to his tail, pelted him with gunfire, and shot him out of the sky. An Aviatik bomber tried to take out an infantry division below, but Kid turned his Camel perpendicular to its fuselage and rained bullets on both the gunner and the pilot before they could react to his quick movements.

More nimble than the Camels, the red triplanes were moving aggressively to take out the Allied squadron, but Milt was outmaneuvering his competitors. Two more red planes were hunting down Lt. Everett, but he cut his speed suddenly and they roared past him. When this occurred the rookie pilot, "Lex" Taylor, dove down and sprayed grapeshot at everyone, missing all his targets and jamming his guns. Kid recognized how obvious it would be to the Germans that this was an inexperienced pilot and he slowed his plane in readiness to defend his colleague in case one of the Fokkers singled out the rookie and charged at him. It happened just as soon as Taylor turned away from the engagement and headed toward friendly territory. One of the Germans spotted the haphazardly flying Camel and singled it out. This was the one with the skull and crossbones on the side of his fuselage, the Great Ace of Deutschland, Rittmeister Hans Eichhorn.

"You won't get away this time, Hank," Kid said aloud to himself. "Today's your dying day, I'm sure of it."

Major Harrison eluded two Fokkers that dove at him from above, watched as they were fended off by three other Allied planes then turned his attention to the pursuit of Eichhorn, who was showering poor Taylor with bullets. Unmolested by any enemy plane, Milt secretly followed the downward course of the red triplane, far enough away to be outside the German's awareness yet close enough that with a sudden burst of speed he might easily be within firing range. Taylor and Eichhorn plunged steadily down to an altitude of 5000 feet until they were within range of ground artillery fire. Weaving back and forth from Allied to German lines a few thousand feet above the Meuse, dodging a barrage of artillery from both sides, the planes seemed headed for a crash in the river. Hans thought his unseasoned prey was soon to be a dead man until he noticed in the periphery of his vision another plane which had emerged seemingly from out of nowhere. Only one man flew like that. He had an American flag taped beneath his flying seat.

"Mein Gott!" Hans shrieked just as the bullets plunged him into permanent darkness and sleep.

The ghostly master from across the sea streaked away across the path of the two other planes before anyone else could fire at him. As Milt raced his plane high into the gray sky, Lt. Everett, close on the heels of the now-dead Eichhorn, flailed the German ace's corpse with several dozen additional rounds of fire. The red triplane flew by itself for several more seconds, drifting further over Allied territory, then nosed itself into a muddy field on the edge of the village of Dun-sur-Meuse. Everett believed that he had been the one to shoot down the Rittmeister, but no one really knew. The German ace had been fired at from so many directions that it was impossible to pinpoint where the fatal shots had originated. But Eichhorn had been dying for some time and today had been merely the official end of his life. He had been dying since the moment the presses of the world had created the myth of his invincibility.

BEATEN SUMMARILY AND THOROUGHLY, the red squadron disappeared, the Allied men headed for their base, and pandemonium reigned on the ground. A mob of people, mostly peasants from Dun-sur-Meuse, rushed to the scene of the downed red plane, chopped it to pieces like vultures grasping for souvenirs, and left little usable evidence for British army examiners to determine what exactly had befallen the late great Eichhorn in his dying moments. They did leave the corpse in a relatively undisturbed state. It was eventually hauled off to Buzancy and placed in a tent barely 100 meters from where Milt, Everett, Taylor and several of the other Allied men returned after the completion of their patrol.

Colonel Tinsley of the British army headquarters staff entered the tent late that afternoon and addressed all the pilots there.

"The Australians are planning to give Herr Eichhorn a full military funeral with last rites and burial in Buzancy. All of you are welcome to come see the body if you wish."

"Why'd we want to do that, Colonel?" Kid asked. "There ain't no joy in looking at a dead man."

"No, no," said Lt. Everett. "I feel it's our duty to go over there. That's the least we can do, now that he's gone. We never met him. . . ."

Carson buried his face in his hands and began weeping while all the other occupants of the tent hung their heads in respect for the deceased warrior. After a few moments of awkward silence, the colonel brought up the next order of business.

"We need a Combats in the Air report. Major Harrison, it was you who downed his plane, wasn't it?"

Milt lifted his hands up as if to suggest he wanted to keep them clean of the affair.

"Colonel, I've never wanted credit for killing any man. I'm here to serve my country and that's what I want credit for—the flying, not for killing people. Everett says he shot the Fokker down, so let him have the victory."

"Is that true, Lieutenant?" Tinsley asked the Canadian ace. "We've got two of your countrymen, McBride and Broussard, who said they fired at and hit the Fokker from the ground. Nobody seems to know for sure who downed the aircraft."

"I'll fill out the report, Colonel," Everett shrugged, still in tears. "Who really cares, anyhow?"

With loathing and dread, the men made their solemn way into the tent that housed the remains of the Rittmeister a few minutes later. It was a disheartening sight, and Carson Everett clutched his throat. Even Milt, war-weary and cynical as he had become, grew squeamish at the sight and his eyes reddened with tears. Lying flat on a table in a navy flying suit was a small, delicate-looking man, his clear gray eyes wide open and several of his teeth knocked out. His thin silky blond hair, like that of a schoolchild, hung down on his forehead and a large gash ran across his chin. The expression of mortal shock seemed to have been fixed to his face, and Milt went over to his body, closed his eyelids and mouth, and conferred upon him a more dignified appearance. He had the look of utter contentment then, as if the burden of vitriol and violence that his brief life had been required to bear had been transferred to the unfortunate souls who had ended that life.

So this gentle, harmless-looking young man had been the demon that had worked up the politicians and the presses of the world into a frenzy! He might have been any man from anywhere; perhaps nothing more than the boy everyone knew who delivered papers or milk while still in school, then married his teenage sweetheart and graduated to the life of a mail clerk or an accountant. But the slim 26-year-long fragment of a life this man had known, a life without marriage or offspring, had denied him the chance to be that. There would be no wild boar hunt, and no meeting with the boy from across the sea now except in death. And there would never be peace—not in the life of Rittmeister Hans Eichhorn.

"I'd bring him back to life if I could," Everett confessed. "That's the impossible part. But ending life—there's nothing to that. This awful, awful goddamn war—there's nothing to it at all." He turned his head away. "I don't want to look him in the face."

"I never knew how he looked," Milt reflected. "Strange how you can destroy something you don't even know about and people say that's patriotism. Well, I'm like you, Carson. I can't look at this any more. Let's get out of here."

They and their comrades left abruptly and unceremoniously, slept in their cold tents, and rose again the next day to resume the insanity that had consumed the lives of an entire generation of able-bodied young men. At Eichhorn's makeshift funeral and burial untold ranks of Allied pilots, nominally his enemies, held their heads down and closed their eyes with all the reverence due a blood brother. For he was first a man, second an aviator, third a warrior, fourth a nobleman, much later a German and much, much later an enemy. On the first three scores he was their kindred, for they were all flying men in war, the first generation of people who had ever been such, and they understood that this was the man whose exploits had mythologized their calling. Hans was buried in a humble churchyard then, away from his countrymen, and not until many months later, when peace finally did return, was he exhumed and given a fit burial for a national hero.

On that occasion, Munich gave him the grandest funeral any figure in that city had ever received, and many mourners in attendance, angry that their hero had been taken away and that his failure had been instrumental in forcing them to accept a crushing peace, began vowing to create other heroes for other times—heroes who would bring them more rewarding results.

CHAPTER 16

Armistice

MAJOR HARRISON CONTINUED DOWNING one enemy airplane after another, but his feats were soon rivaled by the battles of the infantrymen and by Johnny Albritton, who cataloged each and every one of his kills with the precision of an archaeologist preserving a fossil. Quite the master of publicity, Britt had alleged proof that he had downed more planes than any other American by September. Kid was indifferent on the matter. Whether he had downed 10, 50 or 100 was of no matter to him and he in fact had no idea. Whatever the true total, it certainly dwarfed the 12 or so Albritton was claiming and the 11 for which Milt had completed official combat reports. That, however, was unimportant to him.

Life for him hadn't begun with this war, he had no intention that it should end with it, nor did he wish for the rest of his existence to be defined by what he had done here. He expected life to be at its very beginning for him if this war ever ended and he survived it, not to be at its pinnacle. He was pleased Britt, Arky and the other boys were helping to win the war and that if they all continued to enjoy such dramatic success he was soon to go home himself. Yet he believed that, no matter what anyone else claimed, he had actually done more than any other single combatant to bring the empire of the Kaiser down.

Colonel Paul Percival kept hounding Stanton and Lefors to sponsor an all-out combined land and air attack on the German salient at Saint-Mihiel, a village a few miles upstream from Verdun along the Meuse River, and eventually won their consent. The news of the buildup of men and materiel in preparation for the great attack in early September spread throughout France. The most humble cabdrivers in Paris were discussing the upcoming invasion and every newspaper boy on the city's streets seemed to know how many aeroplanes the Americans were planning to use, how many ground divisions were concentrated in the area around Verdun, how many more flying Red enemies were waiting to be sacrificed in the imminent quail shoot of *Le Kid* and his *amies.*

On the evening of the 11th Colonel Percival summoned Milt, Albritton, and a handful of other combat fighters to his quarters at Étain. His freshly pressed green uniform, clanking with a gaudy collection of medals pinned to the lapel of his coat, rustled as he paced before the men and gestured with his hands. His eyes sparkled like those of a tyke on Christmas Eve. An irrepressible smile of satisfaction beamed from his ruddy face.

"Tomorrow morning at five, men," he addressed them, "will start a new page in the history books. If we do it right, you'll pull through it all right and you'll be telling your grandchildren you were here to do it. The pencil-pushers in Washington and the little Napoleons over here keep trying to castrate us, but, dammit, tomorrow we finally get to rain some hell on our sworn enemies. Let's show 'em what aeroplanes can do, men. It's aeroplanes that'll win us this war."

Colonel Percival paused to collect his thoughts. He breathed deeply and went to pull Kid from the ranks of the other flying men, placing his arm on the major's shoulder.

"Here he is, soldiers. Your commander. Wherever this ace goes, victory follows. He hasn't met anybody yet he couldn't beat, and he won't tomorrow, either. Follow him, and we'll get this thing finished."

The boy from Woodvale, jaded by military rhetoric and battle-hardened by continual dances with death, found enthusiasm hard to come by, but he sensed the nervousness in the others that had already been drained out of him.

"And I'm planning on doing it just like Colonel Percival says," he told the other pilots. "I'm raining hell on 'em until they beat a retreat back toward the Fatherland."

The assault was initiated as planned on the following morning and it continued all the next day. Kid and his brigade of 1500 French and American planes, the largest air battalion in history up to that time, bombarded the German positions east of the front. The highways around Metz and Saint-Mihiel were soon covered with the carcasses of horses, the corpses of men, and the fleeing fury of beaten soldiers and retreating vehicles. The American infantrymen closed in on the Germans from north and south of Saint-Mihiel like the jaws of a great serpent. At refueling trips back to the Lorraine and Souilly Aerodromes, Milt and the other aviators gave full descriptive reports of the nature of the German retreat and positions, and this intelligence was used to intensify the attack. On the following day the Allies met with retaliation from Fokkers after they bombarded Metz, but much of the talent in the *Feldfliegartruppen* had already met its demise in the earlier stages of the war, and the young crop of fearless warriors who now constituted the German Air Service was of lesser skill than what the Allied pilots had fought in previous battles. With only a handful of exceptions, the red planes were engulfed by and riddled with the bullets of the vast fleet of their enemies.

When it was over the Saint-Mihiel Drive had dissolved the German presence along that part of the front. Little did the fighting men know it, but the end of the war was near. The only true question among those minds in a position to dictate the course of events was not whether Germany would surrender, but how long it would be before the surrender was made, whether it would be unconditional, and what would be fit punishment for the Teutonic state which had thrust the world into the most horrific conflict civilization had ever seen. Wilson, Clemençeau, and Lloyd George mulled over the issue, Lefors and Stanton casually discussed it, and Percival, though reluctant to take anything for granted, had trouble keeping his imagination from wandering far away from the Western Front, to a future civilian world in which airplanes would have an important place. Kid had the same trouble. While Jonathan Albritton and his boys were proceeding apace with their ever-mounting numbers of kills against the dying military machine, Kid daydreamed about the ship ride back home and what he would find in Woodvale and whether he might ever return to a normal life when the cease-fire came.

WHAT MILT MOST WANTED once he realized the end of the war was near was to revisit and console Lieutenant Everett, who had contracted influenza back in May and suffered another nervous breakdown. Upon recovery he had been appointed an instructor at the Number 9 School of Aerial Fighting, but had fainted in his plane and crashed in August, breaking bones in his back, neck and skull. Ever since then he had been confined in a British army infirmary near Nancy, where he would remain until the end of 1918. In mid October Major Harrison obtained a day's leave to travel to Nancy and visit his downtrodden comrade. A wan and helpless-looking man, beaten down by the intense horrifying pressure of aerial warfare, Carson driveled like a baby when he saw his soul mate enter his quarters and come to his bedside.

"How good of you to come, Kid," he uttered weakly, barely above a whisper. "You didn't have to do this just for me."

Milt leaned down and hugged his lame friend, whose bones ached throughout his body and who winced in pain whenever he got the urge to laugh and therefore kept his face as stiff as that of a mannequin.

"I wanted to see you again, pal, even if it's for one last time."

"Last time? You don't mean you think I'm dying, do you?"

"No, no. That's not it at all. It's the war. The Kaiser's just about ready to surrender."

"Is it really going all that well, Major? News is scarce in here, you know. I just don't have the . . . what's the word? . . . e*nergy* to dig for details."

"It'll be over soon, Carson. The Heinies are flyin' away towards Deutschland like a pack of crows. We knocked all the fight out of 'em."

"WE?" Lt. Everett's face wrinkled up as he tried to suppress a grin that would have jabbed at his nerves. "You mean YOU knocked 'em out. I turned chicken and bailed out. I don't deserve the medals I've got."

"The hell you say, lieutenant. You deserve 'em more than any man. With your nerves and health, you never should've even been mixed up in this craziness."

"They expected me to. The commanders. Also the new kids. I had to stay out there and show 'em what to do, or they would've all gotten killed."

"I know. Same with me. . . . So, how you feelin'?"

Everett put his hand over his chest, as if to make sure that his heart was still pumping.

"Some day I'll get better, Kid. If I live long enough some day I'll feel good again, but not right now."

Milt paused uneasily, clutched ahold of his friend's hand, and leaned a bit further over him. For the first time since he had looked upon Hans Eichhorn's mangled corpse with Lt. Everett he wanted to cry and had difficulty staying composed. To survey the living corpse of a man was in many ways worse than looking upon the remains of a dead one.

"Well, Carson . . . I guess I don't want to stay too long. It's about time I started headin' back."

The Canadian ace tried to elevate his head above his pillow, but he sank down again.

"That's all right," said Kid, "you don't have to try to get up and see me off."

"Let's get together sometime," Everett whispered in a raspy voice. "We'll go flying together some day. You come to Ottawa and I'll show you the country. It's beautiful over there. I can't wait to fly without a man shooting at me."

"I can't wait, either," Milt tried to console him, then he let loose his grasp of the ailing man's hand for the last time. "Well . . . *so long*."

A newspaper in a later generation would reveal to Major Harrison that Carson Everett had died of a heart attack at the age of 46; that he had left the military and bounced around in several futile civilian jobs after the war; that he had even attempted unsuccessfully to start an automobile dealership in an Ottawa suburb. Milt never saw or spoke to him again, and doubted all the while that Everett had stayed alive even one more week until he saw the notice of his death in fine print over two decades later.

GERMAN PUBLIC OPINION WAS growing defeatist. Prince Max of Baden was appointed the new chancellor in early October and his first order of business, at the behest of Field Marshal Hindenburg and Army chief of staff Erich Ludendorff, was to begin negotiations for peace with President Wilson. The news of this leaked out to the Allied men on the front lines, who were emboldened by the first sign of mass weakness by their enemies. Some of the pilots and infantrymen then threw caution to the winds and lost their lives while on the very doorstep of surviving their cataclysmic baptism by fire.

Kid himself, perhaps taking for granted what was not yet made official, relaxed a bit and on one occasion his complacency nearly cost him his life. He frequently flew missions at night to avoid the menacing presence of Fokker squadrons who were assigned to shadow him during daylight hours. Late in October, on a pitch dark moonless night, while on such a lone patrol after dark over the German lines in quest of more balloon kills, he realized that his Spad had been in flight for over two hours, the limit of its fuel tank.

With sudden anxiety he throttled his engine down to the slowest speed that would keep his plane aloft and turned toward the west and friendly territory. A few minutes later he had sunk down to a vulnerably low altitude above his enemies, and then came the flashes from the ground. Deadly artillery fire was coming his way, random grapeshot in the dusk. The Huns smelled his blood. Infuriated with himself, he stifled the impulse to jam open his throttle and continued soaring slowly westward, trying to husband his fuel to its last drop, praying that one last bit of supernatural luck would lead him beyond harm's way.

Soon the artillery fire was behind him, but he still faced an even greater danger: finding a landing place in pitch darkness. He cursed himself for his carelessness. Scanning the black emptiness of space for the bright flares of his home aerodrome, he began to grow desperate. The searchlights were unlit! The recognizable world had vanished! How, after all else he had been through, could his life end this way?

He was too low above the ground to glide a great distance if his motor quit but certainly too short on fuel to open his throttle and burn more of it to gain altitude. From underneath his seat he pulled out an emergency beacon, a Very pistol, which would send out a bright red warning light to his friends and advertise his need for help. He pulled the trigger and the flare shot through the sky just as his engine coughed out its last bit of fuel. He waited in silent despair for an answer. Sometimes to an air fighter in the Great War a half minute lasted an eternity, as it did for Kid on that night. But to someone safe on the ground, it actually seemed like an instant. The aerodrome searchlight came on and to Kid's deep relief he realized he was directly over Souilly! He let out a deep breath, glided down with a dead engine and landed perfectly on the flat field that was home to the Argonne Escadrille. Yet again he had thumbed his nose at the fickle mistress of fate. It would be the last threat of the Great War to the boy from Woodvale.

AUSTRIA AND TURKEY HAD surrendered, and it was Major Harrison's pleasure the next morning to shower the front with newspapers that he hurled over the side of his Spad to the eager doughboys who popped out of their foxholes when they recognized his plane. The risk of deadly strafing by their still-active enemies was a minor inconvenience to exchange for the glorious news that they suspected would be coming from the familiar plane of the ace.

Elsewhere, above the rugged terrain of the Argonne woods, the brilliant orange fire-glow of two burning supply depots spewed black smoke into the leaden sky. German soldiers had set about to destroy their own wares! Determined to leave nothing behind that their enemies might use, they were still on the grounds of the burning buildings, sadly witnessing the end of their attempt to conquer Europe. The roads leading to the east were now clogged with trucks, artillery and beaten Aryan warriors, hastening toward the German border with the limp of defeat.

Reports out of Paris were that the populace there was celebrating, the streets were for the first time in months staying lit up at night, captured German guns and airplanes were being paraded playfully up and down *l'Avenue des Champs-Élysées,* and the yoke of foreign aggression had been merrily lifted off the backs of a population that had suddenly regained its customary *joie de vivre*. The Parisians already anticipated what would be an official fact by the eleventh day of the eleventh month of that year.

The announcement came to the men of the Argonne Escadrille by telephone at sunset on November 11. Milt and his mates were clustered in the mess hall at Souilly, awaiting what was sure to be exceptional news. At the sound of the ringing telephone on the cinder block wall Kid snatched the earpiece off its hook and jammed it against the side of his head while his fellow warriors waited in rapt suspense.

"Major Harrison," came the ecstatic voice of Colonel Percival, "the fighting's over! We won! Germany just surrendered for peace! *C'est le finis de la guerre!"*

"God bless you, Colonel!" Kid cried. "I'll be sure to tell all the boys right away!"

Milt slammed the earpiece back into place and turned to the men, who were poised for a joyful celebration.

"YESSIREE!" he shouted, pumping his fist. "GLORY, GLORY, HALLELUJAH! We stopped 'em, boys! It's peacetime now, the war's all over!"

There followed a rampage of exhilarated men hugging one another, rearing their arms skyward, and rushing in an almost trampling herd to the large field outside. Battery shells were being sent like fireworks into the darkening sky. Men were rushing to their trunks in the barracks, pulling out pistols, darting back out to the field and firing them raucously up at the brilliant sky bursts, then reloading them and emptying their barrels again. From every quarter came the deafening shouts and yelps of happy boys whose death sentence had just been commuted to Life Without the Possibility of Being Shot Down Again. Searchlights and beacons spun wildly like carnival attractions, mingling their glare with the fire and smoke that clogged the heavens. Rockets, bombs and multicolored flares were adding their loud noises and bright colors to the spontaneous riot. Over and over again the happy refrain rang out from the voices of the liberated warriors: "I made it out alive! Nobody'll be shooting at me any more!"

The crazy men rolled a half dozen gasoline barrels out on the lawn, shot holes in them, and ignited the leaking fuel with matches to create a ceremonial pyre. The hue and cry of the celebratory orgy now soared with the sparks of the roaring gas fires. When the heat grew too much, someone remembered the cooling effects of alcohol. Soon there was rum punch and scotch whiskey, the boys were dousing their heads and soiled uniforms with champagne and loosening their strung-tight nerves with booze, and the mess hall became repopulated by tipsy partygoers playing impromptu jazz on the old piano, dancing jigs and mazurkas, hopping and tripping over one another like rabbits in a cage.

The hangovers of the following morning brought severe headaches, but there was no reason to rise early any more, to be prompt or punctual, or to worry if a bit of carelessness might carry with it the penalty of death. The aviators had pioneered a new experiment. They had demonstrated that refined versions of the motorized gliders that the Wright brothers had launched at Kitty Hawk while this war's pilots were all still children could reshape the world. This Armistice would be their own little bit of playtime. No one ever came forth to dispute that they deserved it.

Eventually the time would come for finishing some of the technicalities of the war such as the exchange of prisoners and occupied territory. By then the men who of late had been bitter enemies would stand on common ground again, at long last without malice. There would be civilities offered in the various tongues of the former combatants, the shaking of hands, the putting away of bitter antagonisms. They were now linked more by similarities than differences, the great common bond they all shared being their love of flying machines and their survival of the hazards of operating them, even in the midst of violent warfare.

After the Armistice Milt met dozens of the Germans, who looked with awe upon his towering stature and expressed to him in English their amazement at what he had done. And he was not alone in being treated well by those who for months had aimed to kill him. Throughout the ravaged battle-zone the airplane fighters from both sides enjoyed comparing notes and swapping yarns, discussing plans for the future and relating choice anecdotes of the past. Just as soon as the armaments were put away, many of the former enemy combatants became friends.

BACK HOME, ACROSS THE SEA, the nightmare of intervention whose purpose still confused the ordinary public was over. The boys would be coming home now, to a welcome for heroes. Germany was defeated. Armistice Day was declared. Hurrah, hurrah! Survivors of the puzzling nightmare, shiny-faced lads in their resplendent uniforms, would soon be marching peacefully through parades along the main streets of hundreds of American towns, carrying their empty rifles and bayonets for ornamental show, waving at their mothers and sweethearts and second cousins once-removed, even waving at the conscientious objectors who had shot their toes off and quietly emerged from hiding after November 11. The victory was for everyone, even for them.

The combined Allied forces had devoted 42 million fighting men, four years and *five million casualties* to accomplish the defeat of the Axis; their governments had devoted *$143 billion* to the effort. Now the objective would be to make Germany pay, to shame the Huns and ensure they never tried it again. Wilson, Lloyd George, and Clemenceau were all in agreement. The scourge of Teutonic militarism, the legacy of Frederick the Great, must be stayed for all time by the redoubtable everlasting victory of 1918!

But what of the boy from Woodvale, who had volunteered to leap into the bloody crucible that had terrified so many others? He had emerged from the horror without a scratch. In hundreds of hours of aerial combat he had miraculously been spared not only death but injury of any sort, though he had been in constant mortal jeopardy. Was it not the result of divine guidance? His lapel rattled with medals after France and Britain had decorated him. Lefors, with a tear in his eye, had kissed him on each cheek in the fashion of his country. General Stanton pleaded with him to remain active in the military service, as did Paul Percival. The plea fell on deaf ears.

Civilian life beckoned Kid, and he resigned from active duty two weeks after the Armistice.

"The President has invited you to the White House in Washington, Major," Stanton had informed him at the train depot at Verdun before he boarded to go to Paris and then the ship at Le Havre. "You, Albritton, and our other great heroes. I wish I could be there. Good luck."

Milt saluted the great commander in a formal way, then the general dropped military propriety and hugged the youth. Colonel Percival would not go quite so far, but he put his arm around the shoulder of the ace.

"Keep it up, son. Make the aeroplane America's national bird."

For the first time it occurred to Milt that the powerful commanders who had guided the military machine were just ordinary human beings like himself—a little older and wiser, but with the same aspirations and devotions. They were the brothers nature had never given him and the surrogates of the father he had lost. He felt a little sentimental when he realized it was time to bid them farewell.

"Y'all have been like my family. I . . . I don't know what I'll find after I go back."

NEVER HAD HE BEEN quite so ill-at-ease as on the evening when President Wilson hosted him and a dozen other distinguished veterans of the World War at a White House dinner in the first week of December. The irony of the occasion struck him immediately. Milton Sr. had never been able to get into the Capitol Building; now Milton Jr. would be in the White House standing by the President in bright light, being photographed and congratulated. He was taken by taxi from his suite at the Imperial Hotel on Connecticut Avenue to the inside gates of the residence at 1600 Pennsylvania. When one of Wilson's staff ushered Major Harrison up the marble steps of the first residence his heart was nearly up in his throat. Through the great door he went and into the foyer. There stood the commander in chief of America during the Great War, Woodrow Wilson.

The President wore a black tuxedo with long tails. His face was pale, thin and contemplative. His clear gray eyes, peering through pince-nez glasses, bore the bloodshot marks of fatigue. The war had left lines on his face as though he had been an active combatant in it himself and had poured all of his remaining vitality into its execution. He would not be long in the world after this, and he seemed to sense it.

"Welcome, Major Harrison," said President Wilson, offering Milt his hand. "I'm happy we're both here to share in this occasion."

"Thanks, Mr. President," Kid answered nervously. "I never thought I'd get this far."

President Wilson stared upward at the tall brawny youth and tapped him affectionately on the shoulder. Then he lowered his voice almost to a whisper, so no one else would be able to hear him, and spoke with greater earnestness.

"Always when things were at their worst we knew you would keep fighting. The world will never be able to pay you back for what you did. THANK YOU."

These were the last words President Wilson was to say in private conversation with the boy from Woodvale, for other guests were being shown into the White House and his role was to greet them as they entered his residence. Dinner was French onion soup, roast duckling, asparagus tips with hollandaise sauce, carrots glazed with drawn butter and salad greens with olive oil and vinegar; strawberry cheesecake was for dessert; and everything was served by butlers with sterling silver cutlery and fine china. Conversation consisted of war stories, politics, the League of Nations. The ship for France would soon be carrying the President to the peace negotiations. The commander in chief stood and raised a toast to his guests before dessert. In honor of those who perished, and of their supreme sacrifice for generations unborn. Amen. There was one last round of handshakes with the men of honor and then ushers to take them back into the night.

CHAPTER 17

The Savior of America

TWO NIGHTS AFTER KID'S dinner in Washington, a crowd of politicos, reporters, and high society greeted the arrival of his train at the Terminal Station in Atlanta. By that time he was already confused about his return to the civilian world, wondering where his life would lead him next.

He had sent his mother a letter with explicit instructions for her and the other Woodvale folk not to meet him in Atlanta, to wait until two days later when he would drive back without a boisterous crowd around him. He was unsure if he would know anyone who would be there to greet him in the Georgia capital, but he recognized the first pair of men he saw. The two Hapeville boys who had helped him launch his aerial career were on the landing to welcome him, better dressed than he had ever known them to be.

"It's the savior of America!" cried Chester Dawes, without the slightest bit of irony, shaking his friend's hand. "You never cease to amaze us, Major Kid."

Robert Brackens was sporting a three-piece suit underneath his coat and had a mouth perfectly clean of chewing tobacco. No sooner had Chet finished congratulating the war hero than Bobby did the same.

"Hope I ain't intrudin' on your holiness. It *is* OK for us to touch you now, ain't it, even though you went so much higher than us?"

"Long as them photographers don't catch it on film," said Kid. "I wouldn't want you to ruin my reputation."

"So, how is war?" asked Chet.

"Y'all reporters don't quote me," Milt turned to address the newspapermen, "but it's terrible. General Sherman called it right after he got done burnin' us out of house and home. War *is* hell."

"Even to the Great Ace?" Bobby teased him.

"The only reason I'm the ace is I had to be. Over in that war, if you flew a plane you were either an ace or you were dead."

"Are we safe in quoting you on that one, Major Harrison?" asked one of the reporters.

"Yes, sir, that's all right. Go ahead and put that down and I'll let people judge me on that."

MILT GAVE INTERVIEWS TO the newspaper representatives for a few minutes, posed for photographers and signed autographs for several admirers while young girls screamed and gasped. Tomorrow would be the Armistice parade along Peachtree Street and he was asked to be the grand marshal. He gladly agreed, but he indicated he wanted to cut short tonight's proceedings. He was exhausted and needed rest. The civic fathers had arranged for him to stay at the Piedmont Hotel, in the penthouse suite. Would he ride in the horse-drawn surrey that was waiting for him in the front of the train station, so the thousands who had lined the route from there to the hotel might cheer and salute him? He would be honored to do so, just as long as he got a police escort. That of course had been the plan all along.

Eventually, George Grantland, who always possessed an extraordinary knack for being in the middle of whatever noteworthy was happening in Atlanta, caught up with his old acquaintance and sat in the carriage with him during the procession route. George seemed as happy as a purring kitten curling up on a quilt by the fur of the fattest cat in the neighborhood. Kid was mildly annoyed that Grantland the civilian was bathing in the same limelight as he the war ace, but then he remembered how George always played the publicity game and climbed the ladder. Give this man enough time, thought the aviator, and he would have everyone convinced it had really been he who had shot down the Rittmeister, defrocked the Kaiser, and thwarted the entire Hun invasion of France.

The suite on the upper floor of the Piedmont Hotel was truly extraordinary, and Milt felt considerable pride in realizing that he was occupying the same set of rooms that had housed Stratton Liffey on the night of their brief meeting in 1915. Winning the Distinguished Service Cross and being rewarded in countless other ways for his altruism had temporarily inflated his vanity. He was thinking that his accomplishments had amounted to much more than those of Liffey—that he had left exhibitionism and entertainment behind and had actually helped to shape the history of the world. At just that moment, when the smugness that had been scared out of him by endless months of humbling combat began to creep its way back into him, his telephone rang. It was the operator at the front desk. A Miss Peace wished to see him in the lobby.

He slinked out of his suite and took the elevator down to the lobby floor. Jasmine stood there waiting for him, as gorgeous and seductive as she had ever been, though meek in demeanor and conventional in dress.

"Jasmine!" he kissed her. "You came!"

Tears smeared the makeup on her eyes and cheeks, and she rubbed a handkerchief over her face. Her lips quivered and she bit her lower one before any words came out. His surprise at how much she had changed was exceeded only by hers when she observed the same development in him.

"I gave you up for dead and gone," she whimpered. "I never thought anybody, even you, could come back from that. . . ."

For the first time ever in their strange acquaintanceship he realized unmistakably that she truly loved him, passionately and perhaps insanely. But it was just as unmistakable to him that nothing would ever come of it.

"Milt," she said softly and hesitantly, "I've met a man since you went away. He's a banker. We're going to be married after the first of the year."

He felt as if someone had just shot him, but he tried gamely to hide his emotions. He leaned down and hugged her gently.

"Congratulations," he said. "I wish y'all all the best."

She began crying as she placed her arms around his neck.

"I couldn't wait forever," she sobbed. "And, besides . . . you want every woman. You want to rack up girls the way you racked up kills in your plane."

"You don't need to explain yourself to me, darlin'."

"I know it must seem sudden. . . ."

"Sweetie, you never promised me anything," he said. And then, although he felt as hollow as a rotten tree, he shook her hand.

"We've all gotta live our lives our own way. I'm sure you know what's best for you."

"But it's not what you think."

"I don't think anything. This is what you want. I'm happy for you."

A FEW MINUTES LATER he wished her good luck and told her good-bye, trying to be as supportive and upbeat as possible. Then he returned to his suite. He surveyed the plush interior of his pleasure palace, with the large king-sized bed with the mahogany frame and silk canopy, the chintz pillows and satin sheets; the vaulted ceilings with the floral cornices and the crystal chandelier which hung down into the center of the room; the gold-tinted wallpaper with flowers and leaves inlaid magically into its design. His coat, covered with medals and decorations, was draped over the chair beside the bed. How gorgeous a scene of splendor and accomplishment, he thought, not to have anyone there to share it with him. Back he had come from the Armageddon, where he had outlasted a whole barrage of Satanic assaults, and his reward was a beautiful *empty* room.

He realized he needed to do something to get rid of his discouragement, so he went and took the medal-laden coat off the back of the chair and put it on again, then in full uniform dress and regalia lay on the large bed with his shoes still on.

"The ocean's full of pearls," he consoled himself, "and I ain't near done fishin' yet."

Not a pillow on the bed was moved, nor the spread or any sheet beneath it disturbed. His sleep that night left the bed as unwrinkled and uncreased as if he had never even placed himself atop it. He reposed as soundly on it as if he had been a dead man.

BY THE NEXT MORNING he felt better than he had in months. Today would be a new adventure; whatever happened would be enjoyed and filed away; and tomorrow would again be a virgin blank slate. It was no time to rest on one's laurels. Day-old laurels, in his mind, were as useless as moldy bread. Yet he wore his decorated uniform with pride that morning, donning his leather flying helmet and pushing his flying goggles up on his forehead for extra theatrics. As he rode along the Armistice parade route, mounted atop the rear deck of a city fire truck, waving at the appreciative public, soaking up the rain of confetti that was pouring down from the high buildings that lined Peachtree Street, he began to admire the motorcycles on which the policemen guarding his motorcade were riding. Motorcycles. He wanted one of those for himself. He also admired several of the delectable girls who were screaming themselves crazy as they saw him go by. He wanted one of those, too.

"Let's stop here," he turned and yelled to his driver. "I wanna meet some folks."

The motorcycles screeched to a halt along with the fire truck, and the World War ace gestured for several of the people along the sidewalk to come forward, hoping the adorable lass in the pink dress and flowery bonnet in the front would join them.

"Fellows," he called out to the police ranks along the curb, "let about ten of 'em through."

As Major Harrison had instructed, the police let several people slip through their ranks, most of them young women, and they came to swoon over the ravishing Sky King, the bester of the Rittmeister, the Savior of Old Glory. To his delight, the girl in pink, the cutest dish he had seen along the whole route, broke through and dashed to the side of his car, her hands clasped in prayer and supplication, tears of joy dripping from her eyes.

"Oh, Lord Almighty!" she squealed, "please, please just let me *touch* you, then I'll leave you alone—I promise!"

"I will if you do me one little favor, miss," said Milt.

"Anything, anything!"

"Let me write something on one of your pretty little white gloves."

The girl's face turned pinker than her dress with blush, she cupped her two gloved hands over her mouth in disbelief, then she eagerly ripped off one of her gloves and tossed it up to him. From the inner lining of his coat pocket he pulled out a Sheaffer fountain pen and scrawled on the glove: *245 Lafayette Drive*. Then he puffed on the writing with his warm breath to try to dry it, shook the glove and handed it back to her.

"I'm invitin' all y'all to dinner at my house tonight, darlin'. You and anybody else who wants to come. That's my address. Be there at seven o'clock."

She nearly fainted in shock when she heard his words. The other girls piled themselves up against her to try to read what he had written, and their shrieks of excitement added to the melee. The policemen called for the stragglers to back off the street now, redoubled their efforts to contain the surging mob of spectators who were trying to break through the barricades, and restored order and movement to the parade within the next minute. One of the constables on motorcycle looked up and winked at Kid as he fired up his engine.

"I can't believe what I just saw," the officer teased him. "You sly dog, you!"

"A war ace has gotta enjoy a little civilian comforts, you know."

"Let's don't try any more of them tricks. Next time they break through we won't be able to herd 'em back."

MILT'S ANSLEY PARK VILLA, three miles from the parade route, had grown musty during the year and a half it had remained vacant. He tried opening his casement windows to revive it when he went back to it after the conclusion of the parade, but the cold damp air of the outdoors turned the home into an icebox. By early evening his radiator heaters had restored comfort, the gas lamps outside and the electric lamps within were illuminated festively, and the catered feast which he had ordered from a nearby restaurant, along with its butlers and servers, was in place. It consisted of roasted chicken, potatoes with parsley, buttermilk biscuits and peach cobbler.

The core group that had seen his writing on the girl's glove had spread the news throughout Atlanta that Kid Harrison, the air hero of the World War, was inviting girls to a party at his house. Fourteen women, ranging in age from 16 to 23, took him up on his invitation, all of them resolved to outdo each other in what they assumed would be a competition to determine who would be his bride. Though they were bitterly jealous of one another, they smiled like cultured ladies all the while, engaged in proper etiquette, wore fine white dresses befitting their virginity and did everything within their power to convince him they were the Right Sort of Girl. He had them under his spell. His tales of aviation in the Great War and the adventures of his life at the sprightly age of 22 mesmerized them. The virginity of each and every one of them was ripe for the plucking, but he sent them all away.

"Girls, I know it's hard for all y'all to try to get to know me like this, but I'll tell you what. I'm lonely. Any time you girls wanna visit me individually so y'all don't feel crowded, just stop by, and if I ain't here drop me a note."

He honestly never thought he would see any of the beauties again after his party ended that night, but just being with them had been a diversion for him. For the first time in ages he had been surrounded by attractive members of the opposite sex who spoke his language, who were from his country, and who lived near where he lived. However, he still failed to grasp what love meant to them. The truth was that each girl was convinced of two things when the rendezvous had ended: one, that she would either have him or else turn into a nun; and, two, that the nunnery needn't worry, because the way his eyes had devoured the sight of her throughout that evening made it obvious that he was secretly partial to her above all the others. It had to be that way, or else the family tree would sprout no further branches. No other man would do, not in comparison to the hero who had led a nation into battle then come back and fêted them elegantly in his own home.

Two girls were already back by the next morning, hoping for another dose of the laughter and good cheer he had given them. It was impossible for these two to imagine another chance like this in the future, so they roused themselves early that morning in the predawn hours, perfected their beauty before mirrors, had their anxious mothers fix their hair, and ordered the taxi to drop them off in the cold at 245 Lafayette Drive. When the first girl saw the other one disembarking from another taxi several minutes later at the same spot her heart was flooded by a less-than-benevolent desire to scratch her rival's eyes out and yank out her hair. She controlled this urge and instead smiled artificially and offered her enemy her gloved hand.

"So you had the same idea?"

"Of course. I had a really swell time last night."

"Don't you think we're being a bit obvious? He probably wants more of a challenge."

"I don't care about that. I just thought I needed to be here."

The first girl pulled a piece of striped cloth of some kind out of her purse. When she began unrolling the cloth it was revealed to be a small American flag tied to a miniature wooden pole a few inches in length. She held the flag in her right hand, her hidden weapon to be used to gain a strategic advantage over her less patriotic colleague.

"It's such a wonderful thing, what he did. I waved this yesterday."

Milt was in the meantime readying his Duesenberg for the long and potentially harrowing drive to Woodvale. The tire pressure was right. So was the oil. The battery had water. The fuel tank, which he had run dry before leaving for France so it would avoid varnishing, had three gallons of gasoline that he had just poured in it from a tank in his garage. He would need to stop for fuel somewhere in the city before reaching the dirt roads of the boondocks, where gas stations were virtually nonexistent. Or at least they had been before the war, though what he would find now in this new universe was beyond him. One thing he knew: Woodvale had not changed. It would be the same from now until the end of time.

When he swung open the wooden doors of the barn that now served as the storage place for his horseless carriages, he saw two ladies staring at him out by his mailbox in the front. They both smiled and waved at him, and one also began waving her flag back and forth. It was a great surprise for him to see them there and another blessed reminder of peacetime and America. His vanity puffed up at the sight like a hot-air balloon inflating itself over the flow of heat from its gas blowers, and he went out to meet his two lovely suitors.

"Back so soon, eh?" he called out to them.

They both giggled modestly.

"Where you going?" asked the first girl, the one with the flag.

"The sticks. You gals wanna go with me?"

"Where are the sticks?"

"Out yonder where my Mama lives. I know y'all wouldn't like it."

"Yes, we would," the second girl said. "I'd love to meet your mama. You serious about taking us?"

"No, ma'am. It ain't the place for city gals. You'd just see what a hick I am."

"You're not a hick," said the first belle. "You're very charming and distinguished!"

"If y'all knew me y'all wouldn't think that way. I'm a bum, a weasel. I'm good at killin' Heinies and flying aeroplanes, but that's about it."

Both of the girls laughed.

"I wish you'd take me with you," said the first girl. "Are you sure you were teasing?"

"It's another world out yonder. A lot of pain and regret that way, and a lot of happiness too. Them folks think I'm the savior of the human race. I'm about the only thing they got to look forward to."

"Why, *aren't* you?" asked the girl who had no flag but only her own curly red locks to commend her.

"Aren't I what, miss?"

"The savior of the human race. That's what President Wilson said."

"Well, that was before he met me. The truth is, I'm not."

"What are you, then?"

"I ain't worked out the details of that yet, miss. I'm still trying to decide what I am. But I know I ain't saved nothin' yet. Look at how much is left to be done."

The redhead tapped her partner on the elbow.

"We can come back, whenever he's paid his respects to the sticks."

"Would that be all right, Major Harrison—if we visited you when you came back from your mama's?"

"Anytime you beautiful ladies wanna come on my property, you do that, and if I'm here I'll be overjoyed."

He curtseyed to them both and kissed each separately on the back of her gloved right hand.

"Have a wonderful trip back home," said the redhead. "Tell Woodvale that people in Atlanta think the same way about you."

"Woodvale? I said the sticks. Who said anything about Woodvale?"

"Everybody knows about Kid Harrison," said the first girl. "Someday I'd love to go where you're going—just to see it, just to say I'd been there."

THE ROUGH AND MUDDY route to the aviator's home village, worn with decades of poverty, abuse and neglect, bathed his shiny Duesenberg in an ablution of brown sludge, and by the time his automobile came around the corner of Highway 17, by the fallow field of stubble where his Flying Flivver had last danced for the adoring populace, a startling sight awaited him. The weather-beaten sign had been whitewashed of its former contents and freshened with a new message, artfully painted by the hand of Abigail Yardley. It now read: WELCOME TO WOODVALE. HOME OF R.M. 'KID' HARRISON JR., WORLD WAR HERO. The 196 Woodvaleans then in existence had disappeared from the village's announcement of itself to the world. Now, apparently, there was only one person who had ever lived there who was worth mentioning, and he was coming home to be canonized.

He noticed the new message on the sign first, and then he saw that his car would never make it to 125 Oak Street, not any time soon. From one side of Main Street to the other, in all the finery of dress that would attend a christening, a marriage or a funeral, the common folk who had loved the boy since his first day, for whom his life had been an expression of their innermost dreams, had formed an integrated wall. For the first time in hundreds of years, black people and white people stood together, not on separate sides of the road but in the very middle of it, all to celebrate the common hero who had fought for everyone. Reverend Patterson's booming preacher voice was heard first above all the others.

"HALLELUJAH, LORD! Here comes our boy, who saved the world!"

The black minister's eyes were clenched shut, he had fallen to one knee, and his right hand was held heavenward. The crowd seemed to have a collective urge to engulf the approaching car and bear its driver away on its shoulders like a great tide seizing up a beached whale, but common sense prevailed. It was the white preacher, Reverend Andrew Gray, who stayed the frenzy of jubilation.

"Let his mama go first. Madge deserves this more than anybody here."

The blond matron, who in a different era would have been considered youthful and pretty at age 49, but who dressed, acted and thought like an old woman after a half century of an unluxurious life, trudged through the mud to hail her own little boy, who was now a giant man who had mastered a giant world. Her thick gray corset rustled underneath her ungainly dress, and she held up her skirt as she gingerly stepped over the rocks and craters of the road in her high-heeled laced boots. Two daughters, both grown and with children of their own, followed in her tracks with their husbands and offspring in tow. The returning ace climbed out of his car and gave his mother and sisters tight hugs while the rest of Woodvale stayed back a respectable distance.

"Baby," wept Madge, "you made it back! You're still alive! They didn't kill you or cripple you!"

"No, Mama. No, I got through it all right. And I made sure we didn't lose. We won, Mama. Finally, we won something."

She swayed back and forth in her embrace of her son, rocking his body like a massive oaken cradle.

"I—I'm glad somethin' good finally happened," she said. "They just keep tryin' and tryin' to kill us or wear us down, but we're too strong for 'em." Her eyes grew red now, tears came out and she sobbed. *"I just wish your daddy could've lived to see this. His whole life he tried and he believed."*

"I saw the President—I had dinner in the White House."

"I know. You got to tell me about it later. Tell me about everything."

"No way I can ever tell you everything, Mama. There's too much I saw, and a lot of it I don't even want to remember."

"Don't talk about it, then. It don't matter now. It's all over, you're safe, and you're done with them planes. You can finally settle down now, Milt."

"What do you mean?"

"I mean, now you got all these awards and you can quit flyin' aeroplanes. What good'll they do you now?"

"No telling. But I ain't decided what I'll do yet. I need time to consider it." He turned awkwardly away from her and stared at the attentive throng that was waiting to congratulate him. "Say, Mama, let me go say hello to all the folks."

When the crowd noticed that its idol was finished with his mother it abandoned its self-imposed reserve and swept forward to meet him. He recognized every one of the villagers as if he had never been absent from there, the trivial facts and nuances of their lives still cluttering his mind like old dust. Zeke, Cliff and Blackie made themselves prominent near the front ranks while Shnook, who had shot his toes off to stay home, ducked and crouched low in the back, hoping he might watch the proceedings without being recognized himself. Smiles and hearty handshakes rained on the returning warrior from all the men, and from the women there were hugs, kisses on the cheeks, and beaming acclamations over how fine he looked. Both blacks and whites were speaking to him as though he were a diplomat who would convey their sentiments in translation to those otherwise unable to understand them. Words came slowly to Mrs. Bonniwell, who finally gained Milt's attention after waiting her turn in the long line of people there to praise him.

"What you been up to, darlin'?" Milt asked the gentle widow.

"Nothing, baby doll. Except readin' about you. Oh, I can't believe it was you who was doin' all that! And now you came back. Is it really you?"

Ruth held her hands out like a blind woman who had to touch something in order to convince her mind that it was actually in front of her. Her fingers ran along the side of his cheek.

"Talk to me," she continued. "Just let me hear the sound of that voice again."

"You still ain't gotten another husband, Ruth?"

"Naw, sugar. I'd rather dream about a husband than get one. It's easier to dream."

She turned around and pulled two adolescent children to her side.

"Michael and Sarah, this is Mr. Harrison. Y'all show y'all's respects to the man. . . . This is my son and daughter, you know."

"I'd hardly even recognize 'em," said Milt. "They're twice the size they were the last time I was around here."

"Hi, Mr. Harrison," said Michael. "Did you get scared in that war over there?"

"Sometimes I did, Michael. Everybody gets scared of danger sometimes."

Sarah pulled up both sides of her ruffled dress with her hands and curtsied.

"We glad you came back, Mr. Harrison," she said. "We knew you wouldn't let them come over here and take us over. Long as you were there, we felt safe."

"Why, thank you, Sarah. I don't know if they ever really wanted to take us over, but if they had I wouldn't have let 'em do it."

AFTER TWO DAYS AT his mother's house, Milton began to feel restless again. His mother continued pressing him about his upcoming plans. All he would allow was that he wanted to do something with motorcycles. He never elaborated, but refused to dismiss airplanes from his future. Airplanes had made him what he was, he had survived innumerable assaults in them, and there were sure to be other uses for them in other situations. A flight around the world, perhaps? Madge claimed that would be impossible and suicidal. But he insisted that at the very least he had to humor the populace before he left. They wanted to see him pull his Flying Flivver out of mothballs and launch it over Joe Freeman's stubbled field again, and he agreed to do so. He would place a large wicker basket by the field, invite several counties to watch, request a donation of a quarter and give all the proceeds to his mother. That was an idea. The Great Ace of the Great War. Flying in Woodvale, the birth of the legend. His own plane, the first he ever flew. Reporters would build the story up, and the common folk would trek from miles around to say that they were witness to it. Then he would go home to Atlanta, with another fine memory etched into the consciousness of his native back country.

It was almost like old times. Shnook was too bashful to show his face, but Zeke, Blackie and Cliff, who had all been drafted though never sent into actual combat, gathered to help the mechanical prodigy tune up his machine in Joe Freeman's musty barn. Milt celebrated Christmas respectfully at church and home, but on the following Sunday 4000 spectators came to witness one of the world's most famous aeroplane pilots perform stunts in his little toy. They were simple stunts, almost boring in comparison to the elaborate maneuvers he had perfected with the more sophisticated combat machines in Europe; but stunts that his viewers here thought were beyond belief. He generated over $800 for his mother after barely an hour's worth of flying. There clearly was a future in this, if he wanted to make money easily. But he needed more of a challenge. He wanted something new, something untried. He would go home to his villa for the winter and mull over what the next adventure would be.

"When you decide what to do with your life, tell me," his mother reminded him as he got into his Duesenberg to travel back to the big city.

"The war's over, and knowing how to spin around in a plane and shoot every flying thing in front of you won't help you any more."

"I know that, Mama. I'll do something else."

"Good-bye, child. Sure you don't want to stay?"

"I've always gotta bust out and go somewhere—haven't you learned that yet?"

In January and February he was back at Candler Field with Dawes and Brackens, trying to see if Atlanta would pay to watch him twirl his planes above the racetrack, but the weather was cold and the crowds were small. It occurred to him that the war hero era of his life was past news and his desire to avoid beating that image to death was why he had turned down endorsements and movie offers after his success in Europe.

Something else beckoned, something he had never done before. He wanted to be anonymous again, to be the same scruffy urchin he had been when he had run away from home the first time—to find another new course, to be rejuvenated and challenged. Just how he might do that he didn't know as of yet.

CHAPTER 18

A Motorcycle Journey

MILT HAD BEEN USHERED into the world craving excitement, noise, and motion, but the postwar world had grown staid. It was not permissible any more to aim an aeroplane at a foreigner and flail him with bullets, and the behaviors that were acceptable to the world at large now seemed boringly tame to him.

The Indian Motorcycle Company, the dominant manufacturer of motorbikes for the American military during the war, heard his call. He had turned down endorsements before, but one of that company's most beautiful mechanical ladies had captivated his fancy. In March of 1919, in exchange for allowing his image to appear on a billboard over the Indian Motorcycle dealership on Spring Street, Kid was given a lifetime supply of the models of his choice by the owner of the establishment, Mr. McGowan.

His first pick was the elegant Powerplus Racer, a workhorse with a three-speed side valve engine, a long wheelbase and a cruising speed of a mile a minute. His first stop with his rebellious Powerplus Racer was the racetrack at Hapeville, which he reached after nearly smashing himself into several trucks and cars on the roads along the way as he swerved recklessly into and out of traffic. Every angrily honking horn sent a ripple up his spine. If those irate fools had only known who he was, he kept thinking, how ashamed they would have been! But they had no idea, and that was the joy of it. He took a masochistic sort of pleasure in the realization that fame and glory were so fleeting that a little motorbike ride could make them disappear.

At the Candler Racetrack he sped furiously around the two-mile oval, churning up dust around the corners and taunting the straightaways by pulling his hands off the handlebars and waving them at his two friends. His newly-hatched plan was to stash a thousand or so dollars in cash in his pocket, pack a couple of stray shirts and a toothbrush in a knapsack, leave his swank mansion in Atlanta locked up and his admiring train of women lonely, and take off for a month or two in search of adventure. His intention was to race all the way to California in his motorcycle, then come back. What people he would meet along the way, and what adventure!

"You done lost your mind," Bobby told him when he heard what his friend was hoping to do. "What you think you'll find on the roadside over in Alabama—the goddamn Palace of Versailles?"

"I'll sleep on the side of the road," said Kid. "Just curl up in a blanket in a pine grove somewhere and snooze away."

"You're crazy. You're a rich man and you wanna live like a hobo? What's goin' through your damn mind?"

"I'm tryin' to prove I can do it. I'm gonna take this motorcycle, race across the countryside, and do something nobody ever did before."

"Bobby, you're wasting your breath," said Chet. "He's so excited about being a bum he can hardly hold it in!"

"Man, you got that right," said Kid. "There's somethin' about not knowing what comes next that just thrills me. 'Course y'all slackers wouldn't understand, 'cause all y'all know is soft beds and movie houses."

"Why don't you just shut up?" said Bobby. "Soon as you get mistaken for sugarcane while you sleep in a field down in Looziana and get slashed up into fifty pieces we'll see how soft we are, buddy."

"He don't give a damn about that," Chet replied. "He never did care whether he killed himself or not."

"I sure as hell do care. But I ain't staying home 'cause I'm afraid something bad's gonna happen if I leave."

"I'll tell you what," added Bobby, "Chet and me got more spunk than just about everybody else, but the last thing in the world we'd do is live like savages. Ain't a damn war and several plane crashes enough excitement for a decade or two? If aeroplane twirls don't light your fire, somethin' ain't right about you."

"Nothin' lights your fire if you do it too much," Kid answered. "I done the planes, I done the girls, I done the World War, I done the White House, now it's time I done the spring vacation, Kid-style."

He left at daybreak one Saturday in the middle of April, without telling anyone else. He had been dropping rather heavy-handed hints to his assortment of girl suitors, explaining that matrimony was frightening to him and he needed some time alone and away from the pressure of courting. Again he drained the fuel tanks of his Packard and Duesenberg, again he bolted shut the casement windows of the villa on Lafayette Drive and locked the doors in three different places. His mail would be forwarded to Chet and Bobby's little flat in Hapeville and any bills would be sent by them to his mother, who would pay them with part of the $250 in cash he had left her.

For several hundred miles he sloshed over the muddy byways of Georgia, Alabama and Mississippi. Part of his plan was to sleep outdoors like the pioneers, but he took two nights in acclimating himself to the cool damp night air and barely slept at all. During daylight he amused himself by racing at high speeds, splashing through mud puddles, doing wheelies, and waking up sleepy towns with the loud racket of his machine. By the third night he was so worn out that he could have slept on a pile of gravel. A clump of wet grass under a tree seemed like a featherbed to him by then.

In a Negro shantytown along the banks of the Alabama River west of Montgomery, the natives gathered happily to watch the Powerplus Racer jump back and forth over a large creek. Racing through the settlement, Kid had seen a high stack of lumber and been struck by an idea. He pulled a few long boards out of the stack, wedged several logs under them on each bank of the adjoining creek, nailed the boards and the logs together with a hammer and nails he borrowed from the town blacksmith, and formed two makeshift jumping ramps for his motorcycle. Then, as the natives watched with fascination, he shot his motorbike up the ramp on the near side, catapulted his machine across the water, and landed perfectly on the ramp on the opposite bank. It was such a thrill for him to do it once that he did it again and again. He spent three hours one afternoon jumping that creek for a disbelieving audience.

"Who taught you that?" Huey, the village elder, asked the incognito aviator.

"You know what, Huey? I never done that before I come through this here town and tried it today."

"Naw, man, you kiddin' me!"

"It's true, buddy. I ain't lyin', now."

"You ain't lyin'? Well, then. You *somethin'.* We oughtta tell folks about you so's they can all come watch. Durn, we ain't never seen nothin' like what you doin' over that water."

"Y'all wanna try it? Here, I'll get out of my motorsickle seat and one of y'all can volunteer to do it."

All forty-five of the residents of the shantytown turned their eyes away. Nobody even wanted to look at the crazy white boy for fear that he might try to draft somebody to replace him on his motorbike.

"Aw, y'all are chicken," said the foolhardy stranger. "I'll tell you what, though. Be sure to tell all the folks in the next town y'all done it, and I promise you I won't ever tell nobody y'all didn't."

Huey came over to the tall mechanical daredevil, not knowing he was addressing a world-famous man, and put his hand on Milt's shoulder.

"Can you stay 'round here tonight and have some supper with us? We invitin' you to stay, Mister . . . uh, what you say your name was?"

"Raymond."

"That's it, Mister Raymond. We got us a big hog we done slaughtered and we got enough for everybody. Man, that's gon' be some good eatin' there, boy."

"Sure wish I could stay, Huey, but I got to be pushin' along. I don't want no moss growin' under my feet."

"Where you in a hurry to go?"

"California."

"That where you live?"

"Naw. I just wanna see what it's like. I gotta hurry, you know what I mean?"

"All right, son. You suit yourself. But you welcome to stop in Barlow Bend anytime, young man."

All forty-five people in Barlow Bend, a settlement virtually unchanged since Reconstruction, without electricity or running water, waved farewell to the friendly white boy on the magical two-wheeled machine that was unlike anything they had ever seen before. Eventually someone from a nearby town would hear about the incident and piece together other information and come to the conclusion that it was no ordinary man who had been in Barlow Bend that day. When the news finally came to the villagers about who the white boy really was it became a permanent memory in all of them. Until their dying days many of them would recollect the incident for skeptical listeners and swear that it had really happened.

MILT CAME TO A FERRY crossing of the Mississippi River near Vicksburg two days later. Mr. Wells, the man operating the ferryboat, seemed to have a nervous tic of some kind. He kept swiping at the sides of his face, moving his hands in occult ways behind his neck and across his forehead, and stroking his midriff and thighs in utterly ridiculous ways. While he, Kid, and the motorcycle drifted across the mile-wide sludge of the great river, he continued these bizarre movements with ever-increasing exasperation while his confused passenger tried to ignore him. When at long last they came to the right bank, the Georgia boy gave Mr. Wells a dollar for the ride, and the boatman angrily lifted a gnarled hand with a pointing finger at what he considered the disrespectful youth.

"Damn you, what's that ring you got on your hand there?"

Milt looked down at the ring finger of his right hand, on which he always wore his father's Freemason ring which had been bequeathed to him.

"That's my late dad's ring. He was a member of the Masonic lodge where we come from."

"Didn't you notice all those signs I was makin' to you on the boat? And you didn't respond to one. You ain't got no business wearin' that there ring unless you know the symbols, boy."

"I'm sorry, sir, I ain't a Freemason. My dad was, and he willed this to me when he died."

"If you don't know the symbols you better take that ring off then, 'cause that's a crime."

"Don't you say that to me, mister."

The old troll puckered up and squinted his eyes.

"I'll say whatever I want, young tramp. Who the hell you claimin' to be?"

"Name's Raymond."

"Raymond who?"

"Uh . . . Raymond Milton."

"It's a lie—you had to stutter to make that name up. I oughtta call the police on you. You stole that ring, is what you did."

"Tell you what, old man. You call the police and let 'em try to catch me."

Kid winked at the sourpuss, mounted his motorbike, started it, and raced away on the unpaved river highway on the Louisiana side of the river. The ferocious speed of the machine awed the otherwise bitter boatman.

"Son of a bitch," Wells grumbled to himself. "These kids today don't got no respect for nothin'. A fine world it'll be when these lazy sorry good-for-nothin's outlive the rest of us!"

About an hour later, Kid saw what seemed to be a mirage along the Mississippi floodplain in northern Louisiana. A ramshackle sign by the roadway read "TALLULAH AIRPORT" and an arrow pointed down a cratered path which cut straight across newly planted cotton fields. It was the last week of April and the planting season was upon the land. The very thought of an airport of any kind in that remote outpost was intriguing to the wandering airplane-flyer, and he veered off the main road in his motorcycle to explore this curiosity.

The bumpy path wound through thickets of mimosas, honeysuckles and thorny blackberries on the edges of endless tracts of cotton, but it offered no other signs or hints that it would lead to an airport. A couple of miles into his detour, Kid had an inclination to turn around and go back to the main thoroughfare. But then, amid the monotonous panorama of cotton plants, he saw a collection of buildings bordering a flat unplanted field on the horizon. He raced in that direction like a thirsty camel toward a watery mirage. The tallest of the buildings, featuring a small upper story with arched windows of plate glass that in a few cases had been smashed by rocks, had a burnt red tile roof with cracked tiles and a tiny gasoline pump on one corner.

As the wanderer drew nearer to this brick building he made out the lettering that had been painted in green across its upper story just under the eaves: "TALLULAH AIRPORT." Across the facing of the lower floor of the structure was another sign: "STANDARD OIL COMPANY OF LOUISIANA". Kid saw no evidence whatsoever of any airplanes around the self-proclaimed airport, but at the very least he thought he might make some use of the gas pump, since his motorcycle was running short of fuel.

He rushed his bike up to the filling station, trying to make as much commotion as possible, churning up dust and twirling his Powerplus Racer in a 360-degree circle before he came to a stop. The only person in attendance, a teenage boy sitting on a bench by one of the front doors, was undisturbed by the noise. For quite awhile he had been snoozing away in peaceful sleep with his head bowed down and his cap slid down over his eyes. Kid began pumping gas into his motorcycle's tank while he glanced at the building, the wide open fields and the azure blue spring sky. He heard buzzing honeybees and smelled fresh green vegetation everywhere about him. On one of the windows of the front portals of the station he noticed a handwritten message on cream-colored stationery that was taped to the glass. When his tank was full and he had placed the nozzle back on its hook he went to read this notice:

> WANTED: AEROPLANE PILOT TO HELP WITH AGRICULTURAL EXPERIMENT. GOOD HOURS, COMPETITIVE WAGE. APPLY WITHIN.

The former war ace smirked and walked through the doors. Inside he saw a long counter with a cash register and stools in front of it, and a door which opened to a large empty atrium that he thought would have worked well as a storage hangar for a plane if one had been available. He ascended a creaky wooden staircase to the upper floor of the building and saw nothing there but a sparse room with broken glass on its floor, a modest table and four chairs. The windows upstairs offered a pleasing vista over what from that height clearly appeared to be a landing strip cut straight through the cotton fields, though there were no skid marks or airplanes anywhere to be seen. Back down he went now, and outside. Except for that poor sleeping boy slumped over on the bench, the premises were entirely deserted. Milt wanted to ask what the notice on the window meant and to pay for his gas, so he went and shook the boy.

"Hey, mister, I just filled my motorsickle. Here's two quarters."

Red-eyed and groggy, the youngster yawned, stretched, rubbed his eyes and recoiled from the sight of the grubby, unshaven stranger.

"Don't hurt me, please, I'll git you whatever you want!"

"Aw, I ain't tryin' to steal nothin', boy," said Kid. "Just the opposite. I'm payin' for the gas I done pumped. Here, boy."

The attendant grabbed the two quarters, glanced at them to make sure they were real, and put them in the rear pocket of his trousers.

"It's good money—don't doubt it, fella," Milt continued. "Say, you know anything about that note over there about an aeroplane pilot? Where do I apply for that? I didn't see anybody inside."

"You fly aeroplanes?"

"Sure, I've flown 'em a few times. I'm pretty good at it, too."

Kid's listener looked at him as if he were telling him he had parted the Red Sea with Moses and sailed the seas with Columbus.

"I bet you are," the boy mumbled with as much conviction as if the stranger had just told him one plus one equaled three.

"Well, what's that note about, mister? Do you know?"

"I'll get on the telephone and call the feller that put it up. He's the one that oughtta be handlin' this."

Kid saw the younger man go into the station by the counter, put the earpiece of a telephone to his head, and shout something into its mouthpiece. In the meantime he sat on the bench and propped his elbows on his knees. The boy came out to tell Kid a Doctor So-and-so of Something-or-another and his assistant, some hotshot with a sissy-sounding name, were coming there from the county extension office in Tallulah to meet with him. The war ace nodded, rubbed his hands together, and stared at the ground. Forty-five minutes later, when the scraggly vagabond's patience was just about exhausted, a navy blue 1917 Oldsmobile sedan rolled into the dusty lot of the so-called airport terminal.

Two young men, one a smallish, scholarly man in his mid-thirties, and the other a tall, athletic looking man in his late twenties who wore wire-rimmed spectacles and parted his light brown hair neatly in the middle, emerged from the car. When the pair saw the untidy ruffian on the bench they glanced at each other and at the attendant in ill-disguised skepticism about what he might be able to do for them. The tall man, who spoke in a standard Midwestern accent that betrayed his birthplace in Indiana, offered Milt his hand.

"Hello there, sir," said the Hoosier. "I'm A.T. Bonderman."

The two shook hands.

"Pleased to meet you, Mr. Bonderman. What'd you say your first name was again?"

"My given names are Aloysius Troy, but I go by A.T. I guess my parents must not have been too excited about having me, so they decided to punish me for the rest of my life by naming me Aloysius."

"Sometimes parents are funny that way," said Milt, and then he shook the other man's hand.

"Pleased to meet you, sir," said Bonderman's companion. "I'm Dr. Trevor Reed. What's your name?"

"Uh, I'm Ray. Ray Milton."

"Mr. Milton," said Dr. Reed, "Tommy called us and said you know how to fly aeroplanes. Is that true?"

"Sure is. I've been up in the air a time or two."

"A.T. and I are working for the Louisiana State University Agricultural Extension Service. We've been trying to find an insecticide to kill the boll weevil, and my colleague's come up with an idea. He thinks if an aeroplane scattered a powder of some kind over a field it might solve the problem."

Kid smiled and shrugged his shoulders, as he would continue to do as more and more of the details of this nickel-and-dime operation became apparent to him.

"It's worth a try, ain't it? If y'all get me a plane we'll see if it works. But the weevils ain't out yet, are they? It's just April."

"We understand that," admitted Reed. "We're in the early stages, just trying to see if an aeroplane might fly low enough to dust the plants."

A.T. and Dr. Reed both began squirming to try to find a way to wriggle out of the possibility of involving this apparent ne'er-do-well in their serious scientific work.

"Mr. Milton," said A.T., "where are your credentials? I know you'll understand we want to be sure our equipment's in skilled hands. I learned to fly in the World War myself, but we're looking for . . . shall we say, somebody with lots of experience?"

Milt could barely contain his glee over the charade he was perpetrating on these two men.

"Fellows," he said, "I ain't got credentials with me, but if y'all are concerned about me wreckin' one of y'all's planes, I'll tell you what I'll do. I'll put down a deposit in cash for the full value of a beat up secondhand Jenny, and if I wreck it then you gentlemen keep the cash. But if I carry out the experiment right, then I want my cash back, plus a hundred dollars. How 'bout it, Dr. Reed and Mr. Bonderman?"

A.T. smiled and rolled his tongue around in his cheek before Dr. Reed's appreciative eye.

"Where in the world would you come up with enough cash to pay for an aeroplane, Mr. Milton?"

"I have my ways. Looks can lie."

"I'm sorry," said Dr. Reed, "but if you don't have credentials you can't help us."

"Hold on there, Trevor," said A.T., "the man's making a business proposition to us. It's hard to find skilled aviators and, if this young man happens to be one, so much the better. With his offer, it won't be any skin off our backs if he can't do what he says he can."

Kid pulled out a handful of $50 bills from the tattered pocket of his soiled trousers and brandished them in front of the two agricultural extension agents.

"This prove my point, fellas?"

"I'll be damned," said Dr. Reed. "I reckon it does. A.T., let's see if we can find us a war surplus trainer and watch what he does with it."

KID BROKE DOWN AND stayed in a hotel that night, the finest one in Tallulah, and he yielded to what little civilizing instinct he had inside of him, bathed himself and shaved. It was apparent he would be around for all of tomorrow at the very least, until he could demonstrate his piloting skills for those two suckers and collect on the hundred dollars he knew he would have coming to him. He bought himself an extra set of trousers and an extra shirt at the general store on Main Street, and had the soiled rags he had been wearing laundered at the local cleaners. The lone item that remained dirty in his apparel was his cap, the one he always wore askew, which was so filthy that dust could be wrung out of it like water out of a soppy rag. It was impossible for him to imagine wearing a clean cap, so he left that just the way it was.

When Milt rode his motorcycle out to the pathetic little Tallulah Airport the next morning, Bonderman and Reed were waiting for him in their Oldsmobile, anxiety all over their faces.

"Mr. Milton," said A.T., "I hate to say this, but we can't find any other aeroplane but the one that's in there." He pointed toward the inside of the large storage loft of the gas station building, where Kid made out the features of a biplane through dusty windows. "I sure hope you do what you say you can, because I'd hate to have to find another one."

"Where'd that aeroplane come from, Mr. Bonderman? I didn't see that here yesterday."

"We ransacked all of Madison Parish yesterday afternoon, and that little piece of junk was all we could find. It's one I bought myself last winter from the Army, and we were storing it in some old farmer's barn, just waiting for the right fellow to come along to try to fly it."

"How'd you get it here?"

"We paid the farmer $20 to take the wings off and put it in his truck and follow us over here."

"Why the hell's this place called an airport if it ain't got no aeroplanes?" wondered Kid. "Has there ever been a damn plane that ever landed out here?"

"Not really," said Dr. Reed. "We built it first, then we were hoping the results would come later."

The visitor from Georgia laughed.

"Fellas, I don't like to brag too much, 'specially when I ain't seen what I'm about to get in, but I got a feelin' y'all are about to get you some results."

"Don't get your hopes up too much, Mr. Milton," said Bonderman. "You *haven't* seen it yet."

"Let's go look at it now," said Kid.

A.T. and Trevor led their visitor around to the side of the building, where there was a doorless archway just wide and high enough to allow passage for the plane that was being stored inside. A grimy Curtiss JN-4D, similar to the machine in which Milt had violated Major Simoneau's nervous system at the Rhinebeck Aerodrome in the summer of 1917, sprawled across the concrete floor of the room. It had once been painted olive green but it had now deteriorated to a cow-manure shade of brown. The two entomologists had reattached the wings earlier that morning with the help of the farmer, and it now stood ready to fly.

The war ace walked completely around the perimeter of the plane, stroked his fingers on its fabric, looked at its engine under the cowling, and stepped up on the wing to examine the controls and the seating area. He moved the stick and rudder bar back and forth with his hands, observed the movements of the flaps on the wings and wiped the dirt off the instruments with his bare hands. He quickly concluded his evaluation.

"It's ugly as a possum, gentlemen, but I don't see any reason at all why it can't do what y'all want it to do."

The two agricultural agents showed the self-proclaimed aviator several bags of pulverized limestone that they wanted him to scatter over the cotton fields. This would have a consistency similar to calcium arsenate, the compound shown in their laboratory experiments to be effective in killing the boll weevil, the imported pest which in recent years had decimated the South's cotton crop. The pests were not a problem yet this early in the spring, so dispensing the calcium arsenate now would be a waste; but the limestone would act as a substitute for the purpose of the experiment and also confer the benefit of neutralizing the acidity of the soil once it broke down in subsequent rains.

Kid wondered how the men intended for him to scatter the limestone from the Jenny. He suggested a long rectangular hopper, mounted in such a way on the underside of the plane's fuselage so as not to destroy the aerodynamic lift of the wings, with a screen or mesh on its underside that would enable the powder to seep out during flight. The upper side would have removable covers that would allow more powder to be poured onto the screens when the limestone had all run out. Kid envisioned nailing together four two-by-fours of two different lengths to form a long narrow rectangular frame, then nailing several porous burlap sacks to the bottom of the frame and bolting the frame crossways to the supporting ribs on the underside of the fuselage so that it would stick out like another wing set while the plane was in flight. Then he would fill up the hopper on both sides with the bags of limestone, tie canvas covers to the top of the frame very tightly with jute rope to keep the powder in place, and hope that a suitable amount of powder leaked down through the porous burlap sacks during flight.

"First thing we need to do, gentlemen," he told Bonderman and Reed, "is wheel this bird out, fire it up and make sure it flies."

There was the matter of money. Hadn't he promised them yesterday he would deposit the full value of whatever plane he flew in cash, so in case he wrecked it the investment of the two Louisiana bug experts would still be protected? Indeed he had. A promise was a promise.

"What'd you say you gave the Army for that Jenny, Mr. Bonderman?"

"Five hundred fifty dollars."

Milt undid the flaps of the knapsack he had strapped over one shoulder, pulled out a stack of bills, and licked his thumb. He counted off eleven $50 bills and gave them to A.T.

"I'm trustin' you fellows not to run off with my money, now. If you do I'm willin' to land this bird on the other side of nowhere and keep it for myself."

"That's not even worth discussing," said the tall Midwesterner with the neatly parted hair and wire-rimmed spectacles. "You're the one on trial here, not us."

"Oh, so that's what this is? A trial? You sure?"

"We're waiting to see what you can do."

Together they pushed the Jenny out of the storage room and over to the gas pump, whose nozzle barely reached the tank up by the engine. Tommy, the young attendant, helped them fill the tank and then roll the Jenny about two hundred feet through mud and lush spring grass to the head of the landing strip in the middle of the endless cotton fields. All the while Dr. Reed kept the tail skid up to prevent it from dragging. Tommy was sent over to the gas pump to fetch a couple of bricks to use as chocks for the plane's wheels.

Kid remembered from his experiences with Jennies at the Rhinebeck Aerodrome that their erratic OX-5 engines tended to overheat, so he pulled out his pocketknife and began cutting away most of the engine's leather cowling for ventilation. The exhaust pipes on the JN-4D were short and spewed unusually large quantities of fumes and oil in the pilot's face. He had heard of cases in which these fumes had set fire to the plane's nitrate-coated fabric covering, so on a machine that had seen this much use he figured he would need to be sticking his head out of the cockpit constantly to check the surface of the plane while he flew it. Also, the Jenny was difficult to land with its thin wobbly wings; at Rhinebeck he and a colleague had added special skids to several of the trainers to keep their wings from scraping the ground during landings. That wouldn't be possible today—nor would protection against the spewing oil and sludge, as he had no goggles and his old cap would surely not stay on during flight.

On top of all these nuisances, he remembered the shortcomings of the Jenny's engine. Even in the pink of military maintenance, the 90-horsepower motor would tend to cough before it ran at full strength and the plumbing which circulated water to cool the engine would leak. As he cut away the leather around the engine he thought about all this, not without some misgivings. For all his bravado, coarse masculine talk and apparent defiance of intellectual activity, he was in fact a coldly calculating and cerebral tactician. That was how he had survived the crucible over in Europe. And as he considered his current situation he took nothing for granted.

"Fellas," Kid told the other three men as he stood poised to spin the propellor started, "we usually wear head and eye coverings when we fly these machines, but I ain't got none with me today. A bath in oil and a ruined set of clothes ain't so bad, anyway—'specially compared to what we went through over there."

"What do you mean by that, Mr. Milton?" asked Dr. Reed. "You didn't tell us you . . . who are you, anyway?"

"Nobody special. Just a boy who's real good at dodgin' bullets and flippin' around in space."

Kid winked at Tommy, who was completely alert today and not in the least bit inclined to doze off. Then the aviator primed the Jenny's propellor, leaned into his flying seat to turn on the plane's switches, and went back to hurl the machine started with all his might, ducking when it cranked up and began roaring like an angry lion. It was a loud, uproarious sound and he was just as thrilled to hear it now as he had been the first time he had ever taken a plane up. He doffed his cap and tossed it to the ground near where A.T. was standing, then hopped into the cockpit seat and gestured for someone to pull the bricks out from under his wheels. Flooding the engine with fuel, he felt the Jenny surge ahead, the cool air of the spring morning rush through his hair; saw the little cotton plants in the field to his side shooting by like the rapids of a raging river; and then gently up, up into the sky he went, above the flat infinity of the Mississippi floodplain. Much to his relief, the machine worked perfectly.

He flipped the plane around, came back over the adjoining cotton field, brought the Jenny perilously low to the ground, no more than five feet above it, and rushed it ahead at a constant parallel to the ground, ridiculously low, so low that fully mature cotton plants would have been scraping the bottom of his landing gear. He held this course until he reached the edge of the field, then he shot his plane up, twirled around and came in low again, this time a few feet further into the field, and again he clung to an almost ground-scraping pattern all the way to the end of the row of seedlings.

When he ascended for a second time he decided if he kept this up he might bore both his spectators and himself, so he put his Jenny into a high loop, flipped it completely over, and came down to the cotton field and hugged the ground again. Reaching the outer limit of the cotton field for a third time, he soared heavenward and this time began displaying some of his combat acrobatics, doing a side-slip and a figure eight, rolling up to about three thousand feet and plunging the Jenny into a *vrille* as if he imagined Eichhorn were still on his tail. But he wasn't in France. This was a cotton field in Louisiana, he kept having to remind himself. Down he went, nearly scraping the soil, the little sprigs swaying under his propellor blast as he dragged the plane across the field.

"Good God Almighty!" swore Trevor, looking on at a distance with the others. "I would've thought it was impossible for a man to fly like that!"

Aloysius Troy removed his spectacles, pressed a handkerchief to his eyes as if he were nearly in tears, and spoke with the reverence and solemnity of a religious occasion.

"I saw a man fly like that one time," he said. "It was from the trenches in France. The men said he was one of our boys, but I thought it was God himself. The way he spun his machine and dove through the sky, the way he attacked the enemy fearlessly . . . Trevor, I swear to you this has got to be the same man. There's only fellow on the face of the earth who can fly an aeroplane like that!"

"You don't mean that boy in our plane is—A.T., what would *he* be doing here?"

"Raymond Milton," said Bonderman. "That's his name all right. His given name. Raymond Milton 'Kid' Harrison. That's who's in that Jenny up there, my friend."

Young Tommy was coming up a little bit short of breath. In fact, he was gasping.

"No way," he said. "Ain't no way Kid Harrison would be wasting his time in Tallulah, Louisiana!"

"I don't understand it myself," said Bonderman. "But I know just as sure as I'm standing here we lucked into the best help in the whole world. I almost think it's an omen of some kind—a good omen that we're destined to prosper."

When Milt had completed his third skimming of the ground in his plane he decided to come back for a landing as he had gotten some oil in one of his eyes and it was stinging rather painfully. He swung around to the outskirts of Tallulah and brought the Jenny back down smoothly on the landing strip, its flimsy wings swaying on impact and grazing the dirt slightly but avoiding damage. Having taxied back safely over to where the three observers stood, he shut off the plane's motor and came down from his flying seat. His audience had grown eager to embrace him when they realized his true identity, and they were there to shake his hand as soon as he hit the ground.

"You're Kid Harrison, aren't you?" asked A.T. "There's no mistaking it."

"I could be. But I still don't have my credentials with me."

"It's a real privilege to meet you, sir."

Tommy was the most star-struck and goggle-eyed of the group.

"I gotta be dreaming! No way I had Kid Harrison come up to my gas pump on a motorsickle! That just can't happen."

"It's a rare honor indeed," added Trevor. "Who would've ever thought you'd be out this way on a motorbike, see our notice and be the one to help us? What brought you this way?"

"Just passing through on a little lark," said the aviator, "and havin' some fun at your expense."

"Here's your money back," said A.T., returning the stack of $50 bills to its owner. "We're the ones who ought to be paying you."

Milt put the money in his pocket and began rubbing his oil-stained eye with his shirt sleeve.

"Let's go build a dispenser to put on the bottom of the plane," Kid said, "and see if it'll spread the limestone."

By late in the afternoon, after a trip to the nearest lumber mill and a general store in Tallulah for a few supplies, Milt and his new friends had constructed a makeshift wooden hopper of pine boards, nails, burlap sacks and a top cover of denim fabric. The four of them attached the frame to the underside of the Jenny with large wood screws that were drilled through the wood with the bit of an augur, then filled the frames with the limestone, covered them, and held the denim in place with a rope wrapped around the frame. The burlap sagged under the weight of the limestone and some of the powder began seeping out immediately, but the rig held up sufficiently to withstand the startup and takeoff of the plane.

Milt kept the Jenny low over the cotton field, scattering the powder as evenly as possible over the plants. Some of the lime leaked out through the top cover and some was dispersed in the sky as Milt lifted the plane in his turns, but most of it coated the plants in a surprisingly uniform dousing. It was nearly nightfall by then—time to retire for the day and reflect on what went right—and the experiment had been a stunning success. When Kid landed and dismounted from the Jenny, he met with a round of handshakes for a second time that day.

"It would've taken a dozen fieldhands all day to do what you just did in twenty minutes," said A.T. "And they would've been coughing and sick from breathing the dust, too."

"Too bad there ain't no weevils around now, or we'd try the calcium arsenate and see if that would work."

"We're almost certain it would work, Kid," said Trevor. "We've established in our labs that the bugs won't tolerate calcium arsenate if we coat the leaves of the plants with it."

Milt envisioned a whole fleet of Jennies dusting cotton crops throughout the South, and he saw at once that the idea had considerable promise.

"I'll tell you what, Mr. Bonderman. You keep that hundred dollars I said I wanted from you if this experiment worked out. And I'll give you the $550 you had in your hand earlier today. That'll be your seed money. If this operation works out, you remember my stake in this. You seem to be a man of your word."

The aviator pulled out the roll of $50 bills that had already changed hands several times and gave it back to the pair of entomologists. At the time no one realized it, but the man from Woodvale was making the best investment of his life.

"My Lord, this is more money than most folks in this state have in their entire savings," said the ambitious young Hoosier. "I can't tell you how grateful we are to you, Kid. Don't think for a minute we'll ever forget about what you did today."

"When y'all get this operation started I'm predicting it'll make some money. 'The Lousiana Dusting Service'—I can see it now. Why, if y'all do it right I bet you can make that $550 I'm givin' you in profit every month."

Tommy laughed as though Kid were talking some bizarre nonsense, but neither Bonderman nor Reed saw anything at all absurd about the prediction.

"Why don't you stay here with us and help us?" said Trevor. "You don't have any other obligations, do you?"

"No, sir, but I know my place. I'd just be in y'all's way. I ain't no businessman. If you fellers need any help, you'll know how to track me down."

When Milt left the bug specialists and Madison Parish on his motorcycle, he went about three hours further west, a bit past Monroe, before he realized he didn't have any desire to go all the way to California. As a matter of fact, he didn't even want to go as far as Texas. As a matter of fact, he wanted to turn around and go home. Right then. His chance encounter with the entomologists and his tricks in the Jenny had somewhat bored him with his motorcycle.

"The problem with this thing," he said to himself as he slid to a stop in the middle of a lonely Louisiana road, "is it's just too damn slow!"

So he went home.

CHAPTER 19

Bootlegging

KID HAD TO ENDURE the taunts and ridicule of Bobby and Chet when he returned to Hapeville only eight days after he had set out on his supposedly Grand Tour.

"Damn," said Brackens, "I never knew there was a town named California in Looziana. And I sure as hell wouldn't have thought a war hero would drive four days on a motorbike just to see it."

"Well, you don't understand," said Milt. "You don't know the sort of women in that place. California women. The one I went to see was named Andalusia."

"*Andalusia?*" winced Brackens. "What sort of name is that?"

"It's about like Kid. A totally made up name."

Milt was disappointed by how quickly his wartime renown seemed to fade away. Not because he was proud of it or wanted to be forever remembered for it, but because he'd hoped it would be a springboard for public interest in his other activities. The Atlanta Racetrack was growing ever more dilapidated by the month despite the sparsely attended air shows that were being staged there by Chet and Bobby. Kid and his friends were idling away a stiflingly hot summer afternoon in early July of '19, racking their brains to get themselves out of their predicament. How might they convince their hardscrabble fellow Georgians to part with some of their dwindling cash that summer?

"I bet the public would pay $20 a head to ride with me in a Jenny," Kid boasted.

Brackens scoffed and shook his head.

"Ain't no way. Five's the most you could get out of 'em—and even that's pushing."

"Twenty, I say. Let's give it a try—we've got nothin' to lose."

Chester Dawes, who along with his bosom buddy had grown thin with the recent inactivity around Hapeville, chuckled at the notion.

"Bobby, if Kid says he can get twenty I believe him. We'll put bills all around Atlanta in well-to-do areas. Shoot, to some people twenty bucks is pocket change."

"I'll make it pocket change for everybody," Kid bragged again.

"Even if he's right," added Brackens, "that still don't do a damn bit of good to you and me, Chet. Lookit this sorry place. It ain't fit to bury a dead dog in."

The three young airmen paused to survey the vast clearing around them. It was then at the height of summer and on a Saturday afternoon. Only a few years earlier on such a day, the field would have been awash with the glittering pageantry of swooping biplanes and racing flivvers, and the desolate grandstands would have been teeming with cheering throngs of ladies with white lace parasols and men in starched pinstripes with dappled red and white boutonnieres pinned to their lapels. Instead of this a desert now stood on the edge of Hapeville. The wooden grandstands were crumbling and rotten, the grounds surrounding them were threadbare flats of red Georgia clay baked into cracks by the hot July sun, and the cows who had formerly grazed in the grasslands surrounding the racetrack had snubbed their noses at the property, for it was infested with bitterweed and no bovine would even go near it.

And Dawes and Brackens, for all their mechanical wizardry, had of late failed to win any more of Asa Candler's philanthropy, which was now being doled out to war widows and amputees. Their fleet of airships had dwindled to a mere three. Even George Grantland, the man about town, everybody's friend, the hobnobber with the elite, the plaything of politicoes—even George had lost his interest in the place while Kid had been away. He was too busy planning to run for some type of office—city alderman, sewer manager, associate dog catcher or some such title to propel him through the oaken door of power—to bother frequenting an unpopular spread located out in the boondocks.

"All the fun's gone out of life lately," lamented Bobby. "People used to drink and have a good ole time and come out to watch our planes. Then the goddamn Feds stepped in and turned this into Siberia."

"True," Chet agreed. "Kid, while you were saving the world for democracy the same jack-booted communists who took over Russia sneaked into our country and took over our government too. It ain't right."

"I guess you fellers expect me to solve that problem too, don't you?" asked Kid. "Well, I'm gonna bring the fun back all right. And the money back, too."

"How you plannin' on doing that?" Brackens asked doubtfully.

"I just need one good cargo aeroplane. You got any, Bobby?"

"Just one. That DH-4 mail plane over there."

"How's she runnin'?"

"She's a horse."

Kid shaded his eyes and looked across the field at the graceful biplane that still bore the olive green color and the white star of its military ancestors. He nodded with satisfaction.

"Boys, now that I done toured America it's time for me to visit foreign countries. I think I might import me some precious goods too. Some liquid money."

Bobby and Chet looked at each other with a mixture of joy and disbelief.

"You might do *what?"* they both asked at almost the same time.

"I'm going bootleggin'!" whispered Kid, with a smile almost oozing with sinful mischief.

The idea had occurred to the war ace spur of the moment, but that evening, in the comfort of his Ansley Park villa, it evolved into an elaborate scheme. On a globe in his study he noticed that the Bahamas seemed to be ridiculously close to the southeastern coast of Florida; and from that moment onward images of defiance, danger, and boundless profit intoxicated him like the contraband he was hoping to smuggle across the water. It had been in January of that year, barely two months after he had helped to save democracy, that his own government had in his opinion helped to stifle it with the passage of the 18th Constitutional Amendment, rendering the sale and consumption of alcoholic beverages illegal within the United States. And though he had never in his life had any use for liquor he very definitely believed he had use for freedom; and if the government might do such a thing as this, what might it try next? Was nothing sacred? Was there soon to be an amendment making the flying of airplanes illegal, or the flirtation with pretty girls, or the pronouncement of unorthodox political opinions? All these things might be deadly, bad, or dangerous. There seemed to be no end in sight to the madness. As far as he could tell, there was now no difference between the Congress and the Kaiser, except that one was still in full power and the other was deposed. At bottom, they were all Huns.

He remembered that when he had entertained his retinue of pretty girls last December his caterers had brought two bottles of spirits and that the girls had drunk freely from them. That had been in the olden days, last year, before it had been a crime to drink fermented liquids. He still had a cupful of the stuff left in one of the bottles in his cupboard, and he pulled out the bottle to examine its label.

HARTLEY'S BAHAMIAN RUM
Nassau, Bahamas, W.I.

The words haunted him as if they had been Egyptian hieroglyphics. If he flew there, what would he find? He would simply have to fly there, and by himself, and in a machine large enough to carry plenty of bottles back with him. For four days he studied maps of Georgia, Florida and the Bahamas, planned a route that would be practical for Bobby's DeHavilland 4 biplane, and flew a few practice runs at the racetrack under the eager supervision of his two friends. The DH-4 had been adapted from war use to serve as the inaugural carrier of U.S. air mail in 1918. Its stately double wingspan, powerful engine, sturdy build and graceful contours made it a far more impressive machine than the other dinosaurs Dawes and Brackens had housed in their little hangar in the last two years. To their credit, the pair had poured every last precious cent of their meager savings into the mechanical perfection of their best remaining plane. Kid was guaranteeing them, with the braggadocio that had been his trademark of late, that their eleventh hour gamble was about to pay off with a Prohibition jackpot.

"Boys, the only problem with this machine," he told them, "is it can't carry enough booze to run the Bahamas dry. If it could, I'd do it."

"What's the matter with you?" Chet teased him. "I thought you were a true-blue American hero, and now you're turnin' to a life of crime."

"Y'all are hungry," said Kid, "and I'm about to feed you."

ON WEDNESDAY, THE 16TH of July 1919 the former war ace, who had commingled with generals and supped with heads of state, accepted Beelzebub's latest invitation from the fiery flames down under, agreed to give the devil his sweat and blood if necessary to serve his life of crime, and soared into the very midst of heaven in his DH-4 as if to taunt the Almighty to strike him down. The dust of the deserted Hapeville racetrack, flying up like a storm behind the fury of the roaring biplane, drifted high up into the hazy sky and down onto the empty grandstands. Two lean and hungry young men, aviators themselves, shaded their eyes and squinted into the sun as the silhouette of the biplane disappeared into the southern horizon. Their caps and white shirts had been showered by Kid's dust along with everything else, and their eyes stung with it; but they both felt as if they were little boys again, and it was Christmas Eve, and Santa Claus was going off in his sleigh to bring them back a load of presents.

The aviator had armed himself with maps, compasses, a life vest for a possible crash in the sea, a bag of sandwiches, two thermoses and one thousand dollars in cash. Fortunately, snow and ice were an impossibility on this particular trip. Unfortunately, so were fame, fanfare, the prospects for a medal, and even respectability in the eyes of the world at large. The times, it seemed, had changed, and so had he. He was 22 years old, a hedonist, a charmer, a nonconformist, a war veteran, an adventurer, a decorated hero, a genius, a romantic, a showman and an exhibitionist. Now, to this imposing list of titles, he was aiming to add another: BOOTLEGGER.

His DH-4 could go 350 miles between refueling stops and flew as fast as 115 miles per hour, so he was able to go all the way to Jacksonville, just over the Florida line, before landing. He had never flown so great a distance in such favorable weather, nor had he ever derived such carefree pleasure from simply watching the world drift by beneath him. Half an hour before landing he caught sight of the Atlantic Ocean to the east. Somewhere out there, far out to sea, lay his tropical destination, beyond the billowy white clouds on the edge of the horizon. Somewhere out there lay outlawry, riches and adventure, and the very sight of the navy blue ocean thrilled him.

A crude dirt landing strip on the fringe of Jacksonville and the edge of the Okefenokee Swamp had a gas pump that Kid used to refill his tank. The toothless caretaker, a thin shriveled up man who looked as though he had been in a wrestling match with an alligator and lost, eyed the stranger and his fancy plane carefully.

"Where you goin', mister?"

"Don't know yet," answered Kid.

"Where you from?"

"Can't remember."

"Who are you?"

Milt wrinkled his face up and cast a sidelong look of irritation at his questioner, causing the other man to shrink away and keep his mouth closed. The mischievous scofflaw who refused to answer any questions kept squinting and scowling while he replaced the gas cap, poured extra water in the radiator and examined the Liberty engine for loose tubes and fittings.

"If I give you money now, mister," Kid finally said, "will you please promise me to shut up?"

The toothless man remained obediently quiet while the aviator placed his goggles over his eyes and flung a five-dollar bill at him. After the man pocketed the money he stood by attentively to remove the chocks from under the plane's wheels once the propellor was restarted. Only when the biplane had safely ascended into the semitropical summer haze did he dare relax, for he had been afraid this apparent fugitive was about to kill him and dump his body in the same swamp where the gators who had tried to eat him once before still lived.

LATE THAT AFTERNOON MILT landed at an airfield near West Palm Beach, tethered his plane to a banyan tree with a lock and a long chain, and walked to a hotel in town. Tomorrow would present him with a new challenge: a flight over Northwest Providence Channel and the verdant chain of the Bahamian islands to the capital at Nassau—a trip of only about 200 air miles from West Palm Beach, but a cultural and political chasm away.

He had never seen such beauty as the brilliant cerulean blue colors of the tropical waters over which his biplane passed on the following morning; nor had he ever been quite so enchanted as he was by the countless deserted palm-studded isles with their lush verdure drifting by beneath him. He flew low to try to absorb as many of the vivid details as possible. To think that Columbus himself had never seen that little corner of paradise from the air—to think that his eyes might have been the first human pair that had ever taken in such beauty from such a viewpoint—all this drowned out the sordid nature of his mission.

Two and a half hours into his morning's adventure Kid sighted a cluster of brightly colored plaster buildings hugging a small harbor fringed by sandy beaches. This was Nassau, his destination and the object of his curiosity. The city sprawled up the gentle slopes of hillsides above the sea. In surveying the territory around the Bahamian capital, he saw only one suitable landing place for an airplane anywhere close to town: a long flat swatch of unattended dirt with nothing else to complement it except a solitary gas pump and a ragged wind sock. No people or buildings were around it and it seemed to border closely on a citrus grove. He glided smoothly to a landing, safe among the orange trees. The arrival of the plane generated some excitement in the neighborhood. Two teenage Bahamian boys slid through a bamboo thicket across the road from the citrus grove, and ran to greet the visitor.

"Big, big aeroplane!" cried one, who had seen pictures of the strange machines in the newspapers he used to sell along the Nassau waterfront.

"I bet it came straight from the U.S.A.," added the other.

The aviator cut his engine off and leaped down from his seat, his right hand clenched around the empty rum bottle he had brought from home.

"What you doin' here, sir?" asked the second boy.

"I'm in the import business," Kid answered, "and I hear y'all make some good stuff down here."

"What kinda stuff you mean, Mister . . . hey, what's your name?"

"You can call me Mister X if you like."

"That's a funny name. Who give you a name like that?"

"I did. The name my mama gave me don't have that special ring to it, you know."

"I don't believe you," said the first boy. "You're lyin' bad."

"Why don't you boys tell me your own names?" said Kid.

"I'm Sammy," responded the second boy, "and he's Charlie."

"Got any cigarettes, Mr. X?" asked Charlie.

"Nope, sure don't."

"Got any women?" asked Sammy.

"What sorta fellow you think I am? I said import, not export. I ain't here to trade no women."

"Then what you plannin' on trading?" wondered Charlie.

He held the rum bottle up so they could both see the label.

"Either one of y'all know where I can talk to the people who make this?"

They both smiled wide in flashes of ivory teeth.

"Ah, yes," said Charlie. "You need to see the man."

"Who?" asked Kid.

"Mr. Man," said Sammy. "Our friend. We call him Mr. Man since he got in trouble. He about our age, maybe a little older. He work up there pressin' the cane at the still."

"Let's go see the man, then," said Kid. "Where does he live?"

"We can walk there," said Charlie.

The trek up to see Mr. Man was more laborious than Milt expected, since it was uphill, and he was tired and wearing far too much clothing and equipment for the heat. Sammy and Charlie led him through narrow dirt streets lined with modest plaster huts to a little bungalow with a tall thin boy of about 16 sitting on a wicker chair on the front porch.

"Mr. Man," said Charlie to his teenage pal, "here's Mr. X, an aeroplane-flyer from U.S.A. He want some of your rum."

The thin boy shot up to his feet energetically and with a great deal of enthusiasm.

"You picked the right place, sir," he called out. "You goin' back to U.S.A. in the plane?"

"Yes."

"Then let's be friends," said Mr. Man. "It's lunchtime, so you eat here with us, and we go later in the afternoon to Hartley's."

They were all on the porch by now, and the aviator shook hands with the stranger.

"I got a well and bucket in the back," said Mr. Man. "It's good water, you can stay here, Mister—what's your name again?"

"Mister X."

"*Mister X?* What that 'X' stand for?"

Kid shrugged calmly, as if the answer, though he had never even considered it, would be easy to invent.

"EXCITEMENT."

Everyone in the tiny hut laughed, including Milt.

"That's some name you got there, Mr. Excitement," said Mr. Man. "You and me got some things in common, you know?"

"Wait a minute," interrupted Sammy, "ain't you got no first name, Mr. X?"

"Sure do, boy. It's N.B."

"Enby," winced Mr. Man. "I never heard that name before."

"Those are my initials," said Kid. "They stand for 'Nothing But'."

They all laughed again.

"I tell you what, Mr. Excitement," said Mr. Man, "you got yourself one hell of a name. I think I'll call you Enby, 'cause that don't sound so dangerous."

The foursome ate a lunch of bananas and mangoes, washed down with pure well water that the Bahamians served in cups made of small scooped out gourds. Kid relaxed on a cot for a few minutes, trying to plan out the rest of his undertaking while he had a few quiet moments to think. His host had heard the aviator's intention and, while he thought it was a promising idea, he decided to add a word of caution.

"You better let me buy all your bottles for you, Enby. Listen to me, now. Let me do it, and you pay regular cost. But if you buy it yourself, Mr. Hartley know about Prohibition Law and he charge five time regular cost. Am I right or wrong, friend?"

"You're right, Mr. Man. But how do I know you can be trusted with cash if I give it to you?"

The Bahamian boy stood up from his chair, as if insulted, then shrugged and smiled to himself.

"'Cause you know Mr. Man be in trouble and ain't no way he gonna burn the only bridge he got out of this place."

"What you mean by that?"

"Nothing. You just take me to U.S.A. with you in your front seat and get me out of this place, and I gonna get you all the booze I can."

Kid arose from his formerly comfortable position on the cot and shook his head.

"Can't do that. I could fit fifty extra bottles back there in the space you'd take up."

"You no have the money for the fifty bottles if you buy at Hartley's price."

"And what will I do with you after we land? Or what will you do with yourself?"

"Live and be happy, man!"

Kid began shaking his head again.

"Why me? Maybe I should've just stayed at home and rode around on my damn motorsickle. . . . All right, I'll agree to let you do it. I know where you live even if I don't know what your name is. By the way, what is it?"

The tall thin Bahamian boy waved his finger back and forth teasingly in front of his American visitor.

"Ah, no, we not discussin' that till a later time. I'll let you be Mr. Excitement if you let me be Mr. Man."

Sammy and Charlie stayed at the hut while the two aspiring bootleggers refined their strategy. By one o'clock that afternoon they had ironed out all the wrinkles in their plan, and the four boys, three black and one white, had become good friends. The exertions of all four would be needed to help load rum bottles onto a truck at the storage facility. They all walked about two miles to a sprawling villa overlooking the Nassau harbor, and the aviator handed Mr. Man $500 of American money in cash and sat secretively behind a thicket of oleander. The Bahamian outlaw went up a stairway into the plush apartment where the business's main office was located while the two other boys waited outside on the balcony. A blond and bespectacled Englishman of about 35 looked up from his study when Mr. Man barged into the office.

"Mr. Hartley, I got some money for you today."

The Englishman, seated behind a large mahogany desk, put down his ink pen, removed his wire glasses from his thin ruddy nose, and looked earnestly at his youthful employee.

"What do you mean?"

"A great big order, sir."

Jeremy Hartley narrowed his eyes and rubbed his chin with the thumb and forefinger of his right hand.

"This doesn't have anything to do with the American situation, does it?"

"Oh, no, man. No, sir—no way." Mr. Man tried to smile as brightly as he could. "A local English family from right here in Nassau wants it."

"And which local family might that be? I think I've got a fair knowledge of most of them around here."

"They don't want me to say. You know, it could be dangerous now for people to know, so they ask me not to tell."

With every word Hartley was growing more and more suspicious, but he kept a straight face.

"How many bottles do they want?"

"One hundred and fifty!" the Bahamian proudly announced.

"Good God!" exclaimed Hartley. "What sort of family is this?"

"A very, very beeg family, sir," said Mr. Man. "Lots of brothers, lots of sisters, and lots of cousins, too."

Hartley shook his head and put the end of one of his eyeglass handles into his mouth while the teenage boy tried to smile but looked very uncomfortable in doing it.

"Did they give you cash?"

"Five hundred Uncle Sam greenbacks, man. No weak Bahamian dollars from them!"

"Let me see the money," demanded Hartley.

He examined the several bills, nodded, and gave a bill back to the deal's broker.

"For the 1912 stock . . . three dollars apiece times one hundred fifty is $450, and here's the *family's* change."

"Many thanks, sir. I got two town boys to help me load the truck."

"I'll go downstairs and watch," said Hartley. "And, for your sake, I hope at least some of what you're saying is true and this *family* of yours isn't really a syndicate from New York."

"Why certainly not, sir. They good honest folk from right here in Nassau."

Hartley smirked, though he said nothing more about it. He went down to the basement of the compound while Mr. Man backed up the company's delivery truck to the door and Sammy and Charlie waited to help. Mr. Hartley and the three others worked to count and load the bottles while Kid spied on them through the thicket. When the job was done the boys stayed on the bed of the truck while their friend drove it slowly forward and Mr. Hartley observed them skeptically. As soon as the vehicle was safely out of the proprietor's view, Mr. Man put on the brake and Milton Jr. ran ahead to jump in the passenger seat.

"Good work, Mr. Man."

"Here's fifty dollars back. See—" he pointed rhetorically at the aviator, "—I be an honest man. Now we gonna see if Mr. Enby Excitement an honest man too and if he carry me to U.S.A. in his aeroplane."

Kid took two $5 bills and handed one each to Sammy and Charlie as a reward for their help. It was more money than either had ever made in a whole week, to say nothing of a single day. Now that they had secured their precious cargo, next in the order of business would be refueling the DH-4. To wait until they loaded the machine with contraband before they refilled its gas tank would be unwise. Mr. Man said an Englishman usually stood watch over the landing strip and was likely to be there later in the day. And indeed after Mr. Man parked the delivery truck near the orange grove and the foursome slid through the bamboo thicket to return to Kid's DH-4, the Englishman was there, looking admiringly at Kid's plane. He was fingering its cloth and studying the same olive drab regalia that had served the mother country over the fields of France. Milt quickly retreated back into the recesses of the thicket.

"We gotta get him out of the way, boys. If he's English he'll know who I am and we're cooked."

Sammy and Charlie darted out of the thicket and diverted the Englishman with a fantastic story about a buxom American tourist girl who, they claimed, was sunbathing nude on a nearby rooftop. The Bahamian boys told the Englishman that if he would come with them to the other side of the orange grove, he still had a chance to witness this delicious sight. In his haste to witness this spectacle, the Englishman disappeared completely while Kid and Mr. Man pushed the biplane to the cistern on the edge of the dirt strip and pumped enough gas into it to get it back to Florida. Then they ran back to the truck a few hundred feet away, drove it onto the landing strip and worked feverishly to cram bottles into every nook and cranny of the plane.

Eventually Kid told his friend to sit in the front cockpit and stacked bottles on top of his legs. He knew this would be uncomfortable, but it was the only way he could devise to haul both the rum and the stowaway back with him. At the rate of over one pound per bottle, he feared that with his extra passenger and his own 195 pounds he might exceed the plane's quarter-ton load capacity and have trouble getting off the ground. If so, he would be forced to throw rum bottles out until he was light enough to fly.

Milt had just finished stacking the last rum bottle on top of his stowaway's lap when Sammy and Charlie came back. The boys shrugged as if to say they had done all they could but the Englishman's credulity was nearing its limit. The watchman was still back there on the far side of the citrus grove, pining in vain for the arousing vista he had been promised. The boys had actually done a superb job; the aviator was ready to take off now. He gave the boys the A-OK sign and pointed to the truck. It was their job to return it to Hartley's. Kid put on his helmet and goggles and placed his nimble hands on his propellor blade to whirl it into motion. He paused and looked at his anonymous helpmate in the front seat one last time.

"Why don't you finally give in and tell me your name?"

"You ain't told me yours, neither."

"Yeah, but somebody's gotta be the first to tell the truth, and it's gonna be you."

Mr. Man's eyes flitted nervously back and forth. He kept looking at the old yellowed newspapers the aviator had spread over the rum bottles to prevent oil and gasoline from getting splattered all over them. On the front page of one of the back issues of *The Atlanta Georgian*, the Bahamian boy, who was proud of his literacy with many of his friends unable to read, noticed a boldfaced headline: WILSON RESPONDS TO ALLIES. He glanced jocularly back up at his new friend.

"Woodrow," he said. "My name is Woodrow."

"Woodrow who?" asked Kid.

"*Woodrow Wilson*," the boy answered, trying to keep a straight face.

"That's not your name," Kid grimaced. "That's the President's name. You read that off that newspaper back there. I met the guy one time and, believe me, you don't look a damn thing like him."

"See there, you lyin' too. You expect me to believe you met the President when you down here smugglin' booze? No way."

"Sure, there's a way. In America we say: 'Oh, how the mighty have fallen!' Well, I ain't sure I was ever mighty, but I sure have fallen."

"You mean you really met President Wilson, Enby?"

"I swear I did. Now lemme hear you swear your name's really the same as his."

The Bahamian fugitive laughed.

"It is now."

Milt shook his head and repositioned his goggles.

"All right. At least you answered. I'll call you Woody—I like that better than Woodrow."

"That's fine. People call me Woody all the time."

"Right. And people call me Mr. Excitement all the time, too. You must have really done something terrible. You didn't murder anyone, did you?"

"No, man. Not me."

"You didn't steal or rob anything?"

"No, sir, I didn't do that, either."

"Got a girl with child and now you're bailing out on her, are you?"

"Thank God I am not, sir."

"Then what is it? What've you ever done to get to be such an outlaw?"

Woody paused a few seconds, deliberating whether he should divulge his heinous secrets, then he took a deep breath.

"I been sellin' booze to bootleggers from U.S.A. all year, and I ain't paid a penny in taxes to the government."

Kid grinned and again put his hands on his propellor blade to spin it started.

"That's bad, Woody. Real bad."

"The worst, man. Sometimes they don't get you if you kill. But if you don't pay your taxes, they always get you."

"Don't worry," said Kid, "it's real easy to hide in the U.S.A. And you won't be the first feller who tried to do it, either."

He hurled the propellor twice before it sputtered and coughed then came to roaring, deafening life. The plane lumbered across the barren brown tropical field by itself until Kid ran and hopped up on the footrest on the lower wing, dove into the flying seat, and positioned himself behind the controls. Turning stoically to straighten himself in his seat, he put his engine at full throttle and held his breath in the hope that his plan would work and his escape would be successful. He had just enough thrust to overcome the drag, and his biplane rose into the hot sky, leaving the green shores of the Bahamas to glisten in the sun.

CHAPTER 20

The Most Honest Dishonest Man

BY NIGHTFALL THE RENEGADE DH-4 was within sight of Palm Beach and Kid landed on the very same field he had left that morning. Since he had a far more precarious load this time he took special pains to come down smoothly to avoid smashing either his cargo or his passenger. The American bootlegger left Woody behind to guard the plane while he walked into town and bought the two of them a boxed dinner of chicken and dumplings and pork and beans. They ate in the moonlight when he came back. Milt thought it would be too risky to leave all of his contraband freight unattended overnight, so he and Woody slept coolly and serenely in the grass next to the deserted airfield.

They refueled in West Palm Beach the next morning and again in Jacksonville at noon. By the end of the afternoon Kid was taxiing on the familiar grounds of the Hapeville racetrack after another landing so smooth that not a single rum bottle cracked. He was skilled, but he had also been lucky, for in 800 miles from Nassau to Atlanta he had barely met a gust of wind and had seen almost no clouds. Chester Dawes and Robert Brackens, the two primary beneficiaries of his mission, had been brimming with anticipation for three days. When they heard the familiar rumble of their plane overhead they bounced out of the empty grandstands and ran out into the middle of the racetrack to follow its steadily downward course. They knew as soon as he landed that their friend had delivered grandly on his promise.

"*Holy shit!*" cried Bobby Brackens. "Ain't there nothin' you can't do?"

"Nope," said Kid. "Sure ain't."

"Who's the colored boy?" wondered Chet Dawes.

"That's Woody. He come from Nassau with me. I tell you, he can bootleg with the best of 'em, Woody can. Y'all oughtta be grateful to this here colored boy, 'cause he's gonna make y'all rich again."

The Hapeville boys introduced themselves to Mr. Wilson, who was squirming in discomfort. He had been sitting in a cramped position for hours underneath a pile of rum bottles, and he needed to stretch his limbs, walk and renew his circulation.

"Enby, let me down now so I can breathe again."

"What'd he call you?" asked Chet.

"Why, he just called me by my initials, you know. N.B., short for Nothing But."

Kid jumped down from his flying seat and went over to poke Dawes in the ribs.

"Nothing But what?" wondered Chet.

"*Nothing But Excitement.*"

Brackens launched a stream of tobacco juice down at Kid's feet.

"You're a son of a bitch," he grunted.

"I know it," said Kid.

Milt carefully removed about two dozen rum bottles from the rear cockpit of the DeHavilland and helped his friend stagger out of his seat and to the ground. Chet went over to the stowaway and confided in him.

"Woody, your friend there ain't no normal aeroplane flyer. Don't you got any idea who this man is?"

"Not at all," snapped Woody. "He ain't told me nothin' 'bout who he really is."

"Well, you've been smuggled over here by none other than Mr. Raymond Milton 'Kid' Harrison, my friend: the Great Ace of the Great War!"

Woody's eyes widened with the astonishment of a man who believed he had looked directly into the eyes of the Deity.

"That CAN'T be," said Woody. "Why, what's HE doin' runnin' booze?"

"Times are tough," said Chet. "And he don't think it's any different from fighting the Heinies over in Europe. He wants all of us to be free."

"So it's true he really met President Wilson?"

"You're damn right it is," Brackens swore. "The old feller got down on his hands and knees beggin' Kid to come to dinner at the White House."

Woody walked over to the famed aviator who had given him a free and illegal passport to America. Kid responded with one of his characteristic eye-winks and accepted a handshake from him.

"Congratulations, sir," said Woody. "You are a great man. But I rather call you Enby. That don't make me so nervous."

MILT HAD LEFT HIS Duesenberg in his friends' hangar. Later on, he drove the motorcar out to his heavily laden plane, crammed it full of rum bottles, covered the cache with several burlap sacks to keep any authorities from observing the contraband through his car windows, and drove home to Ansley Park. The problem of what to do with Woody was soon resolved when Kid decided his big house needed a caretaker during his long absences. The Bahamian heard the news in the car's passenger seat as they bore their treasure trove through the middle of Atlanta under cover of darkness.

"I'll pay you five bucks a week to tend my house, Woody. I'll fix up a room for you in the cellar. That fair enough?"

"You very generous, Enby. That's a lot of money."

"There's one condition. If I ever have any lady friends over I want you to stay in the basement."

"Sure thing, man. Them ladies, they like they privacy. 'Specially when they doin' something with a man."

"Also, if somebody ever breaks into my house looking for my booze I want you to knock the piss out of him. Think you can do that?"

"Hey, man. Look at these muscles, Mr. Excitement. Well, maybe not so big, but no ounce of fat on my body. I work in the hot sun since I little. I can be a very mean man if I want."

"So you're good at everything?"

"Everything! That's right, Enby. You said it best. You want me to protect your property, I do that. You want me to cook—hey, my sauces are the best. You want laughter and talk—hey, I know how to say the funny or the wise thing. You want me to fix engine on car or aeroplane—hey, I took course in mechanics at school in Nassau."

"Well, I know you're good at telling stories, Woody, so I guess you've got the job."

Shortly thereafter, the man from Woodvale began to forge contacts in the realm of organized crime. For two weeks after his return from his first run to the Bahamas he combed Atlanta for establishments which might be willing to buy his rum. They were fairly easy to find, despite the Prohibition Law, and at Kid's favorite jazz club in town, The Spinning Jack on Peachtree Street, the booze was still flowing rather freely. But much of it was corn liquor, bitter homemade brews and wine so poor it bordered on vinegar. For his dark, rich authentic Caribbean rum the renegade pilot was expecting a premium price, especially since he figured the speakeasies would all water it down to half its normal strength and still fool customers who were getting used to moonshine.

Milt negotiated in secret with two unseemly mobsters who had gained control of Atlanta's bootlegging business, Mr. Thomas "Ziggy" Cicerello and Mr. Joseph "Nails" Scanini, and they finally settled on a price of $15 a bottle for thirty bottles—an astronomical figure possible only in a black market. Delivery was to be made in person at 9PM Friday August 1 behind the club, at which time Ziggy would examine the bottles, randomly sample the contents of at least one, and, if it proved genuine, tender the cash to Kid.

At nine o'clock sharp that evening Kid's shadowy form emerged from his Duesenberg in the back alley of The Spinning Jack. Brass horns and deep bass fiddles were resonating through the brick walls of the nightclub, and occasionally the bootlegger could hear the singing voices of the scantily clad women that he knew were inside. After a few seconds the dark hulking shape of a man slipped out of a rear door.

"You show me you got the cash," said Kid, "and I'll show you I got the rum."

Ziggy Cicerello pulled out a wad of $100 bills, counted to four and then added a single $50 bill. Milt retreated to his car and pulled out two stacks of rum bottles. He suspected he was being watched, probably by a man with a gun, but he feared little for his safety inasmuch as he knew the men were counting on him to provide more genuine spirits for them in the future and needed to keep him alive for that purpose. The mobster opened one of the bottles, pulled a glass goblet out of his pocket, and filled it from the bottle. He held it up to the light from a nearby streetlamp and drank from it. As soon as the mouthful was gulped down he rattled his head back and forth as if to shake loose rocks out of his ears.

"Whew, Mr. Excitement! You weren't kidding when you said you got that at the source, were you?"

"I'm the most honest dishonest man you'll ever meet, Ziggy," said Kid, taking the roll of money into his hand.

In only a few days Major Harrison had distributed all 150 of his smuggled rum bottles to speakeasies all over Atlanta that had sprouted up like toadstools since January. After taking all his expenses into account he calculated that he had made almost $2000 from an enterprise that involved three days of pleasurable flying and a few hours of offshore and domestic haggling. This exceeded his wages for the entire first year of his military service in Europe, during which time he had amassed more combat kills than any other flyer in his squadron and his life had been in constant mortal jeopardy.

It struck him as bitterly ironic that breaking the government's laws in a fun lark was ten times more profitable than risking life and limb to defend them in a miserable cycle of violence. And he was not alone in his thinking. As a new decade dawned, the feeling spread to much of the general populace that life was too short not to be enjoyed to its fullest; that parties and dancing and drink rather than wars and peace treaties were the cure-alls for what ailed the world.

Suddenly the dark cloud of idleness and poverty that had been hovering over the Hapeville racetrack was temporarily blown away from its skies. Money began flowing copiously into the pockets of Mr. Dawes and Mr. Brackens from a mysterious source. All around Atlanta now there was laughter and spirits and people were having a good time again. Alcohol was everywhere, and nobody seemed to know from whence it was originating.

By the end of 1919 Bobby and Chet each lived in fancy houses over in the well-to-do section of Hapeville, nestled among woodsy hills and babbling brooks. But where was Kid? He was apparently on a sabbatical of some kind and he wasn't seen participating in the air exhibitions that Chet and Bobby were staging in 1920 and 1921. The truth was that he was making one or two runs a month to a tropical island somewhere to confiscate its booze and return home to a life of anonymous profit. Though he never quite ran the Bahamas dry, he became dangerously familiar in those islands, so he had to expand his operations to Cuba and Jamaica by 1921. The law was still blind to his machinations; Mr. N.B. Excitement proved to be the most elusive bootlegger of them all.

HE MIGHT HAVE REMAINED a bootlegger for some time to come—might have grown so complacent with his illicit success in the endeavor that he never tried another new adventure—if not for an accident that befell him in the summer of '21. He was headed for Jamaica on that occasion in the old reliable DH-4. As the light of dawn bathed the familiar racetrack at Candler Field he took off for the tropics yet again. There was nothing to suggest that this would be any different from the three dozen other trips he had made with the same objective. Well-rested, strong and familiar with the territory, he was confident that he would journey 1200 miles that day and land at Montego Bay. So comfortable had the aviator become that he had begun to take for granted that events would fall into place—an unforgivable sin in the fledgling occupation that had consumed most of the energies of his young adult life.

An hour and a half south of Atlanta, while he daydreamed with the world spread out beneath him, his plane's Liberty engine began to cough and sputter. He shook himself out of his stupor and leaned his head out of the cockpit. Nothing seemed out of order, but when he ducked back into his cubbyhole he heard a terrifying explosion from the engine compartment in the front. Hoisting himself up over the instrument panel, he saw the engine in flames.

For the first time in nearly three years, the main events of his life flashed through his mind with the desperation of what seemed the final moments of his time in this world. How many times had he nearly died before—twenty, thirty, a hundred? Yet this might really be the end. The end would surely come some day, and was this to be the way he would leave the world, going to smuggle liquor from a far-off place? In the two seconds that he had to spare to think of anything other than self-preservation, he felt shame. One way or another, he was finished with bootlegging. But he burned to live, and the fire that raged in his heart now took command of him in his fight with the fire that was engulfing his machine.

Caution had no place in such a dire spot. Milt was about eight thousand feet above the ground and he decided he had enough altitude to put the DH into a dive to try to blow out the engine fire. He glanced anxiously down below, noticing the brown serpentine course of what he figured to be the Alapaha River near the town of Tifton. In his civilian flying he never wore a parachute, so bailing out was impossible. He would aim his dive for the river so that, in case the fire continued and he had to jump, the plane would land in water and its explosion might be buffered enough to be kept away from him wherever in the water he happened to dive. Perhaps if the impact of the water didn't kill him he might be spared complete destruction by flames. A few seconds of the lightning-quick thought his profession required had once again given Kid hope to survive what seemed unsurvivable.

He steeled his nerves and put the biplane into an almost directly vertical nosedive while he worked frantically to try to cut off the flow of gas to the engine. He was descending now with terrific force, black smoke was pouring from the engine, and he was unsure how far above the earth he still was. A fatal crash was a certainty unless he either jumped and landed in the river or the fire blew out. By his estimate he still had about twenty seconds before the plane would strike the ground.

Kid was by this point nearly blinded by the acrid black plumes of smoke. But when his count reached ten he noticed the smoke clearing. In three more seconds it was gone and his nerves relaxed in the blessed relief of another eleventh-hour reprieve. His bizarre hunch had been right! His furious dive had blown out the fire! Still, he was so close to the ground that he might not have enough air left to straighten his machine for a smooth landing. He was on a downward glide with a dead engine, the crosswinds were fierce, and his wings were tilting badly. He steered his plane away from the Alapaha River, since he had no more need of water to drown out an engine fire and buffer a crash. This was flat cotton-farming territory, and a cotton field appeared to be his only place to land.

Unfortunately, the winds were swirling too violently for Milt to turn his wings parallel to the horizon and the lower right wing struck the ground, jolted his head forward and collapsed as the plane crashed and rolled over on its side. Because his airplane, like all others of its time, had no brakes Milt had been powerless to stop his momentum. His head had been jerked back and forth in a whiplash injury. But the plane, its fuel supply having been cut off, did not catch fire; and the aviator, though injured, had survived.

He lay semiconscious on his side in severe pain, unable to move himself out of the wreckage though lucid enough to wonder how he would ever recover from this with no one to help him. Only a minute or two later a pair of farm laborers carrying bamboo poles who had been on their way to their favorite fishing hole rushed to the side of the wrecked plane.

"God have mercy!" cried one, seeing the lame and nearly lifeless victim, "the man looks dead!"

"He ain't dead," said another, "but 'less we get him outta there right quick he gonna be, and real soon too."

The two of them tried to pull the helpless pilot from the pile of rubble but he yelled out loudly when they touched his shoulder.

"What's wrong?"

"My shoulder's busted up," Kid groaned, "and my neck feels like it's been snapped in two."

"You need a shot from a doctor?"

"Shoot, they ain't a shot from no doctor can fix this problem. What I need's a brand new body."

"How'd it happen?"

"My engine caught fire."

The two would-be rescuers stood up in confusion, not knowing what to do next.

"I reckon we better leave him alone till the doctor git here," said the bigger of the two. "We'd be just as good at killin' this boy as gittin' him well again, 'cause we don't know what the hell we doin'."

"That's all we can do," said the other. "Just stand here and watch this man suffer. Gosh, mister, I'm sorry we can't do nothin' to make the pain go away."

"That's all right," said Kid. "Y'all are still savin' my life by gettin' me a doctor."

"One thing I know for sure," said the first man. "Them aeroplanes is way, way too dang'rous."

A physician from Tifton was eventually summoned to the scene, and after administering a shot of morphine he extricated the fallen pilot from his wreckage. Kid gave each of the two farmhands a $20 bill for helping him, and they were both so happy that they put their fishing poles up and went home. Diagnosed with a broken clavicle, a separated shoulder, and three cracked ribs, Kid was taken to a local clinic, where his shoulder was set back into place and wrapped and he was given a neck brace. Though there was no hospital nearby, the bootlegger claimed one wasn't necessary. With his intense pain deadened by morphine he insisted he was better and spent that night in a Tifton hotel.

The next morning, a local wrecker drove with him to the crash site and towed the remains of the biplane to a nearby junkyard. There it would begin its new life as a permanent scrap heap, monument to the latest civilian scheme hatched by the restless mind of the returned war veteran.

MILT HAD ALREADY SET both Chet and Bobby up in fine fashion and helped to reverse their fortunes, so they were unconcerned when they saw him hobble off the train at the Hapeville depot. In fact, they found the situation amusing.

"One of these days," Chet laughed, "you'll do something so damn stupid even you can't pull yourself out of it."

"When you reckon that'll be?"

"Might be the next time you try to outfox the feds."

"There won't be no next time. It's time I tried something different."

"Like what?" wondered Bobby.

"Like what we were gonna do before I come up with my plan to run booze. Passenger hopping. I still say I'll pull in $20 a head."

"You're dreamin'," said Bobby. "People don't remember you now. You been in hidin' so long you done let the world pass you by."

"The world won't ever pass me by," said Kid. "You can't pass what you can't catch—and this world still can't keep up to speed with me."

Kid brushed off the notion that anything was wrong with him and he bluffed his way around the suspicions of the Hapeville boys, but he was actually in terrible pain. He hired a taxicab to take him to his house and sent Woody down to retrieve his car. For the next day he tried to recover at home but the pain in his shoulder worsened. Woody kept nagging at him to go see a doctor but met with resistance. The fortunate arrival of a visitor by the middle of that afternoon brought about a different result.

"Enby," Woody called out to his suffering friend, who was lying flat on his back in his bed, "there's a man out in front come to see you. He say his name is George. You know him?"

"Tell him I'm asleep."

"No way. I ain't sayin' that. I'm lettin' him in here and he gonna tell you what I been sayin'. You need to see a doctor right now."

George Grantland, the all-knowing gadfly who had managed to buzz himself between a few whispered rumors and the truth about Kid's activities during the last two years, entered the well-appointed villa, hat in hand. He had finally set his sights on a political office that he had a chance of winning: city alderman from the Ninth Ward. At 32, he was starting to feel seasoned enough to take the plunge into the muck of urban politics. A surefire way of getting elected, in his view, was to promise to sweep the city clean of the meddlesome speakeasies and their attendant train of New York mobsters. Another wild-eyed vision of his, born of the success and fame of the very man he was now visiting, was to make Atlanta, Georgia the aviation capital of the world. He knew Milt would be instrumental in the latter pursuit, and if his sources were speaking the truth he also believed Kid would help him achieve the former goal too. Woody showed him into the room where the lame aviator was sweating in discomfort.

"How you doin', Major?" came the familiar honeyed drawl. Milt leaned up as if to rise to his feet to greet the visitor, as every Woodvalean had been taught from birth to do when even an unwanted guest entered a room, but Mr. Grantland waved him back. "Keep your place there—you're not well, I hear."

"That's an understatement, George. You got any painkillers with you?"

"I sure don't. But I know somebody who does: Dr. Parkhurst, your daddy's old friend. You can't go on like this, Kid. Maybe you don't trust doctors because of what happened to your daddy, but you've gotta let up this time."

Milt wiped the perspiration off his forehead with his hands as George seated himself at his bedside.

"Is that why you came here? To baby me and tell me what I need to do?"

"I can't tell you what to do. It's your life. But I've been hearin' stories about what you've been doing lately. Never mind from who. I just think you're too good to end up like this."

"George, I'm doin' what I think is right."

"Maybe your way isn't the only way, Major. There are a lot of people out there who care about you. You can do good or you can do evil in this world."

"I done my share of what the world calls good."

"And that didn't quite turn out like we wanted it to. Now the Germans are raising a ruckus again over that peace treaty they signed and nobody's happy over there. But you had nothing to do with that. You did what you could and you stuck your neck out for what seemed right and necessary at the time. Kid, I don't know if you have it in you to do that now."

"What, fight in a war again?"

"No, not that kind of war. It's the war between right and wrong. Sometimes it's lots easier and a feller can gets lots richer by fighting for wrong."

"Did I miss something, Georgie? Did you sign up with the clergy and learn how to give sermons?"

"Kid, I'm lookin' out for myself and I need your help. I want to get elected to office and promise to build Atlanta an airport, and what you say goes in this town. I think it would be a good thing for you, me and everybody else if you used your talents wisely."

"All right, George, I get your point. I was thinkin' along those same lines myself."

George Grantland stood up and patted his friend on the hand.

"Good, I figured you'd listen to reason. . . . Oh, and Milt, there's another thing I wanted to suggest to you."

"What is it?"

"Mrs. Warner—Jasmine, that is—just had a beautiful baby girl, and I know she'd be proud of showing that baby off to you. I know y'all haven't talked since she got married, but it sure would be a nice gentlemanly thing to do if you went to see her now. You know, she had two miscarriages and I thought we'd lose her the last time. Here, I'll write her address for you and tell her you're coming."

Though he rarely took any advice from anyone and usually turned a deaf ear to do-gooders and moral uplifters, Milt considered George's advice and he took it to heart. Breaking the law was easy, but what did it prove? The world was not as good as it was capable of being and he had more abilities than most to make it better. He felt tired and weary of trying to fulfill the expectations of society, but what was he, twenty-four years old? There was really no excuse for weariness and fatigue in a man still a month shy of his twenty-fifth birthday. And Jasmine—well, he knew she still loved him, would always love him, would never look at her husband or any other man except in comparison to him. If it bothered him that events between them had happened as they did, then what must she have felt? She was trapped. And two miscarriages, no less. That was news to him. He really did feel an obligation to go see her now. Even the part about Dr. Parkhurst rang true to him, for it was an undeniable fact that he was in agony and needed more morphine.

The doctor was glad to see his late acquaintance's son, expressed his admiration for what the aviator had been able to accomplish, and inquired about what he had been doing lately. He had been flying planes to Florida and bringing back cargo, or so he said. After another injection had deadened his pain Milt felt comfortable again. With his right arm in a sling and his neck in a brace, he told Woody to drive him to the residence at 21 Euclid Avenue, where Mrs. Warner, *née* Peace, was recuperating from the birth of her new daughter, Estelle.

The neighborhood of Inman Park, where the house was located, was dominated by the elephantine wooden mansions of the city's moguls of finance and industry. No gable was too pointed nor was any color of paint too garish to adorn a palace in those precincts. Her house was purple with a wide white-railed veranda in the front, a semicircular macadamized driveway and a wrought iron gate enclosing the compound. It must have had, in the casual estimation of the new visitor, no fewer than twenty rooms. A Negro butler met the Duesenberg by the front portico and escorted Milt into the home.

She lay on a couch in the Byzantine main parlor with her infant's cradle at her side—or at least he thought she did. The woman there scarcely resembled the one whom he remembered from years before. She appeared at least fifteen years older than when he had last seen her in December of 1918 upon his return home from Europe. Her skin was wrinkled, her hair was graying, and, even disregarding the normal bodily changes of pregnancy, she had gained an enormous amount of weight and her figure was sagging. And, worst of all, when she smiled at him he noticed that her teeth were stained brown. An ashtray on the coffee table by the sofa revealed the cause; it was filled with cigarette butts from the woman who had now turned into a chain smoker.

Not only were her teeth discolored and her eyes bloodshot, but her pretty voice, which had formerly had the cadence of a singing bluebird, now sounded coarse and husky. The stench of tobacco and bootlegged gin impregnated the room. It was miserable for him to see the condition into which the formerly ravishing beauty, not yet thirty, had deteriorated with such astounding rapidity. Worse yet was the thought of the innocent baby who occupied the cradle. She had been ushered into this madness. He felt a genuinely selfless love for the little baby, even though he had never even seen her yet.

"Milt!" her mother cried, "How nice of you to come!"

They hugged and he kissed her on the cheek. He leaned down and pulled back the lacy blanket that had been swaddling the sleeping infant. She had a full head of black hair, cherubic features, and dainty little hands. His next act, by a natural impulse, was to plant a kiss on the child's warm forehead.

"Congratulations, darlin'," her mother heard the man she adored say to her. "That's the most beautiful sight I ever saw in my life."

Jasmine broke into tears and for the next minute or so she and the man she loved were locked in a gentle, silent embrace, he using his one good arm to hug her and she trying to control her fervor so as not to wrench his injured extremities. Words would have been insufficient to convey all the joy and pain of the occasion, and none passed between them for awhile.

"What happened to you?" she asked to break the silence, referring to his sling and bandages.

"I still fly planes, and sometimes they still bite back."

A sparkle returned to her eye, the only hint he had yet gotten of her former charm and vitality. The question he wanted to ask her, but never did, was the same as that which she had just posed to him. *What happened to you?* But there was no point in posing it, for he knew the answer already.

"Where's your husband?"

"He's at a board meeting for his bank. He spends a lot of time away on business."

"I see he's fixed you up pretty good. You got a castle all to yourself."

"There's one room that's my favorite. Over here across the way. Come with me and let's go look at it while Estelle's still asleep."

She took him by his one free hand and they went through the main corridor past one plushly furnished room after another, until they reached the library. It had oaken shelves of hundreds of old, bound, never-read volumes and several vintage pieces of colonial furniture. But its most distinguishing features were the oil paintings that adorned its walls. All her own work, they depicted Milt in his airplanes in real or imagined situations. Some revealed his clearly recognizable face, and others were of the planes that she had seen him fly or read about. In the largest painting a red Fokker triplane with black Maltese crosses was shown in the beginning of a tailspin, beneath an olive-green Spad with a white star. This room was her shrine to him.

"You've got a great talent, Jasmine, you know that? You still paint?"

Her head lowered and her face grew sad again.

"Not any more. That was another time in my life. It seems . . . so long ago. I come here to remember."

"What does your husband think of this room?"

"It's his favorite room, too. I told him you gave me a ride in your plane back when you were a just a teenager, but he didn't believe me. *He doesn't think I ever even met you.* He comes in here to dream, too, but never with me."

"Dream? What does he dream about?"

"About flying away and being alone and being the first to do something. About being a 'kid' again!"

With every new statement that came from her lips, the situation was getting more difficult for him to accept. She squeezed him by the one free hand again and looked at him with a wide-eyed earnestness.

"Some day," she continued, "when my daughter gets older, I'll tell her all about these pictures. She'll feel the same way."

"You think she'll have any idea what all this is about?"

"She'll know as much about it as I do."

When he left Mrs. Warner a few minutes later she returned to her recumbent position on the sofa, lit up another cigarette and cried. Milt was scarcely any happier. He was feeling like a soiled piece of cloth that had several times in recent days been sent through a wringer. This latest turn had wrung him dry. He was ashamed that people had been admiring pictures of him on their walls while he had been busy trooping with organized criminals, however silly and spurious the crime off of which they were profiting. And he was regretting the twists of fate that had made him too foolish to bind himself to this woman when she had been ready for him, and her too old to wait for that distant point in the future, if it ever did come, when monogamy might finally have suited him.

Was there no higher calling for him in peacetime? Indeed there was. He had heard it from the mouth of George Grantland. His wings were just as capable of lifting up humanity as of shooting it down. The kid in Jasmine's paintings was still alive and still flying, and he wanted to believe that his best days were yet to come.

CHAPTER 21

Kiss the Weevils Good-bye

THE MAN FROM WOODVALE spent another week recovering from his latest near-fatal crash, and then at just the time when he was ready to embark on a new course in life he received an opportune telegram from the backwoods of northern Louisiana.

> 23SEPT1921
>
> MAJOR HARRISON WE HAVE FINALLY SECURED OTHER INVESTORS FOR OUR OPERATION IN LA STOP NEED YOUR PRESENCE HERE NOW TO DEMONSTRATE OUR IDEA STOP YOUR NAME WILL HELP US SECURE STILL MORE CAPITAL STOP WEEVILS ARE OUT NOW AND TIME IS RIGHT STOP RSVP STOP SINCERELY BONDERMAN & REED

It had been a long while, months perhaps, since Kid had given any thought whatsoever to the fledgling operation in Louisiana to which he had committed his financial support. However, in his current philanthropic frame of mind, he was eager to commit additional energy to the project. If the aim of his life had suddenly become to profit from making the world better instead of worse, then trying to eliminate an agricultural pest that was starving thousands of dirt farmers to near death was now an urgent mission.

Early the next morning he was on the westbound train to Birmingham, Jackson, Vicksburg and ultimately Tallulah. His trunk was packed with fine clean clothes, his face closely shaven, the galluses holding up his trousers taut on his freshly ironed and starched white shirt, and he was wearing a flowing bowtie around his collar. He was expecting and hoping for this to be his first totally harmless endeavor—no killing, no blowing up factories, no chasing after loose women, no rum-running, no showing off in a biplane for the sake of vanity. It would be a new approach to life—but would it be exciting?

Late the next afternoon he emerged from the train at the depot in Tallulah. There stood Aloysius Troy and Trevor, the tall trim Hoosier and the squat Southern scholar, to greet him.

"We couldn't be happier to have you down here, Kid," said Mr. Bonderman, giving him a rock hard handshake.

"How you doing?" Dr. Reed greeted him.

"Tomorrow," said A.T., "we're having a big demonstration on the Tallulah town square. The word's circulated through three or four parishes that you'll be there, Kid, and we're expecting a mob of farmers."

"They're just coming to see you," added Trevor. "They've heard so many broken promises before, they wouldn't bat an eye for us."

"I don't break no promises," said Kid. "What I say, I do."

Milt enjoyed a quiet night in the same ostentatious little hotel where he had stayed before, and after breakfast the next day the two entomologists were parked in front of the lobby ready to chauffeur Major Harrison in grand style three blocks away to the town square. A thousand farmers were there assembled, as if on a pilgrimage to see a prophet who might cure the sick and heal the lame. The plague of the boll weevil had affected their way of life just as the plague of leprosy had affected the peasants of Judea two millennia earlier, and Major Harrison, the slayer of the Hun military machine, was as close to a savior as any of these common folk thought they would ever see.

When Kid emerged from the car there was a flourish of applause from men in overalls and straw hats, waves from plump women carrying pale thin babies in their arms, and the usual screams from adolescent girls. With A.T. and Trevor on either side of him, the aviator was escorted up the steps of a podium, next to the mayor of Tallulah, the head of the local Elks club, the state representative, and four newspaper reporters. One poor farmer, gaunt, old, toothless and in threadbare overalls, was desperate to speak to the war ace. He came to the edge of the podium and said something that was drowned out by the roar of the crowd. Kid waved them quiet and then the man's plaintive voice could be heard by all.

"If you could kill them long-billed insects, sir, it'd save us. They're gonna ruin us for sure."

Kid leaned down and shook the man's hand.

"Sir, be patient. I'm gonna kill 'em. In a few minutes we're goin' out to a cotton field near the little Tallulah air strip, and I want all y'all to come and watch. I'm gonna spray poison on the bugs and save all the cotton plants."

The crowd applauded and closed in on the guest of honor. After a little bit of pressing the flesh and autograph-signing the air hero was ushered back into the motorcar and taken away. It was less than a two mile walk from the town square to the tiny airport, and in a mass migration the downtrodden farm families, some of them without shoes, followed the Oldsmobile on foot to the field.

Before the crowd had arrived on the site Mr. Bonderman and Mr. Reed were showing their visitor from Georgia what his investment now amounted to. Instead of the dilapidated and sagging old Jenny in which he had first demonstrated the possibilities of dusting, they had procured a seemingly factory-fresh Jenny trainer from the U.S. Army that appeared to be in mint condition. And the aviator's makeshift bit of carpentry, the hopper made of two-by-four pine planks and burlap sacks, had been replaced by a specially manufactured one with a steel frame, aluminum mesh, and a lever-activated chute that could be open and shut from the flying seat.

"I see y'all are tryin' to make things easy on me, A.T.," Kid remarked. He was examining the underside of the plane, on which the steel dispenser of calcium arsenate had already been mounted. "And y'all filled 'er with the dust, too."

"That stuff's awful powerful," said Trevor. "One whiff of that and the weevils 'll hightail it down to Mexico."

"Ain't the weevils already eaten up this field, yet?"

"Not this one," said A.T. "We've been hiring sharecroppers to put it out by hand this summer, until we could finally get ahold of you. You left us with just enough cash to buy this new equipment and pay their wages."

"So now what? What happens when I put all this stuff out today?"

"In all honesty," said A.T., "I hope it's a revolution."

Kid propped his arm on the side of the Jenny's fuselage, waiting for the crowd to come, and yawned.

"Well, what are we callin' this new trick we done invented, gentlemen?"

"Crop-dusting. That's the term Dr. Reed and I coined for it."

Milt laughed aloud.

"Crop-dusting. Half of Looziana's about to be entertained by watching me dump poisoned dust on bugs with an aeroplane. Ain't y'all a bit short of things to do around here?"

"It's no laughing matter," said Trevor. "We've put ten years of our lives into this—we'll either sink or swim by it."

By noontime the full crowd had gathered by the dirt strip and the cotton field; the morning dew had dried from the cotton plants and the time was right for the demonstration. The aerial virtuoso, having donned the leather helmet and flying goggles he had brought in his trunk from home, heaved his flying machine into motion. In a matter of seconds the populace was amazed. With every flourish of Kid's flying machine white dust rained down over the sprigs of cotton, bathing them in the insect-killing poison that the two entomologists had developed in their laboratories.

From his seat high in the hot sunny sky he saw the crowd of desperate people in white shirt sleeves, overalls, straw hats and suspenders, shading their eyes from the sun on the edge of the field. Spreading the dust was such a ridiculously easy task for him that he felt a little guilty about absorbing their attention with such a small part of his talent. So when all the calcium arsenate had been dumped from his hopper, he looped his Jenny into the heavens, put it into a treacherous dive, swung it back to the horizontal position and glided down gracefully back to the landing strip. The crowd's silent admiration turned boisterous with the aviator's unnecessary bit of acrobatic showmanship, and they hooted and whistled in gratitude when he taxied over to them, cut his engine off and jumped out of his seat.

"Ladies and gentlemen," Kid's voice thundered, "y'all can kiss them weevils good-bye!"

Dozens of girls were sighing at the ruggedly handsome young savior, and farm gentlemen, chomping down on corncob pipes and hand-rolled cigars with toothless gums, clapped and shouted. A.T. and Trevor were several hundred feet away by the gas pump, unnoticed by the populace. That was just as they had wanted it to be. Milt obliged several of the ladies, gave them his cheeks to kiss and his shoulders to hug. He gestured over to the two agricultural agents, who were walking enthusiastically back in the crowd's direction.

"Y'all can thank Dr. Reed and Mr. A.T. Bonderman for this. It was their idea. I just volunteered to help out."

The two scientists finally received due recognition from the people and the reporters on hand. The reporters. They were important here. Potential investors might read the accounts of this and contribute to the operation. Aloysius Troy was considering how this would play in the papers and he was figuring it would be headlines in the daily tribunes of the one-horse towns of the region. Kid Kills Boll-weevil. It would be an irresistible story. The Louisiana Dusting Service. With five or ten planes, maybe a dozen parishes might be dusted; and with a hundred planes, maybe a dozen states. But that would require capital. The wheels kept turning inside the tall Hoosier's head.

"Dr. Reed," said the same gaunt farmer whose complaint had rung from the town square of Tallulah, "does it really work like it seems to? Do the bugs come back?"

"Not if you keep dusting," answered Trevor. "They can't stand the stuff."

"Don't worry about our integrity, sir," said A.T. "We wouldn't fool you. That's why we brought Kid here. No way Kid would lend his name to a scam, now, would he?"

The lean farmer turned and looked at the sparkling youth whose exploits had resonated throughout the world.

"Naw, sir," said the farmer. "They ain't no way Kid would lead us wrong."

Families in Monroe and Winnsboro, Lake Providence and Bastrop were soon investing some of their savings in the Louisiana Dusting Service, and the concept of using airplanes to spray pesticides on crops quickly spread throughout the South. When Kid returned to Georgia he began spraying cotton and melon fields and peach orchards for farmers around Macon and Albany throughout the fall of 1921 and the spring of 1922. Within months seemingly everybody who was engaged in commercial agriculture anywhere in North America had accepted the idea that airplanes were the best means of dispensing poisons that were increasingly necessary to control the ravages of imported pests in a world of growing international trade and commerce.

For nearly two years Milt devoted most of his energies to teaching fledgling operators how to dust tomato fields in southern New Jersey, snap peas in the Finger Lakes region of upstate New York, cherries in Michigan, potatoes in southeastern Colorado, and other crops in other climes. Suddenly a new profession was created for the hundreds of destitute war veterans who had returned home from Europe in 1918 without a way of using their piloting skills to earn a living.

CHAPTER 22

Twenty Dollars a Ride

WHEN CROP-DUSTING BECAME ALL too common a pursuit, the man from Woodvale decided he needed a new challenge to replace the one he had just answered with such rousing success. Would the day ever come when regular people, not warriors or aviators, might ride in planes? The idea had captivated him for years, and before he had gotten sidetracked by bootlegging and crop-dusting he had planned to test it. How eager would ordinary folks be to ride in a flying machine with Kid Harrison?

"I bet the public would *still* pay twenty bucks a head to go up with me in a Jenny," he repeated his boast to Woody and his pair of Hapeville friends in April of 1923, as he chewed on a toothpick. White dogwoods were in bloom throughout the Piedmont, but Candler Field itself was still a muddy desolation. It had been suffering in Kid's absence.

"Not a chance," Robert Brackens shot back. "We tried everything to get people out here last year, but nothin' worked. People just don't give a damn about us fools."

"They'll give a damn about me," Kid said, plucking the toothpick from his mouth and tossing it into the mud. "Ain't that right, Woody?"

The Bahamian, who loved the man from Woodvale like a brother, flashed a smile of gleaming white teeth.

"Yeah, Enby. We gonna show 'em. They ain't got no gratitude for what you done."

"We've shown him plenty of gratitude," said Chester Dawes. "We'd be a couple of hobos living in a ditch it it wasn't for him. But we've gotta learn to make this business work without leaning on him all the time."

"Once people get the idea they like flying," said Kid, "it won't matter a lick who the pilot is. They'll eat, drink and sleep aeroplanes, and they'll pay through the nose to go up in one."

"Kid," said Brackens, "you still got your head in the clouds. Since you quit bootleggin' we ain't made five cents profit off our air shows."

"If the timing's right, Bobby, this thing will go. You see this field out here—" he gestured with a sweep of his hand at the panorama of dirt, weeds, a tiny dilapidated hangar and crumbling grandstands, "—it won't be long before it's covered with people and flying machines again."

"I'd never put it past Kid if I was you, Bobby," said Chet. "If anybody can do it, it's him."

"You fellers can do it, too. This airfield was invented by Brackens and Dawes, not by me. The little bit that's here now—why it would've disappeared a long time ago without y'all."

"Nobody cares," said Robert Brackens.

Raymond Milton, Jr. took a few steps back and looked down at the ground, rubbing his boot heel in the mud.

"You're wrong," he answered, half to himself.

For $800 Kid purchased an Army surplus Jenny from an aerodrome in the middle Georgia town of Warner Robins, fine-tuned it with his friends and flew it back to Candler Field. He had several dozen bills printed up at a local print shop bearing a grand announcement. During the third week in April he drove to locations throughout Atlanta tacking the notices on shop windows and telephone poles.

COME FLY WITH THE WORLD-FAMOUS AVIATOR!
MR MILTON 'KID' HARRISON
THE GREAT ACE OF THE GREAT WAR
Now Offering Rides to the Public
$20 per ride.
Noon-6PM Candler Field
Sat. April 28, 1923.
Grandstands open 11:30. ALL WELCOME.

For several furious days the man from Woodvale and his three best friends worked tirelessly to clean the sullied grounds of the Hapeville racetrack. Woody proved handy with a hammer and nails, ripping out the rotten wooden boards of the grandstands and replacing them with new ones. Bobby took it upon himself to attack the rampant weeds, thistles and dandelions of the fields around the track with a slingblade. Chet made sure the planes in the threadbare hangar, now numbering only three, all of them Curtiss Jennies, were perfectly tuned up and ready to fly. And Kid—well, the World War ace and former booze-smuggler confined himself to no particular specialty but helped out everybody and did a little bit of everything.

Bobby had a brilliant idea about how to ensure that the grandstands would be full on the morning of the 28th. He recommended to Milt that he hire a sign painter to paint three long canvas banners, to be born on ropes in the air behind the Jennies, with messages announcing the event. On Saturday morning each of them would fly a plane over a different section of Atlanta, circle the ground at a low altitude, and try to buzz up interest among curiosity-seekers down below. Then when the eyes of the landlubbers had been drawn heavenward and they read the message they would surely feel compelled to take the trolley or their motorcars out to Hapeville to witness the spectacle. Why, it would be unfashionable, even unpatriotic, not to witness the famed local aviator, who had made his public presence scarce of late, in his novel experiment.

George Grantland drove out to the field in his new Chevrolet to watch his heroes in their preparation for the big event. He had finally gotten elected to city office as an alderman, and had staked part of his political future on what Kid and his gang were trying to do with airplanes. The voters of the Ninth Ward had been promised that with Grantland's election Atlanta would reap the economic boom of the age of the aviator. Most voters thought the claim preposterous and saw nothing of value in airplanes except as instruments of warfare and entertainment, but they were star-struck by the young candidate's known affiliation with Major Harrison and they gave him their votes.

"Y'all don't worry about how it'll turn out," George encouraged the aerial dreamers. "I'm gonna see to it that this thing works. Twenty dollars is a lot of money, but it'll seem like pennies when Saturday comes around."

When the long-awaited morning finally did come, fifteen thousand people were mobbing the grounds of the old racetrack by noon. Three thousand found seats in the pavilion and many more thousands spilled out into the surrounding territory, positioning themselves on bluffs overlooking the field and offering a clear view of it.

Six large canisters of gasoline had been positioned on the racetrack in full view of the grandstands, along with three big toolboxes prominently on display next to them. Whatever the shortcomings of the Jenny, Kid was determined to have no mechanical malfunctions with other people riding with him. He thought the sight of the toolboxes would give an added feeling of security to the squeamish people who would be coming.

At 11:30 AM three Jennies swooped down from the heavens and landed on the track, and the crowd whistled and shouted wildly when they saw Kid leap down from his seat. Woody, Chet and Bobby quickly added extra oil to the engine of the newest and best machine and refueled its tank. The time was quickly approaching when Milt would either look like a fool or a visionary, for there was no guarantee any normal member of the public would be willing to ride for free with such a nerveless daredevil as himself, let alone for the princely sum of $20, more than a week's salary to many people in those days.

He was assuming that George, who sat on the bottom row of the grandstand with his spectacles and neatly slicked-back hair in place, would come to his aid if no one else volunteered. But what he didn't know was that another man, whose own wife had actually been the first lay passenger to ride in a plane with him eight years earlier on this very ground, was determined to go first today. The Warner family—Knox, Jasmine and their 21-month-old daughter Estelle—were seated next to Mr. Grantland. It was the first time in months that husband and wife had done anything together that gave them mutual pleasure.

Mr. Warner, a rich young man, 37 years old, would have paid a small fortune to tell his grandchildren some day that he had actually ridden in a plane with the kid whose image adorned the four walls of his study. Not only would it be a matter of personal pride with him, but it would impress his fellows in the business community of Atlanta, give him a prestige unique among his circle of acquaintances. As he considered the matter carefully, Knox Warner came to see this as the potential investment of a lifetime, and a bargain for the puny amount of twenty dollars.

Woody came and gave Major Harrison a large megaphone into which to project his voice. Kid doubted he could yell loudly enough to be heard by more than a few hundred of the several thousand people there assembled, but he saw no other way of conducting this event without actually addressing the crowd, at least in the beginning.

"Good mornin', ladies and gentlemen!" his voice bellowed into the grandstands, sending the crowd into a frenzy. "Who wants to go first?"

The gentleman in the front row, the one in the neat navy suit, the upturned white starch collar, the bowtie and the sporty golfing cap, rose to his feet, leaned out over the bottom railing of the grandstand, and waved his hand.

"I do, Major Harrison! Please, sir, let me be the first!"

Milt noticed pale and aging Jasmine and her cherubic little girl next to the man and he assumed that this indeed was her husband.

"Come on out here, then sir," he instructed Knox.

As the man climbed over the railing the aviator drew nearer to the grandstand and noticed Jasmine's face, not beautiful as it had once been but still expressive. Her look was as knowing as the face of Eve when she handed Adam the forbidden apple for his first bite. It was almost screaming, behind a subtle grin: "Give it to him!" Kid came close enough so that Jasmine could see his wink, then greeted Mr. Warner.

"How do you do, sir?" he offered him his hand, "I'm Kid Harrison."

Knox was more nervous in the presence of the boyish air hero than he had expected to be a few seconds earlier, and he was tongue-tied.

"I—uh, it's an honor to meet you, Major," he mumbled, offering a limp, sweaty and fish-cold handshake. "I'm Knox Warner."

"You got your price of admission to Kid's aeroplane with you, sir?"

"Pardon me?" the man shook.

"The twenty dollars."

"Oh," Knox stuttered. "Sure I do." He gave the aviator the necessary bill, and Milt looked up at the crowd, making sure that they were paying close attention. He wanted at least a few of them to overhear what he was about to say to poor Mr. Warner.

"I'll give you two choices, sir. We can do the Tour for Grandmas or we can do the Kid Special. If we do the Tour for Grandmas I'm gonna give you a bird's-eye view of the five buildings of beautiful downtown Hapeville then set you down like a chick's egg on the field. If we do the Kid Special I'll pretend we got a mad Hun on our tail and he's dead set on blowin' us to hell. What'll it be, sir?"

When the peals of laughter were heard resonating from the grandstands, Milt knew he had hit his target. The high society folks from the bottom three rows, the big whales with whom this little fish swam every day, were all listening.

"I'll take the Kid Special," Warner droned with the enthusiasm of someone about to enter a dentist's chair.

"Suit yourself," Kid said.

Bobby Brackens, his jaw chock full of a meaty tobacco plug, appeared from behind the gasoline canisters and gave Mr. Warner an aviator helmet and goggles.

"You'll need these, sir," he told the gentleman. "The helmet'll keep your hair from standin' up on its end and the goggles'll keep your eyes in their sockets."

"Now, now, Bobby," said Chet, coming from behind, "Don't scare the man. Mister, he's just teasing."

The pale white face of Mr. Warner did not seem amused by the horseplay, but Milt put his arm paternally over the shoulder of the much shorter man and reassured him.

"One thing we'll be is safe. Ain't nobody figured out a way to bring me down yet, and this easy lark won't do it, neither."

Warner took off his golf cap and clenched it in his sweaty hand, then donned the helmet and goggles. As soon as he had put on the universal head regalia of the knights of the air, his fear turned to anticipation. While everyone else was mortally afraid to get into a plane with Kid he would be the first to fly. He would gulp hard, take a deep breath and try not to be miserable. Kid led him over to the front seat of the Jenny, helped him mount the footrest on the lower wing and offered him more encouragement once he had climbed into the passenger seat.

"Fasten that seat belt and enjoy it. I'm gonna be behind you controllin' this bird. Hold on tight."

It was too late for scared Mr. Warner to get out of this now, at least without exposing himself to everlasting ridicule for being a coward. He had no choice but to pretend to be a man about the whole thing, and then maybe when it was over the society that was then watching him would be fooled into thinking he had been that all along. The boys had taken out the dual control joystick from the front seat so the rank amateurs who would be riding along wouldn't interfere with the maestro's orchestration of his symphonies, and the banker sat helplessly in his cramped seat.

Mr. Brackens, still chomping coarsely on his tobacco quid, flipped around the propellor in front, ducked and ran away. Noise exploded in the banker's face. The passenger would now experience firsthand, whether he liked to or not, the sensation of being in the death grip of gravity and at the mercy of the calculations of a supercharged human mind and the dexterity of a superskilled human hand.

The baptism of oil and sludge that all participants in the age of the aviator had gotten now belonged to Mr. Warner. His helmet and goggles were soaked with black gunk before Kid had even taxied onto the racetrack. What a racket the machine made, and how it blew the drums of his ears out! The Jenny rolled onto the track now, and all the eyes of the grandstands were poised on the simple biplane as it paused before takeoff. What would the Great Ace of the Great War do to this otherwise rich and pampered man, whose nostrils had never before whiffed the fumes of gasoline and whose hands had never before been blackened with the stains of grease? Suspense was universal among the spectators in the crowd. Just as long as somebody else was in the cramped front seat and not themselves, they wanted Kid to "give it to him" and pull out all the tricks in his repertoire.

The Jenny raced impetuously by the grandstands, vaulted itself into the air, and almost immediately shot up into an almost vertical climb. Kid rolled over, put his plane into a dive, and nosed up before hitting the ground. Then he turned his plane over on its side, did a 360 degree flip of the wings and went upright again somewhere over Virginia Avenue. The banker had already retched his breakfast all over his neat new suit, and his bladder had been no stronger than that of some of the others on their first plane rides with Major Harrison—which is to say, not strong at all, for his trousers were soaked. The crowd in the grandstand shouted in jubilation with the same emotions that their distant human ancestors, the Roman plebeians, had felt on seeing poor Christians being fed to hungry lions in the Colosseum. Kid was eating this little man alive. Any Hun who had been on the tail of Major Harrison on that ride would quickly have exhausted all his bullet belts in trying to hit an elusive, swerving and flitting butterfly.

Up and down he swung his machine, with seeming effortlessness and breathtaking precision. Warner was so dizzy and disoriented he had nearly fainted but his mind was consumed by one recurring thought: he was astounded equally by the fact that men had built machines capable of doing this, that they were actually able to operate them in this way, and that some of them had operated them this way repeatedly for years and had lived to tell about it. After five minutes he thought it miraculous that he was still alive, and yet the man behind him had doubtless done this hundreds of times before without paying God's ultimate price.

At this point Milt decided it was time to let up and allow Jasmine's husband to experience the simple joy of flight. After all, he had taken twenty dollars from the fellow and the very least he could do was keep the man upright for awhile so he could study the ground. The Hun was not really there; it was all imaginary. Thank God, Kid thought to himself, those days of being pursued by enemy planes spitting out machine gun bullets were all over.

It so happened that the lackluster Mr. Warner got two tours for the price of one. He was the unwitting victim of the Kid Special on the first half of his flight, but then he received the merciful Tour for Grandmas over the five buildings of beautiful downtown Hapeville. He was able to relax now and enjoy the view, which he would not have been able to do without his rough introduction. Kid recalled his first few times up in simple flights without acrobatics, and how raw, shocking, heart-rousing and nerve-racking it had seemed to him in the open air, thousands of feet above the ground, with the engine roaring, coughing and spitting and the comfort and security of the earth drifting by below. But he had compressed his passenger's maturation into only a few minutes, and what would have seemed frightening to him if he had not been treated so roughly at the beginning now seemed tame and enjoyable.

By the time Kid landed the Jenny gently on the racetrack in front of the grandstand, Warner felt as if a lifetime of joy, terror, and beauty had been compressed into what the ticking hands of his wristwatch revealed had been twelve minutes. He was unsure whether he wanted to hug the man who had put him through all that or strangle him. There was doubt and confusion in his dizzy mind about nearly everything at that point. The man from Woodvale cut off his motor and went to help his humiliated customer escape from his tight seat.

"Sorry I was a bit rough," said Kid. "But you told me you wanted the Kid Special so I thought I had to give you your money's worth."

"T-thank you, Major. Let's just say it was an unforgettable experience."

"You wanna go again?"

"N-no, thanks," he said, sucking air as far down into his lungs as it would go. "It's somebody else's turn."

Kid helped him back up to his seat and into the tight hugging arms of his little daughter. Jasmine gave him a quick cold peck on the cheek, and then turned her rapt attention to the aviator, with a flush complexion and a happy smile that gave a suggestion of her formerly luscious beauty.

"Major Harrison," she purred coquettishly, "*you're a devil!*"

"Ma'am," he responded as her trampled wallflower of a husband attempted to make sense out of him, "I don't know what you mean."

He winked at her again, setting her aflame, and if she had been granted her most fervent wish then it would have been to fly away with him to their own little exotic and erotic island and pretend that the rest of the world never existed. But her fantasy was never to be, as the workaday world was breathing down the aviator's neck that day. He went out to the track, took up the megaphone from his Bahamian pal, and shouted into it again: "Who wants to go next?"

For a few seconds he regretted having scared the public out of its wits with his flamboyant torture of brash Mr. Warner, and he wondered whether one volunteer was all he would get that day. True to his word, though, another man stood to volunteer. It was Alderman Grantland, the man about town, everybody's friend, the representative of the people.

"Major," he yelled out, waving a $20 bill, "after I saw what your Kid Special's about, I think I'll take your Tour for Grandma's."

Mr. Grantland climbed down onto the track and shook his longtime friend's hand. Milt escorted him over to the still hot Jenny, muttering under his breath: "Don't worry, George. I'll make it so damn easy your granny could eat chicken 'n' dumplin's and swig warm moonshine from the passenger seat."

"That's the spirit, boy. You did it the wrong way with poor ole Knox. We're tryin' to convince these folks plane rides are *easy*."

"I know, George, but I hate fellers who beat me in anything and he wooed away my woman. No matter what, I figured you'd cover me and we'd set things straight."

"Let's do it, then," said the city alderman.

The young politician seated himself in the Jenny's forward compartment, and Bobby assumed his position by the propellor of the plane, ready to spin it back to life.

"Georgy-porgy," the crude Hapevillian taunted Grantland, "you know same as I do Kid ain't got no granny in 'im. You better hope your breakfast's down at the bottom of your gut, 'cause if it ain't this mad dog's gonna topple it like he done with that other poor fool."

"We'll see," the passenger answered without concern, adjusting his newly-donned goggles.

This time the flight really did look fun to the casual onlookers who were otherwise inclined to be skeptical. George waved at the crowd and pumped his fist as the Jenny raced to its takeoff. He was quickly thrilled by the rush of cool air as the machine delicately lifted itself into the sky, slowly turned when it reached 3000 feet of altitude, and glided gently back down to the ground. The attainment of his lifelong dream nearly brought the alderman to tears. To ride through the air with the perfect assurance of safety under the guidance of the war ace's steady hand was pure exhilaration.

"Beautiful! BEAUTIFUL!" he congratulated Kid when the ride was over. "Now that's goin' in style!" He stepped down from the Jenny and began egging on the crowd, gesturing for it to come join him. "Come on, y'all, it's too good to pass up!"

When they saw that Major Harrison's Tour for Grandma's was neither too dangerous nor too bland, the people began pouring out of the pavilion and lining up on the edge of the track in ranks of several dozen with $20 bills pressed tightly in the palms of their hands. This was the most fun Milt had had in years—it beat smuggling booze by a long shot. By six o'clock that evening, when he took up his last paying customer, it had long since become apparent that passenger-hopping was his true calling. He had taken up 36 people in a single afternoon, grossing $720 in a harmless and perfectly legal undertaking. He only ceased giving rides out of fatigue and had to beg people to let him go home for the day.

Woody shouted into the megaphone that tomorrow, if the weather permitted, the war ace would be at Candler Field again to offer more rides.

CHAPTER 23

Kid's Flying Circus

FOR THE NEXT TWO years the man from Woodvale introduced the airplane to common folks from one end of the U.S.A. to the other. He never charged more than $20 for a ride, but, in the true spirit of capitalism, he never charged less either.

He would always locate the square in the middle of his latest and newest American town, lower his Jenny so that its noise would stir up the community, and then do a loop or a wing-over to show them he was no rank amateur and he meant business. The townspeople would gasp as he closed out the loop, young girls would shriek, and just as he brought his flying machine right side up again he would dump out a sack of paper leaflets that would drift down like snowflakes over the center of Anytown, U.S.A.

The crowds would wait eagerly for the first strips of paper to cascade to the ground, and at the last instant a mad scurry of people in the square would net about one person out of every five a leaflet, though all the others would hear the news. COME RIDE WITH KID HARRISON, THE GREAT ACE OF THE GREAT WAR. RIDES $20. TODAY, NOON-6P. COUNTY FAIRGROUNDS.

And then what a hum there would be, and what a rush of enthusiasm from the common people to think that divinity had come to their humble burghs! By noon, without fail, several hundred or several thousand people would amass themselves at the nearest landing strip or the nearest empty fairgrounds. Down came the flying machine from the heavens, and from it would emerge the swarthy hero in his dashing flying suit. Local dignitaries would converge on the scene, pretend to be on long-established speaking terms with this fine American boy, shake his hand, introduce him to their young bashful daughters, and invite him to a late afternoon barbecue on the wide verandas of their sprawling houses.

The ministers from two or three of the largest churches in the town would interrupt their sessions of divine meditation, wheel and honk their way out to the field, and bestow upon the secular scofflaw the Lord's blessings. He would oblige them in his way, make a donation to their congregations from his ample proceeds, and be anointed a selfless philanthropist. The mayor and the sheriff would be there, and they would confer honorary titles of local eminence on him. The key to the city would be his, or a hastily drawn up scroll of calligraphy would proclaim this date as Milton Harrison day in Anytown. The Rotary Club chairmen, the Freemasons, or the Shriners would hear about the occasion. They would pour their $20 bills into the visitor's hand, chase the wind and clouds with him for five minutes, and pronounce him a man of greatness.

But he grew homesick after awhile, and by 1925 he was back at Candler Field trying to help Chet and Bobby embark on another new project. He explained his plan to his Hapeville mates as the three of them sat hotly and uncomfortably in the racetrack's empty grandstands in June of that year.

"Let's round up a couple more Jennies, boys, take out an ad in a few newspapers, and do an air show. We'll call it 'Kid's Flying Circus'."

Bobby and Chet greeted the idea with mental yawns, as if they had just heard their bored comrade tell them he was planning to reinvent the wheel.

"Ain't nothin' special about that, Milton," said Brackens. "Why can't we do somethin' *new?"*

"Man, this'll be different," Kid answered. "This time we're gonna git us some women—beautiful ones—to be a part of the show. Not only flyin' the planes, but out in the open, walkin' the wings in skimpy outfits to drive the men wild!"

"Where you think you can find girls to do that?" asked Chet.

"We'll put out a call for tryouts in our ad, boys. If you reach enough people you can find at least a few crazy enough to do anything for attention."

Not much prodding was necessary to convince the two other pilots that the experiment was worth a try. Within two weeks Milt had taken out paid notices in newspapers in several large cities throughout the country. The words were eye-catching to a young generation for whom the sky was a romantic frontier.

WANTED: AVIATORS AND AVIATRICES
Wing Walkers, Skydivers, Aerialists, Lady Air-devils
For Major Kid Harrison's Flying Circus.
Tryouts in Person
Candler Field, Hapeville, Ga.
Sat. June 27, 1925.
ALL WILL BE CONSIDERED.

When Saturday the 27th came, over two hundred people, a fair number of them women, had ridden the rails from all corners of the country to try to win the war ace's favor. Among them was a young man who had crossed paths with Kid earlier in his life: Robert Francis "Arky" Lattimore, his former squadron mate in the Argonne Escadrille. And there was also another man, previously unknown to Milt, who stood out from the crowd of roustabouts: a tall, soft-spoken Nebraskan of 23 named Thomas "Cy" Carlson, who had a reputation as a motorcycle daredevil. While still in his teens, Carlson had been dubbed "The Motorcycle Man" by his friends. In time, his nickname was shortened to "Motorcycle", then "Cycle", and now it had been pared down to "Cy". Cy Carlson had learned to fly during a stint in the U.S. Army, where he was the highest ranked flyer among his fellow cadets. A man of few words, he felt like a misfit amid the throng of loquacious exhibitionists who had assembled at the Hapeville track.

"You think I've got a chance here, Kid?" Cy asked his host, surveying the surrounding assortment of anxious leggy flappers and wiry and stubble-faced ruffians in flying helmets. "You'll give me a fair read, won't you?"

Kid glanced at the strange display of humanity around him.

"Just try your best, Tom, and if you're as good as Arky says you are you shouldn't have anything to worry about."

So many had come to show off their abilities that the tryouts consumed three days. Chet, Bobby and Kid conducted the proceedings on the scorched earth of Candler Field, ushering each successive claimant into one of their Jennies, spinning it started, and shading their eyes as the machine roared and flipped in the hazy sky. They had already decided that they only needed two more men in their show other than themselves, so the procession of worn out war veterans, penniless crop dusters and jilted air mail deliverers was largely a perfunctory one. Lattimore quickly demonstrated that he belonged among the top rank of the pilots of his day by doing solo stunts that were worthy of the Kid himself, and with a flamboyance which made many of the spectators hold their breath. And Cy Carlson was notable not only for his flying abilities, but for his wing walking. There was nothing that this fool, dancing and dodging and spinning on the top wing with Lattimore as the pilot, was afraid to do. The other men were adequately competent, but Cy and the 27-year-old Arkansas braggart quickly distinguished themselves from the rest of the crowd.

It was in the evaluation of the women where the most uncertainty lay. What an assortment of brash and liberated flappers these girls were, wearing bright red lipstick and pearl necklaces, smoking unfiltered cigarettes and swearing with language so raunchy that even some of the utterly profane men there were blushing! A few of the girls there could not fly planes at all, but just do acrobatic tricks on their wings, show plenty of snow white skin, and offer men the eye-winking prospect of cheap unfettered thrills. Bobby and Chet were lured in by a few of these women, but the man from Woodvale clung to the old-fashioned notion that somewhere, somehow there were a few women who were both ladies and masters of the unladylike task of piloting oil-spitting machines through the air.

Whether they found ladies in the technical sense of the term or not was debatable, but they found five women whose talents were so magnetic and whose looks were so alluring that everything else about them was inconsequential; five beautiful girls who made their hearts melt. They were Arlene Deerfield, Mary Jane Morris, Evelyn Reston, Beatrice Williams, and Katie Lawhorn. All five were from 21 to 24 years old, single, exceptionally skilled both at piloting Jennies and dancing on their wings, and had hourglass shapes that tended to make men think profoundly carnal thoughts.

When by Monday afternoon the runners up had sadly wended their way back to the Hapeville depot, the remaining collection of plucky nonconformists stood in the center of the racetrack, clustered around Major Harrison. The women meshed with Kid immediately, laughing and cursing with gusto. Cy, a good-looking man in his own right, shyly kept a few steps away from the group, his lanky frame leaning against a telephone pole and his steely blue eyes staring dreamily at the hazy sky.

"Come on over here and join the gang," Kid called out to Carlson. "Don't be a stranger."

Arlene walked over to the fearless Nebraskan and took ahold of his hand.

"Come on, cutie. I can't wait till we get started."

She smiled at him and led him by the hand over to the rest of the gang.

"Don't sweat it, Cy," said Kid. "The gal thinks you're great."

When Thomas joined the group and began contributing ideas his bashfulness soon went away and he proved instrumental in deciding just which tricks would be in the show. The ten of them spent the rest of that afternoon discussing the types of stunts they might feature in their shows to capture the public's attention. One suggestion was a midair change of planes, with Arlene or Mary Jane jumping from the seat of one plane into the seat of another one flying abreast of it. Arky promised he would hang upside down from a wing while Kid flew a plane if Kid would return the favor and do something equally absurd and death-defying during Arky's piloting. The man from Woodvale readily accepted the challenge and he vowed not only to hang upside down from one of the planes, but to urge whoever was pilot to shoot the Jenny down low so that both he and another acrobat on the opposite wing could reach down and snatch two hats off the heads of two people standing on the ground.

Cy dismissed these as minor feats and told the others he would leap from a moving car onto a ladder dangling down from one of the low-flying biplanes and climb it while it rose upward. Robert Brackens elaborated on this idea, imagining one of the acrobats grabbing onto a ladder from a speeding boat on a lake or inlet. The women sucked hard on their cigarettes and cursed profanely in agreement. Cy wanted to stand on a top wing and shoot arrows at a target on the opposite side, and asked the two bustiest women of the group, Beatrice and Evelyn, if they would consider playing a mock game of tennis on his upper wing, flourishing rackets on opposite sides of a makeshift net mounted in the middle. Kid applauded that idea but added that the ladies should be as close to naked as the law would allow. As a matter of fact, he noted, the general operating principle of their little show should be to flaunt as much lovely female flesh as possible without risking arrest.

"Bravo, baby!" Arlene cackled when she heard this. "We'll get as naked as you want, any time, day or night!"

"Oh, my god, Kid!" swore Bobby. "Did we die and go to heaven?"

"Shoot," said Milt, "she ain't nothin' but a tease. I bet it'd be easier to crack a black walnut than get clothes off that gal."

Beatrice went over and put an arm over Arlene's shoulders, puffing rings of cigarette smoke into the stagnant air and looking back alluringly at the men.

"You wanna bet, guys?"

"Where'd you ladies come from?" asked Chet. "Finishing school?"

"Now, hold on a minute," said Milt. "Maybe we'd better blindfold Cy and muffle his ears with cotton balls so he don't get corrupted by us white trash."

"Good, get him out of the damn way," said Arky, "so we'll have less competition."

Tom Carlson was as amused by the horseplay as the others, though he didn't feel glib enough to partake of any of it himself. He was wondering how, in the midst of all this frivolity and joking, they would ever be able to muster the discipline necessary to perfect their coordinated skills. He was a worrier by nature, not given to light repartee. Milt went over to the younger man and reassured him again.

"Don't pay us no attention, Cy. Let your guard down, now. They ain't really whores, they're just *joking*. The whole damn thing's for laughs."

"I know that, Kid," he answered, less than convincingly.

In subsequent days the free-spirited group practiced many of the stunts they had considered in their first session and formed a consensus about which ones were most likely to thrill an audience. Milt paid for hotel rooms for the seven members of the troupe who were from outside the area, and tried to keep relations among the women and men in the group as professional as possible. They were all partners and, as Carlson had advised him, they needed to avoid emotional entanglements which would interfere with the business at hand. Though Cy was a lad of only twenty-three, Kid thought of him as somewhat of a throwback, a man similar to what his own father must have been when he was young: serious, duty-bound, unwavering, and committed to his own honorable code of personal conduct. With many young people nowadays drinking, dancing, smoking, listening to loud jazz music and indulging their hedonistic inclinations, he seemed old-fashioned.

The circus members started actual rehearsals later in the week. Milt and Chet Dawes pushed their best Jenny out of the hangar one morning and fastened a wire mesh above the front cockpit to resemble a tennis net. Kid then positioned himself in the rear flying seat and prepared for start-up. Evelyn and Beatrice, clad in tight-fitting flesh-colored suits that were so snug that from afar they really did appear naked, took two large tennis rackets, fastened their helmets and flying goggles, climbed atop Kid's upper wingspan, and strapped themselves into place. Cy and Bobby checked the engine, Arky twirled around its propellor, and Arlene, Katie and Mary Jane sat in the empty bleachers, cheering and whistling as the other girls crouched down during the plane's takeoff.

Kid kept the Jenny extremely low and easily within view of the ground. As soon as he had leveled his plane at about 100 feet Evelyn and Beatrice arose on the top wing, their flesh rippling in their snug body suits as the warm wind buffeted them, and with beautiful grace and agility they began moving as if they were hitting a tennis ball back and forth. When Kid had to turn the plane abruptly to come back into full view of the grandstands the women stooped down to keep their balance and on the straightaway resumed their aerial pantomime and ballet. The pilot brought the Jenny back and forth about five times with smooth effortless ease while the lovely women continued their acrobatics, and then Chet signaled for them to land. He had seen enough to know that this was a superb spectacle that must be included in their show.

After the plane landed and the first stunt had been concluded flawlessly, the other four pilots took their turns at taking up various wing walkers. And so it went for the next two weeks. Milt had never walked on wings before but under Cy's instruction he became proficient at it. He was not graceful and had no dancing or twirling moves, but a steadiness of balance was really all that was required for him to be passable at the job. His utter absence of fear under any circumstances, as well as his indifference to heights, enabled him to keep a steady posture while suspended upside down from a wire several thousand feet above the ground or tethered to the top of a cloth wing that was vaulting through space at eighty miles an hour.

Once his system got used to the sensation he actually began craving it. It was the closest feeling to being a bird that a human being could have: to be thrust into the raw open air with arms and legs outstretched and no machinery hemming one in; to feel the brute force of the wind against one's body with the green quilt of the earth spread out below. All the members of the unanimously eccentric group had the same addiction to speed and danger, and all, without a whimper, gladly took their turns on the wings. Cy was the biggest proponent of safety and showed them all the proper technique for fastening themselves to the wings and bracing themselves on the turns, but safety never came at the expense of showmanship.

IN THE MIDDLE OF of July Major Harrison began posting bills throughout Atlanta, which was to be the first stop of what he hoped would be a national tour.

KID'S FLYING CIRCUS
Featuring MAJ. MILTON 'KID' HARRISON
Chester Dawes and Robert Brackens
And a collection of the World's Best
Aeroplane Stunt Performers
WING-WALKING, SKY-DIVING, ACROBATICS,
DANGEROUS, DEATH-DEFYING MANEUVERS IN MID-AIR!
Beautiful Lady Acrobats and Parachutists!

TWO DAYS ONLY!
Sat.-Sun. July 25-26, 1925 12n-2p
CANDLER FIELD, HAPEVILLE
$1 Adults, 50¢ Children 12 and under. ALL WELCOME.

Another huge gathering formed on the muggy morning of the 25th around the crumbling grandstands of the Hapeville landing field. In the middle of the egg-oval track sat five Jennies, each with two names, one male and one female, painted on one side of its cloth-covered fuselage and "Kid's Flying Circus" on the other.

At high noon that day Kid raced his Jenny up solo to about 3000 feet, swooped down violently to excite the crowd, and, just as he was about to crash, pulled up suddenly, only skimmed the ground with his wheels, and went into a complete loop from an altitude of zero. It was an astounding maneuver and the crowd went wild. After he landed he hopped out of his seat and into the arms of two beautiful girls who had appeared from behind the grandstands.

Evelyn Reston and Beatrice Williams seemed shockingly unclothed at first to the less sophisticated members of the audience. But it was a trick! Soon the gallery realized that the stripped-bare ladies were actually wearing skin-tight flying suits; and then another Jenny, piloted by Tom Carlson, taxied around the corner of the track. It slowed to a crawl, and the ladies put on helmets and goggles and climbed up on top of the upper wingspan. As Cy flew them, Evelyn and Beatrice then proceeded to play their mock game of tennis. Everyone seemed to relish the flawlessly executed performance. After Carlson set the plane softly down on the track, the ladies dismounted and stood to cheers and howls from the audience.

Later on, Arky and Chet were the pilots, and Cy and Kid had positioned themselves on the middle of the top wing of Arky's plane down on the racetrack, braced within about six feet of each other. Chet took his plane up and fixed the audience's attention on him by doing a few acrobatic spins and loops. In the meantime, Capt. Lattimore had lifted his plane gently aloft with Milt and Cy as the wing walkers. He aimed it in the direction of the other plane, which Chet slowed and leveled to enable his partner to catch up with him. A minute later Arky had his plane positioned directly under the path of Chet's plane, only a few hundred feet above the field and easily within view of the grandstands. Chet thrust his right arm over the side of his flying seat, flaunting a sharp hunting knife, and he cut loose a rope on the side of the fuselage that no one had even noticed before.

Down came a ladder from his landing gear, dangling directly over the other Jenny. Kid caught hold of the strand with one hand as soon as it was fully unfurled, undid the supports on his boots with his other hand, and in a few seconds was free, with nothing but his own gloved fists to support himself on the ladder as he was dragged through the air. He clicked his heels together to show the audience that he was on his own. Arky now tailed off slightly to put some distance between the two planes while Milt hoisted himself up with his strong arms, pushed both of his legs through the bottom rung of the ladder and let go with his hands so that he hung upside down from his knees. To his crazy war-hardened death-teasing sensibility, the upside down midair swirl was pure bliss. He extended his arms out so that he resembled an inverted T as the people down below gasped.

But now Arky lifted the lower plane, Kid reached down and extended his arms to reach for Cy, and the upside down war ace snatched the 160-pound acrobat and pulled him out of his braces. The crowd quieted anxiously as it saw the Jenny gradually descend to the track with the inverted man clutching the arms of his fellow wing walker. How would they ever reach the ground safely in such a tangle? Or would they?

Brackens had hopped into a Chevrolet race car that had been sequestered in a remote part of the track, and he was making a lap around the track at the rate of a mile a minute. Now Arky swung his machine down directly over Bobby's racing Chevy, followed it until it was in view of the stands, and Kid dropped Carlson into the back seat of the open air racer. Then he leaned up, grabbed a rung, pulled his legs out from the other rung, and hung right side up as the plane and the automobile coordinated their movements at exactly the same speed. He let go as Cy supported his legs and guided him safely into the back seat alongside of him. As the motorcar sped by the gallery the two wing walkers stood to acknowledge the applause that showered them.

Later in the show, Carlson was braced on the top wing of Arky's plane and Miss Deerfield and Miss Lawhorn were positioned down on the lower wing on opposite sides of the fuselage, each braced against a wooden strut. Arky wore a long flowing red scarf and yelled like a madman as the plane took off. Unbeknownst to the audience, the three wing walkers all wore parachute packs which were not apparent while they were kneeling. Cy had trained himself to be one of the Midwest's best skydivers and Katie and Arlene, under his careful instruction, had mastered the activity almost as well as he had.

As soon as Arky's plane had reached a high enough altitude to allow room for error, but still low enough for the people to be able to see the two women plainly, Katie and Arlene began dancing provocatively, spinning, waving their arms in unison, and caressing the Jenny's wooden struts as if these were aerial dance partners and lovers. The men down below howled with amusement, and the more proper older women, they of the matronly class, averted their eyes. But suddenly there was terror among the people! Arlene had slipped off the wing a full 1500 feet above the field, done a complete backflip, and was tumbling headlong to the ground to her apparent death. Almost immediately after Arlene slipped, so did Katie and she also did a backflip and began a free fall.

The two seemed to fall at exactly the same speed and were close enough to gesture to one another in order to coordinate their movements. The audience was completely hoodwinked by the maneuver. The possibility that the young women may in fact have been wearing parachutes completely escaped them, though skydiving had been promised in the show's billings. In the heat of the moment, however, nobody seemed to remember the billings and there was widespread panic that the two girls were diving to their deaths. For several seconds the onlookers screamed in terror.

Then they saw Cy Carlson topple off of his spot on the top wing and he flailed his arms and legs in theatrical desperation like a nervous insect as he fell. Now the terror among the audience members reached its zenith. All three of the young people might be dead soon, and these spectators in the gallery, all willing patrons of the excesses of exhibitionism, began to feel like guilty accomplices.

About a thousand feet above the track, by which time Cy figured the crowd had endured more than enough of a fright, he and the two women simultaneously pulled their rip cords and snuffed out the audience's anxiety like a bucket of water on a campfire. Two large pink domes and one blue one appeared in the sky over the heads of the three skydivers, each with a white star in its middle. They all glided down precisely to a spot on the track in front of the stands, landing side by side and making the fall appear easy.

Everything went as planned during the first performance of Kid's Flying Circus, and all ten of the performers escaped injury or mishap. It was a great success with the audience. The next day, due to word-of-mouth publicity, twice as many people came. There were special guests in attendance besides the usual gentry. Kate and Ellen, Milt's sisters, brought their families on the train from northeast Georgia to watch their irrepressible brother in action, and Madge came as well, gasping miserably every time her son seemed to taunt his own mortality.

It was the first time she had ever seen him piloting anything other than his home-built Flying Flivver.

CHAPTER 24

Bragging for the Girls

IN THE SUMMER AND AUTUMN of that year, curiosity-seekers from all across the land, many of whom had last heard of Major Kid Harrison when he had been on a barnstorming tour offering passenger rides, basked in the spectacle of his latest itinerant venture. On weekends in that hot dry year of 1925, when booze was illegal, cool air was scarce, and excitement was hard to come by, Mr. Excitement himself was in one town after another to ply his trade, aided by the beautiful, unorthodox and gifted young cast of characters who made up his circus.

Before long, all across the South and Midwest, "KID'S FLYING CIRCUS" was painted on barn roofs and roadside billboards, on drugstore walls and picket fences. Just those three famous words, plus a date and a place, were enough to draw fascinated crowds to watch treacherous feats of derring-do by seemingly superhuman creatures in the sky.

Occasionally they would court disaster, right themselves in the waning seconds of an imminent crack-up, survive with a few bumps and bruises, and brush themselves off for the next trick. Milt was nearly killed three times during the tour. Once he struck a rock on a landing, did a ground-loop, dove to the ground and crawled a few steps before his plane exploded. In another instance the fabric on his plane caught fire in midair and he had to bail out by parachute, captivating the crowd which thought it was a planned stunt, and he narrowly avoided hitting the upper reaches of a cottonwood tree and snapping his neck in two as his chute came down. In the meantime his Jenny burst into an orange ball in midair, bringing the people of Fargo, North Dakota to their feet in a joyous ovation for what they thought was the perfect planning of the maneuver.

The five male performers of the troupe all took various turns tempting fate in a potentially deadly stunt which they performed on water. In a few locales, particularly in the Farm Belt states, the fairgrounds were situated by lakes or rivers, and the troupe would incorporate a trick to take advantage of the picturesque natural scenery. Chet or Arky would drive a speedboat across the water while Kid, Cy or Bobby flew a Jenny with a dangling ladder several hundred feet overhead. One of the men in the boat—and they took turns in a regular rotation to alternate who it was—would grab the ladder, climb all the way up to the landing gear, wave to the crowd as the plane turned back, then climb down as the Jenny descended to the water again and fall back neatly into the speedboat.

Or at least that was the plan. At Sioux City, Iowa in late September the ladder slipped out of Kid's grasp; he tumbled head first into the icy cold Missouri River and was nearly chopped to bits by the boat's propellor before he was able to swim safely ashore a quarter mile away. Arky and Chet, both expert swimmers, each took a spill into water at other times. But Cy never had a single mishap whenever he did the trick. After awhile the rest of the gang was a little annoyed at his perfection. They were all having dinner one night in San Antonio when Brackens confronted Carlson about his apparent indestructibility.

"I'll tell you what, Tommy, you always seem to get stuff right. Even Kid, he's almost died so many times he done lost count, but you seem to glide right on by every kinda danger that comes your way. How's that?"

Cy laughed and blushed a bit at his friend's sincere compliment.

"Bobby, if I knew the answer I'd tell you, but I don't. I study out everything I do in advance and try to plan for all emergencies, but so does everybody else, even the ones that get killed. I guess I'm just clever and a little sly."

"'Sly Cy'," said Kid. "That's what we'll call this man."

When the weather in the South that autumn had finally gotten too cold for the performers to feel comfortable in doing their stunts and for the public to want to turn out to watch them fly, Kid's Flying Circus disbanded. There was some discussion about resuming the show the following spring. However, they had all profited handsomely from their current tour, and monetary need was no longer a spur for them to continue risking life and limb in so foolhardy a fashion. The women performers therefore decided they wanted to move on with their lives and pursue other ventures.

This left the men without the prospect of the beautiful female companions who had made their brushes with danger so enjoyable, and so they too decided to give up the show. Arlene talked the other girls into going out to her native California with her to try to get parts in movies. Chet and Bobby were holdouts and insisted they would put on a show of their own the next year that would tour the South—with or without the others. Cy told Milt he wanted to try to do something useful and pioneer a winter air mail route in the upper Midwest. This sounded wonderfully risky and challenging to the man from Woodvale, and he and Arky decided they would go along with Sly Cy.

"Tom," Kid told his friend after the circus's last act in Pensacola, Florida in November, "you know me. I always like a new adventure. You think carrying mail is interesting enough to keep me excited?"

"We'll see, Kid. If we don't like it we can always quit and do something else."

Major Harrison's stellar credentials as a pioneer of aviation won him the lucrative Detroit to Chicago Contract Air Mail Route in January of 1926, while Arky secured the Louisville to Chicago route. Cy, courtesy of Milt's help, was awarded the run from his native Omaha to Chicago. They all flew DeHavilland 4 war surplus planes that were retrofitted for cargo carrying. Kid knew that model of plane well, for in it he had spent his roguish and clandestine career as Mr. N.B. Excitement, the most successful, elusive and persistent Caribbean booze smuggler in the early years of Prohibition.

The three men achieved an exceptionally high rate of success in delivery that winter, despite crude landing facilities, bone-chilling cold, and haphazard organization by the governmental postal officials who were trying to get the service up and running. Milt stayed in a posh apartment on Lakeshore Drive on Chicago's North Side, invited the two other men to join him at his residence for rich parties with voluptuous flappers, and in general had a wonderfully stimulating period of footloose adventure. At one of his parties, with girls swooning over him, Kid made a boast about what his next great exploit would be.

"Ladies, there's an oil company down in Texas, Champion Petroleum, that wants to give $20,000 to the first pilot who can fly around the world solo in a month or less. That's my next mission, when the weather turns favorable."

Samantha, Catherine, Sheila, Elizabeth and Vicky, the latest worshipers at the altar of the Sky King, sighed with awe at the intrepid roustabout's claim. Not to be outdone, the normally reticent Cy, who still struggled with awkwardness around girls, offered his own boast.

"I never heard you talk about that before, Kid, but if I were you I'd be worried about the competition. There's a hell of a good chance I'll make it around the world before you do, if I decide to try it."

Catherine, the fetching redhead, scoffed at Cy's vow.

"Thomas, darling, let's be reasonable. There's no way you'll do that."

Carlson bristled at the pretty girl's defiance of him.

"Miss, you don't understand," he told her gravely. "What I say, I do."

The tone of Cy's remarks put off the girls, and now they shrank away from him as though he were some type of misguided zealot. Arky tried to take up for him.

"Don't you doubt this man, girls. The only problem with what he says is, I'm gonna beat him to it. It's gonna be Arky Lattimore who circles the globe first."

"Both y'all are crazy," said Kid, setting the adoring girls into laughter. "Neither one of you fellers ever gave a damn thought to the Champion Prize till I just brought it up a minute ago—and now you expect these beauties to favor *you* over *me?* Come on, now."

"I bet you never gave it a thought before now, either, Kid," said Cy. "You're just trying to impress the ladies."

Tom's combativeness threw cold water on the girls' wild mirth. Arky and Kid kept trying to reignite the now staid and sober sex kittens, but without effect. The party broke up within thirty minutes.

"Next time you wanna try to conquer the world, Tommy," Kid rebuked the poor dreaming Carlson as he was leaving, "keep it private, 'specially if there's beautiful girls around."

"You're the one who started it," answered Cy. "You're the one who, out of the blue, bragged you'd fly around the world."

"Right-o, Tommy, I did say that. But there's a difference between me and you. When I said it, they believed it. Of course I'll probably never do it, or even come close, but I had 'em fooled. Remember that about women, now. If you're trying to impress 'em, don't tell 'em something unless you know they'll believe it."

Cy grinned somewhat penitently.

"Sorry about that, Kid. You've just got a natural way with the dames, I guess."

"Like hell I do. They love my image, not me. They wouldn't give Raymond Milton the time of day, but as soon as I got to be Kid, that's when they started getting interested in me. So I play on my reputation, and I've learned a few things in my short little life. If you've got a pretty fish on your line, let her swallow your damn hook, don't jerk it out of her mouth. That's my advice to you, boy."

Milt made a playful balled-up fist and tapped his friend on the shoulder with it in brotherly fashion as Carlson laughed. If nothing else, they had milked a little bit of humor out of the occasion, and it came in handy. The three iron-willed mail couriers kept nearly freezing or crashing to death on their routes, and all of them were forced during the next several months to bail out by parachute at various times to avert fatality.

THE MAN FROM THE WARM Southland had taken upon himself the unwarm task of carrying letters and parcels on a course with landings in Detroit, Lansing, Grand Rapids, Kalamazoo, South Bend, and Maywood Field in west Chicago during the winter months of 1926. To impress the feds, his former adversaries during his bootlegging days, he was wearing a parachute to demonstrate his commitment to safety. In early February he met a blinding snowstorm north of Kalamazoo and momentarily lost sight of the ground. He had been airborne for nearly two hours and calculated that, at most, he had ten minutes' worth of fuel remaining in the tank of his DH.

Without having any means at all of gaining his bearings; without knowledge of the exact location of any landing strips or towns; with only intuition and the reading of the altimeter which indicated he was 3500 feet above the ground, he had to make a sudden decision. Bail out by parachute and lose his mail? To him that seemed a dereliction of duty. Perhaps it was still possible to spin his way out of this impenetrable bank of fog and snow; to right his ship; to husband his dwindling cupfuls of fuel so that if he needed to open his throttle again in a pinch he could; to spot the luminous flares of the Kalamazoo landing strip and bring himself smoothly down to safety. Perhaps. But a life was more important than a few sacks of letters, and his lightning-quick mind realized at once that any prospects for survival other than by jumping were too remote to take seriously. The simple fact was that in the flying machines of his day no pilot could stay aloft long without being able to see the earth's horizon. There were then no instruments to provide a substitute for human eyes and a human sense of equilibrium.

He stepped out on the cowling of his wing and dove into the blinding whiteness of the fog and snow. When he had fallen head first 200 feet or so he heard his engine sputter to a stop and give out, validating his decision to bail out at the exact moment when he had. But he was in grave danger anyway. He had neglected to turn off the switches in his plane before he jumped, and when it began its unmanned spinout in the swirling blizzard gravity apparently pulled some unspent fuel down into its carburetor and the machine roared back to life. Pulling his ripcord, he was yanked back upright as his plane began a dangerous downward spiral, roaring with unguided fury down in the direction of his plummeting chute, its cords, and his helpless body.

The wind blew him about like a weightless leaf in the furious ice and snow, as the tumbling plane swooped around. They were both falling at about the same rate: the man in his parachute and the unmanned plane. With each downward spiral the plane seemed to come nearer to chewing up the parachute and the cords and sending Milt to his icy death. At one point its propellor seemed to brush against the chute before fortunately veering off to make its next revolution. Next time would be God's verdict. With one more loop the machine would either chop the aviator and his parachute apparatus to bits or it would narrowly miss him and give him twenty more seconds of reprieve. Down it came, nearer and nearer. There seemed to be no way he would escape his Judgment Day this time.

But a sudden gale-force blast of wind, acting on his falling form in a completely different way than it acted on the spiraling plane, blew him out of the path of the angry machine before it came around again and he staged another last-second escape from the jaws of death. The plane eventually crashed three quarters of a mile from where Milt tumbled into a snowbank, and, most miraculously of all, its mail was undamaged. A government agent examined the downed plane's fuel tank a few days later and discovered that its original 110-gallon tank had been removed for repair and, unbeknownst to its pilot, had been replaced with a 90-gallon one—a nearly fatal alteration that might have killed any other aviator but the one who had last flown the plane.

On two other occasions during that harsh winter, Kid was forced to leap from his machine when he lost sight of the horizon in a snowstorm. Much as he had done over Kalamazoo, he bailed his way out of catastrophe with his parachute in both cases. Only once out of nearly 1000 flights as a mail courier over the Midwest did his cache of mail get destroyed—a record unmatched by anyone else who had the job at the time.

When the weather finally warmed in late April, the task of carrying air mail turned from an always treacherous and sometimes miserable pursuit to a joyful adventure. There were still the occasional fogs and thunderstorms, and danger was never totally absent from what any aviator did in a flying machine, but the stress of the job was relieved considerably by the mild temperatures and limpid skies of the growing season. The trio of friends compiled better than a 99% rate of success for delivery of mail into and out of Chicago for most of 1926.

Yet in due course the challenges of a mail courier wore thin for all of them and greater adventure beckoned. Within a year's time they had all given up their mail routes to another batch of aviators leaner and hungrier than themselves. Kid was the first to quit. By then he was routinely vowing to fly around the world for prize money and making earnest preparations to do it.

CHAPTER 25

A Moth Conquers Greenland

PRIOR TO BOASTING TO all his Chicago girlfriends about flying around the world, Milton Harrison had never given the undertaking a serious thought. But once the impromptu words had passed from his lips, the idea took hold of him. Why couldn't he try it? As with many of his compulsive ambitions, his motive might have been summarized by a simple question which he kept asking himself: WHY NOT ME?

News circulated in a hurry that the great Kid Harrison had devised another bold plan. To win the $20,000 Champion Prize he wanted to circumnavigate the earth alone in an airplane. A crew of U.S. Army pilots had collectively achieved the feat in 1924, two years earlier, but they had been a large and well-financed group. The Army flyers had stopped to refuel every three or four hundred miles, and in studying their course Major Harrison decided that with a few alterations in their route he could make a full circuit about the earth—a 24,000 mile journey in the shortest great-circle route—in about 30,000 miles.

The sponsor of the prize, the Dallas-based Champion Oil Company, was offering to set up refueling stations at remote locations throughout the world. The only specifications for the contest were that the aviator had to land at least once on all six of the inhabited continents, that the journey must be made in a single plane, that only a single pilot was allowed to fly the plane for the duration of the trip, and that the pilot must return to the point from which he originated no later than 31 days after embarking. Six pilots had already attempted the feat since 1921. All had failed— sometimes from fatigue, sometimes from mechanical breakdown, sometimes from hostile weather. Two had lost their lives in the attempt.

In September the DeHavilland Aircraft Company shipped a brand new Moth, altered to meet Milt's particular demands, to the Hapeville depot. Kid, Chet and Bobby, accompanied by a throng of reporters, loaded it in large crates on a flatbed truck that had been rented for the occasion and hauled it off to nearby Candler Field. There it was publicly assembled before the press, the usual collection of dignitaries, and the local stragglers who had grown accustomed to witnessing miracles on that otherwise ordinary spot of ground. The new aircraft weighed 1240 pounds, had an engine of 60 horsepower called a Cirrus I, a wingspan of 30 feet, flew at around 80 mph, and went about 320 miles on a tank of fuel.

With a machine thus limited to relatively short distances between refuelings, Milt would be compelled to chart a course along island chains to cross the great oceans: Nova Scotia, Newfoundland, Greenland, Iceland and the Faeroe Islands over the Atlantic; and Indonesia, the Philippines, Japan, the Kuril Islands and the Aleutians to span the Pacific. He would in the interim be flying predominantly over the landmass of Eurasia. However, he needed to find some way of touching at least one point in Africa, perhaps in Egypt, and also Australia and South America to claim the prize.

Critics were already wondering why the great aviator should choose so small a plane with such a limited range when technicians were already designing machines with several fuel tanks and a range approaching the great-circle route from New York to London, over 3000 miles, ten times the extent of the Moth. The problem was that these machines had yet to be *perfected,* and to survive a course over foreign lands and cultures, with long stretches over open seas and uninhabited archipelagoes, Milt believed he needed a plane that he might land in or take off from relatively confined spaces. The enormous, unwieldy fuel loads of the long-range aircraft that were then being developed; the difficulty of getting off the ground in them with their massive full weights; the impossibility of landing them in a pinch on the small aircraft carriers that were then in the U.S. or British naval fleets—all this discouraged him from using a bigger plane for a trip that would largely take place over realms where there was no civilization at all.

MILT SPENT NEARLY THREE months in the late summer and early autumn of 1926 ironing out the plans for his trip, making essential governmental and military arrangements, perfecting modifications in the design of his plane, and trying to put on extra weight so that a meager diet of nuts, dried fruit and water for a full month would not leave him feeble and scrawny. He was aiming to begin his journey on his birthday, October 1, a time of moderate temperatures throughout the mid-latitudes, daylight hours of nearly equal length everywhere, and calm winds in most areas where he intended to fly. When he rolled his new biplane from its hangar at Candler Field at the crack of dawn on the 1st, assisted by Chet and Bobby, nearly two thousand sleepy-eyed Hapevillians, as well as scores of reporters, were gathered around the landing strip to see off the local legend.

"Happy birthday," one of the newspaper writers called out to him just before he mounted the seat of his plane. "So how does it feel to be thirty, Major?"

"Same as it does to be twenty-nine," answered Kid. "So far, I don't feel any smarter or older than I did yesterday. Just as soon as I get old and wise, that'll be the time when I quit tryin' to kill myself in these wild rides and all y'all will have to find something else to write about. I hope that won't be any time soon."

Some of the groggy-eyed witnesses would swear many years later that they saw a brilliant white glow around his simple biplane as it soared off the Hapeville landing strip. The true congregation of the faithful, who *knew* that the man and his machine were sacred, were already assembling in the tiny village out in the hinterlands that had given him life. It was to be Milt Harrison day in Woodvale, and though it was a Friday the whole town was shutting down whatever trifling bit of business it ever did normally on a weekday to toast the man whose life had animated its spirit.

When the aviator landed on his customary field next to Main Street, where Bobby Williams had just harvested this year's corn as he had done for the last generation, the townspeople shouted and whistled and they spilled out into the stubble like a rushing creek and flooded the area about his plane. Even Madge finally seemed to have accepted that there was no swaying her son from his lunatic ways.

"I know you're too far addicted ever to give up these things, son," she admitted to him while the rest of Woodvale overheard her. "But if you make it around the world WHAT MORE WILL BE LEFT FOR YOU TO DO?"

"Mama, don't worry," said Kid. "I'll think of something else. I always do."

AFTER HE HAD FLOWN to New York and spent the night at a suite in the Waldorf-Astoria, several newspaper reporters were interested in interviewing him. He held sway in the hotel lobby that morning, jawing with the press and grinning mischievously as flashbulbs popped in his face.

"Why aren't you going in a monoplane, Mr. Harrison?" one of the newsmen asked. "Don't you know that's where the future lies?"

"I'm not living in the future, my friend," said Kid. "I'm stuck in the here and now. And right now the plane I got's the best one for what I'm trying to do."

"What do you fellows think you're proving by all this?" someone asked. "Trains and cars take people over land, and steamships cross oceans."

"Maybe so," said Kid. "But a hundred years ago a horse could cross land and a galleon could cross an ocean. We aren't trapped by what our ancestors did. I don't want to live the way they did. Come to think of it, I don't want to go back to living like I used to live myself, when I was a little boy."

Cameras boomed and popped and pencils scrawled over pads.

"So while all the rest of the world's fat and sleeping," quipped one wiseacre, "you'll be eating nuts and water and trying to civilize the wilderness. Is that about right, Mr. Harrison?"

Kid nodded and chuckled a bit.

"That's it, my man. I guess I just got my priorities straight. First comes aeroplanes, then comes life."

He was assuming that his diet until he came back would consist entirely of what he was now loading onto his small plane at McCormack Field on Long Island. Several burlap sacks full of raisins, shelled pecans and walnuts. Six jars of peanut butter and four cans of soda crackers. Twenty wooden gallon jugs full of drinking water. Two boxes of grapefruits that he had ordered from Florida. He complemented his food with several butter knives for spreading the peanut butter and two wooden bowls into which he intended to squeeze the grapefruit juice and pulp. The rest of the small amount of space he had about him was to be filled with dozens of maps of the regions of the world he was to traverse, an inflatable life raft for a possible crash at sea, four flares, three flashlights, and six canteens that he would keep full of the drinking water from his stash of gallon jugs.

Over five thousand spectators had formed a ring about McCormack Field. It was a surreal scene, quiet and dignified, and most were too far away to see anything but a tiny gray blotch with two arms and two legs as it climbed onto the back of what seemed to be a large brown bird of prey. The morning fog had just now lifted and the first glimmer of sunshine was pouring through the lingering haze. What was it this man was attempting to do—to go around the world by himself in that flying toy? It seemed too absurd to be believed. He said nothing, made no gesture, just casually mounted his cubbyhole while another man spun his whirligig; then he flitted quickly across the mud and tore into the sky. He soared so high so soon that he was a mere speck on the horizon before the well-wishers had caught their breath.

Pundits were wondering about the prospects for the trip's success. In print and over the radio there were cautious appeals to logic and realism. Mr. Harrison, the public was reminded, faced a mammoth task just in crossing the Atlantic, to say nothing of completing his trip around the world. He would almost certainly need a strong tail wind and perfect direction to get beyond Greenland in his little plane. Over the open seas without landmarks he would become a prisoner of his compass, and if it malfunctioned then he might well run his tank dry and miss a tiny but critical island outpost where he had intended to make a landing.

He grew weary and bored for his first few days of flying over New England and eastern Canada. Rarely did he rise to an altitude above 2000 feet, easily following the contours of shorelines, the paths of rivers, the succession of large towns and cities whose geographic situation he had nearly committed to memory through long hours of study. Makeshift landing fields, situated near the bays and inlets where small tankers were carrying gasoline and supplies, had been established by the Champion Petroleum Company all the way up the coast of Labrador and at several points on Baffin Island and Greenland. These enabled Milt to follow the barren coastline of Labrador, where the taiga met the icy sea, in stages up to Hebron, where he nearly collapsed in exhaustion in pitch darkness around ten o'clock on his second day of travel. He had to be helped from his cockpit in the subfreezing night air.

"We've got a cot on our ship for you, Major," said one of the two Canadian naval officers who were manning the refueling vessel at the subarctic outpost. "That's all you'll find in this place—unless you want to sleep in the grass."

"*Grass?*" Kid winced. "What grass? You show me some grass, mate, and I'll show you a goddamn palm tree."

The men tried to talk Kid into sharing their dinner of boiled ham and cabbage, but he was insistent on eating his palmfuls of nuts and raisins, several crackers with peanut butter, and scooping out the pulp and juice of two grapefruits. That was as tasty to his famished palate as just about any other meal would have been—though he was hungry enough to have eaten grass itself that night, if any grass had been growing around there.

THE NEXT DAY'S JOURNEY was even more grueling. That evening at Nûk, the Inuit name for Godthåb, the territorial capital of Greenland, the fishermen, reindeer-hunters and shepherds of the region had brought their women and children out of doors to watch him as he swooped down, slid into the mud, and refueled his plane from a cistern by a long wharf.

He was utterly exhausted now, after hours of monotony over deserted subarctic seas, and in need of human companionship. He put his hands together, placed them against his ear, leaned his head off to one side and shut his eyes. The Inuit immediately understood his gesture. An old man, widowed and living alone with two young daughters, was the first to clutch at his sleeve and lead him into the settled part of Nûk, where Kid slept in a modest cottage on a reindeer hide by a fire as the young women stared at him and wondered what he was doing there.

He never was able to communicate with the girls or their father in any way except gestures and hand signals, but he slept soundly and gave the family some American money, probably of no value to them but still of interest, before he walked back out to his plane at sunrise on the following morning. Strapped into the Moth's passenger seat, and taking up a disproportionate share of cargo space inside the plane, were three empty 12-gallon gasoline canisters. Milt had brought them for just the type of situation he would face after his stop at Godthåb.

During his trek he would have at least two prolonged stretches over uninhabitable land, over Greenland and the Arabian deserts, which would certainly exceed the 320-mile range of his biplane. It would be impossible for him to arrange for any type of outside refueling in such a location. These canisters, filled up at the refueling site just before the leg when he expected to need them, would act as his reserves. At some point over the icecaps of Greenland, he anticipated landing, pouring the 36 extra gallons of fuel into his tank himself, and thereby gaining enough range to reach Angmagssalik, an Inuit settlement on the island's opposite shore.

Several astonished members of the Danish navy, helping him that morning to fill and secure these extra containers to his rear flying seat at the Godthåb landing field, noticed that Milt looked weak and pale. They questioned the wisdom of what he was planning to do that day, amongst themselves in Danish and with him in English.

"Are you sure you want to continue, sir?" asked one. "Nobody's ever gotten from one side of the world to the other all by himself."

"That don't concern me a bit," said Kid. "I haven't cared about what other people did or didn't do for a long, long time now, my friend."

When he took off again the man from Woodvale began what he expected to be as difficult a test of endurance as any he would face on his entire trip. He would try to go as far as he could over the blindingly white ice caps of Greenland, refuel wherever he could, and aim his Moth at Angmagssalik, the nearest inhabited place. The continuous wind chilled him, his head and limbs grew numb, the plane wobbled repeatedly. He had been colder before—at 10,000 feet in wintertime over the Argonne, at any altitude during a blizzard over Michigan or Illinois. But in those instances he had had beneath him the protective embrace of civilization. Even in wartime the friendly side of the Allied lines had never been an impossibly far distance away. Safety in some form or another had always been accessible. But now there was no refuge of man's mechanized industrial civilization anywhere near him. He would survive, if he did so, strictly by bettering the forces of Mother Nature.

On the fledgling medium of radio masses of listeners in America were hearing reports that the Great Ace of the Great War, the erstwhile barnstormer, crop-duster, wing walker, skydiver, mail courier (and, though almost no one knew, *booze-smuggler)* was shaken and depleted of energy, possibly over the interior icecaps of Greenland by now, where no human being had ever been before. . . .

Somewhere on a white wasteland with his whereabouts unknown, three hours after his last stop, Kid landed on an icy plain hemmed in by distant crags of glacial mountains. His mission was to try to pour the extra three cans of fuel into his tank. The Moth slid like an ice skate when it came down, and after it spun around to a stop Milt cut off its switches and groaned as he tried to climb down from the cockpit. He was barely able to lift the cans, each weighing only about 70 lbs. and with two-foot-high dimensions, up out of the rear seat.

He dragged them over to the front of the engine, and spilled an excessive amount of the volatile gasoline on his gloves and clothing as his wobbly hands poured the fuel into a funnel he had placed in the mouth of his tank. When he had finished emptying the third and final can he collapsed. Reeking wet fuel soaked his arms and the front of his coat; the ice stung like acid and the subfreezing air numbed his face, hands and feet.

All around him now was nothing. For as far as he could see, from one uninhabited extent of the horizon to the other, there was blindingly white ice under a cloudless sky so intensely blue it seemed to belong to the atmosphere of another planet. He thought about how beautiful Greenland would have seemed to him had it not been so intent on killing him. He staggered back up and restrapped the empty canisters back in his passenger seat, then he lunged at the propellor blade and with a primal yell tried to hurl it started.

The ice-cold sharpness of the blade cut through his worn leather glove and pierced the flesh of the four fingers of his right hand. He angrily pulled off the tattered glove, threw it to the ground, and curled up in pain while he balled his bloody hand into a fist. Blood was spurting out and dripping onto the ice. Without bandaging the cut he tried to push-start the propellor again, but his weakened arms could barely lift themselves to touch the blade, let alone fling it around. His hand bled on the propellor and he leaned down and wiped it on the ice, staining it blood red, before retrieving his glove and putting it on again.

It was useless to fight now, he thought. He stretched out on the ice, supinely on his back, trying to gain strength from the force that dwelled in the sky where his squinting eyes, glazed with rime and ice, stared longingly. He would wait there until the spirit moved him to try again. And if the spirit never came then he would never move, but just congeal into a stiff corpse with his inanimate biplane as the sentry to his unmarked remains until the continents of the earth collided again and the ice of Greenland thawed. He would lie there and wait.

In due course—it might have been minutes, it might have been an hour, he could not tell—the spirit did move him. He suddenly heard a far-away voice from a distant corner of his childhood memory. "*Just when you start to count a fellow out, that's the time when he usually jumps up and surprises you.*" On a spur of the moment he staggered to his feet, charged again with all his might at the propellor, and whipped it around. It coughed briefly, hesitated, then roared back to life.

He took a deep breath. Yet again he had staved off the fate that must eventually claim him as it would all others. He had recut his clotted wounds while spinning the propellor started again, and he shook his bleeding hand back and forth while he repositioned himself in the pilot's seat then wrapped his hand tightly with gauze out of his first aid kit. Soon the man and his machine were soaring aloft again above the frozen lifeless wilderness, the shadow of his plane flitting across the empty ice like a mysterious ghost far below him.

His blood remained on the spot where he had landed. It would always be there on that arctic desert where nothing ever grew or decayed, lived or died. Always on that tiny spot on the icecaps of Greenland would be the mark of human blood, signifying that a man had been there once, long ago, and would never be there again.

AFTER ANGMAGSSALIK, A BRITISH Navy aircraft carrier was to refuel Major Harrison at a point in the Denmark Strait about halfway to Reykjavik, Iceland. Having traveled nearly 250 miles since takeoff from the Greenland coast, Kid caught sight of a dark spot of gray on the nautical horizon. The HMS *Cotswold*, bearing a long platform on its quarterdeck, soon came clearly into view, the Union Jack flapping from its masthead. Piles of sandbags, weighing down rows of heavy steel wires, were positioned at the end of the deck to act as arresting gear. In the steady northern mists, the Britons had been unable to keep the deck dry. But by a stroke of good luck the winds were calm as he landed, though he skidded clumsily on the wet slick steel hull for several dozen yards and dissipated his momentum only after plowing into the cables of the arresting gear.

After dismounting from his plane, the freezing cold aviator wanted to soak in a tub filled with hot water for about an hour, then to continue on his mission without further delay. The British seamen tried to dissuade him from this hasty attitude. They told him he might get frostbite if he kept this up. They warned him of incapacitation, amputated limbs, disfigurement and death—all to no avail.

"Did it ever occur to you that you might die from this trek, sir?" asked a thin and freckled sailor who looked barely old enough to shave.

"Not really," said Kid. "I don't expect to die."

"You've got to, one of these days, don't you? Or are you immortal?"

"Naw, I ain't no immortal. It's just that I won't die—not on this trip."

CHAPTER 26

Around the World Solo

IN A MERE TWO days Milt was past Iceland, the British Isles and France, and had traversed the entire Mediterranean all the way to Turkey. Warmer weather had worked wonders for him. Now his only concern was hunger. Nuts, crackers and grapefruit only went so far. What he wanted presently was a juicy steak dinner with biscuits and honey and a wide slab of cheesecake for dessert. Unfortunately, there was no such luxury in his immediate future.

What he lacked in physical nourishment, though, he tried to make up for in excitement. In the process of landing on the African continent in Egypt he was planning to have a private romantic rendezvous. The green ribbon of the Nile valley led him southward to the modern capital of Egypt, a densely packed mass of white plaster buildings and thronging pedestrians in veils, fezzes, turbans and flowing robes. Long before he recognized much about Cairo he made out the storied profiles of the pyramids a short distance upstream from it.

He flew low over the city, buzzing up the interest of the populace and proclaiming his arrival for the teeming masses of Egyptians. Cries of disbelief and pointing fingers followed the path of his plane. When he came to the gleaming white stone structures at Giza, the Pyramids of Khufu, Khafre and Mankaure, he lowered his flaps, cut his throttle and circled all three at close range, lovingly studying their details, zigzagging from one to the next. Not far to the south he saw the Sphinx and flew as close as he could to her antiquely mutilated face, hauntingly near so that he might have leaned over and brushed his hand against her forehead had he been walking on his own wings, and then he twirled around and examined her lion's body from high above.

Afterwards he landed his plane on the hard flat sand at the eastern base of the pyramids and climbed up on his top wing and watched the sun set in the western horizon, enjoying a long wordless contemplation of ancient glory. He made his bed on the sand that night, sleeping in peace and contentment as gentle breezes drifted up from the banks of the Nile.

A day later he had crossed the Suez Canal and Sinai Desert to Palestine, following the footsteps of Moses; looked down on Jerusalem, the Mount of Olives, the Holy Sepulcher and the Wilderness of Juddah, following the footsteps of Jesus; crossed the Dead Sea and entered Transjordan at Amman; and continued over the desolation of Arabia. He was forced to fill his extra canisters with gasoline at Amman in preparation for another self-refueling stop in the middle of nowhere.

On this occasion it would be at a Bedouin oasis called Ar Rutbah, where men in white cloaks and beards gave him a belatedly friendly welcome and offered him camel's milk and feta cheese. Not since the Great War had they seen any flying machines, and though they mistrusted Milt when he first appeared he eventually made them understand, by way of showing them all his maps of the world which he had stashed away in his cockpit, that he had only peaceable intentions.

THE DESERT AIR WAS hot and clear, the flying was beautiful and the visibility was unlimited. He followed the Euphrates to the Persian Gulf and stopped for fuel at Kuwait. Tonight would be one without rest. The moon was bright, the contours of the desert shoreline were easy to recognize and follow, even in the dark, and the Union Jack was strung up at regular intervals on ships and consulates clear across eastern Arabia, Iran, India and the southeastern peninsula of Asia.

At Bahrain he landed in the dark, stripped naked, and bathed blissfully in the saline waters of the Gulf. As there were only men about even in the daytime in that Islamic domain, he cared little about whether anyone might have seen him. After seven days and nights of travel in a cramped seat he felt entitled to give free rein to his impulses on the ground. His healthy and well-shaped form seemed perfectly in its element as he swam back and forth in the turquoise water under the predawn moonlight. It was past two in the morning, and the refreshing swim had the same revivifying effect on him as a three-hour nap. He had no towels with him, so upon emerging from the water he put his flying clothes back over his soaking body and let them absorb the moisture from his skin.

By sunrise the Moth had stopped at Dubay and continued past the Strait of Hormuz and was following the southern shoreline of Iran toward India. Another British aircraft carrier, the HMS *Nelson*, awaited his arrival at 25°North and 60°East, a few kilometers off the shoreline of Iran in the Gulf of Oman. He felt more comfortable about landing on a floating vessel by now, having done it once before, and the English boys who manned the ship saluted him upon his arrival.

The legend of the man from Woodvale had spread like a brush fire. The Great Ace of the Great War, the fearless barnstormer and wing walker from the Southern back roads of the U.S.A., kept plugging away at his joystick, ignoring hunger and sleep, single-mindedly determined to conquer the world with the aid of a crude little machine, a few maps, and an erratic compass.

The sights, sounds and smells of India burned themselves indelibly into his brain. Disgusting filth, crowdedness, squalor and destitution alternated with brilliant lushness, fertility, teeming, swarming life, and extraordinary scenery. The heat on the ground was suffocating and stifling. It reminded him of summer back home, except that the stench of rubbish and fecal matter seemed to be more widespread, and the flies a lot more aggressive, and the cows extremely full of their own sacredness.

RADIO LISTENERS IN AMERICA were getting used to a communal routine each night as they sat comfortably in their living rooms and heard the accounts of Kid's far-off adventures. The aviator was at Calcutta in India. He was at Rangoon in Burma. He was at Bangkok in Thailand, had narrowly avoided a crash in a precarious landing at Singapore, and had kept on all the way to Djakarta in Indonesia. On some nights he was sleeping and on others not. He was pushing himself as hard as humanly possible. Men and woman who did not understand his language and whose heritage and culture were totally different from his were beseeching him, through translators or through gestures, to go more slowly.

Maybe it was not possible for an aeroplane to go around the world with only a single person behind its controls. Maybe it would never be. And what was the point? Trains and cars took people across land and steamships crossed oceans.

He had slept at a clean inn in Jodhpur, nearly in exhaustion, but had again gone another two days without sleep between Calcutta and Djakarta. Two weeks into his trip he had arrived at Kupang on Timor island in the south of Indonesia; the same Timor Island on which the notorious Captain Bligh, after a mutinous Fletcher Christian had thrown him off the HMS *Bounty*, had completed a 4000-mile trip in a lifeboat 137 years earlier; and was the accomplishment of Major Harrison not akin to that of Bligh? But to expect the aviator now to circle the rim of the Pacific in another two and a half weeks and go all the way down to South America before returning to New York—was this not asking Bligh to make it completely back to England in the same lifeboat?

As he rested on a hammock at Kupang, basking in the setting sun over the Indian Ocean, Milt was confused, hungry, and slightly delirious but in no mood to cut short his chase. One good night's rest, eight hours—that was all he needed. One night of sleep, then two more weeks of grueling, grinding flight. Two beautiful island girls from the French-run inn attended to him. He kept telling them he wanted them to massage his back, which was covered with saddle sores from countless hours of confinement in his leather seat. That was all he wanted from them—to rub his back and hold his hands. He was too weak for conversation and even smiles, but, by the blessings of fate, he did attain his eight full hours of sleep that night and by the next sunrise felt as if he were starting his voyage anew.

He eventually touched down at Darwin, at the northern tip of Australia, and continued north for several days over the islands of the Pacific. North of Manila, in the Philippines, he had trouble finding a landing spot over the Ilocos Norte province. He circled about the town of Laoag and, for the first time in his journey, he ran his plane's tank dry and had to glide down in a small field with a dead engine. Just as the arrival of his machine had generated crowds in dozens of other locales throughout the world, so it did here too—though it was an entirely unannounced arrival.

A large group of Filipinos—mostly women, children and the elderly—from a nearby barrio quickly came to his rescue. One young sable-eyed girl who said her name was Conchita Ramirez led him to her auntie's bamboo hut and offered him a seat on the divan while she went to fetch him a gourd of water from the backyard well. The neighbors crowded around the threshold of the house, craning their necks to peak at the activity inside. One aggressive woman, who later said her name was Violly, kept smiling while Conchita, who was the only one there with fluency in English, inquired about the American visitor's airplane as he sipped the cool water from the small gourd. Finally Violly slipped in a momentous question.

"Do you like to eat rice?"

"No, thanks, ma'am," said Kid. "This cool water's all I want right now."

"I don't think you understand what she's asking," said Conchita. "She's not offering you rice now but she wants to know if you like eating it."

"Ma'am, I don't eat rice too often, but if you gave it to me now I'd probably like it. Heck, right now I'm so hungry if you fed me the bark of a tree I'd say it tasted good."

The barrio served him a feast of rice and pork over a bonfire in the dark. Conchita, her auntie and three cousins abandoned their hut to stay with neighbors that night and gave the stranger carte blanche to do as he pleased alone in their home. Sweltering in the tiny cabin's heat, he began to understand why natives of the tropics had worn little more than loincloths before their contact with Europeans. He removed all his clothes and tried dousing his body with a cold cotton cloth that he soaked in a pot full of water. As fatigued as he was, sleep came quickly if not comfortably after his back and midriff had been drenched with the water.

What he craved now, most intently, was *ice*. His dreams were filled with it. Only a few days earlier his whole world had been made of ice and he had been on the verge of being entombed in it. Now it existed as a precious commodity in his imagination, a substance of more value than gold. When he was cold he seemed to forget that he had ever been hot, and now that he was hot he couldn't seem to remember ever having been cold.

A jeepney driver transported one of his empty canisters to Laoag the next morning and brought Kid back some gasoline which he used to restart the DH Moth. He offered the Filipinos American money for the help they had given him, but they flatly turned him down. How to repay them—that was what gnawed at his conscience as he flew off to what the natives had told him was the nearest place to refuel, a landing field on Bangui Bay. But their greatest time of need was yet to be, and the greatest thing anyone could do for them he would, in another generation, return in an airplane to do.

BY WAY OF BATAAN Island, Taiwan and Okinawa he reached the enchanting city of Nagasaki, in extreme southwestern Japan, before that day had passed. Around the picturesque blue harbor of Nagasaki a thick mantle of leafy vegetation, curling up hillsides, glowed with every known shade of green and, with the approach of autumn, faint glimmers of gold and orange. The bright structures of the town radiated a brilliant light, as if this were the Oriental version of the New England Puritan's city upon a hill.

The sound of an American plane buzzing over Nagasaki brought joy and happiness to the people who were there to witness its landing. Formerly walled off from foreign society by imperial decree, the Japanese had embraced the West in the last 75 years and this latest arrival signified that their land had become a pearl on a string that now ran throughout the world.

CHAPTER 27

Closing Out the Loop

THE CONE OF *FUJIYAMA* appeared on the Milt's horizon early in the afternoon, and he soared above 12,000 feet, exposing himself to subfreezing blasts of air for the first time in two weeks, in order to fly directly over its snowcapped summit. From there it was but a few minutes to the airfield on Tokyo Bay, where the Japanese Emperor was present to witness his landing.

When Major Harrison touched down at Tokyo to appreciative welcomes from the several thousand Japanese who were there to witness his arrival, an interpreter informed him that the Emperor wished to bestow upon him a gift. Kid felt as mangy as a stray mutt, unshaven and soaked with oil, grease and gasoline, but he thought it wise not to snub royalty. So out he came from his flying seat, removing his helmet and goggles, and he followed the interpreter to an elderly man dressed in a woolen three-piece suit. Standing next to the Emperor was a very young man in another woolen suit, and a youngish woman in her early forties, wearing a long white silk dress. These, the foreigner was told, were the Crown Prince and Empress of Japan.

Milt placed his hands together in Japanese style, bowed his head and genuflected before the dignitaries. The Emperor said to him through the interpreter that he was familiar with the aviator's career from the last war and he considered their meeting a matter of personal pride. Kid answered politely that the real honor was for a commoner such as himself to be allowed to meet and converse with royalty. The Empress gave her son a small birch box which he opened to reveal the token of appreciation that the Japanese people were presenting Major Harrison.

Inside was a long silken band, on the end of which was an *origami,* a 12-year-old Saitama prefecture girl's creation of folded rice paper in the shape of a bird with two long wings. The little girl emerged from the crowd, genuflected, and was chaperoned back to her beamingly proud parents. The Crown Prince made as if he wanted to place the band over the pilot's head, and Milt leaned down and allowed him to do so. They then shook hands.

"Your Majesty," he said, "if I fly back to America with this I'll have a hard time not crushing it. It gets rough up in the air, sir—especially when you're trying to get across the Pacific Ocean alone in a plane."

"Ah," said the Crown Prince in English, not even waiting for his interpreter's translation, "you keep it here." He gave Kid the birch box, opened its lid and pointed inside. Photographers were blitzing the scene and the two young men from exceptionally different backgrounds chuckled and bowed their heads at one another.

The Emperor, through his translator, mentioned half-seriously that Major Harrison must be a direct heir of Commodore Perry. But the man from Woodvale replied, humbly, that as far as he knew the best his ancestors ever did was lose a war and an election and overfarm a few fields of hard red clay in a poor section of America. The Emperor thought this a funny joke in translation and he laughed, but the pilot had meant it as no joke.

The Emperor, whose knowledge of America was limited, thought it obvious that this man had descended from a direct line of warrior-gods or explorer-gods, and was simply putting into practice the intense precepts and disciplines of a youth filled with rigorous education as befitted the nobility of his land. Was not Woodvale the site of some noted temple of some kind where apprentices in all the various arts and sciences of America went to meditate and commune with great masters? It seemed not unlikely to the Japanese monarch.

THROUGH SHEER FORCE OF will Milt reached Nemuro on the eastern edge of Hokkaido, Japan's northernmost major island, near midnight that night. He had been hearing voices for the last few hours, and seeing blurred double visions of things, his teeth chattering in the fierce cold of the increasingly high latitudes. Constant noise, deadening boredom, hunger pangs and exhaustion were turning him into a wreck of a man. He had put up a game front for the Japanese royal family, but he was feeling more and more like a beaten man, someone destined to give up an ambitious undertaking when it was only half finished.

Japanese women were extremely attractive to him, and it was quite obvious that large numbers of them felt the same way about him. He had a fleeting urge to seek out a prostitute in Nemuro to restore his feeling of communion with the human family, but he feared reporters, publicity, shame, the ill opinion of the world. Instead he was helped to a cozy inn, given warm tea, and attended by three *geishas*, who were as close to prostitutes as a respectable man in the glare of an international spotlight might go but offered no sexual favors.

They prepared a warm bath for him, sent his soiled clothes to be washed in the middle of the night, massaged his back and sore legs after he wrapped his midriff in a towel, and served him a traditional Japanese dinner of various items that he wouldn't have normally allowed to come even near his mouth but that he now devoured like a famished wolf. He paid them lavishly with his dwindling supply of American cash before falling suddenly into a deep, comatose sleep which lasted seven hours, until the women knocked on his door at 10AM and stirred him back to life.

KID MADE STEADY PROGRESS over the Kuril Islands of the U.S.S.R. and the Aleutians of Alaska during the next several days. The Soviets, former allies of Major Harrison in 1917-18, had agreed to man refueling stations on otherwise barren islands in the Kurils. Chairman Joseph Stalin, casting a wary eye on China on his southern frontier and the maelstrom of instability in Germany to his west, was looking to make powerful diplomatic friends in the event that he needed them in the future, and he offered no objections when the request was submitted to him by the Soviet Navy to help the American pilot.

Milt did not encounter a single English-speaker while he flew over the chilly and woebegone isolation of the Kurils and the Kamchatka peninsula. He was able to communicate via hand signals and facial expressions with the glassy-eyed Russian seamen, manning small refueling tankers on deserted islands, who climbed up to help him from his plane when he landed on permafrost-hardened bluffs above the sea. They gave him paper and a fountain pen, and motioned for him to autograph his name. They offered him cigarettes, which he diplomatically turned down. No cigarettes? Ah, America grew fine tobacco. How about vodka? There was nothing to rival Russian vodka. Kid realized the closer he came to finishing off his job the more souvenirs he would be accumulating, so he accepted the vodka. If there was one thing he knew very well it was flying over water with bottles of spirits about him in DeHavilland biplanes. He had never acquired a taste for the stuff, but if he ever ran out of gas he thought maybe he could pour the bottle of vodka into his tank and run on that for awhile.

The conditions were too dark and cold in this region for extensive periods of night flying, so Kid stopped in the main urban center of the Kamchatka Peninsula, Petropavlovsk-Kamchatskiy, a gray town full of pudgy women with large red spots on their cheeks and heavy furry hats, and razor-thin men with pale complexions and icy blue eyes. He gathered that the townspeople were making somewhat of a fuss over him, since they cheered him when he landed after dark, they led him with some fanfare to a hotel, they offered him cigars, caviar and more vodka, and they seemed to be carrying on in their language about what he had done. He recognized that what they were feeding him was fish of some kind, but he had no taste of it. His hunger was so consuming that he was inhaling food without bothering to chew it or let it linger on his palate long enough to determine its flavor.

The scenery of the wild northern extremity of the world was breathtaking, and it was this untamed beauty that mitigated his boredom the next day as he flew north along the coastline of Kamchatka Pensinsula. He turned east across a desolate empty sea again, and stopped at the last outpost of the Old World along his itinerary, the Kamandorskiye Ostrova islands, Soviet territory on the edge of the Bering Sea. He brought his Moth down on the taiga by the sea, taking care to avoid rocks which might have destroyed his landing gear just as he was on his home stretch, and was aided in refilling his tank one last time by star-struck Russian-speaking men.

Three and a half hours later when he landed on Attu Island, the westernmost of the Aleutians, he was back in U.S. territory. The seamen were waving American flags and cheering him in English, and he nearly wanted to kiss the ground when he stepped down from his plane.

"Congratulations," said one of the refueling tanker's crewmen. "You made it!"

"Hallelujah!" Kid cried, falling to his knees and clasping his hands together melodramatically. "How'd y'all like to celebrate by taking some nasty imported Russian vodka off my hands?"

The men drank his bottle dry at Attu, and he followed the spectacular chain of Aleutian volcanism, one snowcapped cone after another towering over the pure blue sea, for as long as he could recognize the chain, until darkness had long since descended over the wilderness of water and mountains, and he stopped to rest at Unalaska, on the island of the same name, 1200 miles and 17 hours after he had begun that morning on the Siberian mainland.

He flew along the Alaskan coastline for two more days, staying overnight at Anchorage and Ketchikan, a weary traveler too numb to care much for the extraordinary procession of two-mile-high glaciated mountains and unpeopled fiords that drifted by under his wings. Only one more day of mountain flying remained: the fiords of the Coast Ranges of British Columbia to Vancouver, then across the low mountains of northern Washington to Spokane, then the Bitterroot Range of Idaho and Montana, and the railroad tracks, the endless railroad tracks to the Great Plains around Billings, Montana. . . .

At Billings the enfeebled man, worn down by the vast dimensions of the world; frayed by the vibrations of millions of cylinder explosions in his machine as it circled the earth; confused by alternating bouts with heat and cold, by the swirl of languages, customs, cultures, landscapes, coastlines and peoples; malnourished by a meager, monotonous diet for the better part of a month; and staggered by the weight of the expectations that it seemed the entire human race had placed on his shoulders—at Billings the man from Woodvale collapsed on the dusty landing field after he brought his plane down in darkness yet again.

He was too proud to let anyone carry him from the field without at least a second try at self-sufficiency, so he waved off the men who wanted to help him and simply lay on the hard-packed dirt a few steps from his plane, curled up in a fetal dream, his ears clanging with the tintinnabulations of endless mechanical noises, his eyes bloodshot, his nose runny, like a pummeled schoolboy who had lost a bout with the playground bully. Now he knew why men had died trying to do this. What amazed him was that he had made it this far and was still alive. Perhaps just barely alive, but still . . .

When he awoke the next morning, nearly at noon, he was in a clean bed. Some men had carried him off the field in a stretcher, propped him up in a taxicab, and taken him to the Western Star, the finest hostelry in Billings. His stomach ached with starvation, but within seconds after reawakening his consciousness was flooded with joy. *He was in America!* He could cram his mouth with American victuals now, flirt with American flappers, talk American slang, fly over American towns. Gone was the exhausted despair, the prostration that was near death. A good night of sleep had served to rejuvenate the man from Woodvale. Was he ready to close out the loop, now that he had come this far?

"Don't count me out, men," he told a gaggle of reporters after he downed a platter of flapjacks, eggs and sausages at the diner in the lobby of the Western Star. "*I may be gittin' a little old, but I'm not dead yet.*"

It was October 26, the twenty-fifth day of his voyage. Seven more days remained for him to touch South America then return to his starting point in New York City. He was getting such a late start on this day that he was only able to advance two states, to Sioux City, Iowa, before darkness brought his journey to a halt. For the first time in his 25 days of globetrotting he encountered a thunderstorm, over the South Dakota prairie, and he flew directly through it, his Moth being thrashed about like a windswept leaf, his eardrums nearly blown out by thunderclaps. Anything for a little excitement for Mr. Excitement. Following the railroad tracks and the Missouri River eastward had bored him nearly out of his senses, but a near-brush with death perked him up nicely.

He was heartened the next day by the most alluring destination to someone who has long been away: HOME. He was able to fly in a day's time all the way from northwestern Iowa to the hardscrabble cow pasture in Hapeville whose cozy familiarity had been sweetening his dreams across several days, continents and time zones.

At Candler Field he recognized for the first time how seriously the people at home were taking his excursion. Seventy-five thousand people, the largest assemblage that had ever gathered there, welcomed the homegrown hero as his machine came down just as the orange glow of the autumn sunset was flickering out of the horizon. Police had to restrain the crowd and, per Kid's orders, he was carted away by motorcade to his house and his property was guarded by patrolmen while he slept.

In subsequent days he landed twice on a U.S. aircraft carrier in the Caribbean as he flew to and from Barranquilla, Colombia. He followed the Eastern Seaboard up to New York and landed at McCormack Field on the afternoon of November 1. The Champion Prize was his. Frenzied specta-tors broke through the police barricade and surrounded his plane when it sputtered to a halt in New York. An enterprising radio reporter was first up on the wing and he thrust his cumbersome microphone into the aviator's face.

"Major Harrison," he yelled above the commotion, "what are your impressions on circling the globe?"

"If the Lord made all that in six days," said Kid, "He must've had one hell of a factory!"

CHAPTER 28

Hollywood

AFTER HE FLEW HOME to Georgia several days later, a parade was given in Major Harrison's honor in the center of Atlanta. And after he made his triumphant return to Woodvale he was practically elevated to sainthood. It was quite overwhelming to him, actually. He fell a little bit into the doldrums. What was next? At every stage of his life, having conquered one more mountain or slain one more demon, he was always confronted by the same vexing dilemma: how to slake his ever-present thirst for more action, more excitement, more discovery.

His mother and other kinfolk were still happy to live in Woodvale, and one of Kid's former housemates had now joined them. Woody lived out that way now. During Kid's Flying Circus, the Bahamian had met and befriended Rev. Patterson in the segregated grandstands at Candler Field. Just before Milt embarked on his long journey, Woody had been offered and had accepted a job as caretaker of the First AME Church of Woodvale. This meant that Kid was all alone when he returned home, and he rarely saw any of his old friends—even Chet and Bobby, who seemed determined to prove they could prosper without him

Milt did nothing of any consequence for several months after he returned from his round-the-world trip. With only one exception there was nobody around Atlanta who seemed to notice that his inactivity was bothering him. Alderman Grantland, his eyes still fixed on the horizon of the heavenly future when pigs would have wings and cows would jump over the moon, was curious to know what Kid's next great undertaking would be. And so, like an annoying uncle nobody wants to see, with stern warnings and pious preachings, George dropped in unannounced on his old friend one day in late February.

"You think you're done now, Kid—just 'cause you made it around the world once?" Grantland lectured the aviator as they rocked on the wicker chairs on the chilly veranda behind Milt's house. "You're only thirty years old—you might live a long time into the future. You gotta do something besides rest on your laurels."

Kid had worn down the toothpick on which he had been nibbling to a soft pulp, so he pulled it out of his mouth, turned it around and began nibbling on its hard side.

"How many times you been around the world, George?"

"What difference does that make? I couldn't even make it across the street without help."

"Well, I think you oughtta jump off your high horse, Cap'n, and see if you can do better than this here lazy son of a bitch."

"Again, Milton, that's beside the point. It's not about what I can do, it's about you. You flew around the world in a month, but who says that's the fastest anybody's ever gonna do it? You believe that?"

"Hell no. It won't be six months before somebody else does it in half the time."

"Why can't it be you again?"

"I can't do it all, George. It's humanly impossible. I gotta step aside eventually and live a regular life."

"And is that what you want?" George asked. "You want to sit back and live a regular life while somebody else does something amazing in an aeroplane?"

The alderman's question seemed to strike Kid in a particularly touchy spot, and he underwent a sudden change of heart. He plucked the toothpick from his mouth, stood up out of his rocking chair, and went over to the concrete balustrade of the veranda, hurling the toothpick defiantly into the grass of his backyard.

"You kiddin', man?" he turned and answered his friend. "Nobody beats Kid Harrison in an aeroplane. NOBODY."

For once in his life he proved to be wrong. Six months later, while he and some engineers at Vandermeer Aviation, a Charleston, S.C. aircraft company, were still perfecting the *Aeroniña*, a monoplane which they expected to fly nonstop across the Atlantic Ocean, their plans were scuttled. A little-known Midwestern ex-barnstormer named Charles Lindbergh flew nonstop from New York to Paris in 33 hours and claimed the $25,000 Orteig Prize. Overnight he became the most famous figure in the brief history of aviation.

"I gotta admire the boy for pulling it off," Milt was telling Mr. Vandermeer on the morning of May 22 of '27. "But . . . if we'd had two more weeks . . . hell, *one more week* . . ."

"We'll never know," sighed Vandermeer. "Why don't you go anyway, just to prove you can do it?"

Kid squinted at the old man as though he had just uttered the thoughts of a lunatic.

"For what? *To come in second?* In this world, coming in second ain't a whole lot better than coming in last!"

WHILE SLIM LINDBERGH BASKED in all the world's attention, Kid finally thought of a way to make himself useful again. Though he had only intermittently taken much interest in business in his haphazard life, he remembered having given those two entomologists in Louisiana $550 for a crop-dusting operation in 1919, having helped them build it into a profitable company, and having left them to their own devices while he chased after other will-o'-the-wisps and competitors moved in and began to crowd them out. What had become of the Louisiana Dusting Service these days?

Aloysius Troy Bonderman and Trevor Reed had moved to Monroe, Louisiana, and Kid cabled them in early June to request a meeting. A few days later he flew the newly-finished Aeroniña down to a dusty landing strip in the middle of northern Louisiana. The two entomologists were on hand to congratulate the aviator on last year's bit of globetrotting, and listened to his suggestion. It was time they laid off the boll weevil business and started carrying passengers. Somebody like old man Vandermeer in Charleston would be available to design a suitable plane for them, and as to the seed money for the endeavor, well, Milt pulled off his leather jacket in the stifling heat and removed a manila envelope from one of its interior pockets. He took out several bound stacks of bills from the envelope and threw them almost tauntingly down to the ground.

"That's $13,000," said Kid. "After I paid off the manufacturer for this here airship, the thirteen g's are all that's left of the prize money that oil company gave me for flying around the world. We've gotta do something to pump some life into this sagging old maid of a company we got out here. Let's use this to try to get a passenger outfit going."

"Where?" asked A.T.

"Candler Field, gentlemen."

"Who the hell wants to go there? What's it near?"

"Atlanta."

"Atlanta—what's Atlanta near?"

Kid began laughing as he kicked up dust with his boot heel and a cloud swirled about the money he had thrown on the ground.

"*Nothin',*" said Kid. "Nothing *yet.*"

Mr. Bonderman nodded and stared down at the remnants of the prize money the celebrated flying man had poured all his heart and soul into winning.

"You're right about one thing, Kid," he admitted. "It's a crowded field of dusters now. If you put three cows in a field where there's only grass enough for two, they all get thin."

"I just thought of a new motto for us, gentlemen," said Milt. "If the grass really is greener on the other side of the fence, soon we'll make it *our* side. We'll call our new outfit the Gulf Coast Air Transport Company."

His mind now populated the universe with airplanes laden with happy fearless passengers going from one point to another, planes continually landing and taking off and going somewhere. As he flew his own aerial toy back east the next day, it occurred to him that this was the first practical scheme he had ever concocted. It would not be some useless piece of exhibitionism, but practical, necessary, vital to the future of civilization.

There would be no spins and loops and wing walking tricksters and screaming mobs of people begging some poor lean barnstormer to push his joystick one step closer to the grave. It would be, in a word, a *respectable* pursuit, designed toward the furtherance of human potential. He had convinced himself, by the time he plunged down to the lowing cows of the scrawny fields surrounding the Hapeville landing strip, that his time on the earth would forever after be devoted to utilitarian aims. His resolution stayed intact for several days, until a mysterious telegram was delivered to his Lafayette Avenue villa late one afternoon.

28JUNE1927

MAJOR HARRISON CONGRATS ON YOUR FLIGHT AROUND THE WORLD PERIOD ALL THE WORLD OWES YOU PRAISE PERIOD I AM A MOTION PICTURE PRODUCER FROM CALIFORNIA AND AM STAYING TONIGHT AT THE GEORGIAN TERRACE PERIOD I WOULD BE HONORED TO MEET YOU OVER DINNER AT THE HOTEL TOMORROW EVE AT 7 AND DISCUSS A BUSINESS PROPOSITION PERIOD RSVP PERIOD BEST REGARDS GARRETT HAWKINS

Milt had never heard of this Hawkins, though he realized he needed someone else's advice before he decided how he should respond to the telegram. Perhaps this man was a bigwig of such stature that to ignore him would be a mistake. Kid drove over to Alderman Grantland's residence in the Ninth Ward and asked the man who shared a peculiar friendship with him if he felt this Hawkins was a real person or a stalker. George recalled having read about this man. He was very young. He was a tycoon. He had produced one or two dreadful picture shows that had flopped miserably at the box office. He was now making a movie about airplanes in the World War. Another dreadful movie? Possibly. But a very expensive movie. It made sense for such a man to travel two thousand miles to meet with the ultimate authority on airplanes in the World War. The alderman thought the telegram was legitimate and that the aviator should answer yes. Business was business. At worst, it would be a wasted evening. At best, it would preface a momentous new period in the evolving life and times of Mr. N.B. Excitement.

Kid sent a message to the enigmatic Mr. Hawkins at the Georgian Terrace Hotel accepting the latter's dinner invitation for the following night. The Georgian Terrace had long since supplanted the Piedmont as the Atlanta hotel where the finest people stayed, the finest parties were held, and the finest deals were made. Young Hawkins, six months shy of his 25th birthday, had been the heir of his father's shipping business in Long Beach since age 19. A request by an old family friend for financial backing for a movie had lured the young mogul into show business in 1923, and once he had dabbled in it he had become addicted to it. He had lavished vast sums of money on a pair of mediocre pictures before being inspired to undertake a project about his second love, aviation, to be entitled *Fire and Air.*

For this latest venture, which Hawkins defiantly promised would be the greatest motion picture in the history of the cinema, he was serving as the producer, director and screenwriter. With ravenous and dilettantish abandon the spoiled millionaire had devoured the society of southern California. He had thrown heaps of money at beautiful women, directors, cameramen, stuntmen, extras. Already he had spent some $3 million on the production—over a half million dollars reconditioning 93 World War fighter planes and nearly as much money building airfields throughout the Los Angeles basin.

As the producer and director of the epic silent film, he had insisted on countless retakes and absurd attention to detail, sometimes idling his entire production for hours until he got cloudy skies and placing his cast on all-night call in the elusive quest for a rainy night in the semidesert climate. A preview audience for the silent film had rated it a $3-million dud and Hawkins was seething. It was apparent to him that he needed two new elements in order to fulfill his bold claims: audible dialogue, which was new to movies as of that year; and a big name, of which he had ridden the rails 2000 miles east in search. Money was no object. He needed the *imprimatur* and the guiding hand of the great Kid Harrison, and he would secure it at any and all cost.

When Milt entered the hotel's tea room that evening he noticed a tall, thin, slack-jawed clean-shaven young man in a tuxedo approaching him. He thought it must be the busboy coming to ask for his autograph and had a notion to turn around and leave the room before he could be cornered. Other people would recognize him and a throng of autograph-seekers and well-wishers would cluster around him at a time when he simply wanted to discuss a little business with a millionaire. However, before he could turn and leave the room, the figure he took to be the busboy called him out by name, under his breath, inaudible to the others around them:

"Mr. Harrison, I'm Gary Hawkins."

Milt looked up, amazed that someone so young occupied the position that George had claimed this man did. He shrank back in surprise, a fact which did not escape the young tycoon's notice.

"Pleased to meet you," Kid extended a handshake to Hawkins and greeted him.

"Caught you off guard, did I, Major?"

"You might say so. I was expecting somebody with a few more wrinkles than you got."

"Let's sit down over at the corner table, where we can't be overheard."

The plush room had deep red carpet, thick burgundy velvet curtains with wide sashes against its windows, and kerosene lanterns overhead. The two men made their way in the dimly lit room to a corner booth, and snacked on tea and scones while Hawkins made his offer.

"I've never been one to mince words, Major," he said, "and I won't now. I'm making a movie about aeroplanes and I need you to be in it. If I don't spice this thing up and get people into the movie houses to watch it, my name's gonna be disgraced in Hollywood. I can't afford to fail."

Kid crossed his arms and looked skeptically at the newcomer.

"Just how do you think I can help you, Mr. Hawkins? I'm no movie actor."

"I need a technical adviser, somebody to perform and supervise tricks in planes. What I've got so far after months of work isn't exciting enough. I need stuff to wow the public. Hell, I need to drum up publicity by announcing you'll be flying in the film. You understand, sir?"

"Sure, I understand," said Kid, trying to downplay his interest when in fact he was intrigued by the prospect. "I'm just wondering what the compensation's gonna be."

"Seventy-five thousand in cash up front," Hawkins announced, "and one percent of the gross box office receipts."

Milt whistled and shook his head.

"And what do you want me to do for that—kill myself?"

"No, I just want you to pretend California's France, and a bunch of hungry and underemployed barnstormers in the sky with you are the Kaiser's airmen."

"That won't be hard to do."

"And I need you to do it soon, before I'm tarred and feathered and ridden right out of that town."

"Give me two weeks, sir," said Kid. "To say good-bye to my mama, my mistresses and all the bums who drag on my coattails."

"It's a deal then," said Hawkins. "Let's shake on it and have some dinner. It's on me."

Several days later Milt drove a brand new automobile a local Atlanta dealership had given him in exchange for endorsement, a chrome-covered Hispano-Suiza roadster, over the familiar byways of northeast Georgia until he was in his home village again. To the citizens of Woodvale Lindbergh's flight had never even happened. There was still only one aviator in the world who mattered in those parts. The sign on the outskirts of the village, constantly evolving along with the career of its subject, had recently been repainted by the artistic brush of Mary Ann Yardley, who was in her sixties now but still steady of hand.

WELCOME TO WOODVALE
Home of Raymond Milton 'Kid' Harrison, Jr.
WORLD WAR FLYING ACE AND PIONEER WORLD TRAVELER

Soon after Milt's Hisso roadster turned the corner and came to a stop on Oak Street the news spread among the villagers that he had come home. Woodvale's citizenry quickly gathered around the front porch of Madge's house to fraternize with the poor doctor's son whose obsessions with flying machines had now spread to an entire world. All of the familiar characters were on hand. Rev. Gray was not as spry as he used to be, nor was Joe Freeman, and Rev. Patterson had a bad heart and could no longer roar out his fire-and-brimstone sermons. But Shnook Adams had lost all shame for having shot himself in the foot, and he stood in the front ranks. And Zeke, Blackie and Cliff, all married to local girls and with children of their own, were also there to marvel at his company.

Woody, Rev. Patterson's protégé, had undertaken the ministry himself and was in the process of becoming the Pastor of Woodvale's African Methodist Episcopal Church, but he abandoned all pious reserve when he saw his dear friend again. He slapped hands with the aviator, hugged him and nearly broke down in tears. Ruth went even further. The world seemed different after the Woodvale boy and his peers had helped to shrink its oceans and mountains into insignificance. There was no point in repressing her feelings any longer. When she saw Milt she wrapped her arms around him and, in full view of the entire town, kissed him tenderly on the cheek.

"I don't care what anybody else says," Ruth muttered with her cheek pressed against his. "*I love you.*"

She held his hand for awhile longer while he awkwardly made small talk with various white and black folks. He had a grand announcement to make.

"Y'all, I'm goin' out to Hollywood next. A rich movie producer out there wants me to do stunts for a picture about aeroplanes."

The 193 living Woodvaleans seemed fascinated by the idea of Milton Jr. in pictures, with one exception. Madge considered the project cheap and tawdry.

"I thought you were through with circuses and tricks," she said. "That man's tryin' to take advantage of you—I wouldn't trust him!"

Several villagers laughed, but Milt knew exactly what to say next to win his mother over to his cause.

"Aw, Mama, acting ain't the worst thing I could do. What about tax collectors and Prohibition agents? What if I turned into one of them? Shoot, acting's better than at least two other professions—maybe three, if you count prostitution."

CHESTER DAWES AND ROBERT BRACKENS were absent from Candler Field doing a barnstorming tour when Kid left later in the week. He was aiming to establish a new transcontinental flying record in the Aeroniña with a nonstop run from Hapeville to Los Angeles, a route that had never before been flown without a stop. Departing in the wee hours of the predawn, he flew 18 hours and 10 minutes without mishap, touching down at Clover Field in Santa Monica a little before 8 pm on the night of July 11.

Hawkins had reserved a penthouse suite for Kid at the Golden Rose Hotel in Beverly Hills, where he was welcome to stay for the duration of the time he was to spend working on *Fire and Air*. But first there was to be a coming out party of sorts for the famed aviator—a luncheon the next day at the Wildwood Studios in Culver City at which as many movie personalities as the brash mogul could round up would be present, along with a necessary complement of press members. Several of the luminaries who received a call from Hawkins agreed to be on hand to meet Major Harrison. Milt took extra care to smooth down his cowlicks with pomade that morning, shave closely, and fasten the cuff links on the tuxedo Garrett had sent to his suite. A navy blue limousine appeared in front of the Golden Rose at 10 that morning, and Kid was surprised to find the tycoon himself in the back seat when the chauffeur opened the car door for him.

"Don't worry about any of this bullshit, Kid," Hawkins told him. "This kind of stuff is part of the business out here. The bigger a splash you make, the more people show up to watch your picture."

"I sure hope it works out that way, Gary."

When the aviator emerged from his limousine inside the studio gates scores of reporters, photographers and press agents crowded around to capture his reaction once he began mingling with the talented collection of household names who were there to pose with him. Charlie Chaplin, Douglas Fairbanks, Mary Pickford, Norma Shearer, Clara Bow, Harold Lloyd and Lon Chaney, among others, were standing a few steps away from the limousine. Milt put his hand over his eyes to shade out the bright sun and squinted at the welcoming party. He was hoping not to botch any of the conversation he figured Gary wanted the press to overhear between the stars and himself. Hawkins escorted Milt first over to Loretta Lindstrom, the best known gossip columnist in Hollywood, who seemed determined to be the first to meet and greet the new Kid in town.

"How do you do, Major?" Miss Lindstrom thrust her hand at him to be shaken. "Do you mind if I ask how Mr. Hawkins talked you into this madness?"

"That's easy to answer," said Kid. "He promised me I'd be running this town in a year if I came out."

The blond maven, older-looking and heavier than she fancied herself, smirked with a face plastered heavily with makeup.

"To be fair," she said, "we ought to put up a sign at the outer limits of Los Angeles County: 'Abandon all hope, ye who enter here.'"

"Oh, that wouldn't keep me out, ma'am," said Kid. "Matter of fact, that would make me even more determined to get in."

The next edition of the *Los Angeles World* featured three pictures of the outing on its front page and in the accompanying story the paper's reporters celebrated the juxtaposition of eccentric characters which had occurred on that day, under the headline: KID MEETS HOLLYWOOD. *Serendipity* magazine delved more deeply into the nuances of the occasion. Its version of the story revealed that the amoral shipping tycoon who had hired Major Harrison for his film had apparently arranged for a half dozen of the most sensuous young starlets in Hollywood to make themselves available to the aviator in his hotel room. What scandal, what outrage!

No matter how it had come about, whether by the force of his personal charm or the money and power of the Long Beach millionaire, Kid found himself delightfully surrounded by lovely girls wherever he went in southern California. With the palm trees, the ocean breezes, the sunshine, the floodlights and the girls, the world traveler was having no trouble at all in making himself comfortable there.

Though Gary had led Milt to believe they were in a breakneck battle against the calendar to rework his movie and make it a sensation, the visitor from Georgia spent all of his first week and part of his second in Los Angeles giving flying lessons. Not to the other cast of stuntmen or to anyone who would actually be appearing onscreen, but to Hawkins himself. Kid shrugged and accepted this turn of events as standard procedure in the land of the Angels. The playboy had already handed the aviator a check for $75,000 with no conditions attached. His picture be damned, he was determined to milk the full value of his investment out of Major Harrison while the latter was still responsive to his massive ego.

"I've always wanted to fly one of these things," Gary revealed to him early the morning after the luncheon in Culver City, pointing at a reconditioned Jenny parked on a newly-built landing field he had spent $20,000 to carve out of a junkyard. "Let's take her up, shall we? Show me how it's done."

"Ever done loops and spins, sir?" asked Kid, thinking back on the track record of regurgitations that novice riders in his planes had compiled with him behind the controls. "It ain't quite so easy as it looks."

Hawkins rubbed his impeccably shaven upper lip with his thumb and forefinger and put a leather helmet and flying goggles over his head.

"I'll be the judge of that. Let's go."

Something about the way Gary had answered him grated against Kid's nerves, and he wanted to make sure to seize the millionaire's attention in the subsequent flight. If anybody needed to have the fear of God put in him it was this young punk. The man from Woodvale wanted to make sure the man who had been born with the silver spoon in his mouth gagged on it before they came back down to the earth again.

He told Hawkins to stand out in front and start the propellor, expecting him to shrink back once he saw the ferocity of the spinning blade and heard the engine's eardrum-shattering roar. But Gary whirled the propellor violently into motion, stepped a little bit off to the side, and unflinchingly held his ground while a handkerchief from the outer pocket of his leather jacket was blown halfway to San Diego. He almost seemed to relish being a cigarette puff away from getting chopped to bits like a head of cabbage. There was a snarl, almost defiant in its ignorance of danger, fixed on the expression of his face. Kid was impressed. This was the sort of man who might actually retain hold of his breakfast once they blasted off into the sky.

The San Gabriel and Santa Monica Mountains, barren and high, and the Pacific Ocean itself, endless and serene, formed the backdrop for Milt's joyride over Los Angeles and its suburbs with Hawkins in the front seat. It was no gentle breaking in. He spun and dove with such fury that his passenger thought several times he was sure to come out of his seat. But the rush, the swirl and the agitation acted on Gary in a totally different way than it had on all the others before him. Every deadly loop and fierce dive and climbing spin was a syringe injecting a blissful drug into one of his primary veins. A little bit of medicine made him yearn for more, and he was a full-blown addict by the time his maiden air voyage with the ace had concluded. Far from making him queasy, the trip had in fact roused a deep hunger in him for more of the same.

"Hot damn!" cried the young millionaire when they landed in the reclaimed junkyard. "That beats screwing any dame ten to one! I've gotta get so I can fly one of these machines alone!"

Milt accommodated him. Day after day the addiction continued, with Hawkins gradually assuming familiarity with the controls and proficiency at using them under the master's careful instruction. It was only after a full week, by which time the tycoon had showed surprising promise at piloting, that there was even any mention made of *Fire and Air.* The principal actors and technicians, scattered in confused limbo throughout southern California, were at a loss to make use of their unexplained idleness, as were the hundreds of anonymous extras. After nine eight-hour days of instruction by one of the world's best pilots, Hawkins reluctantly remembered that his big-budget flick had completely stalled while he had been indulging his playboy obsessions.

"Kid, I really like you," he told Milt after he made his first solo flight. "I like you better than any man I ever met. If any other producer ever offers you more money to work for him, just tell me and I promise I'll top him."

"Well, thanks, Gary," said Kid. "What do you do, boy—go in your cellar and print more money when you need it?"

"No, it's hard to get. But when you've got it and you're trying to move heaven and earth, results usually come fast if you throw it around a bit."

"When are we moving heaven and earth to get your movie finished, Gary?"

"Aw, hell, I guess we can start bright and early tomorrow. I'm telling everybody to meet me in Riverside."

BY SUNRISE OF THE next day, in the empty desert near Riverside, California, Curtiss Jenny biplanes stretched seemingly from horizon to horizon. Hawkins and his tripod were positioned to capture the awe-inspiring spectacle of fifty beautiful flying machines, painted in the regalia of the warring armadas that a decade earlier had done battle over the Western Front, as they soared and spun through the sky.

The other pilots, most of them lean and restless war veterans and barnstormers willing to do almost anything for a little extra cash, had been bowing and scraping to another famous aviator whose presence on the movie lot Hawkins had never bothered to mention to Milt. Rather than the $75,000 he had dumped at Kid's feet, the millionaire had secured the services of this man for a mere $40,000. He was none other than Robert Francis "Arky" Lattimore, whose term in Kid's Flying Circus and subsequent career as a mail courier had made him a folk hero of sorts.

The poor unknowns who had been trying to emulate Lattimore's deadly tricks for the camera had taken him to be as worthy an authority on aerial acrobatics as anyone they would ever meet. But when they observed a black Fiat 520 sedan raising a dust cloud across the shimmering mirages of the desert until it screeched to a stop, and a chauffeur open a rear car door for a tall man wearing a ragged tan leather jacket, they realized Arky was soon to be put into the backdrop of their attentions.

"God bless us," said one, "I never thought I'd see it happen, but it's true. It's Kid! He's here!"

Though he felt a bit upstaged by his rival, Lattimore was grateful that now he would have an equal partner during his most extraordinary aerial maneuvers. When Milt walked over to Arky and the group of other pilots, they surrounded him with joyous handshakes and back slaps.

"*Arky!*" said Kid, surprised to see him there, "how'd you get out here?"

"Same way you did, Milt. By turnin' into a celebrity."

"Did Gary wine and dine you too?"

"Don't he do the same for everybody?"

"I done spent the last week teaching the maniac how to fly. He refused to do a damn thing on this movie till he could actually fly a plane himself."

Arky spat on the sand and crossed his arms.

"That don't surprise me a bit. With Gary, you just never know what might come next."

Another half hour or so of yawns and twiddling thumbs on the part of the airmen elapsed while Hawkins argued with Kyle Norton, his cameraman. The tycoon wanted for the morning sun to get high enough so that the camera wouldn't be directly facing it during any of the aerial footage, but Norton said that was unimportant since he would be filming every scene with the sun at his back anyway. But the director was adamant. He made his way over to his cast of flying men to explain to them the urgency of the situation. This was to be one of the climactic scenes in the movie, when the Allies, led by Kid and his comrades, were to subdue Arky and his brigade of pseudo-German desperadoes. One by one, Kid's squadron were to shoot down rival planes, and, one by one, Lattimore's men were to retaliate until only two leaders were left: Major Harrison, though he was to go by the fictional name of Bill Strong, one of the two British heroes of the picture; and Arky, who was being asked to fly as Rittmeister Hans Eichhorn.

In the end, of course, after the two aviators had exhausted every last acrobatic stunt they knew for Norton's camera, Kid would finally prevail and send Lattimore's plane down to a fiery extinction in the desert. All this was to be part of the new, extravagantly beefed up footage which Gary was hoping would salvage his picture. The rather insipid love story involving two English fighter pilots and a pampered society girl would now have an added element of violence, with sounds of crashes and explosions enlivening what was originally planned as a silent movie.

No one could guess how long it would take to film this particular sequence, but Milt volunteered to speed up the process by flying a few of the planes that were to be shot down in various takes, and Arky did likewise. Before long, almost half the aviators on the lot were superfluous.

They were anxious to start, but even after Gary was satisfied with the position of the sun there was a further delay. The heroine of the picture, a busty blond bombshell named Pernilla Lamb whom Hawkins had plucked straight off the cheerleading squad at Pasadena High School, was lingering in her dressing quarters. At the moment Miss Lamb was Gary's dearest female morsel, they were copulating like frisky wild goats, and she was being promised the glistening immortality of film stardom by the wealthy maverick. And every one of her queenly vanities was being satisfied, no matter how absurd and time-consuming.

Hawkins had an idea that he wanted to film her in the midst of a screaming fit in front of a backdrop of warring planes in the sky. Just how a woman throwing a tantrum was interesting or relevant to the story, or in any way realistic with dozens of bombing planes overhead, was a mystery to all the stunt pilots. But Pernilla wanted it and Gary demanded it. The time dragged on. The desert sun was merciless and the men were sweaty and uncomfortable. At 11AM Miss Lamb still dawdled in the tent Hawkins had built to accommodate her, and the director signaled for Kid to come over to him.

"She'll be out soon," said the millionaire. "Don't worry."

"She'd better be, Gary," said Kid. "I didn't come all this way to stand around doin' nothing. The other guys won't tell you this, but I will. This is crazy, and it's gotta stop."

The director pushed his hat back off his forehead and poked his chin out.

"Are you questioning my authority?" he asked curtly.

"Yes, sir. And I'm a-sayin' your money tree don't have enough leaves on it to shade out the hot sun while you kiss some teenaged bimbo's ass."

The outpouring of mirth from both the pilots and Hawkins himself was nearly suffocating. Gary slapped the Georgian affectionately on the back.

"Kid, if we didn't have censorship I'd sure as hell find a way to use that line in our new talkie. As it is, why don't you go over to Pernilla's tent and see what you can do?"

"Damn right I will. I've seen it all now—fifty aeroplanes grounded by one woman's makeup!"

The aviator's boots crunched on the hard-packed sand all the way across the field to Miss Lamb's muslin tent. The other flyers, as well as Gary and Kyle Norton, were waiting with baited breath to see just how the famous man would vent his anger in the presence of a lady. Southern boys still believed in chivalry, didn't they? Down South, where Milt was from, no man would go and attack a lady, would he? This would be an unprecedented event, and all were anxious.

Kid stopped short of barging in on the tent, but stayed close enough so that his voice might be easily heard from within.

"Miss Lamb," he uttered in a soft and urbane tone, almost mockingly ironic, "—Miss Lamb, all us boys are really excited to see how you'll look today. But if you keep us waitin' we may get too hot and decide to go cool off back in town, and nobody will be here to *gasp* when you come out!"

There was a momentary pause, then the woman inside said:

"Who are you?"

"Raymond Milton Harrison, Junior, ma'am. The papers call me Kid. Maybe you've heard of me. I fly aeroplanes for a livin'. But I tell you what, I was so durn excited about working with you on this here picture show I just couldn't stand it. But now . . . well, I think I'll go on back to Beverly Hills with the other boys."

Kid made exaggerated stomping steps away from the tent, his boots crashing like anvils as he walked away. His all-male audience was in the thrall of his every movement. He hadn't gone ten paces away when Pernilla's voice shot out from behind the tent.

"Come back here, Major Harrison!"

Milt grinned at all the men, then returned to the tent. When the fresh morsel knew Milt was at arm's length from the front of her quarters she suddenly peeked out through the flaps, revealing only her beautiful young face.

"You *wouldn't,"* she said coyly to him. "You wouldn't leave me here all alone, Mr. Harrison!"

Like a father extending his hand to a wayward toddler, Milt turned the back of his palm to her and wiggled his fingers for her to come grab it. She leaped from her tent like a leopardess and was soon enveloped by the grip of his hand. Like seasoned lovers they strolled hand in hand over to Kyle Norton's tripod.

"Let's fly some planes now, boys," Kid told his comrades. "Soon it'll be lunchtime."

ALL THE MEN WHIRLED their propellors around and flew their Jennies with violent precision in the skies above Riverside in imitation of the wild death dances many of them remembered from firsthand experiences earlier in their youths. Miss Lamb did her cacophonous hysterics for the camera while the men spun and dove at one another, firing blanks and toying with nitroglycerin to simulate real explosions. For many exhausting and dangerous days the hot-tempered Hawkins rode hard on the men to push their simulated violence to its foolhardy limit. Kid took up Kyle several times to enable the cinematographer to capture bird's-eye views of the mock battles on film. Hawkins was ranting and raving with tyrannical perfectionism.

"God dammit," he would growl, "you guys look like a bunch of Sunday school students out flying kites! We'll get ourselves hissed right out of the movie houses if we try to palm this shit off as the World War!"

Hawkins averted an out-and-out mutiny by showing several of the men the rushes from the recent days of filming. To their trained eyes the squadron battles *did* look staged, it was true. The casual viewer would have had no inkling of the true nature of air combat by exposure to them. There was little or no hint of the bloody bullet baths and scorching detonations which these veterans had witnessed and survived in real life. A sappy love story was not what would distinguish this film. It would rise above mediocrity and salvage some of Hawkins' millions strictly on the basis of how graphically it reproduced the mind-numbing speed and heart-stopping danger of open-cockpit fighter planes engaged in machine-gun battles with other open-cockpit fighter planes.

With the stakes raised so high by the boisterous demands of the director, Milt sat down in his hotel room one night, sketching out with paper and an ink pen a plan for making the filmed explosions more lifelike and breathtaking. Just as he had done his most creative brainstorming as a fighter pilot in Europe at night while everyone else slept, sometimes suffering from insomnia after his supine hours of planning and calculating in the darkness of his bunk, so now did he have a frenzy of ideas in predawn solitude. By sunrise he was convinced he had found a way to resuscitate Garrett Hawkins' cumbersome whale of a movie.

With Lattimore's help he picked out the most rundown Jenny on a lot in the San Fernando Valley, tied gunpowder sacks to its struts, doused its wings with ten gallons of oil and fifteen gallons of gasoline, and taped a long string wick leading from a gunpowder sack to the side of its fuselage. His intention was to take up this flying time bomb and ignite it from his cockpit with a match before bailing out, off camera, by parachute. With Arky as his pilot, Kyle Norton would be running his camera from the seat of another Jenny hovering nearby to film the stupendous explosion, and seven cameras would be running simultaneously on the ground to capture the resulting downward plunge of fire.

It turned out magnificently. Scenes of Kid and Arky firing gunshots would be intercut with the earthshattering explosions of the plane Milt was sending to a crash in the desert. When he rose to 10,000 feet above the valley floor he struck a match and then transferred the flame to the long kerosene-doused twine which extended inside his cockpit, protected from the open-air winds. Seconds were then life or death. He bailed out immediately, flailed his arms and legs in a free fall for several thousand feet while his unmanned plane tore through the sky, and pulled his rip cord once he saw the explosion and verified that he would be clear of any of its repercussions.

A lucrative but disastrous precedent was thus set. From then on the obsessive Hawkins demanded that every other crash and explosion must follow similar techniques. In the next few weeks Kid would repeat the treacherous stunt more than a dozen other times in variously decked out planes over all kinds of terrain. To try to moderate the tycoon's lust for pyrotechnics, Milt suggested that Kyle capture footage of lead pellets being traced across the fuselages of midair planes to simulate bullet-strafings, and thereby introduced a new fixation for Hawkins. *Fire and Air* would from that point onward feature one bullet-strafing after another, one fireball of death after another, actors writhing in apparent death-grips as bullets were seemingly splattered across their torsos and makeup-smeared faces.

Remembering his *drachen* attacks, Kid further imagined a dirigible pierced by a nighttime bomb. Gary went wild over the idea. The centerpiece of the film's aerial footage became the nighttime scene in which a torpedo dropped by Kid in darkness over a floating airship sliced through it like a fire-breathing knife and incinerated it in a rain of cascading ashy particles. A massive burst of fire would rage across the screen, and as an added touch several ground cameras would follow the burning airship as it plunged to the desert floor on the Riverside lot.

Inevitably, the lust for spectacle produced casualties. Three men had died on the set prior to Milt's involvement in the project. When another one burned himself to death while trying to do Kid's flying time bomb stunt, leaving behind a wife and two small children in Kansas, Milt withdrew into his hotel room in seclusion for several days, in protest against the young director's manic hunger for sensational effects at the expense of real human life. Hawkins had to come in person up to Kid's suite at the Golden Rose and plead for a second chance.

"We're almost done, Kid," he tried to encourage his best stunt pilot. "You can't abandon all the magnificent work you've done up to now."

"I ain't done a single magnificent thing since I got out here," Milt answered sadly. "All I've done is fake a lot of violence and death, when the truth is I hated the real thing when I had to see it. Maybe when you're a little older you'll understand what I mean. I used to think I couldn't do anything wrong. Now it don't seem I ever did a damn thing right. Every accomplishment of mine's been written on water."

"Major, I'm shocked at this," Hawkins goaded him. "*You*, of all people, feeling sorry for yourself."

"It ain't sorrow, Gary. It's just realism, man."

"Well, this is different. When *Fire and Air* comes out it'll last forever. A hundred years from now people are gonna watch in awe at your world of aviation and say, 'So *that's* what he was about!'"

"You're a damn snake oil salesman," said Kid. "There's never been a picture show anybody remembered longer than six months. Even Mr. Griffith's flick about the Klan—nobody's seen that in years, and after the Negro riots died down nobody talked about it, either."

Hawkins stood up from the velvet chair on which had been attempting to conduct a calm persuasion of his idol. He pulled a silver cigarette box out of the pocket of his white silk jacket and offered a cigarette to Milt before yanking one out for himself, lighting it up and puffing on it with a flashy air of exasperation.

"The past don't matter a lick," the brash tycoon snapped back at him. "It don't mean we can't be the first to do something, and you should know that better than anybody. Won't you come out to the set tomorrow and let's put a wrap on this? PLEASE."

Seeing Garrett Hawkins grovel to him in such a way was somewhat pleasing to Milt, and he agreed to return to the set. He rode the limousine out to Riverside the next day to try to stage a few final stunts for Kyle Norton's camera. Hawkins, however, had not been pleased by the tenor of the previous night's conversation. When Kid pulled up he saw that in the last week the moneyed director had imported some reconditioned Spads and Fokkers into his fleet of cinematic aircraft. One of the Fokker triplanes was dolled up in the exact regalia of Eichhorn's red plane, complete with the white skull and crossbones on the side of the fuselage. This red replica was now buzzing around the air over the lot while thirty bored stunt pilots leaned idly against their planes.

"What's goin' on?" Milt asked Lattimore.

"Well, see that there plane out yonder?" Arky pointed to a parked green Spad with Kid's name painted under the flying seat. "A couple of hours ago Gary was flyin' that and pretending to be you. Now he done took to thinkin' he's the goddamn killer Hun, and he's circlin' around like a butterfly."

"That's *Gary* up there in that bird?" Kid winced.

"Yup. The one and only."

"You reckon maybe I could pretend to be me, too, Arky, take that old Spad up, and shoot down the fake Rittmeister just like I done the real one?"

"I don't know. Maybe he's rigged the Spad with blanks and put real machine guns and bullet belts into the Fokker. With Gary, you just never know what might come next."

Milt turned around and walked back to the limousine that had so recently deposited him on the field.

"And with Kid you don't know, either," he said to the others as he walked away. "So long, boys. I just sweated out my last little drop of patience with that maniac."

Hawkins ranted and raved and cursed the ingratitude and unfaithfulness of his apparently former hero when he realized Kid had quit the movie project, and he vowed never to speak to him or have any further dealings with him in the future. And Kid began openly accepting the amorous invitations of Pernilla Lamb, a frequently naked and worshipful guest in his hotel room, who found him far more handsome and charming than the self-centered director.

Up until then Milt had always tried to quell the interest she had in him by reminding her that no one would ever have so much money as Garrett Hawkins, no one would ever exert more influence over show business than Garrett Hawkins, no one would ever cut so wide a path across the world at so young an age as Garrett Hawkins.

Now he told the splendid but brainless beauty, happily reciprocating her advances, that Hawkins was married and he was not. And if a millionaire would cheat on his own wife—one whom he had sworn on the altar to love and cherish forever—then did she honestly think he would treat *her* any better?

CHAPTER 29

Fire and Air

THE RUMORS BEGAN SWIRLING around Kid's alleged contributions to the revised version of *Fire and Air,* though Hawkins labored interminably over minutiae without releasing the film. Other directors, producers and creative people around Los Angeles had heard that Gary had finally found the few key elements his project had been missing before and that these elements were mostly bound up in the aerial mastery of the Great Ace.

The man from Woodvale remained ready and available in California, and other filmmakers began calling him. Aviation was the craze of the day, and one of the figures who had made it such was in their midst. If he had reversed the course of the mogul's monster, what might he do for their ventures? He quickly moved out of the suite Hawkins had been providing him, rented a mansion in a swank part of west Los Angeles and listened to their offers.

At Elixir Studios Benjamin Yarrow, a frustrated ex-barnstormer and stunt pilot who had turned director, had been inspired to make a picture similar to *Fire and Air.* Its plot, to the extent it had any, would be a trite rehashing of the two-men-fighting-over-a-woman concoction Hawkins and others had rendered a mainstay of the aviation pictures the Los Angeles studios were then turning out. To be called *Flight,* this would be a silent epic about the combat flying of the World War. The studio had assigned Harriet Lee, a huge starlet of the day, dubbed "The Honeybee" for her sweet yet dangerous sex appeal, to play the heroine of *Flight.* Two American chaps, kindred spirits to the English brothers of Hawkins' film, would fight over her. Drawn into battle over France, they would wallow in interludes of emotional treacle in their efforts to woo her between the true spectacles of the production, the battle scenes.

How high would the studio bosses go to win Kid for those all-important battle scenes? It was merely an unfounded rumor that he had a contract of exclusivity with Hawkins, wasn't it? The public falling out between the Long Beach tycoon and the Great Ace emboldened Benny

Yarrow to arrange for a meeting with Major Harrison at the Benedict Canyon home the aviator was renting. After two months in the muck of the motion picture business, Milt understood how the game was played. Any discussions on any subject would revolve around the all-important ingredient of money. Yarrow was thrilled to meet his hero in person. Most of the hardscrabble flyers of the last decade who had had dreams of glory had idolized this man, and now, through a quirk of fate, the filmmaker was in a position to hire the great aviator to work for him.

"Sounds great, Ben," Kid replied to the notion of helping out with Yarrow's movie, sizing up the director and finding him, in every visible way, free of the kind of messianic egotism that had alienated him from Hawkins. "But I'm sure you know what I'm about to ask next. I'll flip my planes around to wow your audiences, but what's the compensation?"

The accountants at Elixir had slaved over the correct numbers to wave in his face. They knew from word of mouth that Hawkins had paid him $75,000. It would be shameful and probably futile for their august company to offer him any less than some independent dilettante. They were confident he would take what they would be offering.

"A hundred thousand?" asked Kid, trying to keep a straight face. "For what, two months of work?"

He didn't want to seem too anxious or otherwise he would make them think he might have been had for less.

"But you won't be working every day," said an anxious Yarrow, envisioning the fizzling of his great epic without Kid. "Sundays off."

"Whew! . . . You make it real tough on me, sir, but . . . shoot, I guess I'll accept."

THE ACTORS ON THE set of *Flight* were frequent spectators when the planes were dodging and spinning for the cameras. They watched the methods Major Harrison used to bring about some of the special effects with great admiration. He repeated the gunpowder sack explosions he had used on the other movie lot for this one too. He demonstrated some of the textbook combat maneuvers, the *vrilles* and *retournements*, for the other stunt pilots who had either never perfected them or who had lost them through disuse. He borrowed Hawkins' idea of pellet gun fire to simulate bullet-strafings. To the delight of the paid gossipers in the press, he and Miss Lee were entranced by each other, though they never had any other than professional relations.

When *Flight* was released it became an instant sensation. Since *Fire and Air* was still unfinished despite having been in production for several years, the public had never experienced such a true-to-life depiction of aviation. Though many thousands of people had by then witnessed the types of flying circuses Kid himself had produced, they had done so from distant stationary vantage points. With the use of close-ups and rapid intercutting from a wide variety of angles, film was able to magnify and glorify the speed of the planes, the delicacy and grace of their operation, and the terrifying precision of their movements in wartime.

Though only his flying appeared onscreen and never his recognizable face, his assortment of lady friends carried on about him as if he were another Valentino. Arlene Deerfield, formerly a performer in Kid's Flying Circus, lived in nearby Santa Monica and began openly courting him. She fancied herself the lady who would eventually get a diamond ring from him. Which other girl of his could fly planes too? Which other one understood his mind and eccentricities the way she did? She was beautiful, vivacious, talented and, as she saw it, tantalizingly close to winning the lifelong beatitudes of matrimony with him.

For years Arlene, like countless thousands of other girls around southern California, had been trying to get her foot in through the door of show business, with minor success. An ability to fly planes well was not a particularly desirable attribute to help a beautiful woman break into motion pictures, since men might fly disguised as women without a film audience's ever knowing the difference. She had made appearances as a bit player in a handful of silent pictures as a beautiful wing walker and aerial acrobat, but had made no inroads to true stardom. However, all that would change if she ever lured the man from Woodvale into conjugal bliss—or so she believed. Her latest idea was to write a screenplay for a talking movie about airplanes, one that would star the two of them, and circulate it among her friends around town to help her get it produced.

Kid was trying emphatically not to get ensnared in Arlene's web. He would not make love to her, would dine with her only occasionally, telephone her no more than once a week. Though he did find her desirable, he stayed away from her for a good reason. He knew the more deeply he got buried under her spell the harder it would be for him to avoid marriage—which, in order to be successful, would forever end the type of life he had enjoyed for all of his civilian adulthood. Now was not the time for him to give that up. Would it ever come? Maybe, but now was not the time.

FOR THE NEXT TWO years Milt went from one film project to the next—over a dozen different productions, all talking pictures and none approaching the excellence of the silent *Flight.* Since the going rate for his services had now been set at $100,000 a picture, he was well on his way to becoming a millionaire himself. His masterful flips in Jennies, Sopwith Camels, Fokkers,

Albatrosses and Spads became almost as familiar a feature on back lots around Los Angeles as sunshine, blue sky and palm trees. With the exception of the airplane stunts, he regarded most of the projects for which he was risking life and limb as mere foolishness, and never even bothered to see any of them in their entirety with the exception of *Flight* and *Fire and Air*, which was not to be released until 1930. Such forgettable dramas as *Flying Desperadoes, Kings of the Air, Squadron Commanders, The Armada of the Armistice, Wings at War*, and *The Bombing Patriots* were churned out like so much pap with his name appearing just after those of the director and the main stars in the credits.

At the various premieres he squirmed in his tight tuxedo, guilt creeping over his conscience like some newly caught virus. He sweated in embarrassment and, before the first reel was even finished, he would slip out of the theater with whichever goggle-eyed female worshiper he happened to be twirling on his arm. He felt especially guilty when, almost chin deep in money himself, he heard the news in October of 1929 that Wall Street had crashed.

While he was raking in a fortune by contributing to cinematic cotton candy, the poor common folks among whom he had been born and reared had been plunged into the worst poverty in generations. He had rarely paid mind to his old acquaintances since his descent into Los Angeles, but he began writing his mother in Woodvale more frequently—to reassure her, to protect her from whatever illusory demons were hovering over the isolated back roads of northeast Georgia.

November 4, 1929

Mama,

I'm sending you a check for $1000 this month instead of $500 like I've been doing. I understand lots of people have been making runs on banks lately and maybe a bank's not the best place to put money, but they'll still cash checks won't they? If the Toccoa Community Savings & Loan is in danger of running dry, just cash this thing and put the money in a shoebox in your closet where nobody will find it. I'd send you cash if I trusted people not to steal it, but I don't. Especially now, when people have got so little of it.

I know you think $1000 is a ton of money and you wonder why I give you so much, but, Mama, if you only knew how much money these fools out here give people for being in pictures you'd wonder why all you got was the crumbs. I don't even want to tell you what I'm getting for cutting up for the cameras in aeroplanes. Really, it almost makes me blush to think about it.

Even if you can't spend all this—and I know you can, especially if you go to a big store in Atlanta—you can give some of it to other folks around Woodvale who are down on their luck. Don't worry, there's plenty more coming. Next month you'll get another check for the same amount. With people starving and foreclosures on land around there, I know the money will do somebody some good.

I hope Kate and Ellen and their families are doing fine. Give them some of this money and tell them I'm trying my best to cancel the reservations everybody out here seems to be making for me in Hell. I've decided there's one thing Los Angeles leads the world in, and that's whores disguised as actresses. Of course I won't touch any of them, Mama. You know that. You know what kind of god-fearing man I am, don't you?

Don't believe any of that gossip y'all read about me over there. The rumor mill out in these parts now has me and Harriet Lee carrying on like a couple of lovesick jaybirds. I don't think I ever even put my arm around that poor gal when we worked together on that movie, and I've seen her maybe five times in the last year. But according to some folks she should be having my tenth kid by now. And they get PAID for writing this stuff?

Many days I get homesick and wish I was back in Georgia. I'm a Southern boy in my heart. I was born there and raised there and no matter where I go that's still what I am and what I'll always be. It won't be long before I leave this place and come back. Wherever in the world I've gone I've still always had an itch to go home. I just wish there wasn't so much poverty and suffering out yonder. I've got an idea some day it won't be like that and people will be trying to go there instead of get away from there. I want you to use any leftover money to help make that happen, if you can.

Love, Milt

Arlene Deerfield finally succeeded at winning a producer over to her cause in December of 1929. He was pudgy, balding and middle-aged Mack Stein, a specialist in silent adventure films who was still struggling to make the transition to sound. He had long wanted to make a movie about aviation, but had never secured a big enough star to make the idea feasible. Arlene was telling him she had written a script about the adventure and romance of a male and a female pilot and that Kid Harrison would agree to play the part of the man in the drama, to be entitled *The Hawk and the Dove*. The marquee would read STARRING THE GREAT ACE! On that basis alone, Arlene assured Stein, the box office would be flooded.

But could Major Harrison really act? His Southern drawl was likely to seem absurd next to the ersatz British accents that were then in fashion among Thespians of the stage and screen. That was fine, Arlene said. He didn't have to say much—only enough to deliver on the promise of the marquee. A few dozen lines, perhaps. How much talking had Al Jolson done in *The Jazz Singer?* Not much more than that. But that was different, Stein protested. Sound was brand new then and now it wasn't. Finally, Arlene reminded him that the plot and dialogue were unimportant in a talkie about spectacle, love and adventure. The airplane tricks, the love scenes between the famous aviator and a beautiful woman who flew planes herself, the loud sounds of roaring propellors on the soundtrack—all this would be enough to guarantee a promising return at the box office, would it not? Stein mulled it over for a couple of days then got back to her. Yes, indeed. He was betting *The Hawk and the Dove* would fly.

Though Milt was growing increasingly unhappy with how his flying talents were being wasted by Hollywood, and though he doubted he had any acting ability whatsoever, he agreed to appear in Arlene's movie. He had a deep and abiding affection for her and wanted to help her get started in a career in show business. He knew that was important to her and, if his time in Los Angeles might serve to do anything except enrich his personal bank account, it would be his one selfless legacy if he helped make a woman he liked a star.

For several weeks thereafter Kid was not himself. Arlene led him by the hand every which way, to one loud party after another, to social events and picnics and press conferences. One night she dragged her beau to a premiere of the most recent of the productions that had featured Kid's aerial stunts, *The Royal Flying Corps.* This was a drama about a squadron of English pilots in the World War and their efforts to gain discharge for one of their hospitalized comrades so that he might return to Coventry and marry his beloved sweetheart. The hero of the story was played by an actor named Reginald McClain and the heroine by Phoebe Farnsworth.

Tears nearly leaked from Kid's eyes as he was forced by Arlene to sit through the wretched spectacle—not tears of emotion, but tears akin to the pungent chemical reaction of one exposed to a sliced raw onion in a hot and unventilated mess hall. It distressed him greatly that his aviation scenes were routinely being ruined by the maudlin and self-aggrandizing overacting of Miss Farnsworth and Mr. McClain. And there was another distraction in the theater. Earlier that day Arky Lattimore had eloped to Reno with the succulent and busty Miss Farnsworth and gotten a quickie marriage, and Milt sat uneasily next to the two of them in the theater, the new bride's meaty shoulder pressed hotly against his while she necked and petted with Arky for almost the entire seventy minutes of the picture. During one particularly intimate embrace between Mr. and Mrs. Lattimore, Kid leaned discreetly over to Arlene and whispered:

"Except for the aeroplanes this picture ain't no good at all."

"It's that way in all aeroplane movies," she answered, squeezing his hand. "But it won't be in ours."

"Just as long as we keep Arky's new wife out of it, I like our chances."

"SHHHH!" Arlene giggled.

"Let's get out of this firetrap," said Kid.

They abruptly sneaked out of the dark theater, went back to Kid's Benedict Canyon mansion and consummated their intimacy. The two of them were different from all the other crazies in filmdom, Kid told her. It was one thing to score with a cute soft bimbo like Pernilla Lamb or Phoebe Farnsworth, but Arlene was a girl of stature and substance and Kid felt a real sense of accomplishment when she became the latest mark on his bedpost.

MACK STEIN HAD LOFTY hopes for *The Hawk and the Dove.* Kid and Arlene would both emote for the camera as well as do their own flying. Whatever one thought about his totally green acting skills, Major Harrison unquestionably had the good looks to compete with any prized stud in Los Angeles. The plot would concern a wealthy heiress, disowned by her family for abasing herself at the feet of a flying male ne'er-do-well, and her attempts to surpass him in flying ability. It was hardly more original or intriguing material for a story than the usual stuff the studios were then turning out. But Stein thought he had seen sparks flying between Harrison and Deerfield in person and was hoping to capture their scintillations on celluloid.

Arlene was one of the most accomplished female aviators of her time and had been acknowledged as such long before anyone had ever even heard of the latest darling of the press, Amelia Earhart, though now . . . Stein started hearing Hollywood whispers. Several executives were wondering why he hadn't snagged AMELIA EARHART rather than Arlene to play opposite the Great Ace. Didn't he care about boffo box office? What was the matter with him? It had to be that he was sleeping with Arlene. There was no other explanation for his blindness.

Despite his original hopes, Mr. Stein realized two weeks into the filming of the non-flying scenes that he was getting almost nothing of interest when Milt and Arlene were in front of his camera. The sad fact was that the dramatic talents which the two of them had were improvisational and unsuited to a medium which required them to follow a prepared script in intermittent takes. It was a minor problem, easily able to be corrected. The two of them would fly, and a couple of experienced players would be plucked out of the stable of Imperial Studios to do the acting in their places. When the director showed Milt and Arlene the rushes of themselves from the preliminary scenes they both saw at once that the acting experiment would be a painful embarrassment if it continued any further. Milt asked Stein if he might speak with him in private, and Miss Deerfield excused herself quietly and sulked her way out of the screening room.

"Mack," said Kid, suppressing a grin, "I don't think Arlene oughtta hear what I'm about to ask you. How much will I have to bribe you to give me that roll of film so I can go burn it?"

Stein laughed uproariously.

"I'll gladly give it to you for free, Major. And I'll also gladly throw in a set of matches to help you get started."

Arlene went home to her ornate Santa Monica mansion, the product of her late father's success during the Southern California real estate boom of the Teens. She locked her door shut and buried her face in the pillows of her canopied bed. She wept helplessly, like a bride jilted at the altar, an expectant mother miscarrying her first baby, a flower girl robbed of her bouquets and pushed face-first into the dirt by a heartless thief. Her dreams of success in the fantasy world of the arts had been shot down. The Muses, so notoriously stinting in their apportionment of inborn talent, had withheld from her the gifts that she had deluded herself throughout her life into thinking she had.

And even as an aviatrix there was one better. She would never be as good as Earhart . . . *never.* It was different with *him.* The idea of acting was a joke to him because his first and only love was flying planes. *And no one was his superior in the seat of a flying machine.* He wouldn't even marry her, either . . . she meant nothing to him. She was his love slave, his toy. . . . Here she was, barely noticed by anyone, beautiful and childless and husbandless, twenty-eight years old—and he was world-renowned, handsome, perfect in every way, able to laugh at his failures, thumb his nose at danger, dust himself off after a crash, thrive in solitude. But she was no quitter. There was always a way to be a star, and she would bleed her veins dry and stretch the fibers of her soul to their snapping point to be one herself. Life was simply unlivable without stardom. Not men, money or the joy of spinning on a wing could rival the intoxications of fame.

She was in Stein's office early the next morning, a Friday. With manic determination she was suggesting that the director film her most innovative stunt on the following Monday night. It would be a nosedive in a white

Jenny biplane, portrayed in the film as a nighttime event but originally planned by Stein to be shot in the daytime.

"The night scene?" he asked the beautiful young woman with the strange demented face. "We're shooting that in broad daylight and darkening it with special filters."

"No, we aren't," Arlene pleaded. "I'm a brave woman and I don't need to cheat. Let's do it my way, Mack." Unconsciously she clasped her hands together as if in prayer and propped her elbows on her lap in her chair. Noticing her desperation, Stein was hoping an escape hatch would miraculously appear in the floor of his office so that he might slide out of there and avoid having to confront the problem this woman was posing for him. He asked her to let him think about it for a day or two, then he would let her know if he could rearrange his shooting schedule for her.

Everyone in the cast and crew spent an anxious weekend worrying about whether Miss Deerfield would survive the treacherous stunt she was insistent on doing. Stein himself decided late Saturday that he wouldn't permit her to do it on his watch, but when he visited her at home in Santa Monica on Sunday she said she was going to do it the next night whether he chose to film it or not, and she would quit the movie unless he did film it. Stein decided it was pointless to fight against such stubbornness in a grown woman who had been flying for ten years, so he prayed for the best and prepared to go through with it.

Later on Milt appeared on Arlene's doorstep, trying as calmly and as rationally as he was able to talk her out of her plan. But her heart was set and adamant. She began accusing him of jealousy and of wanting to keep her in submission to him. She was his lover, but never, ever would she be his slave. Stardom might not have suited him, but how dare he stand in her way to prevent her from achieving what meant the entire world to her! He began regretting having taken her to bed with him. Everything had been better before then. He had suddenly become a caretaker to insanity, and, no matter how lovely and feminine the package, it was frightening to him.

"So what if the camera don't love you?" he argued with her. "You fools out here never even heard of the real world. Show biz is just a game. It's fun, it's play, it's a way for people to get away from their problems. But it ain't real. There's more to life than play."

"Don't insult me like that!" she retaliated. "Everything's always about you and your ambition, and never about me!" She continued whimpering and wailing in a very disturbing manner that was difficult for him to watch. He quickly turned his back to her, took his hat off the rack and coat from the closet, and made hasty steps to her door.

"You oughtta be ashamed of yourself!" he turned and said to her angrily. "Millions of people are starving in bread lines. Millions more have suffered or gotten killed by violence and disease. Women and harmless little children, lots of 'em. Innocent folks, who ain't done nothin' wrong their whole lives. What right have you got to bellyache? Them folks can take anything and still smile and be optimistic. What's *your* excuse?"

TECHNICIANS SPENT THE NEXT day positioning five 100,000-candlepower arc lights, designed to illuminate Arlene's Jenny in the dark winter sky, around an empty field in the San Fernando Valley. Arlene was to plunge to the earth from 2500 feet, ignite magnesium flares on her wing tips to simulate flames, and spin violently to a crash, bailing out by parachute at the last moment. The stunt was her own idea, and she insisted on doing it herself. Her Jenny had been painted white so it would stand out in the darkness.

At 8:00 PM on February 10, 1930, the daring aviatrix was in the final stages of her preparations to go up. She had appeared on site at seven, looking strangely cheerful and radiant. Milt and Mack were lulled by her unexpected effervescence into believing sanity had returned to her. Before she mounted her seat, breathlessly eager, she hugged Kid and kissed him softly on his lips. Her eyes sparkled in the moonlight, her movements were sprightly and limber. She said to him: "After tonight you won't have any doubts about my skill and preparation."

Stein overheard the comment and remarked to Kid, when he had walked to the edge of the landing field, "She seems much better today. I think she'll do fine."

A crowd of several hundred gathered on the chilly grounds to watch her soar heavenward. Shortly after takeoff she became invisible in the thick pall of darkness. Soon her white plane emerged in the beams of illumination cast by the arc lights at about 3000 feet of altitude. The cameras captured her as she swayed and rolled for several minutes, then ignited her flares while the spectators held deathly quiet. At about 2000 feet she began diving like a shot goose, spinning furiously toward the ground. Many of the observers covered their mouths and gasped. Suddenly the plane caught fire—and everyone recognized it as real fire, too, rather than magnesium flares.

"Good god!" yelled Stein. "What's she doing?"

The Jenny hit the cold ground in a fiery explosion, the flames leaving no remains of the plane or anything in it.

"Where's the parachute?" asked one member of the crew. "Did she bail out?"

Kid took a few halting steps toward the fireball of the wreckage, then stopped cold in his tracks. He stared in a stunned trance at the flames as they devoured all traces of the plane, the only sign of life in him the tears that began forming in his eyes. The L.A. County fire trucks which had been standing by in case of emergency rushed out into the field and began spraying the destruction with their hoses, eventually dousing the blaze into a pile of ashes. There was a rush of people out to gawk at the incinerated remains of the woman and her plane, but Kid turned his back on the wreckage and silently began walking away.

To join the mob would have been pointless. Airplane crashes were nothing new to him, and he instantly recognized the ones that were survivable and the ones that were not. Parachute jumps were also not new to him, and he was thoroughly familiar with how one looked and the path it might have taken if it had ever actually happened or been attempted. What was new to him was the pointlessness of the particular crash he had just witnessed. He needed time to consider what had just happened and, if possible, expunge it from his memory.

His sights were set straight ahead, on the Rolls Royce sedan that he enjoyed driving about the hills and vales of Southern California. Straight to his house in the dark western canyon, straight to his bed, straight to oblivion—that was where the Rolls would lead him. It would have been a perfect night for intoxication if he had been so disposed. But that would have served little purpose except to delay the inevitable. Tragedy had to be confronted, swallowed, digested, or life could not go on. He was determined, as he had always been, that life should prevail over death.

When he soared above Clover Field in his beloved Aeroniña the following morning, having abstained from contact or conversation with any other human being since the crash from the previous night, the world seemed littler than before. He had previously observed the outrageous cheapening of human life for questionable political and social ends, and now what he wanted to behold was only the vastness of the world and not its smallness. His steady diversion of the last three years, between money-making dives for the cameras, had been leisurely flights in Warren Vandermeer's toy above the still pastoral Lotus Land of terra cotta roofs, blue ocean breakers, tawny hills and irrigated orchards that hemmed in the steadily fattening adolescence of Los Angeles. Today he was trying to compose something in his mind to summarize a life while he flew alone through the blue sky above the mountains, the ocean and the teeming newborn metropolis.

Two days later what may have been Miss Deerfield's remains, dug at random out of the large indeterminate pile of ashes at the crash site, were interred in Santa Monica, under a headstone which bore an epitaph that the sky had written for him.

ARLENE MARGARET DEERFIELD
1901-1930

She soared into the night

And left us weeping—
Hail! conquering woman of flight,
Now sleeping.

He hated funerals and decided then that he would never want one for himself. The rehashing of good times turned bad seemed to serve little purpose to him. He paid his respects to the family, to the meddlesome press. If Stein still wanted to complete his picture, Kid agreed to stay on and finish his obligations. Then he was sure to go home. He began to think how little his present life had to do with airplanes and how much more it had to do with mirage and illusion. He wanted to do something real. He didn't know what other real feat he might accomplish in a plane that he hadn't yet accomplished, but it was becoming obvious to him that flying for the cameras was not very fulfilling and, moreover, was not advancing the cause of aviation in as great a measure as he desired.

The *cause*—that was becoming more important to him as he got older: the service of airplanes to humanity and the world at large. He wondered if airplanes might survive into the lifetimes of his children, if he ever had any, and, if so, just how they might be useful. Surely, there were more benign uses for the machines than warfare, bootlegging and exhibitionism; more dramatic ones than crop-dusting and carrying mail; more useful ones than setting speed and distance records. A beautiful young woman of great talent had been killed in her prime now. Whether she had had psychological defects or not, the exhibitionistic nature of what aviation had become had contributed to her death. Even before Hollywood, there had been Kid's Circus, and she might just as easily have died during their show as out here if her luck had been worse.

The thought even crossed his mind after Arlene's absurd death—though it was never more than a passing thought—that he might give up flying airplanes altogether and turn his attention to charitable endeavors as a newly minted millionaire, maybe as a philanthropist around Woodvale during these times of trouble. He pondered this half-seriously, knowing all along that he had no choice in the matter. He simply could not live unless he flew. For eons man had lived on earth without being able to fly; but Kid was thinking he may have been the first man who ever had to fly in order to live. So in one form or another the airplane would remain at the center of his life. The only question was where he would next take it and what he would next do with it.

A MAN OF HIS WORD, Milt stayed in Los Angeles for most of 1930, completing a breathtaking assortment of tricks for *The Hawk and the Dove,* which would be his last movie. At the film's premiere he sat next to Mack Stein in the upper gallery of the Sepulveda Theater in west Los Angeles and digested the first half of the pulpy show as manfully as he could, trying hard to stomach the idle nonsense of the two imported players who had replaced him and Arlene onscreen and nodding approvingly at the exceptional piloting feats over which he had had direct control.

Stein had left Arlene's actual death flight in the film, and just before it was to be shown he nudged Milt on the elbow and excused him to leave. Pressure from the studio bosses, and not Stein's own judgment, had demanded that the lurid scene be included. The public had heard about the incident, and the notorious stunt, courtesy of human fascination with death, was responsible all by itself for a huge box office take for an otherwise mediocre film. The trite argument had been made by the studio bosses that Arlene herself would have wanted the scene to be included—she would have liked nothing better than for the show to go on. But the question had never been thus posed to her: "If you die in a stunt do you want us to include footage of your death to lure curiosity-seekers into the theater?" Though there were no direct messengers to deliver the question to her in the next world, those in the here and now took it upon themselves to answer for her, favorably to their own interests: YES.

Not long after this, *Fire and Air*, the *raison d'être* for Kid's career in show business, was finally released by Garrett Hawkins, to the catcalls of most critics but to the delight of most of the public. Gary had undergone a change of heart after he had seen the result of his tireless labors finally completed. He wanted to apologize to Major Harrison, tell him he had no hard feelings and give him the credit he deserved for helping to transform a $5 million money pit into a spectacle that had the potential to thrill the world.

Milt, Arky, Gary and most of the glittering stars in Hollywood's constellation appeared at the Sepulveda Theater to watch the much-ballyhooed opening. Over dinner in the adjoining restaurant after the show the swaggering tycoon, vindicated after years of struggle, glowed in the adoring stares of beautiful women, studio heads, press mavens and Loretta Lindstrom, the dean of all gossip columnists. There had been a method to Gary's madness. The airplane scenes in *Fire and Air,* true to his word, had been awe-inspiring. For years to come the product of the dilettante's imagination would continue to captivate audiences. Not the story itself, but the damn-the-torpedoes-full-speed-ahead nature of the flying scenes, which had resulted in the fatalities of four stuntmen. Though Hawkins had spent $5 million in the production of his movie, more than anyone else would spend on a single picture for many years to come, he would eventually take in $10 million in receipts.

"Kid, I was young and foolish a couple of years ago," the penitent mogul said to Milt while Miss Lindstrom stood admiringly by and overheard them. "We've all got our growing to do, you know."

"I'm glad you've mellowed with age, Gary," Milt answered the 28 year-old. "You've gotten so damn old lately I hardly recognize you."

Kid left Clover Field in his Aeroniña the following morning, carrying nothing but the clothes on his back. Los Angeles had made him a fortune but had left him bitter. When he had landed there three years earlier it had offered him a cornucopia of possibilities, and his arrival had been attended by great fanfare and celebration. Now, as he left, no one seemed to care, and his plane buzzed its way in solitary flight into the golden glow of the eastern horizon.

CHAPTER 30

The Birth of the Airlines

THE MAN FROM WOODVALE thought he had landed in the wrong spot when he touched down at midnight in Hapeville. Had he lost his bearings and somehow gotten detoured to civilization in his search for the familiar emptiness of nowhere? A new hangar had been built on the premises, with shops and a diner. Actual runways had been carved out of the dirt, the old grandstands removed, the outline of the egg-oval racetrack effaced in the name of progress. All forms of bovine nourishment had been stripped clear of the areas where flying machines were attempting to land and take off. And, most impressively of all, beacon lights now illuminated the field, courtesy of George Grantland's shameless brown-nosing of the feds the last time they had been in town.

When Milt returned to see the new setup the next day in broad daylight it occurred to him that the new terminal had been built as if its architects actually expected *people* for some reason or another to be passing through it. For what reason? No other airfield in the nation had a terminal for passengers built next to it, and even this one had no real passengers yet. There were no crowds to celebrate his arrival home, but what greeted him was even better. It seemed as if his old friends had been reading his mind by telepathy across the wide expanse of continental geography, had acted on his wild dreams, and had built him a marvelous theater for the staging of his next drama.

"Before the end of the year," Chester Dawes told him, "we're aiming to carry passengers to a different place."

"Where?" asked Kid.

"Don't know. Wherever they want to go."

"Whether they like it or not," said Robert Brackens, "we're gonna be flyin' 'em somewhere. Even if we gotta do it at the point of a gun."

"We won't have to," said Kid. "They'll do it 'cause they like it and need it. I'll find somebody to step in and help us, and we'll make it work."

"Oh, I forgot," said Brackens, "you got all the money now and whatever you say goes."

"Even before I made off with half the loot in Hollywood, boys, whatever I said went around here. And don't y'all forget it."

ATLANTA'S CITY FATHERS had arranged for Charles Lindbergh to come to town and celebrate "Lindbergh Day" in Major Harrison's absence. Loudly cheering throngs had greeted Slim's motorcade, motorcycle escorts had followed him wherever he went, important banquets and meetings had been held to honor the Lone Eagle, and he had addressed a crowd of 20,000 at Grant Field, the football stadium at the Georgia Institute of Technology. George Grantland was almost apologetic when Kid brought this up to him a few days after he was back at home.

"We'll give you an even bigger day than Slim," the alderman promised Kid. "We'd've done it before now if you hadn't bolted for Hollywood."

"I don't want y'all to do *anything* for me, Georgie. Hell, I'm just a dumb ole country boy who got a few lucky breaks in his life, so what do I know? I don't want a parade for me and I don't want a Milton Harrison Day. And, for god's sake, don't y'all dare try to name any street or any other damn thing whatsoever around here for me. I'd rather let Slim do all the suffering."

When Lindbergh came back to town a few weeks later he was given just the sort of honor Kid was afraid somebody would try to confer upon him as well. To commemorate the Lone Eagle's visit, Mayson Avenue, an otherwise nondescript thoroughfare in the northern suburbs connecting two of Atlanta's principal roads, Peachtree and Piedmont, would be renamed Lindbergh Avenue. It was a routine that had been repeated in countless other places in the previous three years, and the young aviator tried his best to invest the occasion with novelty and enthusiasm. Milt stayed quietly in the background, hoping the public wouldn't see him and get the idea he had suddenly become an historical relic.

Not long after coming back to Georgia he sold what was, by a millionaire's standards, his *small* house in Ansley Park. He then bought a castle on Peachtree Battle Avenue in the northern suburb of Buckhead with $80,000 of his $1 million fortune, and quickly adjusted to people who came to stare at him not because of his looks or because he had flown around the world or because he had smuggled booze or slain 100 Huns in battle or even appeared in motion pictures. They were coming to stare at him now with one thought in mind: "So THAT'S how a millionaire looks—Lordy, what we wouldn't give to have his money!"

In those depressed times thoughts of money were never far from the minds of the mass of people. Every time Margaret Harrison deposited one of Milt's $1000 checks in the local bank in Toccoa it was the largest amount deposited at that institution by a private investor at any point during that decade. As a matter of fact, had it only been *one-tenth* that amount it still would have held the distinction.

He was shortly in negotiation with a man named Jerry Lithgow, the owner of a small company called Lithgow Aviation which, by dint of the combined efforts of Chet, Bobby and George, had decided to lease the shops in the new terminal at Candler Field and inaugurate passenger service. Kid promised he would pilot the first few passenger flights to foster interest and trust in the operation, then turn the flying of the planes over to however many wing walkers, displaced Hollywood stuntmen, penniless acrobats and World War veterans he and his partners could scrape up from among their circle of acquaintances.

By the early part of September, Lithgow had recruited several down-and-out crop dusters and circus performers to pilot his fleet of four Curtiss Condors, biplanes seating half a dozen passengers with two propellors on opposite sides of the fuselage. An advertisement in a local newspaper informed the public of the entrepreneur's intention:

Lithgow Aviation
Announces Inaugural Passenger Service Sept 4*
Atlanta/Miami and Atlanta/New York and Points in Between.
Two Daily Flights!
Safe and Reliable Aircraft.
Purchase tickets in Person at Candler Field.

*Inaugural flight to Miami to be flown by Maj. Milton 'Kid' Harrison.

On the appointed day in September Kid stood behind a makeshift wooden kiosk inside the small but comfortable Quonset hut that was the terminal building, hoping some people would come and pay to fly in his plane. He was attended by Dawes, Brackens, Grantland and Mr. Lithgow. They had deliberately failed to post a time for either of the departures in the newspaper, not knowing how many would come to fly with them and, if so, when would be the time most convenient for their schedules.

By noontime the hut was crammed full of people, most of them celebrity-watchers only there to catch a glimpse of Kid, along with a couple of dozen newspaper reporters. Not until 2:30 did someone who actually wanted to go on a flight identify himself. Lofty visions of a packed-full

Curtiss Condor on the inaugural flight were obviously in need of being scaled down somewhat, from a glorious total of six passengers to a sobering total of one: a middle-aged briefcase-carrying businessman named Stearns.

"I need a ticket to get to Miami by tonight," said brave Mr. Stearns, stepping up to the desk. "Can y'all fly me there?"

"Why, of course we can, sir," said Milt. "We're stopping in Macon, Savannah, Jacksonville and West Palm Beach on the way there. You mind?"

"Not as long as I get there before midnight. What do I owe you?"

Milt pulled a figure from his imagination.

"Fifty dollars for one way passage, sir—one hundred for a round trip."

Stearns pulled a fifty-dollar bill from his wallet and handed it to the aviator, who appeared ready to pocket the money into his own flying suit without hesitation, though he in fact passed it to Lithgow.

"I'll wait to see how it goes before I commit to the round trip," said Stearns.

By three o'clock Stearns had climbed into the seating compartment through the rear door behind the wings, and Kid was giving him instructions before takeoff. He was holding up a parachute pack and forewarning the poor layman of the dangers that might lurk near in the future.

"Put this on during the flight and if we run into trouble don't worry, this thing'll come in handy."

Milt helped the man strap the parachute to his back and put a helmet over his head to protect it in case he was thrown from his seat. The sight of the thin bourgeois man wearing headgear and parachute apparatus was laughably ridiculous, but Stearns seemed game for the task and he followed instructions meticulously.

"Major Harrison," he said, "I'm trusting one hundred percent in your reputation. I never did a single adventurous thing in my life before now, but—well, you know what they say. You only live once."

Stearns took off his uncomfortable and apparently superfluous helmet and parachute pack after the first landing in Macon. At Savannah another businessman, paying the arbitrary sum of $50, hopped on to go to Miami. Two more got on at Jacksonville, and by nighttime the wires were hot with the news of the successful venture. Five businessmen had arrived safely via Kid's Curtiss Condor at Miami. "Like a majestic eagle alighting from the clouds," wrote one turgid reporter in a Miami newspaper, "the machine coasted down smoothly into its new nest in history in the late summer gloaming." Kid checked into a hotel and looked forward to tomorrow's return flight from Miami back up to Atlanta.

All six seats were full then and passengers had to be turned away at all of the intermediate stops. The curiosity-seekers who were doubling as paying passengers would frequently lean into the aisle during the course of the flights and try to study the mysterious workings of the famed maestro behind the controls. At Candler Field by that afternoon over two hundred people were in the tiny brand new terminal to try to ride next. By then the other workaday pilots of the carrier were mobilized and ready to carry the torch that Kid was passing to them. And Lithgow, inspired by the poetic bombasts of the Florida journalist, had decided to rename his outfit "The Eagle Air Transport Company".

"Thanks for riding, y'all," Kid personally greeted each of the passengers as they filed out of the fuselage and went down the wooden steps that had been rolled up against the door. "Tell your friends about it, and you come back now."

Robert Brackens and Chester Dawes helped fly the Atlanta to New York route up the eastern seaboard until Lithgow had hired enough pilots to manage the steady procession of flights, but soon the heroic Hapeville duo, like their comrade Major Harrison, retired into the background. The millionaire had given assistance to the Eagle Air Transport Company *gratis,* but he had an ulterior motive. He had ample money to invest and he was hoping for an important stake in whichever carrier gained predominance at the Hapeville landing field. And he wanted to lure A.T. and Trevor, his Louisiana duster friends and business partners, into moving the center of their operation to Candler Field.

He was finding that being so well off financially was not in any way cloying to his hunger for more money. On the contrary, to the millionaire the most important goal was to get his next million. By the end of October two other air transport companies, Columbian and Allied, were offering passenger flights out of Candler Field, one of them going all the way to Los Angeles after a series of stops.

When Milt flew the Aeroniña out to Monroe, Louisiana to check on the progress of the outfit that he had renamed the Gulf Coast Air Transport Company, he was taken aback by the brisk progress the business had made under the stewardship of the tall bespectacled young Hoosier. One of A.T.'s secretaries had suggested shortening the name from "Gulf Coast" to "Coastal", and the far-seeing Bonderman had followed her advice. Now, going by the name "Coastal", the infant airline had begun a passenger route from Dallas, Texas to Jackson, Mississippi with stops in Shreveport and Monroe. With a fleet of four Travel Air S-6000B airplanes, each carrying five passengers and one pilot, humble Coastal had kept its head above water.

"Kid, we grossed $3500 on passengers alone last month," bragged Aloysius Troy, accompanied by Dr. Reed's nod of approval. "Also, the dusters went to South America last winter to spray the vegetable fields and coffee plantations and we pulled in a couple of thousand that way." Mr. Bonderman paused, as if to give full consideration to the gravity of his next words before they passed from his lips. It was not a time to speak frivolously and without due estimation of the power of one's opinions. "I do believe," he went on, "we're the largest unsubsidized air fleet in the world. Not one penny of Uncle Sam's money's in our pocket."

Unimpressed, Kid spat on the weed-strewn dirt of the Monroe landing strip.

"A few thousand dollars in a month ain't squat, A.T., and you know it. What are you payin' your pilots with—Crackerjacks?"

"They're getting a decent wage of $200 a month—which how many others are getting nowadays?"

The man from Woodvale remained unimpressed.

"I told y'all Candler Field's where the future of aviation is. You turned your nose up and asked what the hell was near Atlanta—but, shoot, last I checked Shreveport and Jackson and even Dallas ain't about to be confused for no centers of the universe."

Trevor Reed laughed momentarily, then clamped his mouth shut when A.T. glared at him. Mr. Bonderman, his white sleeves rolled up in the still-hot sun of mid October, removed his eyeglasses, wiped them with the edge of his shirtsleeves and replaced them on the bridge of his nose after he had seemed to weigh the matter in the fast-spinning sprockets of his mind.

"Major, let's don't fool ourselves. Atlanta's in the middle of nowhere too. Dallas has oil, but what's Atlanta got? Coca-cola—you think that's any kind of rival to petroleum?"

"It's got me," said Kid. "And a lot of the people in this world who tried to look past me have gotten themselves six feet under the ground—or else would rather be six feet under than where they are now."

For one of the few times in his life the entomologist was forced to concede a point.

"Okay, I'll grant you that much," shrugged Bonderman. "It's got you, the expert at proving the rest of us geniuses wrong."

ALOYSIUS TEMPORARILY SUSPENDED Coastal's Jackson to Dallas run, and Kid flew one of the all-metal Travel Air passenger planes across the ailing Southland to the Hapeville haven where absurd dreams were still plausible. All three Atlanta newspapers soon bore the notice that the local activities of Eagle, Columbian and Allied Air Transport Companies were to be augmented by that of unheralded Coastal, whose lone saving grace seemed to be that Kid Harrison was its principal financial backer. Tiny, lowly Coastal, the operation that had introduced crop-dusting to the world, now dared to rear its head in the crowded marketplace of passenger-carrying aviation. It almost seemed to be in defiance of the precepts of the mastermind of the company—the grazing of an extra cow in the pasture when there was already too little grass for the cows that were there.

"We've got to go about this from a new angle," the Hoosier told Kid when he emerged from the train at the Hapeville depot. He was preparing for the first time to set eyes on the rural tract of land on which the war ace was pinning his company's hopes. "This business with passengers will be totally different. Everybody's got the nuts and bolts, but we'll have *people.* Otherwise, the big boys will run us into the ground."

"So the other guys won't have people, A.T.? How will they run their operations, with livestock?"

"Figuratively, yes, they will. They'll be treating their people like beasts of burden. But our people will be a part of an extended family. Once they get with us they'll stay. It won't be like a job or work, it'll be cut from the same cloth as life at home."

"I'm not sure I'm following you there," said Kid. "This ain't no kindergarten. These fellers in our planes are gonna be a bunch of wing walkers and Hun-killers. A Sunday picnic don't exactly thrill us daredevils."

The former entomologist put his arm over the aviator's shoulder.

"Maybe I can't explain it, but I'll demonstrate it to you over the course of time."

KID WAS BEHIND THE controls for Coastal's first passenger flight out of Candler Field, just as he had been for Eagle's. The Travel Air S was scheduled to go from Atlanta to Birmingham to Jackson, Shreveport and ultimately to Dallas. Mr. Nick Fiedler, a prominent Atlanta department store owner, was the only member of the public on the plane when it left the field bound for Birmingham, and he seemed well enough pleased by the experience at first. But then the small plane encountered a thunderstorm, was thrashed about like a floating scrap of paper, and Kid turned to the north to try to flee its swirling winds.

He eventually diverted to Chattanooga, landed and parked on the dirt runway by the Tennessee River while the ominous black clouds and ferocious winds from the southwest seemed to be following in his direction with ever-increasing speed. He was nearly beside himself with disappointment. It was the maiden flight out of his home field for his fledgling company, and the news would be about the passenger scared senseless, the diversion, the stranding of the passenger in an out-of-the-way locale. He was almost afraid to turn around and check if Fiedler were still back there or even still alive. Gamely he did so, saw the passenger sitting quietly in his seat staring skeptically at him and recalled some of what A.T. had told him about the way to run their business. He made his way back to the cabin and addressed Mr. Fiedler.

"You all right?"

The passenger adjusted his tie and pushed his fedora back off his head.

"I am now, Major. I never thought I'd fight in a war, but I think I've just been in one."

"I sure am sorry about all this, sir. The way things look now, we might be stuck up here all night. Believe me, this is not how we plan on doing things with Coastal Air."

"That's all right, sir. If I've got to get there by train, I'll do it. I was just hoping this new way would be better and faster."

"Well, we're aiming to make it that way, but sometimes . . . I still think, no matter what, you'll get to Dallas sooner by stickin' with me than going by train. I been on some long runs and I never came up short yet."

"Of course I know all that," said Fiedler, a gray-headed man with a peppery mustache and tired, flinty eyes. "It's a part of our history books now, what you've done."

When it became obvious that the weather was too inclement for them to fly anywhere else that night, Milt looked for Fiedler's grip in the stowage compartment so that he would have the necessities for checking into a hotel and continuing on the trip the next day. To his mortification he found the bin in the belly of the Travel Air totally empty. He sweated over what excuse he might give Fiedler for losing his bag. For the first time in a long while he felt badly embarrassed.

"Sir, I can't find your bag," he said bluntly, "but you wait right here in my plane and I'll do something about it."

Fiedler crossed his arms and began pouting in a way that seemed to herald a volcanic eruption soon if things continued along their current course. Milt darted from the plane and went into the shed by the landing field where there was both a telephone and a telegraph line. He dialed up the field in Hapeville, got hold of Bonderman and quickly explained his dilemma.

"God dammit, A.T.," he scowled, "if we don't locate this feller's bag, we're finished! Do something, anything! Go get a bag and fill it with golden nuggets if you have to, but get us something, and fast!"

Kid heard loud yelling, even though Aloysius was trying to muffle the mouthpiece with the palm of his hand. Milt also thought he heard crashing boards and broken glass through the telephone, though that may well have been a product of his distraught imagination. Five minutes later the Hoosier's voice, calm and steady, returned to the earpiece.

"I've got his bag here, Kid. With all those reporters raising such a ruckus, we forgot to load it before you left. Give him all his money back, put him up in the best hotel in Chattanooga, buy him dinner and tell him his grip's gonna be delivered to his room by first thing tomorrow morning."

Milt went back to the incipient volcanic outburst that was Mr. Fiedler in the Travel Air, trying his best to put a pleasing slant on the unhappy situation.

"You're bag's in Atlanta, sir," he said apologetically. "We'll have it here by tomorrow. I forgot to load it when we left. In the meantime, here's all your money back for the flight, and we're putting you up in the fanciest digs in town till the weather breaks."

Milt pulled four $10 bills from his pocket, handed them to Fiedler, and helped the older gentleman dismount from the plane. It proved to be one of the happiest episodes in the prosperous department store owner's life. For free he had the company of one of the world's most famous pilots in the taxi into Chattanooga, over dinner at the best restaurant in town, and for breakfast the next morning. And he arrived in Dallas, with three other businessmen who had hopped aboard at intermediate points, at about the same time as if he had ridden the rails from the start.

This Coastal Air Transport was the best thing going, Fiedler was thinking to himself. Despite the delay and the hassles he loved the experience. Even if someone else besides Kid had done all the maneuvering, there would have been something picaresque and fantastic about the adventure. It was like being in a covered wagon along the Santa Fe trail, panning for gold in the Klondike, planting maize at Jamestown. Fiedler's conscience began bothering him that he had been so close to an angry tantrum on the night before.

WOODVALE'S BEST-LOVED SON had not visited there in nearly four years. When he returned for Christmas in 1931 he was sobered to find many of the upstanding characters of his youth wizened and debilitated by age. Joe Freeman was barely able to walk, and Rev. Gray and Rev. Patterson were both in equally ill health. The pillars of the community nowadays had been the mischief-makers when he had been coming along: Zeke, Shnook, Cliff and Blackie. They were all family men now, with school-aged children who seemed to herald a brighter future for the community.

The most sought-after man, among those who currently lived there, was Woody. He had taken over the sonless Rev. Patterson's ministry at the First African Methodist Episcopal Church while the elder man prepared himself for death, and was the closest thing the community had to a biographer for its most famous native. The Bahamian would fill the air constantly with anecdotes—all of them amazing but none of them, in light of the extraordinary personality they were describing, beyond the realm of possibility—about the man he knew as N.B. Excitement. Then others in the worn out village, hearing of the Great Ace's newly-minted millions, would endow him with an almost supernatural quality.

Most popular of all, of course, was Madge: the mother of the character around whom much of the settlement's gossip and most of its identity revolved. No one suffered or starved in Woodvale. The millionaire's $1000-a-month stipend, after it had satisfied her modest wants, was being doled out among the less fortunate Woodvaleans in accordance with need. After this many years of her son's generosity, Margaret scarcely needed any more of her son's money. These days, only $20 or $30 of it was usually left for deposit into her account in the Toccoa Savings and Loan by the end of each month.

Ruth had become a virtual recluse, tending after her sick father and mother after her own children had married and gone away. No passion or joy in life had she, save in her imaginary encounters with Major Harrison, the man she loved more than any other. In those impossible visions, known only to herself and her maker, age and race vanished in the unbridled freedoms of joy and discovery. In the innermost sanctity of her locked room, with her two elderly and dying parents asleep in another part of the house, she would disrobe before her dressing mirror and admire her 46-year-old body, which she imagined any normal man of 30 or 35, white or black, would enjoy looking at almost as much as she did.

MADGE HAD A PICNIC for the town on Christmas Eve day, which was warm and pleasant. Woody and his family along with Ruth and hers were invited, and no one seemed to notice or care that Kid was helping to integrate the world. White folks and blacks alike had finally migrated to the same side of Oak Street now and were gathered around the guest of honor.

"Enby, I bet you anything you goin' back to Hollywood soon," said Woody as he helped his friend roast pork barbecue over hickory splints in a big kettle drum cooker. "Man, you a natural born entertainer."

"Naw, I ain't," answered Kid. "I'm doin' serious work now."

"It's about time after all these years you settled down," said Madge, who was still disgusted by the notion that her son never seemed to take any advice she gave him. "There's lots of pretty girls around who'd make perfect wives for a rich man like you."

"Shnook, what's your boy drawin' over there?" Kid asked, pointing at Matthew, his friend's 8-year-old son, who was a perfect reason for Milt to change the subject. The youngster was making a drawing with a set of Crayolas on a bare sheet of paper. His father, now 35 years old and still with a limp from having shot himself in the foot to avoid Wilson's War to Save Democracy, stood and hobbled over to Matthew. He began patting the child on the head and running his fingers through his thick brown hair. Shnook was working in the textile mill in Eastanollee for $2.50 a day, and proud to have work when almost no one else did. He was holding his head up high these days, and he adored his little boy.

"Aw, Milt," said Shnook. "It's about the only thing he ever does. He's drawin' another picture of you in an aeroplane. That's all he talks about, day and night. Woody done rurned that child with all them stories he tells about you. He'll draw a dang picture of one of your planes, then he'll put right underneath it, *'Mr. Excitement takes over the world!'"*

Milt's boyhood friend laughed, revealing a mostly empty set of gums with a handful of black and decayed teeth, and wheezed out a phlegm-filled cough, aggravated by a smoking habit that he had had since age fifteen. Milt stood from his picnic table, wiped his mouth with his cloth napkin and went over to little Matthew Adams, who was carefully coloring a surprisingly well-drawn sketch of a biplane with a green crayon. His tongue poked out and he seemed to be in an almost trancelike state of concentration. When the boy saw his idol standing next to him he put the crayon down and handed him the picture.

"It's a present for you, Mr. Excitement. Now, will you tell me another story?"

Kid thanked Matthew for his artwork, and the large man lifted the little boy up with his strong arms and put him in his lap. Ever since Milt had been in town this boy had been asking him to tell more stories about N.B. Excitement like the ones he had heard from Woody. This one would be about the flyer who shot down another flyer named the Riding Master just as he was about to attack a beautiful far-away city called Paris. There was also the story about the little boy who taught his daddy how to drive a flivver, who flew a plane through a snowstorm and won an air race, roamed around the countryside on a motorcycle and slept in grass and scared people because he drove so fast. And there were stories about circuses in far away places, flying alone across oceans and over mountains, going completely around the world and meeting emperors and sheiks and Sphinxes. And then there were stories about California and beaches and dream girls and explosions and swimming pools and parties with a hundred different kinds of foods.

Never did one story end before little Matthew was begging the great big man to tell him another one. The one consuming thought in the boy's mind was that some day, when he grew up, he wanted to be Mr. N.B. Excitement himself and do everything the boy in the stories did. His clear, fresh wide child's eyes scarcely blinked while he heard the words passing from the war ace's lips. When Milt finally put Matthew down he felt sad and a little guilty, knowing the little one would now have to suffer from his forced return to reality again.

After the holidays Kid left Woodvale to return to Atlanta, and the heartbroken village, dreading as always to see him go, settled into the usual patterns of its existence, in which one thought was never far beneath the surface: "When's Milt coming home again?" But for many years to come he would make his presence scarce there.

CHAPTER 31

Love, Politics and War

WITH HIS FORTUNE ALREADY made while much of the world suffered during the '30's, Milt branched out into other areas in which he had previously had no interest. He was in demand as a public speaker. In the next decade he would persuade the elected officials in several municipalities to build airports. A new president, Franklin Roosevelt, had taken over Washington, aiming to give work to the able-bodied unemployed masses and alms to the poor. New air carriers were begging for his attention. George Grantland paid a visit to Kid's Atlanta mansion with Jerry Lithgow to discuss airline matters in the spring of '33, and offered Major Harrison the chairmanship of Eagle Air Transport, hoping that a famous name at its helm would help the struggling company win FDR's favor.

"It wouldn't work for two reasons," said Kid. "Number one, I don't want the job. And, number two, I ain't no businessman."

"Won't you recommend anybody else, then?" asked Lithgow, who was still the acting chief of Eagle. "You know of anybody?"

"I'll talk to Johnny Albritton," said Kid. "I correspond with him from time to time and see him every now and then. He's better at business than any flying man I know."

Milt had been hiring himself out to a few of the new airlines, piloting Ford Tri-motors and Curtiss Condors to map out routes over remote sections of North America. But he was always most partial to the two airlines that he had helped to start: Eagle and Coastal. He had total confidence in the leadership of Coastal, and if he happened to be successful at talking Britt into taking the reins at Eagle he would be equally satisfied by the management there. The two of them met over dinner at Jekyll Island, where Albritton had a home, and Milt made him an introductory offer to run Eagle Air. The fellow ace accepted.

"But Britt," warned Kid, "try to lay off FDR. I know it ain't my place to try to order you around or in any way suggest you don't know every damn thing you're doing, but what good does pissing off Roosevelt do?"

"What good does it do?" Johnny scowled. "I'll tell you what good it does. It lets the public know what's at stake. He's not there for life. In three years the voters can have at him again, and I want to make damn sure they pay attention this time."

"They paid attention last time, Britt. They decided Robin Hood's just the feller they need to lick the unemployment lines. The more he robs from us and gives to them, the better off they'll be."

"Socialist bastard!" fumed the former car racer. "We used to be among those poor folks, you and me both. And how did we get to be where we are now? By gettin' down on our hands and knees like beggars and collecting money in a hat? Of course Roosevelt don't know any other life except servants and mansions, the blue-blooded snob! The quack! The day I kiss his ass will be the day I blow my brains out with a .45 caliber revolver!"

Milt was tired of trying to kick his way through the brick wall of Mr. Albritton's convictions, so he gave up the effort.

"You do it your way, then, Cap'n Johnny," he said while his fellow ace sloshed some ice water around in his glass. "I know you'll help Eagle turn a profit somehow or another, and I know you'll help bring jobs and people to Georgia."

"We'll get our profits all right, I guarantee you that. I'll win if it kills me, I will."

Soon the pious axioms and folk wisdom of the self-made chieftain adorned Eagle's circulars and pamphlets. Every penny was a building block to a fortune. It was better to do without material than to spend on credit without money. No one was working so much that he could not work still more. Timeliness was next to godliness. Lateness was a sign of sedateness. A government check was no different than a pacifier put in the mouth of a spoiled and bratty child. The reason there were only twenty-four hours in every day was that the Good Lord thought twenty-five hours would be too many for one person to work in one day. The reason the Good Book said God rested on the seventh day after creating the world in six was that the Good Book wanted to leave a way for mankind to outdo God in at least one way by outworking him. Installment plans and manholes had one thing in common—they both conducted the careless into sewage pits. Governments had two purposes: to fend off invaders and to disappear once the invaders were dead. Taxes and Satan were both the misbegotten children of evil. A woman in the workforce was like a peacock in a mud bath. Burning dollar bills with a match was a better way of getting rid of money than leaving lights on in empty rooms, because burning a bill wasted no electricity. The company leader who fattened up off his employees with a high salary was worse than the cardinal who castrated his choirboys. Either of two things resulted from indecision: death or blindness.

The employees at Eagle quaked while the company's profits soared. At any given moment, and for any reason, there was liable to be a tirade issued by the Big Boss in the event of a flagrant violation of one of his precepts. A dressing down by the taskmaster in full view of other workers was a thing to be dreaded worse than a quart-sized dose of castor oil. His eyes would glint like burnished points of steel, his lips quavered and his voice roared with Jeremiads of sarcasm and denunciation. There was only one way to do a thing right, and you either chose to do it that way or to do it the wrong way, which led back through the door which would slam behind you on your way out. It was very easy to go from hero to zero. There was no finish line to anything in life. A mirror was meant more for looking over your shoulder to make sure no one was gaining on you than it was for looking at yourself. And last of all, the most important thing. Nothing was more important that aeroplanes.

The extraordinarily rapid rise of Eagle Air Transport under Jonathan Albritton's stern discipline was a great surprise even to Milt, who profited handsomely from the carrier's success. Johnny's favorite saying was indeed no exaggeration: he really was determined to win in whatever he did, or to die trying. With such military ferocity as a lucrative precedent for airline management, the other carriers quickly began to copy the examples set by Albritton. One such company, however, was not Coastal. Poor, struggling, southern, Louisiana-proud Coastal, led by another son of the Midwest who viewed the world somewhat differently than the erstwhile war ace, still plodded along at its old pace, innovative in nothing since its introduction of crop-dusting, cautious in its approach, wary of bold moves and comfortable with established formulas.

There was a saying about catching flies. More of them came for honey than for vinegar. To catch them was a worthy pursuit, and necessary to the furtherance of commerce and civilization. However, it must be done carefully. Britt seemed to put all his emphasis on the size of his fleet, where it went, whether it operated on time, how many people it carried. Personal popularity was to him as fleeting and unsubstantial as morning fog. But the Hoosier thought sweetness would be a better bait than acidity for a new fly-trap to be put on virgin ground. While Britt seized the reins of power, rammed the bits in his horses' mouths and whipped them into motion, A.T. favored a more leisurely approach to the fledgling airline business.

In the meantime, though he was fattening up off the hefty profits of Eagle's spartan operation, Kid felt more of a kinship in his soul with the Louisiana dusters, the "wooden axle outfit," as the bigger carriers were contemptuously calling them. Oh, Coastal, little Coastal, birthed in the dusty cradle of Tallulah! Of all his interests, unsung Coastal was the sentimental favorite of the man from Woodvale.

"Let's put ourselves on the other side of the counter," the Hoosier would tell Milt when they were discussing the business of the wooden axle outfit. "We have a responsibility over and above the price of a ticket."

Unfortunately, the lowly airline rarely sold any of its tickets, and several times bankruptcy seemed imminent. Still, the former entomologist kept his faith and sustained the faith of those working under him. Coastal had 224 employees, and he knew certain details about the lives of all of them. He knew where all of them lived. He knew the names of all the members of their immediate families. He knew their habits and preferences. He probably knew their political and religious convictions, where they recreated themselves, all the urgent matters pertaining to their health and well-being.

When Coastal had 500 employees he still knew them all. When it had 1000 his memory had expanded to include all of them. No matter how many newcomers he admitted into his fold, his brain continued to carve out untrodden territory within itself in which to store away photographic impressions of each and every one. His ear, hearing a fact or a name a single time, absorbed and transmitted it to an easily accessible passageway of his mind where, at some distant point in the future—maybe a month, a year, or five years later—it might be yanked immediately out of its hiding place at first bidding. Not a single time was he ever heard to criticize an employee publicly, though from time to time he would escort a pilot or a bag loader or a stewardess attended by a chaperon into his cramped cubicle in the corner of the Quonset hut at Candler Field and emerge several minutes later having apparently chastened the person in question. Whenever he noticed a new member in his workplace—someone about whom his ravenous memory had yet to absorb personal information—he would always introduce himself, modestly add he was the president of Coastal Air Lines and ask the rookie: "So, how long have I been working for you?"

He became so beloved by his employees that they actually pooled their savings and bought him a new Cadillac, though he persisted in driving his trusty and clunky old Buick out to the Hapeville headquarters for the rest of his life. He never wanted the people under him to think that he was any different from them. His achievements were their achievements; their failures were his failures. One set of rules applied to everyone, himself above all. Monarchy had been a spur to revolution in most of the places where it had been tried, so why in the world of business should it be a model for success?

GEORGE GRANTLAND BECAME ONE of Bonderman's closest advisors when he finally yielded to Milt's pressure and moved Coastal's headquarters to Hapeville; and Franklin Roosevelt, though politically distasteful to the Hoosier, was being ardently pursued as an ally. How would Coastal ever win the blessings of the Hyde Park aristocrat? It was a question not long in existence before an obvious answer presented itself.

"Kid," A.T. suggested one day in his tiny office, "why don't you arrange to have a chat with FDR next time he visits Warm Springs? You can put in a good word for Coastal with him and explain who we are."

"He won't pay any attention to me," said Milt, "at least not on that subject. But there is one thing he *might* do for me."

The aviator sent a short letter to Roosevelt requesting a meeting with the President on his next sojourn in Warm Springs during the Thanksgiving holiday of 1935. The wheelchair-bound commander in chief mulled over the matter for awhile before he decided it would be politically advantageous for him to have the meeting. When Roosevelt's train pulled into the tiny depot in the middle Georgia village where he customarily spent every Thanksgiving, Milt was ushered by the Secret Service over to the railcar, down from which FDR, supported by braces and crutches, swung onto the landing.

The President was never photographed in his wheelchair, but just as long as he stood upright news photographers snapped streams of pictures of the two men on the depot landing at Warm Springs. Milt and FDR had a friendly conversation for a few minutes before Roosevelt hinted he needed to be moving along.

"One more thing, sir," said Kid, realizing he hadn't yet brought up his main subject.

"And what might that be, Major?" asked FDR.

"It sure would be nice, Mr. President, *if Woodvale got electricity*."

Before Christmas of that year a crew of ten workmen, driving trucks and hoisting poles up with heavy equipment, had strung up an electrical line connecting Woodvale to the rest of creation. For the first time now there were mechanical ways of cooking, of washing, of running fans, of illuminating darkened rooms along the dusty byways of northeast Georgia—ways that bettered the age-old hand-driven instruments that had sustained life in most of the world since the dawn of civilization.

Woodvale was getting to be a certified metropolis now. When it staged a 40th birthday celebration for its best-loved son on October 1 of '36 the sign on its outskirts could glow in the dark. Its streets were flooded with electric light specially tinted for the occasion with all the major hues of the rainbow. Older residents who remembered all the important events of his life took pause to reflect that they were all getting precariously old themselves, for the man they still called 'Kid' was forty.

A 52-year-old coffee-colored beauty, the daughter of the longtime pastor of the Woodvale AME, which was now presided over by the Rev. Woodrow Wilson, kept her distance from his party, trying to nurture the secret crush she still had on him. And though everyone else seemed to be having a wonderful time, Margaret Harrison was not entirely happy about the situation. Her son was forty years old, had never even considered proposing to a woman, and was surely on the verge of truncating the family name.

Matthew Adams, Shnook's boy, was now tall and thin and fourteen, about the same age Kid himself had been when he had first seen an airplane. The young stripling wanted Milt to show him how to operate a plane, to give him instruction in aeronautics, to help him realize his ambition to be exactly what Major Harrison had been. Milt gave the boy a hundred dollars and told him to ride the rails to Hapeville the next weekend. The next Friday afternoon he met the youngster at the depot in his Bentley motorcar and rode to the field with him.

When Matthew donned Kid's old helmet and sat in the legendary Aeroniña, his entire body tingled. No heaven existed but that; there was no joy in the world that could reasonably be called joy in comparison with that. For an entire weekend Milt lavished the boy with advice and baptized him in the mists of the clouds. He was an apt pupil, and there seemed little doubt that within a few years he had the potential to be a sky-devil of the same order as Brackens, Dawes, Lattimore, and even the Great Ace himself.

When young Matthew left town Sunday night to return to progressive and electric Woodvale, and all the routine tedium of the ninth grade at the one-room schoolhouse there, and all the country ways of his kinfolk—when Shnook's boy left Atlanta, Kid for the first time in his life began to ache in his heart that he had no family of his own and no true son to guide through the maelstrom of the advancing world.

THROUGHOUT THAT AUTUMN KID was preoccupied by politics. George Grantland, the Julius Caesar of the Ninth Ward, had fancied himself mayoral material and chosen to take on one of the old entrenched lions named Charlie Kent in a race to determine who would be the next mayor of Atlanta. It was a race full of slime and slander and buffoonery so exaggerated that it seemed more a farcical Vaudeville act than a real-life political campaign. George's trump card was the Great Ace of the Great War, the Girder of the Globe, none other than Kid himself.

Milt was an ardent supporter of his longtime friend, appeared at many of his parties, gave speeches on his behalf, and rendered the outcome of the election, no matter how muck-befouled George became, a foregone conclusion. It was at the election-night celebration of Grantland's ascension to the mayorship that Milt saw the image of the most beautiful girl he had ever beheld in his life, while a live jazz band blared out its hopeful tunes, balloons wafted up to ceiling rafters, streamers shot through the air, and cigar-chomping reporters pecked away at their typewriters.

He had been swept off his feet only once before, long ago, by a young Jasmine Peace. All movement, vitality and noise seemed suspended by this latest brunette beauty. The way she had been looking at him from across the ballroom made it obvious to Milt that she was setting her traps for him. At the first opportunity he made his way through the ranks to introduce himself to her.

"My God," she swore, pretending just then to have noticed him, though she had in fact been staring at him for a full half hour, "it's Kid Harrison!"

"Yes, ma'am," he said, "and who might you be?"

"Juliette Fairfield," she said. "I'm Estelle Warner's best friend. You know Estelle? Her mom's got all those paintings of you on her walls."

He kissed the back of her hand and she began fluttering her eyelashes.

"Tell me," he went on, "is that how you know about me—those paintings?"

"Of course," she purred. "I can't believe you're just as handsome in real life."

His heart nearly beat itself up into his throat.

"H-how old are you?" he mumbled, almost afraid to hear the answer.

"Er . . . uh, I'll be sixteen soon."

In the blind unreasonableness of hope, aroused by the womanly curvaceousness of her figure, he had been hoping she would say something like twenty-five.

"Sixteen soon? Don't that mean you're fifteen now?"

She nodded yes, smiled with her ruby red lipstick, puffed out a perfect ring of cigarette smoke into his face, and tried as hard as she could to smear her newly-sprouted sexuality all over him. She giggled, leaned her head back and squinted her eyes. In her adolescent visions, she wanted the powerful older man to take her and teach her things.

"Well, sweetie," said Kid, "if you keep puffing away on them things like that, it won't be long before you look older than I do."

She giggled again, imagining that to be the highest compliment any man might give her. Apparently, this man was very interested in her. Apparently, her beauty was irresistible. Afraid her parents or George or Jasmine or some other old goat might see her making a spectacle of herself in front of him, Milt excused himself from young Juliette's presence after that, saying something about needing to ask the mayor-elect an important question. The prematurely curvaceous beauty was left positively thrilled. For days, weeks, months, years, the encounter would be fodder for her imagination, an indication of just how high she had already climbed in the hierarchy of the adult world. There was a glimmer of hope that she had a fighting chance in the ultimate challenge to bag the richest, handsomest, most famous man she had ever seen in her life.

CAPTAIN JOHNNY HAD AMBITIOUS plans for his Great Shining Fleet, as Albritton liked to call his company. The Hyde Park aristocrat, far from being annihilated in his first bid for reelection in 1936, as Britt had prophesied, had himself been the annihilator. The election of 1940 loomed as a watershed in the history of free government, in Britt's mind. The birth of big government was the death of free enterprise, he reminded Eagle employees in a pamphlet during that summer. To trade freedom for bread was the same as trading the living for the dead. Thrift was the only fit yardstick for success. Most importantly of all, ignore the interventionists. America first. Ignore the insane maneuvers of foreign despots. We have been in the cauldron and we have gotten scalded, so we dare not go back.

Mr. Albritton adopted a new dear friend, Republican Wendell Willkie, challenger to the two-term incumbent president. On the steel fuselages of the immaculate Great Shining Fleet, the war ace was unabashedly forthright in his political preferences. He ordered Eagle's mechanics to paint, in bold red letters on the sides of his planes, 'ELECT WILLKIE'. He corresponded warmly with the Republican challenger, made substantial campaign contributions, and foresaw glorious results on that upcoming momentous day, the first Tuesday after the first Monday of November of 1940, when the drug of socialism-slavery would at last be drained from the bloodstream of the oppressed common American people.

"The goddamn idea of it!" scowled Captain Johnny, when anyone prodded him on the subject of the upcoming campaign. "Not even George Washington went for a third term. This heathen thinks he's too good to abide by the standards of Washington, Jefferson, or Jackson! We've got ourselves a dictator just the same as if we were in Germany!"

But Jonathan Albritton's opinions put him in the minority. The American public seemed to want continuity and stability. Poverty and want may not have been eradicated by the Rooseveltians, and bread may have still been scarce for many of the American people; but at least it was *their* bread and they enjoyed it on *their* land, and no one was yet threatening to take it away from them. So the precedent-setting third term was awarded to FDR by the electorate, less overwhelmingly than before but still decisively.

Now was not the time for bold moves or shifts in direction. Stories abounded about Adolf Hitler, the charismatic dictator who had taken over the reins in Germany; about how, in defiance of the terms of the Treaty of Versailles, he had rebuilt the armed forces of *Deutshland* into a terrifying Juggernaut, vowing to usher in a new era of worldwide Aryan domination;

about how he had swindled Josef Stalin and Neville Chamberlain, annexed Austria and the Sudetenland and attacked Poland. Some had seen newsreel footage in movie houses of his frenzied and masterfully staged orations from the Chancellery steps in Berlin. It seemed dangerous to allow an untested president to engage in dealings with this man.

Major Harrison had stretched his heart, nerve and sinew to their limits in his youth to destroy the Kaiser's war machine. And yet the world was in demonstrably worse shape now than it had been before. Kid was already disposed to look ill on the spectacle of German militarism, but the stories he heard about the Nazis, preposterous to some though par for the course to him, angered him to his boiling point. If only he had been younger . . . if only . . . Now it would be up to kids to fight, mere whippersnappers fresh out of high school who had no firsthand knowledge of what he did, kids who . . . but had *he* not been a child in the last war? Had he not, despite the shortcomings of youth, found a way to muster the deepest and most self-sacrificing strains of courage to defend his convictions? If his whole life had been about showing others how to do that which was difficult or dangerous, why should it now not be the same? There was still the possibility of something new, something untried.

While Milt was building up intense resentments for the spreading despotisms in Europe, and an equally intense determination to do whatever he could to thwart them, some of his peers were urging a calmer approach. Charles Lindbergh had been traveling around America making speeches advocating pacifism. The clamor for war from some circles, Colonel Lindbergh announced, was being fanned by "the British, the Roosevelt administration and the Jews". The greatest threat to the future of civilization, he stated in one ill-advised address, was from the nonwhite races who were threatening to crowd the whites into submission. Slim aggravated matters by traveling to Germany to receive a medal from Hitler and the head of the Luftwaffe, Herman Goering. He was caught on film shaking their hands and commingling with them in a friendly and sympathetic fashion. Roosevelt, hearing the news, was quick to denounce what he considered the preposterous gesture and severed ties with Lindbergh.

Yet the drumbeat for pacifism was heard from other quarters as well. Captain Johnny, emphatic in his opposition to U.S. intervention in the second version of the World War, found it impossible to understand his friend and fellow veteran's stance on current events.

"If I didn't know better," he told Kid over lunch one day as he was passing through Atlanta, "I'd say you had amnesia. Ever since you and FDR had that get-together I think you been brainwashed. All that pap coming out of you sounds just like a war poster. What are you, a shill for the Democratic Party? We got two big oceans on either side of us, and if they wanna play ball in our park let 'em come and get massacred over here. But until that happens let's get our own house in order."

"I wish I saw things like you do," Milt answered. "But I've still got that bitter taste of the Hun militia in my mouth. I was over there and I saw what it was like. So were you, but maybe it's you who've got the amnesia. If you ain't scared of Heinie militarism and what it can do to the rest of the world, then apparently your memory's not what it used to be. Them boys know how to fight, they're fierce, they ain't scared of nothin' and they'll kill everything in their path like savage animals without a bit of remorse."

Britt sloshed around some of his ice water in his glass, looking dreamily down at it, as was his habit.

"All that's true, Kid," he replied. "But they won't cross an ocean to get to us. Hitler don't got the slightest interest in us. He never set foot over here, he don't consider us to be a part of his sphere, and we could go to hell for all he cared, just as long as he took Eurasia and mowed down every Jew and Slav in his way."

BY 1941 TINY, PLUCKY Coastal, still struggling to make payroll on the first and fifteenth of every month, received glorious news from its financial backers, Kid Harrison and the Citizens and Southern Bank of Georgia: an application for a loan of $600,000 from the bank, with a portion of Major Harrison's estate offered as collateral, had been approved. With this money A.T. Bonderman bought five brand new DC3's, the premier passenger-carrying aircraft of the day.

From now on, Coastal patrons would be traveling in high style in planes sixty-four and a half feet long and with a wingspan of almost a hundred feet: 30,000 pounds of chromed steel. With a range of 1500 miles, a normal cruising altitude of seven to ten thousand feet and a speed of nearly 200 miles per hour, the twin-engined monoplane, introduced in 1935, had sleeper berths for 14 people, day accommodations for 24, soft fabric seats, engines mounted on noise-buffering rubber insulators, and on-board dining service. Supposedly, the plane's cantilevered wings had been engineered to withstand being driven over by steamrollers, and its range and speed would enable it to avoid the most jarring elements of weather.

Milt put one of the DC3's to the test just as soon as he got behind its controls at the Douglas factory in Los Angeles. Mr. Bonderman, Mayor Grantland, several reporters, and representatives from four prominent Louisiana families who backed Coastal sat in the back while Kid piloted the DC3 smoothly over the western deserts and prairies. But the passengers were nearly scared out of their wits when the intrepid daredevil flew directly into two thunderstorms over Texas and Alabama en route to Candler Field.

Ron Rice and Drayton Darnel, two Coastal pilots accompanying the Great Ace, wouldn't dare to suggest that he change course to avoid the bad weather. Instead they quietly gritted their teeth and sweated nervously as the DC3 was jerked back and forth, as thunderclaps shook the sides of its fuselage and bumpy air pockets nearly yanked the floor of its seating compartment out from under them. After the direct penetration of the first thunderstorm, the bespectacled Hoosier stormed into the cockpit.

"Dammit, Kid, what're you trying to do, kill us all? That was the worst experience I've ever had in an aeroplane."

"What was?" Milt shrugged.

"I'm serious. Can't you find ways around those things when you see 'em coming?"

"I ain't trying to go around stuff, A.T. I'm goin' in a straight line. That's faster and better, and if people are chicken, let 'em stay home and ride in streetcars. This here's a flying tank, it's designed to shoot right through weather, and I ain't about to sidestep a little commotion in this warhorse."

By the time the second thunderstorm approached, a death-like pallor descended over the passengers as streaks of lighting shot through the sky by the windows and loud booms of thunder pierced the eardrums of the poor suffering riders in the back. Kid had never before felt so comfortable in the midst of chaos. While everyone else on board had final thoughts about loved ones and unfulfilled promises and last words, he was already looking ahead eagerly at the approaching clearing, anxious to find another storm into the center of which he might aim his steel torpedo. When the second bout with violent weather for the DC3 passengers was mercifully at an end, several of them considered going up to the cockpit themselves and demanding that Kid give up the controls to the other two pilots, though they never worked up the nerve to do it. Much to Milt's chagrin, though to the delight of everyone else on board, the weather was perfectly clear the rest of the way to Atlanta.

When the prized DC3 finally landed and was chocked safely in the large tin hangar the city had built for the Coastal fleet at the northern extremity of Candler Field, A.T. called a meeting of all 35 of the company's pilots. Rice and Darnel were of course already there, and they were soon joined by Stoffelmyre, the wing walker who had lost an ear and gotten dashed on the side of the head by shrapnel when he crashed into a barn in Missouri; Rellison, the Hollywood stuntman who had burned half his body over Burbank by igniting the wick by his cockpit two seconds too soon before bailing out back in '29; McMaster, the insatiable womanizer and boozer, who was nevertheless so good a flyer in military air shows and training maneuvers that FDR was proposing to offer him a captaincy in the Navy before Coastal came calling; Gentry, the polar explorer who had been stranded once in the Yukon while trying to map out the coastline of the Arctic Ocean, subsisting on reindeer meat and boiled grass until located by rescue party; and Norm Shepard, the newest member of the fold, hired only last month, the pride of Albany, Georgia, a former peanut duster and mail carrier; and on down the line. A more crusty and hardboiled collection of young men the world had scarcely before seen. Now these gritty rogues in their leather jackets and flying helmets had been summoned by Kid and the boss to convene in the hangar and hear a brief pep talk.

"Boys," said Kid, pointing at the first plane that had ever been profitable by passenger fares alone, "now *this* is an aeroplane!"

After all the whistling and hooting died down, Aloysius Troy addressed them in a more serious tone.

"It's make or break time, fellows. If we don't turn this business around and make Johnny Albritton start sweatin' a little with Eagle over there, we'll all be out of a job and this thing's going back to the C&S bank."

Milt examined the bedraggled ranks of the men, patted Norm the rookie on the back, and reassured the corps of pilots.

"When we get out of here, men, let's go out and tell all our friends about flying. Tell 'em how fast and safe it is. Your mamas, your sisters, your distant cousins that you ain't seen in ten years. All of 'em need to spread the word and pack this here beauty to the gills—or else I'm out a fortune and all y'all are back to stunting and dusting."

Perhaps the gamble of borrowing so large an amount of money to get so fancy a set of airplanes might have backfired on the brass of lowly Coastal if not for a tragic accident that befell its main competitor at almost exactly the same time as its own acquisition of the DC3's. For years A.T. had bragged of his company's perfect record of safety: no fatalities in thousands of passenger flights. Until 1938 Albritton boasted of an even more remarkable record at the much-larger Eagle: 144 million passenger miles flown in the previous seven years without a single fatality. But a DC2 crash at Fort Lauderdale in January of that year ended Eagle's unblemished record, and in June of 1941, as a DC3 sleeper carrying Albritton himself and nearly a dozen others made its approach into Candler Field, it clipped into some trees on the outskirts of Hapeville, crashed in flames, and killed nine passengers and its two pilots.

Britt was severely injured himself, and it appeared that his hold on life, put to the severest challenge countless times in his exemplary career as a race car driver, fighter pilot and adventurer, would finally slip from his grasp. For weeks he teetered on the brink of death in the intensive care ward at an Atlanta hospital, with smashed bones in his legs and charred and mutilated skin. Every day the heartbroken Kid, who loved Britt when many others seemed to detest him for his bullheadedness and irascibility, went to pay his respects. During his visits he rarely saw anyone else visiting the fellow war ace and national hero. It was true, what Captain Johnny had said. It was easy in this world to go from hero to zero.

"You're gonna come through all right, Britt," he would encourage his friend in his private suite as the wounded man's dazed and bloodshot eyes looked helplessly at the ceiling above him. "I know you've got the strength—you're stronger than any ten average men."

Mr. Albritton would breathe in slowly and calmly, not daring to show effeminate emotion, or to feel sorry for himself or to go against the grain of his own philosophy of self-reliance and self-determination in the face of mortality.

"Thanks for knowing, Kid. You understand that, even if nobody else does. We're brothers, you and I are. I'll win if it kills me—you know I will. But it won't."

Eventually the indestructible war ace survived the unsurvivable. He was sustained by the boundless zest for life and courage that was privy to him and a select few others in the age of the aviator. A whole year passed before Britt was even able to return to work, and he walked with a limp for the remainder of his life. But he lived. To the delight of some, and to the regret of a few, the stern taskmaster who dwelled in the chivalries of his own imagination returned to the captain's chair of the Great Shining Fleet

But the public was skittish. Any mishap at all, let alone one of such lurid and disastrous consequences, was bound to leave an opportunity for scrappy little Coastal, with its still-perfect record and new set of DC3's, to win over an otherwise skeptical public. For the first time in the era of passenger carrying, Coastal finally stemmed the flow of red ink and turned a healthy profit. The Hoosier's homespun wisdom began to assume an almost biblical authority, and Britt, as he recovered, began to break a sweat. Maybe there was more to those good old southern Louisiana dusters than he thought. Maybe they would stay in Eagle's way forever.

IN THE MEANTIME, KID had a new interest in his life, and indeed she made him feel like a kid again, though he was 44 years old. Juliette Fairfield, the cigarette-smoking 15-year-old sexpot from Grantland's inaugural party, was now 20 and trying to live apart from her parents. All of the younger men she had dated had fallen short of her lofty expectations, so she began dropping by Kid's mansion, flirting with him, and letting him know she was interested and available. Also, she kept dropping hints that despite appearances to the contrary she was still a virgin. That was the only way she felt she even had a chance with him. Those old-fashioned sorts of men, she thought, had their girls for play and girls for keeps. She was trying to convince him she belonged in the latter camp. What bothered him was that most of the pretty girls he had known who had had cigarettes in their mouths by age 15 had also had plenty of other things in plenty of other places.

But he soon started believing her. He asked her to dinner with him at his favorite neighborhood bistro, and by their fourth date he was already thinking about the ironic possibility of being married to a girl who had originally been attracted to him by Jasmine's paintings.

"Your folks probably won't like this one bit, darlin'," he told the bubbly young belle, whose charms made his blood sizzle as if he were a teenage boy again. "I'm old enough to be your . . . uh, your *older brother*."

"You are not, Kid. That's not true. If I had an older brother I'm sure he'd be way older than you."

"Really? Maybe you've got a future career in politics if you're that good at stretching the truth."

"So what should we do, pretend we're not in love just because of what's on our birth certificates?"

"That's the problem. Birth certificates. I don't have one because they weren't even around when I was born. That's the way it is with me. Just about everything you can think of, sweetie, has come along since I was born. How much can we have in common?"

"We've been getting along very well, no matter what you say."

"That's true," he said. "But some day I'll be either prematurely dead or an old fossil that you'll have to pry out of a rocking chair with a crowbar, and then how heroic will you think I am? Are you, a hot young thing, prepared to watch me turn into a shaky old man?"

"Yes," she said, squeezing his hands. "Maybe I'm foolish, but that's what love means to me. There's only one man for me, and that man is you. No matter what happens, I'll still feel that way and you'll always be alive in here. " She put both of her hands over her heart.

And, of course, having heard this, he was left with only one possible decision. He *had* to marry her.

SHNOOK ADAMS' BOY, Matthew, had taken too seriously the legacy left him by his home village's greatest figure. Whatever Kid had done, Matthew wanted to do himself. Prohibition had ended years earlier, so running booze over the Caribbean was no longer the fortune-making instrument of outlawry it had been in the heyday of Mr. Excitement. And the Angelenos had seemingly lost their interest in airplane pictures, so the prospect of following the master's air trails to Tinseltown was a threadbare one. Being a world explorer and traveler had lost its feasibility now with much of the world at war. Being a war hero like Kid would have been grand, but the U.S.A. had so far steered clear of the overseas fray. Which exploit of the great ace remained to be duplicated? The only one that came readily to mind was what the young Adams boy actually ended up doing: being an aviation fanatic around Hapeville, sleeping outside in the grass in the summer, or on the hard floor of a hangar under the wings of an airplane in winter.

Nineteen years old and full of energy, young Matthew had graduated from Jennies to the complications of DC2's and DC3's, all under the apprenticeship of Chester Dawes, Robert Brackens, or Milton Harrison himself. With the rulers of the realm at his beck and call, and with the financial support of Milt, who was using the idle planes of Coastal's fleet which happened to be parked in its hangar, Matthew had logged 200 hours of time in the latest and best equipment, and was as skilled behind the controls of contemporary aircraft as many of the active members of Coastal's corps of pilots.

On one occasion, when Mr. Bonderman saw the young Adams boy curled up in the weeds like a wino napping away a warm afternoon in front of Coastal's hangar, he had a mind to call the police and have him hauled off. But then he remembered that Kid had described this boy to him and asked him if he might offer him a position with the company. The Hoosier seemed skeptical about whether that would be in his best interests as he went to shake the boy out of his sleep.

"Are you the boy who knows Kid Harrison?" asked A.T.

Scraggly and unshaven, Matthew roused himself and quickly rose to his feet to respect his elder.

"Yes, sir, Mr. Bonderman, I am."

"Are you from Woodvale too?"

"Yes, sir. Born and raised in the shadow of Kid."

"Do you know how to fly planes? Major Harrison said you did."

"I do, sir. Ever since I was a little bitty boy that's what I've wanted to do."

"How'd you like a job with Coastal Air Lines, young man? A flying job."

Shnook's boy's mouth went totally dry and he gulped.

"I don't think you'd want anything to do with me, sir. I don't have any education."

"On the contrary," said Aloysius Troy, "you've gotten the best of all possible educations. The fellow on the throne of the airplane heaven actually came down from the clouds and blessed you. If Kid said you're good material, you're good material. Be in my office tomorrow morning at nine sharp—clean-shaven and with your shoes shined, please."

YOUNG MATTHEW NOW HAD the boy's place in the man's world that had long ago belonged to none other than the Great Ace himself. He was one of the fleet. His reputation as a skilled pilot grew quickly and his youth made him a prime resource to Uncle Sam after the Japanese attack at Pearl Harbor in 1941. He quickly volunteered for military service, joined the Marines, and enjoyed three air victories in his Grumman F4F Wildcat monoplane over the Pacific Front before being shot down over northern Luzon in the Philippines, ambushed by a Japanese battalion, and shot five times in the back of the head at point-blank range in February of '42. His remains were shipped homeward, across the vast sea, for interment in the family plot behind the First Baptist Church of his native village.

Woodvale had never experienced a darker hour. The doleful funeral procession wound its way into the church, and Milt and five other somber pallbearers carried the casket to its bier, leaving the twenty-year-old boy's body to lie placidly in the box that would be its eternal bed. The greatest of all the Woodvaleans fell apart like a shattered eggshell. For only the second time since his own father's death, and the first since Arlene's crash, despite all the other tribulations throughout his life, the usually dry-eyed man wept.

The slain boy had drawn pictures of him with crayons, had dreamed of doing just what Milt himself had done as he sat in his lap listening to his life's stories. John "Shnook" Adams, who had shot off his own toes in 1917 to spare himself a similar fate, had lost his only boy in a worse war a generation later.

Soon John's weeping friend, who had gone willingly—though it now appeared futilely—into the middle of the tempest in 1917, had dry eyes again. The job had not been finished last time. The loose ends of the great anarchy had never been tied together. It was time now to end the madness.

"Don't worry, John," Milt told the bereaved father when Matthew's remains had been buried in the cold dark ground. "They thought your son couldn't fight back, but they were wrong. *I may be gittin' a little old, but I'm not dead yet.*"

CHAPTER 32

South Pacific Air Force

FOR MONTHS AND EVEN YEARS the prospect of another terrible war had haunted the man from Woodvale, and the temptation to join the America Firsters and ignore the worldwide upheaval had been great.

What, after all, had anyone in the U.S.A to gain by joining in the mass carnage and destruction of another foreign war? It was *their* problem; so *they* were the ones who needed to solve it. Just so long as North America was at peace, what business had we in meddling in the affairs of overseas tyrants? Why should a new generation of promising boys be sent to the senseless slaughter or degradation that he knew would await them? The question had teased him and danced about his skeptical mind.

Milt considered the matter philosophically until the first week of December of 1941. Then philosophy went flying away like a ghost into the cellar of a large old haunted house. Some said Roosevelt had gotten warning signals about the imminent attack on Hawaii and had done nothing to stop it, convinced that the attack would reverse public opposition to a war effort the President believed was necessary. Kid thought that was unprovable, and he saw it as a moot point anyway. The attack had happened, and Roosevelt hadn't been in the planes dropping the bombs. And in February, when he saw the stiff corpse of young Matthew Adams, he realized that he had to be not only a supporter of the retaliation, but a participant in it himself.

Violence would have to be answered in the only way it understood: with more violence. And he personally was in no position to hide behind age or wealth or the laurels of the past. Never had his life been checked in its progress by the complacent memory of past accomplishments, and now was not the time for his old habits to change. A boy who had once bounced on his knee had become a victim of the insanity, and he felt partly to blame for it. Perhaps he was too critical of himself, for he had hardly been idle since the last war. The problem, it seemed to him, was that he had not done enough. Always, for as long as he lived, he would feel compelled to push himself to further and greater heights; to aim his sights as high into the heavens as it was humanly possible to go.

It was far different for him now than in the last war, when he had been humiliated by Sergeant Gilmore as a new enlistee. Nowadays the President himself would lend him an ear if he called. Churchill would meet with him, and the Führer and the Emperor—one who had personally fought against his side as a private in the last war, the other who had welcomed him on friendly terms in peacetime—would both want in the worst way to kill him. That was of little concern to him. Long ago the fear of losing his life had left him. In fact, a condition of relative safety was more alien to him than one of imminent danger. He was bound to die at some time or another, and what better way to go than this, by fighting a pair of the most bloodthirsty regimes in the history of the world?

He made a special trip to Washington to confer with the President at the White House and ask a favor of him. He wanted reinstatement into the Army Air Corps and assignment to the Pacific theatre in the bulwark against the Japanese advance on the Philippines. That was where the young man who idolized him had perished, and where the cruelties of the aggressors were most excessive.

Roosevelt was warm to the idea. The boost to the morale of the armed services with the Great Ace himself back in the fold would be inestimable. When Milt was told he would be granted the rank of colonel, he stood and saluted the Commander in Chief.

"If there's anything I've learned in the world, Mr. President," he said, "it's that if we don't keep fighting and struggling for what we know is right, there won't be any America left. There will always be people who hate us and who'll do everything they can to kill us."

"Always," said Roosevelt. "The struggle will never end."

COLONEL HARRISON RETURNED HOME to Georgia in one of the Eagle DC3's which only fifteen months earlier had sported a sign on its fuselage endorsing Roosevelt's opponent in the last presidential election. He found that before he left to serve in the Second Great War another woman would be begging him to stay home. Not his mother, for she had years earlier learned that all attempts to sway his mind in anything were totally futile. But this time his sweetheart, who had been inspired to love him by the very same woman he had loved before the first war, was pleading earnestly and desperately for him to stay behind.

"You'll be a marked man, Milton!" Juliette cried. "Those horrible monsters will come right after you. They'll shadow you."

"No, they won't," said Kid. "They have bigger fish to fry. And even if I knew they would, that still wouldn't keep me from going."

His fiancée wiped tears from her eyes with a white handkerchief.

"All this will be yours," he said, "no matter what happens. I'll revise my will just as soon as we . . ."

She leaned up and pleaded with him one last time, as he felt a twinge of pain shoot through him: *"How could you leave me like this? You don't have to go, not at your age, not after what you've done."*

"Yes, I do have to go, darling," he told her gently, pushing her hair off her forehead. "Come over here and let me read something to you."

He took her by the hand and walked with her over to the large oaken bookshelves which guarded the corner of the room. It was so out of character for him to read to her out of a book that she was both shocked and speechless. Still more astounding to her was his choice of literature. He pulled the ancient, dusty, antebellum King James Bible of his father and grandfather off the top shelf, and turned to a page he had bookmarked. In all his years of churchgoing with his mother and sisters only one scriptural passage had ever worked its way verbatim into his memory. It was Reverend Gray's mainstay, Luke 12:48. Though he knew the passage by heart he thought reading it aloud to his young sweetheart from its source would make a deeper impression on her than a recitation out of his head.

"'For unto whomsoever much is given,'" he quoted, *"'of him shall be much required: and to whom men have committed much, of him they will ask the more.'"*

She looked with amazement at this side of him which she had never known existed before, as he continued to explain his personal moral code to her.

"If I have a heavy burden, dear, it's because I've got shoulders that can carry it. Of course I haven't always carried my load, and many times I've done a fine job of serving the wrong master. But that was in the past. I've always felt one person matters in this world. That's what my parents and their parents felt, and their actions proved it. And I think my life demonstrates they were right. One person *does* matter. One person *can* make a difference. Now the world's about to get overrun by tyrants who don't respect the rights of the individual. Well, I don't want today's children to live in a world like this when they grow up. I don't want them to go through this nightmare all over again and see all of what I've had to see. I want them to have a happy and a safe life—a better one than what I've had."

MILT AND JULIETTE, unbeknownst to any of their relatives, were married on the night before he left for the Far East at a quiet ceremony in his large home. He promised her a more colorful betrothal and a full-scale honeymoon when he came back. And he assured her that he would be back. She was only twenty and he had turned forty-five four months earlier. A quarter of a century earlier, when he had first been shipped off to war, he had been her same age, twenty years old, and she had not even been a dream in anyone's imagination. How much he wished he could make her understand, and yet how impossible it was! Some day, though perhaps not until she was even older than he was now, she would understand. Maybe then she would explain it to others so that they too would know.

He flew on an Eagle sleeper to Los Angeles, met up with the crew of the U.S.S. *Monticello* at Long Beach, and presented his papers and commission to Admiral William Parsons at dawn on the day of the carrier's embarkation to Hawaii, Guam and the Far East. The famous Colonel quickly became a favorite of the rank-and-file seamen onboard the transport vessel during its voyage. Many of the green recruits listened to his stories of air combat in the First Great War as though he were telling them a tall tale antedating Noah and the Great Flood. And indeed the previous quarter of a century had brought revolutionary changes to aircraft and aircraft design.

In 1918 most of the best fighting planes, with the notable exception of the steel-ribbed German Fokker D.VII's, were of completely wooden frames and cloth coverings. Limited to only 160 horsepower and 117 miles per hour, the vessels had been armed with two machine guns, had cockpits open and exposed to the rigors of the elements, and no radio or mechanical means of communicating with other pilots or military officials.

But now, in 1942, planes were all of steel frame; at high altitudes their operators could wear oxygen masks; engines were rated over 600 horsepower and could achieve speeds approaching 400 mph; they had ignition-controlled cockpit-activated starters, sparing their pilots and mechanics the deadly manual propellor spins of old; and the pilots were able to stay in constant contact with others through radio and, with the development of radar in its infancy, were fast approaching an ability to track and shoot at targets they were not even able to see.

Instrument panels now enabled "blind flying", the guidance of planes without any dependence on sight readings of the horizon or surrounding elements. In Kid's and aviation's early youth, the airplane flyer could not maintain his equilibrium without a visible horizon. Air combat thus had become less a matter of pilot versus pilot as machine versus machine. Skill and strategy, though still important, had become secondary to engineering. The days of the great knights of the air were gone. In their stead were air soldiers: winged fighters who were nearly as manipulable and coordinated as regiments of infantrymen.

By the time Col. Harrison reached the Philippines at the end of the week the Japanese had already seized control of the two main U.S. Military posts on the islands, Clark Airfield and the Subic Bay Naval Base; and the American military forces were in retreat, to Java and Australia. Milt was assigned to Las Palmas Field, a makeshift air base near the Lingayan Gulf on the west-central coast of Luzon, and named commander of the South Pacific Air Force (SPAF), a squadron of nerveless holdouts intent on recapturing the Philippines from Japanese occupation.

Las Palmas had been bombed twice in the past month, escaping serious damage only because the Japanese had apparently placed a low priority on devastating a base where nothing seemed to be happening. But now, with the relocation of the SPAF, that was certain to change. The likelihood that the modest airfield would stay intact long was remote. Still, General MacArthur and others held out hope. If anyone could hold back the tide of the invader it would be the Great Ace, who had rarely failed at anything he had ever tried.

AT LAS PALMAS, MILT was introduced to the current war's new machinery, the Lockheed P-38's and Grumman Wildcats. With twin propellors, one on each side of the fuselage, and a glass-enclosed cockpit, these machines were the latest in military aeronautics, capable of blasting by the 300mph threshold. So great a thrill did the enormous speed and wizardry of the new airplanes give him—so finely and precisely did the sophisticated instruments work in comparison with some of the cow-crates of his past—that he nearly forgot about the death and destruction that had brought about their development.

The young boys of the SPAF had been skeptical about whether the "old fellow", as they called him, could handle modern planes. The first time he spun and dove in a P-38 over the tropical blue waters of the Lingayan Gulf, after a scant half hour of instruction from one of the young captains, he put those doubts to rest. However, the sobering fact was that he had gotten to the Far East too late to help repel the Japanese from Clark Airfield and Subic Bay. The Imperial campaign of assault had been ruthless, murderous, and completely effective, and when Colonel Harrison saw the results of the enemy's success on the addled young soldiers around him he tried to reassure them.

"You've trained thoroughly for all this, boys," he addressed them as they stood at attention before the first sortie he was to lead. "And if we all stick together and do our best, we'll make everybody back home proud. And I say 'we' because, no matter what happens, I'm gonna be right in the middle of it. I may be an officer, but I'll never ask you to do something I can't or won't do myself."

Despite his reassuring air, Kid was appalled by the reckless might and cruelly devastating coordination of the Japanese forces. In the Philippines they were wreaking havoc on the conquered native populace. Villages throughout Luzon were being pillaged and looted, woman and children slaughtered. Newborn babies, precious in their unknowing innocence, were being pierced with long metal knives and their carcasses strung up like fish on trotlines, hung from the rafters of smokehouses. Young Filipino women, in order to avoid the ever-present scourge of rape in the wake of their heartless predators, were taking hog bladders under their dresses and, on the approach of would-be assailants from the militia of Imperial Japan, gouging the bladders with razorblades so that the blood poured out and covered their midriffs between the thighs and below the navels. Nothing less than the sight of a completely gored woman would hold back the repeated violations.

To the thus-brutalized Filipinos the man from Woodvale, the millionaire and movie performer and world-traveler, was no less than a god, just as he had been along the Western Front to the French populace in 1918. Once he was outside the confines of Las Palmas Air Base, he was welcome at every corner and along every byway. There were no strangers. Many still recalled having seen his plane during his voyage of 1926. He wondered whether some people in Japan might secretly be harboring similarly warm memories of that trip, or if there, as in many other of the warring nations, the past had now been either completely erased or altered to suit the designs of the current ruling class.

Kid humored the Filipinos whenever he went out among them, usually in the nearby village of Dagupan City near his base. He accompanied the sick and the elderly to faith healers who promised to reverse their fortunes. He accepted invitations to lunch in tiny hovels and ate rice, pork and *lumpia*. If he had leave enough he sat down to card games with elderly men, gambled copious pesos on poker and blackjack, presided over several cockfights in which the screaming rabble of spectators drowned out the screeches of the chickens. He led the people to know that he was one of them. It was not true that he was royalty. He had been born in a poor village, just as they had been; had fished and butchered animals and shot quail and attended cockfights and worked in a cotton gin and blacksmith's shop. No soft child of privilege was he. He'd been born fighting, and he'd continue fighting till the end.

He had ingratiated himself with the common people, and it would be the common people who would provide safe harbor for him in his greatest time of need and save his life. During his first five weeks in the Philippines, Colonel Kid and his brigade of youthful acolytes in the South Pacific Air Force achieved 27 kills in their skirmishes with Japanese Zero fighter planes, while sustaining only four losses. Milt himself downed six planes, becoming an ace in both of the World Wars. Most important of all, he and his mates successfully parried a half dozen Japanese air raids and extended the precarious existence of the Las Palmas base for at least another month.

But the Japanese were elsewhere achieving almost total air and naval victories. They had staged a successful preemptive air raid over Darwin, Australia, where Kid had landed in 1926; invaded Bali and New Guinea; forced the British evacuation of Rangoon in Burma and the Dutch surrender of Java; had sunk the U.S.S. *Houston*, the largest American vessel in the Pacific theater; and also the *Langley*, the first U.S. aircraft carrier in the region. They had even gone so far as to attack the U.S. mainland, with a shelling of an oil refinery near Santa Barbara, California.

There was no question that Colonel Kid's side was losing. Perhaps the man from Woodvale was too small to make the slightest difference.

THE EMPEROR, THOUGH REMEMBERING his cordial encounter with Colonel Harrison sixteen years earlier, had no qualms about considering him a mortal enemy now. Times had changed. Now the cherished soil of *Nippon* herself was at risk. Kid had to be killed. He was only one tiny man in a world of billions, but he had proved to be a deadly thorn in the side of the last war machine to fight against him, and only when his superinflated pride had been destroyed would he be prevented from replicating himself on the impressionable blank slates of the American boys who were watching everything he did.

The SPAF had downed an unusually large number of Zeroes, it was true, and the attempts to seize Manila Bay and Bataan had been slowed. But not for long. One man did not amount to much in the world, and this man, a scourge to the Empire, would soon be removed from the unswerving path of the Emperor's war machine.

One person did not matter. That was what this fighting was about. One person did not matter in Germany, in Italy, in Japan, in Russia. It was only the state that mattered. The personal effects of an individual—his family, his property, the fruits of his labor—were only so much fodder for the state, to be consumed or annihilated as the state dictated. What mattered was the homeland, the fatherland, the inanimate soil.

The last foreign power to threaten Japan had been Kubla Khan in 1281. He had been repulsed by a fortuitous storm of such violent dimensions that Khan and his entire Mongol fleet had been blown away. Divine forces had seemed to be behind this favorable cataclysm which had spared Japan. Japan must have been the Chosen Land to have been spared by the "divine wind", or the *kamikaze*. The flying machines which bore the young men of Japan aloft were now serving the *kamikaze*, the divine winds. It was not they who mattered, but the inanimate dirt and rocks of the land, the wealth of territories, the soul of the great Emperor himself. Mother Nippon was small and needed new territories to enrich her economy: petroleum, timber, foodstuffs, precious ores and metals, coal. The lives and deaths of the kamikaze fliers would be subsumed entirely by the needs of Japan and the Emperor, by the omnipotent forces of the Buddha and Shinto. To die was what the life of an obedient servant was about, not to live.

The Japanese High Command had detailed information about the size of the SPAF on the Lingayan Gulf in western Luzon. No more than a hundred aircraft, mostly P-38's under the guidance of Colonel Harrison, had been reported in action. The Imperial militia literally had men and material to burn. Their mission would be to wipe out this contemptible unit with two hundred Zero fighter planes, torpedo the Bataan peninsula west of Manila, seize Manila Bay by land, air and sea and expel the Americans from the Philippines.

On April 3 the Japanese bombarded the U.S. and Philippine forces at Bataan in just such a manner as the High Command had envisaged. Milt had been visiting with wounded children at a clinic in Dagupan City when he heard the familiar air raid sirens and saw the Japanese flying in formation on the northern horizon for yet another air attack on his little landing strip. He immediately recognized this attack as one which would dwarf all the others. "God dammit, they mean business this time," he thought to himself.

He ran through the panicked streets of Dagupan City back to the base and saw men scattering like ants around the hangar and concrete runway. The bombing had already started. Men were ducking and the runway was being cratered by explosions. There was no time to organize a plan to lead an effective counterpunch. It would be every man for himself, impromptu strategizing from plane to plane by radio, and massive casualties for sure.

For the first time in his career as a fighter pilot he realized that the enemy was going to achieve an almost total victory before he ever even went airborne. No matter: he had come into the world kicking and fighting, and he had no intention of leaving it with his tail between his legs. And there was always that chance of escape—he may have been getting a little old, but he wasn't dead yet.

Only about fifty planes out of the SPAF fleet ever made it to the air in the feckless attempt to intercept the Japanese assault on the Bataan peninsula to the south. Milt was among the first to go airborne over the base, and he was able to shoot down three Zeroes by soaring to 18,000 feet without being detected by the enemy, hiding in the cloud cover while they circled to the southwest, and pouncing on the trailing Japanese in the formation before retreating to the clouds above Manila Bay, some eighty miles to the south. By this time over thirty of his comrades had followed Colonel Kid's lead into the deceptive cloud banks under which the Japanese, in need of visibility for their bombers, had been ordered to fly.

Kid was able to take out four more Zeroes by sneak attack, and his fellows a total of fifteen, making a remarkable twenty-two enemy aircraft eliminated in less than half an hour. But technique and strategy could not long forestall the might of the superior numbers of the enemy. By radio the Japanese had communicated the situation to their colleagues in the next formation, and the next wave rose to 20,000 feet, above the cloud bank, to take out the Americans once they emerged from cover.

With their ranks swelled by the repositioned members of the first wave who had avoided being shot down, the latest cluster of enemy aircraft outnumbered Colonel Kid and his men by a ratio of better than four to one, and they began raining death down on the defeated heads of the South Pacific Air Force. Milt tried to fight as gamely as he could, but when he saw several of his squadron mates shot down and noticed a cluster of six Zeroes swooping down on him from overhead he realized he had but one choice. Milt yelled over his radio, hoping at least a few other pilots of his squadron might hear him:

"Boys, we gotta dive to the ground, hope they don't follow, and bail out, or we're dead meat."

The great master of aerial acrobatics deliberately put his P-38 into a controlled downward spiral, hoping the Japanese would think they had hit him and not break formation to follow the downward course of his plane. And, indeed, the current antagonists, making the same mistake as a few members of the Kaiser's *Jagdstaffels* a generation earlier, were fooled into thinking the man from Woodvale had already been shot down.

Anticipating what would happen upon landfall, Kid had aimed his dive at the coastline of the peninsula's western shore, trying to avoid the thick vegetation of the interior that would doubtless be full of Japanese and treacherous for parachute landings. Before the P-38 struck the ground and exploded he jumped out and, though dizzy and disoriented, guided his parachute down clear of obstruction into some soft mud by an estuary near Bagac Bay on the western coastline of the Bataan Peninsula.

No sooner had he landed than he realized a Japanese company of foot soldiers had seized the area and was on patrol. Kid grabbed a Bowie knife from a sheath on his belt, cut himself loose from his parachute apparatus, and dove into a bamboo thicket before the enemy could catch sight of him. The Japanese commander heard scurrying sounds from an indeterminate direction and fired a few potshots hoping to get lucky, but he never actually saw the American ace.

Milt hacked down the thinnest reed of bamboo that he saw while he heard Japanese shouts and gunfire and explosions in the woods around him. He fashioned the reed into a straw of sorts, about two feet in length, and submerged himself completely in some brown muck for about half an hour, breathing through the makeshift pipe, until the Japanese commander and his battalion gave up their pursuit of him and the sounds of shells and gunfire had died down in the immediate vicinity.

For the rest of that day, in fits and starts, Col. Harrison walked nervously up the coastline of Bataan, ducking into sloughs, bogs or thickets when he heard airplanes or gunshots. Unarmed except for his Bowie knife, and with no food or water, and adrift in an area rife with enemy forces, he knew his hold on life was dangling by the most precarious of threads. At one point he was spotted by a Japanese U-boat a half mile out into Bagac Bay, and he was forced to cut into the brush in the direction of skirmishes. Japanese voices were everywhere about him, though far enough away not to hear his scurrying through the brush, and he knew he would need to think of some bizarre and unconventional method of hiding in order to avoid them.

He came to a clearing in the jungle where he saw the corpses of seven soldiers—three Americans, three Filipinos and one Australian—strewn within a few feet of each other around a small murky shallow pond that could be waded across in a few steps. The enemy was surrounding him. He realized that unless he played dead until nightfall and sneaked out in search of a town under cover of darkness, he would have no chance of surviving. So he dragged the seven corpses into a pile and hid under one of the rancid dead bodies just as a Japanese regiment emerged from the thick brush and entered the clearing.

His only hope was that they would have no more regard for a pile of dead Allied soldiers than they would for a pile of dead rats and make no attempt to identify them. He heard the footsteps of three of the Japanese and held his breath while they kicked at the corpses, kicked at him and began goring the corpses with their bayonets. He felt a bayonet point jab completely through the body on top of him and graze his leather jacket above the navel as he held his breath in. After Milt had endured about five minutes of this disgusting, dehumanizing horror, the men gave up the search of the bodies without ever bothering to move the corpse off of him.

The stench of cold dead rotten flesh had been revolting in the extreme. What were these people—animals? No, they were worse than that. To call them animals would be insulting to animals. In the anger of the moment, no atrocity of retaliation seemed too severe to him.

The man from Woodvale removed himself from the thicket, weakened by thirst and hunger, and limped along the coastline of Bataan while elsewhere on the peninsula the armed forces of Imperial Japan were beginning what would culminate a week later in the infamous "Bataan Death March", the herding of 76,000 Allied prisoners of war 60 miles across the baking heat of the tropics without food or water to their internment camps. Twelve thousand of the prisoners would be Americans and 5000 would die in the march.

Colonel Harrison struggled ten miles up the shoreline in complete darkness, before finally coming to Morong, an occupied village near Subic Bay, where he saw an old Filipino fisherman. He pleaded for water and was soon helped by the fisherman's daughters and grandchildren, devout Catholics who made the sign of the cross to acknowledge the miracle of his survival. They hid him with blankets and pushed him in a wooden cart to their barrio.

"Ang manga dakilang Americano," the fisherman had told his friends and neighbors, "*ang taong ipinanganak na may pakpak, at tagapagligtas nang bangsang Pilipinas!"* It was the great American, the one who was born with wings, the savior of the Philippines!

Kid had learned a few words of the native Tagalog language for use in emergencies. He kept saying, *"Tulungan mo ako! Parang awa, tulungan mo ako!"* Help me, help me, please!

Within a few minutes the Filipinos throughout the village were aware that Colonel Kid was in their midst and needed aid. Not knowing any Tagalog, the Japanese occupiers were totally unaware of what was happening. Before dawn the banana farmer Romeo Delacruz brought his mule-drawn wooden cart to fisherman Pedro Mendoza's hut, covered Colonel Kid with banana leaves, and bore a tiny hole in the side of the cart with an auger so Milt could breathe. He then smuggled the American to his friend's gas station in Morong, where a truck marked "LUZON PRODUCE COMPANY" was waiting to transport him secretly to the U.S. Embassy in Manila, which took him in later that afternoon.

PRESIDENT ROOSEVELT, HEARING THAT the indestructible ace had been given his umpteenth new life, escaped being taken prisoner and, though shot down, had downed ten more Japanese planes and delayed the full onslaught of the attack on Las Palmas long enough for hundreds of servicemen to take cover and be spared, awarded him the Silver Star ribbon and commissioned him a Brigadier General.

Lady luck had once again been on the side of the man from Woodvale. She had always been his most prized mistress in times of crisis. Had he flattered her enough, bedecked her with sufficient jewels, and promised her an adequately lavish estate? He had not. He had always taken her for granted like every other adoring woman in his life, dared her to find a worthier man, and never yet been called up on his dare. And he knew that, even after her bailing him out this time, he would continue to treat her that way. For he still knew only one way to live, and that was with his heart banging like a jackhammer against his ribs.

CHAPTER 33

General Harrison

THE PRESIDENT SUMMONED GENERAL Harrison to the White House after his latest escape in the Philippines. From Manila he was flown to Washington via Honolulu and San Francisco.

"We're transferring you to the European theater, General," FDR informed him. "The Prime Minister wishes to confer with you on a matter of particular urgency."

When he arrived by plane in the bombed out rubble of London, a sobering wreck of a city, in July of 1942, the man from Woodvale realized more concretely than ever before the extent of this war's carnage.

In 1917 when he had traveled through France by train, only a few dozen kilometers from the front, he had been unable at a cursory glance to detect that a war was even happening. It had been possible in those days to confine the violence to the actual military theaters of action. Now, due entirely to the accelerated development of the machines he loved, it was no longer possible to separate military and civilian spheres from the homicidal tentacles of mass warfare.

London, the seat of empire, the nerve center of the nation that had fathered the very ideas of representative government, jurisprudence and civil liberties that were now under siege throughout the world, was in ruins. A decade of nonaggression treaties and fashionable espousals of pacifism and appeasement had allowed a ruthless war machine to reemerge on Continental soil. A monomaniac from across the English Channel in Berlin, ignoring the insignificant separation of water in the current age of the aviator, had sent his airmen to detonate the British Isles into submission and, but for the stirring rhetoric of the current Prime Minister, would probably have sapped the morale of the Britons along with their physical landscape. But the same monomaniac had then made what would prove to be his fatal mistake. He had declared war on the United States.

An armed motorcade accompanied General Harrison's taxi from Heston Airfield into central London. Winston Churchill was quick to offer cigars and cognac to the globetrotting idol, the "fearless rascal", as he called him affectionately, upon the latter's arrival at the quaint quarters of 10 Downing Street. Photographers and well-wishers were everywhere. The cheers and shouts for the American were almost fanatical. But some of them were undoubtedly also for Sir Winston, whose slogans and speeches had proved him the master of the native English tongue.

In the depressing and nerve-racking gloom of the recurrent air raids much of the joy of life had fled from the Londoners. Everything had seemed hopeless, the struggle to survive futile. Suddenly, as if from behind a dissipating black cloud, the sunshine of greatness now beamed upon them: an old bulldog, one of the very few who had penetrated the shams of the enemy chieftain from his beginnings in the beer halls of Bavaria; and the valorous American hawk, the perpetually youthful Kid, whose wings and talons had once already rid their neighborhood of its vermin. With the two of them (so the hopeful rabble prayed and swore) nothing was impossible, no challenge too daunting to surmount.

"No smoke and no liquor, General?" Churchill asked the American, after Milt turned down his offerings of cigars and cognac. "Trust me: they might be your salvation."

"No thanks, sir," said Kid. "It's too late for anybody to salvage me."

The two went into a conference inside Churchill's flat. The situation on the Continent was gravely serious, Churchill informed the American general. There was the matter of the Führer's newly opened death camps, which the Prime Minister described in greater detail than had been previously elaborated. Also, the Führer's elimination of all opposition, even within his immediate circle of toadies. His ultimate design: *Weltmacht oder Niedergang*. World-power or ruin. A thousand-year *Reich*, dominated by the Nordic fairy tales of the Nazi religion. His desire to bring all of Germany and the rest of creation down with him if he should fail.

But, more to the point, there was the matter of his new airplanes. British intelligence indicated the Luftwaffe was nearly ready to begin manufacturing a new type of aircraft engine which would function by means of jet propulsion. If this was true (and German engineering had always been exceptional, so to slight this bit of intelligence might be fatal), then Hitler's air force might soon have planes which could almost literally fly circles around any Allied planes at unheard of speeds perhaps approaching the sound barrier, in which case the result of the current war for the Führer was almost certain to be *Weltmacht.* The British and Americans were also close to perfecting jet propulsion in their laboratories, but in this current climate the six month technological advantage of the Germans amounted to eons. Might General Harrison do some reconnoitering about the air battle zones, determine the nature of these jet aeroplanes, if they existed, and, perhaps the impossible, *find some way of stopping them?*

"Mr. Prime Minister," said Kid, "I can't work any miracles, but one thing I know. I'll either stop them or die trying to."

"That's the very reason I asked your President to send you here," said Churchill. "You really mean that."

A SOCIETY OF FLATTERERS and obsequious bootlickers had formed a circle about the Führer's presence in the subterranean bunkers of Berlin. The whisperings of the outside world occasionally penetrated this inner sanctum, as they did shortly after Kid's meeting with Churchill, when Josef Goebbels, the Nazi minister of propaganda and the caretaker of the Hitler myth, took aside his friend in the Reichchancellery.

"Er ist in England jetzt," said Goebbels. *"Herr Harrison!"* Mr. Harrison was in England now.

"Herr Harrison!" Hitler repeated with a mixture of interest and animosity. *"Ich erinnere mich an 1918"*. The Führer well remembered 1918 and was eager for revenge. He thought it unlikely the Luftwaffe would be entirely efficient with so skilled and experienced an adversary pouring all his energies into disrupting it. They had to kill this man. *"Wir müssen diesen Mann töten."*

AS SOON AS GENERAL Harrison established his quarters at Hythe on the Strait of Dover, nearly within sight of the northern extremities of France just across the water, he and his 41st Fighter Group staged one successful air raid after another over the Ruhr region of Germany and some of the Nazi strongholds in occupied Belgium and France.

The young American lads who were under Milt's command were amazed that General Kid, as they called him, a man who was the same age as many of their fathers, had all the rambunctious courage and exuberance of a twenty-year-old lieutenant. When they observed his unflappability in the face of the horrendous violence of their theater of operations they interpreted his behavior as somewhat of a dare to them, as he himself had stated it: "You boys play it safe if you like, but I ain't restin' till I get me some fresh and tender white meat: the Führer's ass on my grill."

They all laughed boisterously at his wisecracks and instinctively followed his lead at a moment's notice in order not to disappoint him. "If this is a battle of willpower, men," said Kid, "we got 'em whupped."

Every new day revealed to the young fighter pilots another of the Great Ace's riveting anecdotes about the olden times when the world was young and the skies were empty. It was always another adventure, another bit of whimsicality and derring-do, another instance of aiming high and flying still higher, of thumbing his nose at the insanity of the world beneath him and defying it to prevent him from rearranging it to his own liking.

"Let's remember who's got the real power here, men," he would encourage the youngsters when he began to suspect that ugliness and terror, which had nearly overwhelmed him a generation earlier on his first exposure to warfare, did not vanquish them. "It ain't some old goat in a bunker who's afraid to show his face to the world or let the world have at him in a fair fight. It's all of us, the soldiers, the fighters. We control what happens in all this."

Both example and words were his tools. The P-47 planes which his squadron flew had frequent skirmishes with the Messerschmitt 109's and the Focke-Wulf 190's of the Luftwaffe. There was still no sight of what Churchill had mentioned: the jet fighters which could allegedly approach the speed of sound. Kid ceased to expect that he would ever encounter any of them, at least during the course of this war. He began to think that the Nazis themselves had fabricated the rumor about the jets to create a smokescreen for something even more sinister. Hitler was too impetuous a personality to be holding such a weapon back, if he really did have it

And if the Nazis ever did develop such planes, the results might be devastating. Milt explained to his men, and demonstrated for them, the importance of speed. Whatever one had to do to attain greater speed in the air was what one must do in order to stay alive. Acceleration, climbing, and maneuverability were important for a fighter plane, but if it lacked speed in combat it was a deathtrap. Who could stand a g-force of 7? The man from Woodvale, in his swerves and dives, proved that he could. How about a g of 8? He raced the P-47's around until he was convinced that was possible as well. There would be no higher a g than 8, he decided after he and his men had bombed Dusseldorf: not in this war, not with this equipment. Most of his understudies shrank from going above 7, but the importance of diving fast and turning fast was impossible to overestimate. Many green rookies, after only fifty hours of air time, were trying maneuvers beyond their capabilities, compelled by the urgent demands of their missions. Memories of their tragic, violent deaths were recurring visions in the distracted minds of the surviving fighters from both sides.

Kid kept insisting on life, no matter how he was brought to tears by the loss of one man after another. He had been through it all before—the first war to end war—and now he had lived to see it repeated and grown even more murderous. To the aviators, it was a simple matter. The dogfights of 1918, flown in small circles at 100 mph with one man as his own marksman, navigator and pilot, were now being waged in bigger circles at 300 mph, with multiple crews specializing in navigation, gunning and piloting; but they were still dogfights. You surprised your opponent, you maneuvered your plane to his tail, you tried to get an advantage in altitude, you aimed your guns carefully at him, and you killed him. Either that, or he did the same to you and you got killed.

In the old days, maybe it had been better and rawer. No oxygen masks or closed cockpits. No one at a nearby base vectoring and directing you by radio as you conducted your mission. You could smell your enemy back then by the oil he burned. Today's closed-cockpit fights were more impersonal and in some ways more savage. You attacked with such overwhelming speed and precision that sometimes you killed your opponent before he ever even saw you. But outfox him and kill him you must; that necessity would never change.

The Allies bombed Dresden and Dunkirk to rubble, invaded Normandy, and profited from the Führer's myopic military vision, suspicious and insular habits, and rank absolutism. In the course of the war which he had started to eliminate the Slavic empires to his east and extend the domain of the Nazis all the way to the Asian shores the Führer never once visited a bombed out city. As he saw the glorious empire of his precious Reich put under siege and ever more failures from his air fighters, the Nazi chief ordered the beleaguered head of the Luftwaffe, Hermann Goering, to produce better results, or there would be mass executions of officers, their families, their children.

But soon there came good news to Hitler's ears: the weapon that might turn the tide of the war and perpetuate the Thousand Year Reich. A new aircraft pushed aloft by jets rather than propellors had indeed been developed by Luftwaffe engineer Wilhelm Messerschmitt. The Führer summoned Messerschmitt along with the greatest existing German ace, Adolf Galland, whose kills rivaled those of any of the late Kaiser's aces in number, over 100. The Nazi dictator prepared to make a decree which, once uttered, would forever after occupy eternity intact as the indelible wisdom of Aryan godhead. A Hitler decree, *Der Befehl des Führers,* was ever thus: like an Oriental potentate, he was never to be doubted or questioned, and his orders, by virtue of the very fact that they had once emerged from his infallible mind and passed through his pious lips, were unalterable in the face of all changing evidence and conditions.

Hitler asked Messerschmitt if the new plane would carry bombs and, if so, of what weight. Messerschmitt, who had not envisioned the plane as a bomber, hesitated. Yes, Führer, it would carry bombs, maybe two bombs of 500 kilos each. The chief Nazi smiled delightedly. *"Mit diesem Flugzeug kann ich die kommende Invasion stoppen!"* he vowed. With this aircraft he would stop the coming Allied invasion. The Führer ordered the manufacture of 1200 of the planes as bombers rather than as fighter planes, against the private inclinations of both Messerschmitt and Galland, who looked at one another behind Hitler's back and rolled their eyes. *Der Befehl des Führers,* the leader's command, had been given.

One other command must be executed as well. "*Herr Harrison! Wir müssen diesen Mann töten!*" Galland and Messerschmitt were equally perplexed by the latter decree. If espionage and terrorism had failed to bring down General Harrison yet, and the latest innovation was to be used to bomb ground targets rather than engage in one-on-one plane-to-plane dogfights, how were they to destroy Kid? Neither one of them, as they valued their own lives and those of their families, gave the slightest outward hint of their interior questions, but just listened to and nodded at the latest *Befehl.*

"*Ich habe Vertrauen in Ihnen,*" the Führer encouraged Galland. He had confidence in him.

WHEN GALLAND FIRST FLEW the single-seat jet prototype, the Messerschmitt 262, the product of the famed German engineering which, despite the insanities of Nazism, had enabled Hitler's war machine to terrorize much of Europe, he remarked to his friends that it felt like being pushed by angels. Nearly 200 miles per hour faster than any other plane in existence, it astounded the Allied airmen when they first saw it in flight in the summer of '44. When General Harrison, piloting a P-47 Thunderbolt over northern Belgium, encountered a long, gray condor-like phantom Me262 shooting through the air like a comet he decided to radio his other squadron mates and tell them they needed to return to England and plot a new strategy.

"Good God!" he cried. "Did y'all just see that? Where the hell did THAT come from?"

During the course of the next several weeks the men of the 41st began encountering more of the elusive Me262's in combat and began to worry that the Führer had a whole fleet of them about to roll off his assembly lines. Half a dozen of the men did not survive the encounters, and fears arose that all fighter pilots who encountered the 262's in conventional aircraft, even the Great Ace himself, would ultimately give up their lives in the vain attempt to repulse them.

Galland and others, by subtle hints, had suggested that a token number of 262's would be helpful as fighters, and Hitler, on an interim basis, had agreed to manufacture a few dozen. If the jets did impressive enough work in their test phase as fighters, the High Command of the Luftwaffe reasoned, then the Führer might realize the wisdom of ordering more of them to be manufactured and revise his decree.

War materials in Germany were growing scarce, and every bit of chrome-nickel and steel used in propellor blades had to be husbanded as carefully as possible. Galland and the other Luftwaffe aces in whose command the 262's were being placed felt as if they had to score in a big way to convince the Nazi leadership that a large enough production of the new planes would win the war. Every battle was critical, every downed enemy a doubly prized feather in their caps.

At every stage in his life when life itself had seemed lost to him, Milt had found some form of redemption. The Allies had taken Normandy back from the Nazis, but this latest salvo from Berlin, it seemed to him, might well be one for which there was no answer. Long ago Gen. Percival had envisioned a world in which airplanes alone would win wars, and Kid's first few encounters with the 262's left him wondering if perhaps that day had not dawned already and Hitler had been the beneficiary.

Churchill and Roosevelt had said the British and Americans had nearly perfected jet technology on their own and within a few months might have a prototype for a fighter jet. But a few months would be too long. With enough of the new planes the Luftwaffe would have such a marked superiority that it alone might reverse the course of the war. At stake? The course of world history and the very existence of the Führer's terror state.

General Excitement knew, and he had preached to his men, that speed was everything in the air. A slight advantage in speed was inestimable in an air battle, but a *two hundred knot* advantage was overwhelming. He kept trying to boost up the spirits of his confused men, promising them he would think of some way of doing the impossible yet again—of nullifying, with propellor-driven planes, the rocket-force of jet propulsion.

"What the hell are we gonna do if they keep firing them flying comets at us, General?" asked Captain Flannery, one of the best young fighters in the 41st. "I know you're good—but, god dammit, nobody's that good. There's only so much you can do if the other guy has better equipment."

"We don't know yet if their equipment really is better, Captain," said Kid. "Sometimes the team that scores first isn't the better team. Sometimes a smaller and a slower competitor can beat a bigger and a faster one, by outfoxing him."

HE TRIED TO SEEM CONFIDENT for the next few days, but his doubts grew steadily. Whom should he ask for help? Where should he go for advice? For that matter, where had he *ever* gone for advice? As far as he was able to remember, nobody had ever actually given him any that he had followed except for maybe Stratton Liffey or his father, who on his deathbed had told him to keep flying airplanes. And he would have kept flying them anyway, regardless.

So it would be entirely up to him. He stayed awake night after night in his quarters at the Hythe Air Base, worrying and planning, just as he had done at Souilly in 1918; as he had done when smuggling rum and performing in air shows; as he had done as a little boy concocting his superlative schemes to fly away from Woodvale some day and conquer mountains, oceans and continents. But this time the worries were the most serious of all. WHAT IF THE OTHER SIDE WON? How much would anything he or anyone else had ever done matter then? WHAT IF THE OTHER SIDE WON?

Suddenly an incident from his childhood flashed through his mind. He must have been about nine years old. A storm had struck Woodvale late in January and an inch-thick crust of ice coated all the countryside for miles around. At the crack of dawn that morning a haggard and desperate-looking man, Silas Yow, had rapped on the front door of 125 Oak Street and pleaded with Dr. Harrison to brave the elements and come with him to the other side of the village, where he was afraid his wife had the influenza back at his house. His mother had urged his father not to go, claiming he would be risking his own life by venturing out in the ice, but he had brushed her off, saying: "I know how to get around in this stuff, dear. I'll take my time. The faster you move, the easier it is to trip and fall."

All that morning Milt and his family were bitterly cold, and they huddled against the fireplace, their hands outstretched to absorb every beam of warmth coming from the hearth. It wasn't enough. His mother asked him to go outside to the woodpile in the backyard, break up the ice on the logs with a hammer, and bring back as many hickory splints as he could so the fire would finally be hot.

After he wrapped himself in several layers of clothing and put on his boots, he went out the back door and stepped gingerly over to the woodpile. He chiseled and scraped away the ice and began creeping repeatedly back and forth between the stack of logs and the house, each time carrying a log in each mitten. But the cold was ferocious and his fingers were growing numb, so when he had grabbed the last two logs he needed he made a mad dash back to the house, lost his footing and fell. He nearly impaled himself against one of the logs and was knocked almost unconscious when his head struck the ground. Of course his father was summoned from the other end of the village to come and minister to him as he lay woozy in his bed.

"Your mama says you were doing just fine, boy," his father said to him, "until you started running. Sometimes you can go faster in life by going slower."

Now, forty years later, half a world away, and with all of civilization on the verge of disintegrating, the man from Woodvale kept thinking about falling on the ice as a boy and hearing his father's words as though they had been uttered only yesterday. *The faster you move, the easier it is to trip and fall. Sometimes you can go faster in life by going slower.*

EARLY THE NEXT MORNING, General Harrison called the boys of his squadron out to the main hangar at the Hythe base.

"Men," he addressed them, "I've been out of school a long, long time, but I do remember something called the law of inertia. Isaac Newton, was it? Was he the one who thought of it? I'm not sure, but that's beside the point. What it means is this. If something is moving, it tends to keep moving. If it's at rest, it tends to stay at rest. In other words, the faster something goes, the less able it is to change direction suddenly. On the other hand, the slower something goes, the more easily it keeps its balance."

None of the boys seemed to know exactly what he meant, so he elaborated.

"I'm thinking we can neutralize the speed advantage of these flying rockets if we catch 'em while they're either trying to pick up speed quickly or throttle it down quickly—in other words, during takeoffs, landings and dives."

CHAPTER 34

Kid Versus the Axis

GENERAL HARRISON WAS READILY willing to put his theories into practice, and later that afternoon he flew his P-47 on a solo sortie over the English Channel.

One of his theories, the by-product of his childhood memory of slipping on the ice at just the moment when he started running, was that the law of inertia might be used by the slow to gain advantage over the swift. His other theory was that very few German aces were actually left and that Hitler's new supercharged Me262's, manned mostly by novices who had been forced into service by the attrition of the Luftwaffe's more seasoned pilots, were no better than a work in progress.

He spotted three of the 262's attempting to stage a surprise attack on Allied bases. He lured them all into dives which were beyond their capacity to sustain, and each and every one of them went crashing down into the sea. A propellor plane could spin and flip in ways that a jet plane could not. A tortoise, through guile and cunning, was capable of outracing a hare.

The men of the 41st, upon hearing of the Great Ace's success on his solo mission, cheered with relief. In the ensuing weeks they would all participate in a mass waylaying of the phantom jets near their air bases at Bremen, Essen and Wiesbaden. Kid never allowed the boys under him to take anything for granted, though his daring escapades had melted away most of their inhibitions. But the German Air Service would prove incapable of doing anything to stop them. The Americans converged and hovered around several different Luftwaffe landing fields and mowed down the vulnerable 262's as if they were clay pigeons at a shooting range.

Galland ignored the Führer's orders to single out General Harrison and never met him in a face-to-face battle; and, unlike the unfortunate Hans Eichhorn, he survived a Great War to befriend his former adversaries for generations into the future. But almost none of his colleagues joined him. The spooky court of flatterers in the underground passageways below the Chancellery in Berlin was growing continuously more desperate. Mr.

Excitement would not die. *Der Befehl des Führers* had been aimed at him, but without success.

There were some people who could not be pushed aside. One of them had mastered Model T's on dirt clay roads as a child; worked in cotton gins and as a blacksmith's apprentice as a teen; slept outside in swamps and prairies; smuggled warm moonshine in back alleys; done motorcycle wheelies in shantytowns; put a flivver engine in a crate and flown it over cornfields one decade, then over oceans and ice caps the next. Of tougher fabric no human being had ever been made. The greatest obstacles were to him nothing more bothersome than burrs clinging to the sides of his socks. The Führer had declared war on him and his peers. That had been the cataclysmic miscalculation by which the rest of history would judge him.

Yet all did not seem lost in those dank corridors beneath Berlin, where the High Priest of Nazism kept vigil over his dying ruin. On Friday April 13, 1945 there came glorious news. At his middle Georgia hideaway in Warm Springs the American commander in chief had collapsed and died on the previous day. The fires of a burning Berlin blazed in the hypnotic eyes of Dr. Goebbels when he received the news on the steps of the Propaganda Ministry. *Herr Reichsminister, Roosevelt ist tot!*

A telephone call was placed immediately to the Führer's private line in his subterranean vault. It was the turning point, *Mein Führer.* Friday the 13th. *Roosevelt ist tot.* The Führer heard the news of Roosevelt's death with ecstasy. It was the beginning of the great reversal! The Thousand Year Reich was near at hand!

Horoscopes prepared years earlier were brought down to the subterranean passages for perusal. Remarkably, they predicted the beginnings of the war in 1939, continuous victories until 1941, a series of setbacks reaching their disastrous nadir in early April of 1945, then, dramatically, sweeping victories by the end of April which would culminate in a peace by August and an eventual rise of Germany to greatness by 1948.

But astrology failed the most high of Nazi holies in his dark bunker. The angered Soviets surrounded Berlin, shut off the city, and began bombing it to rubble. General Harrison and his peers from countless other American towns and backwaters, whether by land, sea, and air, paid no heed to the pomposities of the Führer's myths, and they moved into western Germany and seized various Nazi strongholds.

After a somber birthday celebration in his bunker on April 20, the Führer realized that all hope for victory was lost and he dictated a last political testament and personal will. In it he blamed the German people for being unworthy of his high ideals. The slogan *Weltmacht oder Niedergang* had now been resolved in favor of the *Niedergang.* Like a sacrificial corpse on a great Viking funeral pyre, he wanted the Fatherland now to burn itself to extinction, for none of it deserved to stand without him. He denied ever having wanted war, blaming the outbreak of the current war on Jewish politicians and their sympathizers. He was refusing to turn himself over to the Jews, to be made a spectacle of, and was choosing death on his own terms.

On the morning of April 30th the master poisoned his dog, took a poison capsule along with Eva Braun, his former mistress whom he had just married, and shot himself through the mouth. He ordered several canisters of gasoline to be doused on his and his wife's corpses and for the bodies to be burned in the Chancellery garden. His philosophical comrade Dr. Goebbels, despite his terrified wife's protests, poisoned his own six small children, and took a poison pill with his wife later. The cyanide pill, in fact, became the panacea for the Nazi dignitaries who were cornered by the steel-nerved Allies who had brought down their demented creation: Heinrich Himmler, the master of the Secret Police and the concentration camps, bit one in the Berlin suburbs as he tried to escape, as did Goering in captivity at Nuremberg, and several others.

The six-shooters and the rum-runners and the wing walkers from the new and decadent nation across the sea had prevailed again. Nineteen-eighteen had returned. The boy in his Spad was now nearly a fifty-year-old man in a P-38 flying at twice his former speed; still he soared over the war-torn land, still he survived. Corporal Hitler had never had a chance to shoot at him in 1918, and Chancellor Hitler had never succeeded at getting someone else to do the job for him in 1945.

"Der Chef ist tot," said the Führer's servants when they realized one of the smoking corpses in the garden belonged to the late Chief. Cigarettes, forbidden in Hitler's presence while he lived, came out again, and laughter and levity returned. The Chief was dead. An Admiral Doenitz announced on German radio the next day that the Chief had died fighting like a warrior at the head of his troops, but the lie fell flat. There had been no such uncharacteristic conclusion. Rather than face earthly justice, the Chief had ducked out with a bang, surrounded by the last remaining fragments of his genocidal cult.

AT THE END OF APRIL Milt and his squadron mates, the vanquishers of the Luftwaffe jets that were Hitler's last chance at air supremacy, landed at Garmisch-Partenkirchen in the Bavarian Alps near the southern frontier with pre-war Austria. There, along with a company of the U.S. Army, they overtook Hitler's retreat at Obersalzburg.

With relief and, if not jubilation, then the intense satisfaction of seeing a difficult and hazardous task realized, the men of the 41st Squadron combed through Hitler's Alpine chalet on a chilly spring day. Far away from the gas chambers, the bombed out cities, and the stuffy bomb shelter where its former proprietor's carcass was smoldering at that very moment, the retreat at Obersalzburg seemed elevated above and isolated from all mortal cares.

Kid and the two members of his squadron who worshiped him above all others, Capts. Flannery and Halsey, were scavenging though Hitler's study by a panel of windows. The spectacular view outside was of knife-edged peaks, glistening glaciers, and, now at the dawn of springtime, green foothills of myriad colorful wildflowers. They found several of the late dictator's architectural drawings on top of a desk, confiscated three of his watercolors from an adjacent easel, and discovered a movie projector in an adjoining room which had apparently been used as a private theater in which Hitler had indulged in one of his favorite pastimes of watching films.

"Say, look here, General Kid," said Halsey, pulling out a stack of cream-colored stationery from one of the desk drawers. "I think I'll write my sweetheart a letter on one of these."

He handed Milt one of the pages of stationery, on which the Führer's personal letterhead was embossed. It consisted of a large eagle with outstretched wings perched atop a circular garland inside of which was the outline of a swastika; underneath it was the name ADOLF HITLER. The young pilot removed a fountain pen from his pocket, marked through the name at the top of the page and wrote CAPT THADDEUS HALSEY beneath it. Then he took about one third of the sheaf of papers and offered it to General Harrison.

"What do you want me to do with this, Captain?" asked Kid.

"You'll think of something. The bastard ain't here for you to roast on the grill, so this is all we've got."

The men had no idea what had actually happened to Hitler at his death, nor would anyone among the Allies know definitively for years into the future. They only knew that an announcement had been made over German radio that he was dead and that, apparently, this was as close as they would ever get to him.

"I want a few sheets as a souvenir, Thad," said Flannery, who helped himself to about half of the remaining stack.

"Watch this, boys," said Mr. N.B. Excitement, his youthful grin returning to his war-weary visage. He had found a box of thumb tacks in another drawer. "I only want one page."

Milt sat down in Hitler's plush roller chair, borrowed Halsey's fountain pen, and wrote a message in boldfaced print on his lone page of stationery. Then he stood up and tacked the notice outside the door of the former Führer's private chambers:

THE NAZI GOING-OUT-OF-BUSINESS SALE—
ALL ITEMS 100% OFF!

GENERAL HARRISON WAS SUMMONED back to Washington after the German surrender in May. The new president, Harry Truman, conferred upon him the most prestigious American military decoration, the Medal of Honor, in recognition of his unswerving bravery and humanitarianism in both of the World Wars. Then he informed Milt, bluntly, that his services were no longer needed to prosecute the war in the Pacific.

"Is this another way of telling me I'm fired, Mr. President?" Kid asked him.

"Hardly," said Truman. "Far be it from me to stand in your way. But I don't want you to get killed, not after what else you've done. You've gone so far beyond the normal line of duty it's ridiculous."

"Sir, at the very least I want to go back over there. I can tell there's something big in the works."

"You just go over there and observe and stay out of the fray—and if you still get killed then, by golly, it'll be a damn shame, but if the good Lord wants to get you He'll come and get you."

"Observe? What good's that?"

"Even a prized cow's got to be put out to pasture in time, General. I don't mean to be indelicate, but, as country boy to country boy, I can't think of a better way of phrasing it."

With a reluctant heart, the man from Woodvale, feeling a bit superannuated and unnecessary, was sent to Guam. There he exchanged pleasantries with the appreciative boys who were now doing the flying and fighting, signed autographs, smiled for the cameras and plucked gray hairs from the side of his head before a mirror each morning when he shaved. It was no fun to be an institution. Far better it had been in the olden days—to be an up-and-comer, a rebel, a young green stud.

He went island-hopping to build up troop morale for the better part of two months, from Guam to Iwo Jima to the Samoans, Okinawa and back to the now-liberated Philippines—a circus attraction of sorts, the conqueror of cotton fields, county fairs and low-lying clouds, the slayer of political dragons, a well-worn relic of a vanishing world.

Then in early August, completely off his guard, he heard the news that the U.S. military had dropped the most powerful bomb ever engineered on Hiroshima. And three days later Nagasaki, the very city over which his plane had passed a generation earlier, suffered the same fate. He was flown there the following week to survey the damage after the Japanese surrender. It was the most terrifying devastation he had ever witnessed.

But, as the war-sickened general knew from his own experience and as history had served to illustrate, heat could quickly turn to cold and cold to heat; light to darkness and darkness back to light. And, just as he had once yearned for Greenland while he sweated in India, and longed for the jungle while he froze on the subarctic ice caps, so might sorrow today become joy on another page of the calendar; and hatred in one season quickly turn to love in the next.

Memories were sometimes erratic, but his stayed powerful. For as long as he lived he would remember, vividly, the cruel wasteland of Nagasaki on that day. But just as vividly had he remembered the sight of another day at an earlier period of his life: the same place observed from the air with the same pair of eyes in the carefree peace which had preceded this horrendous war.

He hoped to live long enough to see that which was ugly and violent today again turn beautiful and peaceful. It had happened before, and he believed history would repeat itself.

<u>CHAPTER 35</u>

Homecoming

UPON HIS RETURN HOME to peacetime in the late summer of 1945, the man from Woodvale renewed affections with his sweetheart. He had already legally married her just prior to having left, but for ceremonial purposes he married her again after he came back. Marriages between returning veterans and their fiancées were commonplace during that heady time. The groom in this case, however, was considerably older than most of the others at age forty-nine.

After all the testimonials and banquets given in his behalf throughout America; after Woodvale had tried to perpetuate its idolatry for him by renaming itself "Harrisonville", despite his dogged and eventually successful refusal; and after the world was again apparently safe for democracy and the skies once again peaceable for the travel of airplanes, he decided to try to settle down to domesticity for the first time in his life.

His lovely young wife waited at the foot of the graduated ramp under the door of the Eagle DC3 that brought him back to Candler Field from Washington. She was before all of the thousands of other screaming Americans who were there to witness his historic return—before Mayor Grantland, before Brackens and Dawes, before A.T. and Woody and Ruth; even before his mama Madge. It hadn't happened! She hadn't stopped loving him because he was almost fifty! She was still there for him. He was glad she was there. It all proved that he may have been getting a little old . . . well, he had shortened the thought to just that. He may have been getting a little old.

"Welcome home, brave soldier!" she said sweetly, and threw her arms around him and gave him a long and intimate kiss. "You made it back! I can't believe you made it back!"

They hugged for a long time after that, and swayed in each other's arms, and closed their eyes and were quiet.

"'Course I made it back, darlin'," said Kid. "I told you I'd be back, and I always do what I say I'll do."

GENERAL HARRISON AND HIS pretty bride left for their honeymoon in his Aeroniña in mid October and flew about the land for two weeks with no particular destination in mind. They landed in stubbled fields and abandoned fairgrounds, at big city airports and on country dirt strips with no other accoutrements but moth-eaten windsocks; in Barlow Bend and New Orleans, Tallulah and Dubuque, Chicago and Minneapolis. They flew west to Montana, south to California, back east again to Palm Beach in Florida, and north all the way to Maine. They would always stay in the best hotel in whichever town they happened to land for the night, dress elegantly and dine lavishly, and make passionate love in the honeymoon suite.

More happy times were ahead. After years of toil and trouble, ferment and discovery, challenge and triumph, the man from Woodvale felt he had earned the right to enjoy his existence rather than defy it. For what purpose he had been spared, if any great purpose remained, he didn't know. But that he had survived another terrible war seemed to him to signify that fate meant for him to do more great things in his future. His life had never seemed so meaningful as when he became a father for the first time at age fifty. Little did he know or suspect it, but he had barely passed the halfway point of a term on earth which even then seemed to have been several lifetimes compounded into one.

He cradled his newborn son, born in the first week of December of 1946, tightly in his arms when he first saw him in the waiting room at the hospital near his Peachtree Battle mansion. He was the first Harrison who had ever been born in a hospital, this tiny creature was. So wide the little one's eyes were, so blank the stare: a complete innocent brought into a world of unspeakable joy, beauty, cruelty and wonder.

How much he wished he could convey to the creature—how much of what he had seen and felt—how much of what he was! Raymond Milton Harrison the third. With big green eyes and a full head of brown hair just like his daddy. A tough and brawny little kid, with a hefty paunch and built like a rock. The little waif never could pronounce either of his given names. The closest he ever came, at least before he was four, was "Mitt". And so the family took to calling him Mitt, because that seemed appropriate for such a rugged little fellow.

Barely a year later a daughter, Alexandra, was born; then, seventeen months after that, a second daughter, Melissa. It occurred to Milton that his own father had died at age 56, not much older than he was now with three toddlers. At that point he realized that he was unlikely to survive to see much of the adulthood of any additional scions of the family tree, and the three that he already had were taxing his patience to its limit, running rambunctiously all about the house. So, by mutual consent, he and Juliette decided they would produce no more children.

From the beginning, there never seemed to be any question about which child drew the bulk of his attention. He loved his girls, but the boy—well, the boy was a miniature version of himself. Little Mitt was so cuddly and adorable that when he went in public women would often stare at him and come to ask his mother if they might hold him—and the attention was not of the perfunctory kind that people will frequently give to small children in the presence of their parents to try to humor the parents. That was the sort of attention Alexandra and Melissa got. But Mitt was everybody's little prince.

Even men were smitten by this little boy. They would come to slap hands with him, hoist him up in their arms, and laugh when he turned his eyes coyly away. The boy was a born flirt, as social as a politician and as happy as a fat kitten in a rocking chair. He was as close to royalty as any American boy would ever be, so they said: the namesake and lone son of the emperor of aviation, the celebrated war hero, showman, wing walker and globetrotter, the airline tycoon and tyrant-killer.

But, alas, it is not easy to be the child of one who has walked on clouds and trampled on dictators. When Mitt was a small boy and preciously cute and his father every day smothered him with hugs and kisses, the world seemed to be one vast glorious playground. The big man could rarely even walk out to his mailbox without the little one's waddling behind him, following everything he did, making the same expressions as his father, going just as far out into the grass as his father did; then, when he saw his father turning to go back, following his footsteps to go back inside. For awhile the boy was totally satisfied and considered it marvelous to try to be the mirror image of his father.

However, when Mitt was seven years old he began to realize that to do *everything* his father had ever done might be somewhat more difficult than he had previously thought. He was learning to read, and his family had gotten a newfangled thing called a television. And it seemed to him that every time he saw people on the television they were people his daddy knew or had encountered in some way; and every time he saw a newspaper it either mentioned his daddy or featured somebody his daddy knew, or reported something that was somehow related to something his daddy had done or said.

He knew his daddy wasn't the President. That was Eisenhower. But he also knew that every time President Eisenhower came to Georgia to play golf at the Augusta National Golf Club his daddy was playing with him. In fact, it occurred to him that his daddy had only learned to play golf very recently, and only to socialize with people like the President.

There were stories about Mr. Grantland and Mr. Bonderman, who had recently moved into a mansion in an adjoining neighborhood. Eventually Mitt realized that these were no ordinary men. Grantland was mayor, and

Bonderman ran Coastal Air Lines, which in its own way was flying circles around its competitors. One day Mitt overheard his mother and father discussing a board meeting for Coastal which his father had attended. In it there was a discussion about how the board was considering buying out Eagle Air Lines and merging it with Coastal. The mayor was sitting on the company's board of directors along with his father, but apparently his father was the one who made the decision. No, Coastal and Eagle would not merge. It was that simple. His father decided, on the spot, that a multimillion-dollar transaction would not happen, thereby altering the entire history of an industry, a city, a state, maybe even a nation and a world. He heard his father recounting what had been said at the meeting.

"It'll be a disruption of Coastal's culture, A.T.," his father told one of the men. "Britt still hasn't gotten his labor unions under control."

That settled it. Mitt found it remarkable that with such apparent ease and finality the issue was resolved. Everything his daddy did seemed so cut-and-dried, so matter-of-fact. There was never any doubt that he would do exactly what he wanted to do. That Britt was another famous man who ran another airline, wasn't he? All these old people who did things a long time ago and kept visiting his father and calling him—this Mr. Brackens, this Mr. Dawes—what were they about? When Mitt asked about this his father always devoted a minimal amount of words and elaboration to the answer, calling them people he knew from way back and adding no other details.

The youngster often suspected that what his father didn't tell him was far more worth hearing than what he did tell him. Apparently, life had always been that way for his father. There had always been meetings with the powerful, hobnobbing among the rich, and adulation from the famous. It was hard for Mitt to understand why. What was so remarkable about airplanes? They were just machines that flew.

"That boy needs discipline," Kid told Juliette when Milton III began to grow noticeably aloof from his parents at age twelve. "We ought to take him out of Waltham and put him in GMI."

Mrs. Harrison offered little resistance to the idea. Waltham Academy had been a coeducational preparatory school for blue bloods, but the Georgia Military Institute, situated in College Park not far from Hapeville, was an all-boys boarding school with an international reputation for rigidity. The problem was that Mitt had had things too easy, Kid thought. Back when he was coming along and they used corncobs in outhouses and there was no electricity and he taught his daddy how to drive a Model T and then enlisted in World War I and shot down the ace of the Jagdstaffel 7 and . . . by this time Mitt usually tuned his father out. That was ancient history.

There was a new vocabulary word which one of the masters of literature at the Waltham Academy had taught the seventh grade students there. *Irrelevant.* Mitt took to the word like a camel to a watering hole.

Irrelevant. Those absurd old-fashioned stories about walking ten miles to school through snow and living in an outhouse made out of logs and sailing around the world with Columbus in the *Niña*—those were irrelevant.

Only one time had Mitt ever found any relevance in anything in his father's early life, what little he knew of it. It was the only time he had ever seen his father cry. When he was about eight he had seen his father holding a yellowed newspaper in hand and poring over a picture on the obituary page. The article, from way back in 1948, concerned a heavy-looking woman who had died of a diabetic seizure. The headline read:

MRS. JASMINE WARNER, 56, FIRST WOMAN
TO RIDE IN A PLANE AT CANDLER FIELD

"Why are you so sad, Daddy?" Mitt had asked him. His father, embarrassed at being seen by his son in such an emotional state, quickly doused his eyes with his shirtsleeves and feigned a sense of calm.

"Oh, nothin', Mitt. I just remembered going to the lady's funeral, that's all. I helped to carry the casket."

"Who was she?"

Milt sniffled like a child, doused his reddened eyes and runny nose again, and tried to stiffen into a stoical pose.

"Just an old friend to the family. It's—well, you're a little too young to understand."

"When will I be old enough, Daddy?"

"I don't know, son. We'll see."

That was all his father had ever told him. For a flickering moment the boy had felt a stirring sense of sadness and curiosity about what had so moved his father's soul, but that flicker was quickly extinguished. What was it about his father that made him close his heart to the one creature above all others on earth who needed to see the inside of it? Were there things of which his father was ashamed, dark secrets which haunted him with guilt? Where had been the passion and the adventure in his life? What had molded him into what all these strangers now respected? As an eight year-old Mitt had not thought of this, but in his adolescence, as he looked back on the incident, the questions plagued him.

THE DISCIPLINE OF MILITARY school had little effect on Mitt. A time or two per month he was made to run laps around the outdoor track encircling the football field, usually for sassing his teachers, carrying a switchblade concealed under his uniform jacket in class or smoking in the boy's washroom. He was twice caught smoking marijuana, a fact which, in light of his father's high standing and immensely deep pockets, was hushed up.

As a day student in what was predominantly a boarding school, filled with the problem children of the famous and near-famous from as far away as South America, Mitt was able to smuggle in contraband luxuries—drugs, liquor, even fast girls from College Park High, the public school a few dozen blocks away—during his time outside the confines of the GMI campus. His father tried to take a more personal interest in his upbringing, suggesting interesting outings for them to do together, but the two of them apparently had almost nothing in common.

Mitt hated airplanes. And every time his father suggested they go hunting or fishing or to a ballgame or to meet one of the stalwart stallions of the old guard who populated the elder man's circle of acquaintances, Mitt winced like one who had been offered a glass full of spoiled milk. He much preferred hunting down the freewheeling hussies at College Park high, downing highballs with his friends, and sucking on reefers with the Brazilian cadets at GMI. He was far and away the most popular student at the institute among the other boys—a hellion who could get his hands on all the good stuff and all the cute girls.

When an instructor caught Mitt cheating on an algebra exam in the Fall term of his junior year in 1962, a crib sheet with all the formulae taped with cellophane under one of his arms, he was threatened with expulsion, a fact which thrilled him. He was hoping against hope his father would put him in a coeducational school of some kind, or else send him away from home to another boarding school where he might indulge his boundless appetites for girls and intoxicants with even less parental supervision than he currently faced.

What he really wanted was not to go to school at all, just to join a rock and roll band as a drummer and drift around the world and conduct orgies with fast women and stay in fancy hotels. When his father was telephoned by the school administrators about Mitt's latest act of mischief he felt humiliated and came to take the boy home. He was so angry he wanted to strangle his son. Even at 65 he considered himself capable of beating the 6-foot-tall 15-year-old punk to a pulp.

"I'm tired of all your shenanigans," Kid told him in the family's new silver Cadillac as he drove him home. "You're nothing but an overgrown spoiled brat."

"Like hell I am," Mitt snapped back. "You stop and let me off here on the side of the road, and I won't ever miss you. I don't need you a damn bit."

"If I left you on the side of the road," said Kid. "you'd be in jail by the end of the night. You're staying with me. We're going way out yonder to the country."

It felt like a death sentence to the rebellious young miscreant. Hours and hours they traveled in the silver Cadillac, though one sleepy country town after another, to a place so far out in the boondocks that Mitt had no inkling of where they might possibly be. He had never been this far away from civilization in his life. Soon they drove past a brand new large white metal sign that had recently been erected by the state highway department to replace the dilapidated old wooden one which had been on the verge of collapse.

WELCOME TO WOODVALE
HOME TO GEN. R.M. 'KID' HARRISON, JR.
WORLD WAR I AND II FLYING ACE
AND PIONEER AVIATOR

Mitt had heard stories, veiled references to this backwater, from his mother, though his father had never brought him here. His grandmamma was still alive, 92 years old, and living in the same house where she and his father had both been born. She came to Atlanta to stay with her son and his family every holiday season at the end of December, returning home after the arrival of each new year, so Mitt was familiar with her. The teenage boy kept deathly quiet as the car came to a stop in front of the old house at 125 Oak Street. They were going inside.

"Your grandma won't like it a damn bit when I tell her what's been going on," Milt told his boy. "I been hiding it from her, trying to keep from worrying her. Now you're going in there with me, and you'll have to face the consequences and see the pain a poor old lady will be in when she hears about what's become of her own flesh and blood."

He got out of the car and slammed the door shut. He went around to the passenger's side and crossed his arms, waiting on Mitt.

"You first," he said.

The boy nervously climbed out of the car and went to the front porch and knocked on his grandma's front door. A shriveled up old white-haired lady in a plaid dress limped to the door and opened it. She lived alone, but every day Rev. Woodrow Wilson came and checked up on her, and Rev. Wilson's teenage daughter, a recent high school graduate trying to save up money for college, prepared her meals and did housework for $50 a month.

"It's my grandbaby!" Madge yelled excitedly when she saw the Adonis-like teen whose handsomeness made her tingle. "Milt! What're y'all doin' here?"

Madge had grown hard of hearing, and her son had learned to lean down into her ears, yell, and talk slowly when addressing her:

"MAMA, YOU'RE GRANDSON'S BEEN ACTING UP LOTS WORSE THAN I DID WHEN I WAS A YOUNG'UN. HE'S SMOKIN'

AND DRINKIN', EVEN TAKIN' DOPE. HE'S GOING AROUND WITH BAD GIRLS, TOO."

Madge paused and looked at young Milton Harrison the third. Within seconds her eyes were pouring out droplets like a leaky faucet. When the three of them went inside, she sat in her musty old chair, draped a multicolored quilt over her lap, removed her spectacles and whisked tears from her eyes. In her old age her nerves had grown eggshell-fragile, and she was as apt to cry as a newborn baby.

"I'm real sorry to hear this, Milt," she said, removing her spectacles, rubbing her eyes with a handkerchief and blowing her nose. Then she looked helplessly at Mitt, who wanted to crawl under a bed and hide. Kid continued cataloging his son's misdeeds with unfortunate detail while the eyes of Grandma Madge continued pouring out tears, and Mitt began to feel like a viper with fangs. He shrank steadily further down in his seat, until soon his chin was resting on his chest and his backside had nearly slipped completely off the edge of the chair.

"Young boy," said Madge, "I waited a long, long time for my son to have children. I never thought it'd even happen. Don't ruin it for us, now. You're the only grandson left to keep alive the family name. We all struggled a long, long time for everything. *They always tried to keep us down, but we always beat 'em in the end.* Let's don't beat ourselves."

When they both hugged Madge a few minutes later, Mitt felt ashamed of himself. His father said nothing to him as he drove them through the Negro shantytown in Woodvale. There was one nice old house just behind a church, and his father stopped in front of it.

"Let's go meet an old lady friend of mine," Kid said as his son looked at him in complete bewilderment.

They went into the clapboard wooden house with the immaculate lawn and garden, and were met by an older attractive black lady whom Mitt saw kissing his father and hugging him. The teen's ears rang and he thought his eyes were blurry. The subject had never come up between them, nor had he ever heard any mention of it in the conversations his parents had had amongst themselves and their friends, but *he had always assumed his father was prejudiced against colored people.* But it was obvious that this woman adored him and that he adored her. Something seemed very much out of place to Mitt.

"Son, this is my girl Ruth. She ain't as spry as she used to be, but she ain't bad for a 78 year-old, that's for sure."

Trim and fit, Ruth might easily have passed for a woman fifteen years younger than she was. In her permanent widowhood she had turned to gardening to give her life meaning. The acre surrounding her late parents' home had become a haven for apple, peach, cherry and pecan trees, vegetable plants, ornamental flowers of all kinds, and exotic colorful trees and shrubs. She had learned to combat loneliness by her communion with the living things of the earth. Mitt stared at the brown hand which held his father's white hand as the two sat together on the couch inside the house. She wore an elegant white dress, had a piano in her house and her late father's college diploma on her wall.

"Boy," said Kid, "this lady here helped operate on your granddad the night before he died of appendicitis in 1915."

Mitt wished his father would go into more detail and explain exactly what had happened in that instance. Soon the black woman rose from her seat and came to look down at Mitt, beaming as if she had been the one to bring him forth from her own womb.

"You look just like your daddy, child. Just beautiful. Don't let your daddy down now, boy. His name's like Jesus Christ in this town."

Ruth and his father embraced one last time before they left. Maybe they would never see each other again. Maybe they were trying to make up for what was lost and what could never be regained. The boy was sure there was too much in this for him to understand. A few minutes later they went into the nearby church and a black man with a hefty paunch was hugging his dad.

"Enby!" cried Woody. "You finally came back, man, and you brought your boy with you!"

The pastor of the First African Methodist Episcopal Church of Woodvale shook Mitt's hand and patted him on the shoulder.

"Son, your daddy's the man who brought me to America," said Woody, who had a wife, four children and eight grandchildren of his own. He was balding now, fifty-nine years old, with gray hairs on the sides of his head above the ears, but still jocular and full of enthusiasm.

"What does 'Enby' mean?" asked Mitt.

"'N.B.', for 'nothing but'," said Woody. "That's what he said his name was when he came to run booze down in Nassau during Prohibition. Nothing But Excitement."

"So that's where the name Mr. Excitement came from!" cried Mitt in what was by far the happiest moment of that whole day for him. "Now I know!"

Woody and Mitt laughed, but Kid would have preferred that Woody not divulge that precious bit of information—especially now, as he was trying to wean his son from bad habits.

"What's smokin' reefer compared to bootleggin'?" Mitt wondered, and continued laughing, though Woody stopped.

"Now, don't be smokin' no dope, boy!" Woody chided him. "I hope that ain't what you been doing."

Late that night when Milt and Mitt had returned home, there was a renewed kinship between them. The boy wanted more exposure to the ghosts of his dad's storied past, but his father had gone as far as he cared to go. Something about his early years bothered him—the violence, the roughness, the coarseness, the rawness—and at his present stage of life he wanted to distance himself from it.

CHAPTER 36

Fallen Son

FOR AWHILE, THE OUTING in Woodvale seemed to have a genuinely benign effect on Mitt. He was attending class regularly, abstaining from alcohol and the burning cannabis leaf, even talking respectfully to his teachers and avoiding the company of the loose and frolicsome floozies of College Park High.

Mitt returned to GMI and for the next three months was a model student, impressing the administrators but disappointing the ruffian cadet boarders whose idea of fun had become whatever Mitt had decided to smuggle into their rooms, whether animal, vegetable or mineral in nature. But the concept of rebellion kept growing in the energetic mind of Milton the third. If his dad had been Mr. Excitement in the old days, then why couldn't he, his son, be the same today?

On the occasion of his 16th birthday on December 9, 1962, when his father presented him with the keys to a brand new 1963 navy blue Corvette convertible, Mitt's pent up lust for excitement suddenly burst loose from its bounds. He was the new Mr. Excitement. After class that day he ran hurdles on the school track, swiftly like the Olympian athlete nature had predisposed him to be. Mr. Edwards, the GMI track coach, was certain he had found the next champion runner. At home the birthday boy shared a cake with his parents and two sisters, Alexandra and Melissa, and a pair of spoiled rich neighborhood buddies, John "Stump" Hestlemeyer and Bradley "Edge" Tucker.

Still a few months shy of the watershed of their 16th birthdays, Stump and Edge had both suggested quietly to Mitt out by the front curb that they all secretly cruise off that night in the Corvette for a little nocturnal adventure. The temptation was too great for even the reformed version of Mitt to resist. In the wee hours of the next morning, when everybody else was sleeping, the trio would embark upon an automotive safari of daring and discovery.

"Let's go break into my dad's country club and steal some liquor," Mitt whispered to his comrades on the landing by the front door of his house. "Y'all be out back by the basement door at three in the morning."

"What if your dad hears the 'Vette crank up?" wondered Edge.

"He won't," said Mitt. "I'm telling him I need to get some pencils and paper for my tests tomorrow at the drug store up the road, and when I drive back I'll park the car out by the street. It's so dark he won't ever notice."

"Cool, Mitt," said Stump. "But what if he does look out and asks you why you didn't park it by the front?"

"Dammit, let's don't worry about him. He's irrelevant. I know how to handle him."

Young Mitt never got to sleep that night. Anticipation throbbed through his veins, his ears rang, and the admiration of his two friends for his bravery in going through with this scheme was thrilling to him. This would be his initiation rite of sorts, his passage to manhood. Times were different, and nowadays boys needed drugs, girls and cars to prove they were men. Being orderly and square just didn't pay enough of a dividend in excitement. Old people didn't understand that; their lives were old-fashioned and a long time ago there was nothing to do and no reason to be curious about anything.

The old man was just incapable of understanding. Why, his version of excitement, it probably amounted to smuggling a few bottles of white lightning across Miami Beach, turning himself over to the police, and spending a night in the slammer. Modern excitement would be *real* excitement. Breaking the law when everybody thought you'd turned over a new leaf. Being a thief and a rebel, even though your dad was a part of history and knew every president since Lincoln and you were expected to be this earthshattering kid when there was really nothing left to do, nothing to fight for, nothing to discover, nothing to be the first at.

His dad had sounded very corny that night, just as Mitt seemed to be going to bed: *"Son, you've got everything going for you, your whole life ahead of you. I wish I was your age again."* And then his dad had hugged him as if he had been a little baby, and kissed him on the cheek.

AT THREE THAT MORNING, a bitterly cold and moonless night on the cusp of winter, Mitt slipped out of his bedroom on the lower floor of the house, carefully undid the latch to the door to the rear patio, sneaked through the shrubbery and grass of the front lawn of the old mansion, and met his admiring disciples, Stump and Edge, by the navy blue Corvette.

"Let's drive with the top down," Mitt goaded the boys.

"You kidding?" cried Stump. "It's cold as Alaska out here—we'll freeze our butts off."

"Shit, you think this is cold?" Mitt said. "This ain't nothing. No wind, no ice, nothing but blacktop all the way to River Hills."

"Once that car starts moving there's gonna be plenty of wind," said Edge. "And I bet it's gonna be you who puts the top back on just as soon as you feel it."

"Hell no, I ain't putting no damn top back on," said Mitt. "Don't you know my new nickname? *Mr. Excitement."*

"Cool," said Stump. "I like it. How'd you come up with it?"

"I didn't sleep a wink tonight, so I thought I'd pass the time by thinking of something that fit my personality."

Mitt pulled the canvas top off the seating area of the convertible, started the engine, and off the boys went, exposed to the elements, freezing cold, nearly to the point of frostbite, but none would dare to try to return the top to its place. They were too old for that; they were men now, not sissies. Mitt wondered if his dad had ever withstood anything as cold as this.

He followed the predawn emptiness of Peachtree Battle Road and Northside Drive through the moneyed and woodsy splendor of the city's northern suburbs, all the way to the Chattahoochee River. A few miles outside the core of urbanization, nestled along the rolling banks of the river, lay River Hills Country Club, a private and patrician enclave where many of the local lions, the titans of finance and industry who included his father, were golf-playing members. It had eighteen holes, lakes, azaleas, dogwoods, towering pines and oaks, the imprimatur of Bobby Jones himself (another bastion of the old guard), and was said to be modeled after Augusta, where the Gods, Eisenhower, and Almighty Dad played.

The clubhouse and its grounds were encircled by a black wrought iron gate, but Mitt had brought a key to a side entrance used by the groundskeepers, and he and his two friends slinked out of the Corvette after he parked alongside the secret entryway. He had caddied enough times for his father to have a rather extensive knowledge of the layout. There would be a still pond by the 14th hole once they slipped through the rhododendrons, then an azalea thicket in a pine grove opposite the pond, and, beyond the azaleas, lurking in the depths of darkness, the multigabled sandstone castle which was the clubhouse.

Down in the cellar, where only a few influential people ever went, were the billiard tables and the wet bar with an astounding collection of fine wines and imported liquors. What made this plan all the more exciting and dangerous was, as Mitt well knew, the presence of an armed night watchman who usually stationed himself after midnight by the door to the bar and billiard room.

"Y'all do everything exactly like I say to," Mitt whispered to Stump and Edge. "When we get to the basement of the clubhouse I'll break the glass of one of the windows with a rock. If I don't hear the guard stirring, I'll jump in and start lifting out cases of the good stuff one by one. Then you guys carry it back through the gate and put it in the back seat of the Corvette."

The plan was to stash all the alcohol in the woods behind Mitt's house, cover it with leaves, invite about twelve gorgeous girls to a party at Edge's house the following weekend when his parents went out of town, get all the girls smashed, and bed all of them down. When the girls asked where the boys got all the liquor, Mitt would brag about breaking into the most exclusive country club in Atlanta, evading an armed gunman, and staging a dramatic getaway in his open-air convertible. Then he would reveal to the awestruck bobbysoxers his new nickname. *Mr. Excitement.*

"You sure you know what you're doing?" asked Stump, with a little skepticism. "*I mean, we're unarmed.* What if the guard sees you? What will he do?"

"I'll just tell him who I am," said Mitt. "I'll say who my daddy is and how I'm just having a little fun 'cause it's my sixteenth birthday."

"What if that don't impress him?" Stump wondered.

"Aw, shut up, Stump!" said Edge. "Mitt knows what he's doing. What are you—*chicken?"*

There was no answer. No, no, they weren't chicken, the boys thought to themselves. But as they skirted the edge of the pond whose black water matched the appalling murkiness of the moonless sky they all became nervous. Mitt had a premonition of danger when he saw the familiar colors of day shrouded in the colorless grays and blacks of darkness. He was going into an unknown realm and it was terrifying to him. For the first time in his life it occurred to him, wrenchingly and suddenly, how humbling it was to go on a path never before taken on a mission whose outcome was uncertain.

Some words from his father—words which he had heard from him long ago, he had forgotten exactly when—began to echo in his memory. *The secret to beating the odds is always knowing you can, while at the same time always fearing you won't.* He wished at that moment that his father had been there with him—he wanted his father to tell him how he had done it. What was the secret to controlling this ever-present fear? What was the secret?

It was too late to stop now. An external force beyond his understanding had overthrown his willpower. Even if he had wanted to, he would have been unable to stop. Mitt continued to lead the other two boys around the rim of the small lake, through the pine straw and azaleas, to the small rectangular window at the top of the cellar room where the vast fortress of the clubhouse castle met the ground. He couldn't find a rock anywhere around him, so he took off one of his shoes and smashed the window with it, removing all the remaining particles of glass with his fingers to keep from cutting himself when he squeezed through the sill. He was barely able to fit his body through the opening of the small window, and when he leaned his head into it the darkness was so complete that he thought if he tumbled down it would be into a bottomless abyss. He heard nothing, no stirring of the night watchman.

"How is it?" asked Edge, keeping his voice in a whisper. "Is it okay?"

"I can't see," said Mitt, with his heart beating like a jackhammer against his ribs. "I—I hope if I jump I land in the right place."

"We'll hold your legs and ease you down," said Stump. "You don't have to jump in cold turkey."

"No, no," said Mitt. "I gotta do it by myself. I gotta be the one . . ."

He thrust himself through the small opening with his hands, fell hard on an unseen wooden table and knocked three chairs loudly to the marble floor. The middle-aged night watchman, Horace "Hock" Sims, heard the clamor and opened the door to the room. The light switch was too far away for him to reach—perhaps he had but a second or two. In the near total darkness he made out the black shadow of a tall well-built man and yelled out, fearfully and anxiously:

"Halt right there, mister! Put up your hands!"

Mitt did as he was bidden, and held his arms straight up. But in the darkness Sims thought he saw the youth reaching for a weapon in his pocket and, fearing he might be shot at unless he acted quickly, he pulled the trigger to his gun.

Within a fraction of a second the bullet passed under the victim's right armpit, pierced his heart, and emerged from the body under the arm on the other side. A dull thud signified the collapse of the corpse onto the floor. Sims' blind aim had been far truer than he would have hoped if he had been able to see his target's gesture of surrender.

The two boys outside, hearing the gunshot, took off running for the Corvette and never looked back. Edge had the car keys and, though underage, he drove the two of them somberly home with the convertible's roof closed and parked the vehicle by the street where Mr. Harrison had last seen it the night before. Then the two of them scurried away like scared fugitives back to their houses without telling anyone else what had happened.

When Sims finally turned the light switch on and looked at the dead boy he shuddered at the thought of who it appeared to be, but when he called the police to the scene he said nothing, offered no speculation. The youth had been carrying no form of identification.

EARLY THE NEXT MORNING a proud father went down to his son's room, as he occasionally did, to wish him well for the day and let him know how grateful he was to have him. Finding the bed empty and the disheveled sheets cold, he returned up the steps to Juliette and asked with some degree of concern:

"Where's our son?"

For the next three hours of increasingly miserable uncertainty they scoured the house, called friends and relatives, the school, the jail, the drug store. Edge and Stump, the only available eyewitnesses who knew the whole story, had gone to school as if nothing had happened and were unavailable to give the information that the bewildered family needed to know. Finally, at about ten-thirty on the morning of the 10th, the chief of police called Kid by telephone.

"Mr. Harrison, would you kindly come down to the station?" he asked gently. "There's somewhere I want you to go with me."

Juliette's complexion was ashy white and the touch of her skin was as cold as stone. With a limp hand she saw her husband off; with nervous hope she prayed that he might rescue joy from despair.

He could not. The police chief, saying nothing, drove him to the county morgue, where, out of a grisly row of cabinets, the chief opened a door and pulled out a long pallet. There before him lay the remains of his only son, who was dead at the age of sixteen.

CHAPTER 37

Minding the Children

FOR THE REST OF their lives Mr. and Mrs. Harrison never spent a day without the thought of their son. They saw him as a baby crawling on their floor; they imagined his doll-like toddler's eyes, two twin green emeralds shimmering like jewels. They heard the mischief of his boyish laughter, saw his swift muscular athletic body clearing hurdles on the school track, felt his warm soft infant head leaning against their shoulders, imagined the soft feel of the plump newborn cheeks that had existed once but which time and accident had obliterated.

There would never be a recovery from his loss. Nothing that anyone might do or say, no breakthrough of peacefulness and loving-kindness upon the earth, no memory of greatness past or aspirations of accomplishment in the future could replace what had been taken away.

The father and the mother drifted apart. She wanted to pursue legal action against the night watchman; he to keep it all quiet, insisting that no courtroom verdict would give a smidgen's worth of relief for the pain. Hock Sims had been assigned and armed to protect a piece of property. Someone had forcibly broken into the premises after dark, someone who had foreknowledge of his presence as an armed guard. What was the night watchman to assume? Milt could see the dispassionate force of reason through the cracks in his emotion. His wife could not.

She insisted they take the case to court, and her obstinacy resulted in their having to cut open the scabs on fresh wounds repeatedly until there was no chance that the scars on them would ever heal. The press coverage of the trial was an embarrassing nuisance, and when the jury sided with the defendant the pain in the Harrison family was nearly as excruciating as when they had first witnessed the sight of their boy's body as it was being slid out of its cubbyhole in the morgue.

What Juliette could never forget, and what reached the point of obsession with her in her recurring bouts with depression for the rest of her life, was the memory of what her husband had done the first time he had encountered Hock Sims in the courtroom; Sims, the same man who had shot their son dead while their son was lifting his arms in surrender; Sims, the author of her life's endless agony. She witnessed her husband, a proud fierce man who had stood firm against horrors his whole life, *shake the man's hand*.

"*Mr. Sims*," he had said, as the night watchman hesitated and trembled in anticipation of a violent backlash, "*religion's never been for me, but I forgive. I know you didn't mean to do it.*"

How many times she would revisit the incident to him, how many times he would bolt from the room, slam the door shut, and go out on his own to avoid the thought of it! At the funeral every friend he thought he had, and many he didn't realize he did, came to try to console him. Mr. Bonderman ordered his company's catering truck to appear in front of the Harrison home and supply all the edible goods needed for mourning, redemption, and commemoration. Bobby and Chet, Shnook, Zeke and Woody, all aging men now, carried the casket of the ill-fated golden boy. As the boy's father struggled with his wife and with the memories of his past, and as doubts crept up in him that his life had mattered at all, his friend Woody had a conversation with him that reverberated through his mind for months and years to come.

"Enby, you always got to remain Mr. Excitement. I've known you forever, and I know can't nothin' keep you down."

"What else is there, Woody? You tell me. I'm old and I've killed my own son. *I* did it, by ignoring him and by going around thinkin' I was important. My boy's the one who had it right. He always said I was irrelevant."

"You can't blame yourself," Woody consoled him. "You've come too far to throw it all away now. There are other things to do."

"What can I do now? You tell me."

"You know what'd be good, man?" said the aging Bahamian, with a sparkle in his eye. "I want you to build a DH-4 aeroplane just like the one you brought me in. Only one of 'em's left—and it's in the Smithsonian. No single person ever built a machine that big. But you can do it, Enby—I'm sure if anybody can do the impossible it's you. You can build one yourself and say, 'See, that's what I did for my boy. There now.' Before I go, Enby, I want us to go on one last ride. And he'll be in there with us—your boy will, I mean."

ONCE THE IDEA TOOK hold of Milt of yet again trying an impossible thing—of building a replica of a DeHavilland 4 biplane with his own hands in his own workshop—it took total possession of his bereaved and beleaguered soul. He was tired of city ways and city people, and purchased a 200-acre tract of rolling pasture on the outskirts of Woodvale, hoping to retire there with his family, build an ornate home with a large hangar and workshop beside it, and create another miracle.

His depressed wife and his complaining teenage daughters, alarmed at the prospect of boredom in the boondocks, hated the idea. As a compromise he decided to have a house and workshop built in the distant suburbs north of Atlanta, on a wooded bluff overlooking the Chattahoochee River, closer to the country club where his son was killed than he would have preferred, but still far enough away that he never went in it again or even drove by it.

The girls could stay at Waltham Academy, a 30-minute drive away, while he could hide himself away in leafy trees. With imagination he could pretend he was nowhere near the scene of the death of his son. At least he couldn't hear traffic noises and he had no worthless neighbors like Stump and Edge. And he spent his quiet hours studying blueprints he had personally obtained from the Smithsonian Institute in Washington, D.C.—the plans for the antiquated airplane he was hoping to reproduce.

He tried to smother his two daughters with love and attention in the absence of his son. He opened up to them as he never had to Mitt. It worked only partially because the whole world seemed to be falling apart. Leaders were being assassinated, rockets were being shot into outer space, and his two girls were teenagers who had made the no-good discovery that there was such a thing as boys in the world.

Most of these boys seemed to be long-haired scoundrels to the aging relic of the last century, and his scowl was effective at scaring them off. But one of them he liked—young Dean Wellesley, a junior at Wofford College in South Carolina, who had met Alexandra at one of her school dances. The college upperclassman worshiped at his shrine. He knew almost everything there was to know about Kid Harrison, wanted the general's autograph on pictures of old airplanes, and aspired to fly planes himself.

"A fine, fine boy," Kid said to Alexandra. What he didn't know was that, at 18, his precious beauty of a daughter had already sacrificed her virginity to the 20-year-old Wellesley and would soon be conceiving his child. Alexandra would only laugh. He was wickedly fine indeed.

When Milt saw that his daughter had gotten herself with child as a result of Dean's ardent affections and they had eloped and gotten married he realized he had a problem. What to do about Dean's lack of employment? Juliette suggested that he teach Dean how to fly an airplane and ask Aloysius Troy to do him a favor and give the boy a chance as a pilot with Coastal. Kid said his friend was in ailing health and he didn't want to impose on him in that way. Juliette asked who was more important, his ailing friend or his daughter and future grandchild.

"Tell me, Dean," Milt asked the sweaty-palmed father-to-be in the main sitting room of his new mansion in the woods, "how'd you like to learn to fly aeroplanes?"

The college man was shaking like one with delirium tremens. He had gotten himself into a very thorny predicament. Did he really have a choice?

"I'd love to, sir. How do you go about doing that?"

"Let's go out to Robin Field tomorrow and I'll teach you how in a Cessna 150. We'll fly all day every weekend during the summer to build your hours up, then we'll get you in through the door."

Wellesley was tense but thrilled. At Robin Field, a paved landing strip in a remote part of western Fulton County, Milt had been renting out a hangar where he housed his own private jet. Here, in several dozen sessions ranging from two to four hours, the old warhorse of aviation, soon to be 70, passed on his knowledge of the mystic science of the air to the sponge-like absorption of his young pupil. During the weekdays of this period Wellesley took the final few courses he needed for graduation from college with a degree in mechanical engineering, and during the weekend he logged his hours with General Harrison to try to qualify himself for some sort of a job. They got along swimmingly; Kid did all the talking and Dean did all the listening and nodding.

By the end of August of 1966 his son-in-law had logged a little over 200 hours in the Cessna jet, and Kid told his wife the boy was ready.

"Are you crazy?" Juliette asked her husband. "They'll never hire him with that."

"It ain't *they,*" said Kid. "It's *he.* And, oh yes, he damn certainly will hire him. He will if I ask him to."

Kid trotted out the shiny silver Cadillac, made the long trek southward to Hapeville, and went up to his longtime friend's office. For years now it had been occurring to him that the accelerated pace of change in the world was bothersome at best, and traumatic at worst. The bookends of his life had been losing a father and a son; the filling from in between was being steadily eroded by progress and age.

Britt had been thrown out of the captain's seat at Eagle at the end of 1965, and Kid had responded by divesting himself of all his stock holdings and involvement at that company. Lately, word had circulated that A.T. was in poor health. When Milt saw his enfeebled friend for the first time in over a year his frailty shocked him.

It was disheartening to think that time stopped for no one. Here sat the Hoosier who had taken an aerial bug-killing operation, a wooden axle outfit, and transformed it into a business that now ruled an entire region of the greatest nation the world had ever known; but gone was the sense of energy and passion that had used to dwell within him. Instead there was an old, tired man who seemed out of step with the turbulence around him.

He spoke more slowly than before; his trademark eyeglasses magnified his tired eyes; his jowls sagged; his full-throated laugh had turned sardonic. No longer did he know all the names of all his employees and the names of their wives and children and where they went to church and what they ate for dinner. The wear and tear of the years had dimmed his abilities. But his old friend's request for his new son-in-law was granted immediately.

"Tell him to be here bright and early Monday morning," said Aloysius Troy," his hair combed, his shoes shined, his college diploma in hand. If you say he's Coastal material, he's Coastal material."

"The youth of America, A.T.," said the man from Woodvale cryptically, and then his old associate broke into one of his wry chuckles.

"Ah, yes," he said, "the youth of America. I'll tell you what, Milton. I wouldn't trade our youth for theirs, would you?"

"Shoot, you kidding me? My boy used to say I was irrelevant, and that's how all these kids nowadays think of us. We don't mean squat to them."

Mr. Bonderman paused and crossed his bony hands, as if a bitter thought had just passed through his mind.

"Maybe that's our fault," he said. "Maybe we were better at doing things than talking about ourselves. At any rate, it's too late now to change. And why should we? I think we gave a pretty good account of ourselves on this little sphere."

"You think so?" asked Milt. "Sometimes I wonder if my life has meant anything at all—if anybody in the future will even care what I did. I don't care a lick about being remembered, but I'd like to think in my own little itty-bitty way I helped make the world a better place. But the people who outlive me will be the ones who determine that."

It felt awkward for the two of them to look back and try to analyze past accomplishments. Neither felt comfortable in any other temporal place but the here and now. Milt rose to his feet to say good-bye before the conversation might drift further into the reminiscence that was alien to both of them.

"So long, friend," said the chairman, standing to shake hands. His facial expression struck Milt because in it he realized a sense of finality. This was a man who sensed he was soon to die and his eyes were cloudy with emotion. It was not a pleasant realization and Kid tried to downplay it. Matter-of-factly he accepted the handshake and left the office. His premonitions were proved eerily true when, four months later, the old Hoosier entomologist and crop-dusting emperor died of heart failure at age seventy-six. It was to be one of many deaths of old friends in the next several years as the lions of the old guard were toppled by death from their pedestals.

THIS CHEERLESS PROCESSION OF deaths and extinctions, of old times vanishing amid the speed and clamor of new, of today looking worse in rose-tinted comparisons with yesterday—all this seemed to be put aside when Alexandra bore her child. Life had renewed itself. Just when the ancient Kid had apparently lost all his audience now he had a new one. The little boy looked just like his uncle and his granddaddy in the long ago time. Timothy, they named him. And two years later Alexandra bore his first granddaughter, Teresa.

By now everybody he had ever known well in Woodvale was dead, except for Woody, Ruth, Shnook and Madge. His mother's longevity had proved the most remarkable of all her many attributes. For her 100th birthday in September of 1969 Milt brought together all the offspring of all his old friends—as well as everyone in his own family. The other old people in the village had been preparing Grandma Madge for her big party. Ruth was a spring chicken of eighty-five with perfect hearing, and she fancied herself as looking not a day older than sixty-seven. Yet to Madge Ruth was the same age as herself. Each afternoon, always at one o'clock, Woody's son drove Ruth over to 125 Oak Street, and the two old ladies, one black and one white, had a visit. Ruth knew to stand and yell so the nearly-deaf matriarch would understand her.

"MRS. H, YOUR FAMILY'S ALL COMIN' TOMORROW, SO YOU BE SURE TO GO TO BED EARLY TONIGHT AND DON'T READ ALL THE FUNNIES IN THE PAPER!"

Madge, occupying her chair with her yarn quilt in her lap and her gnarled hands clasped together, pursed her lips and chewed on her toothless gums.

"Sure will, Ruth," she said. "I promise I will."

The next day, when her son arrived back in Woodvale, he told all the other members of his family out in front of the house that his mother needed to absorb things gradually. She still hadn't been told what had happened to Mitt, seven years after the fact. Her Woodvale neighbors had discreetly confiscated the newspapers during that time, and the family had always insisted that Madge not visit them in Atlanta after that. When she asked about Mitt she had always been told that he went off to the University then struck out on his own for adventure in the mountains. "Just like his daddy," Madge would beam proudly. Nobody ever worked up the nerve to tell her the truth. Milt knew she would die of heartbreak if she ever heard it, and he didn't want the gruesomeness of the tragedy to spread to the weakest of all possible victims.

"Now, y'all," he was telling all the clan—his wife, daughters, son-in-law, his two sisters and all their children and grandchildren—out on the concrete porch before they went inside, "Y'all, let's go in two or three at a time so she won't feel ambushed. Allie, you take baby Teresa in your arms and I'll take little Timothy by the hand and just the four of us will go in. Mama still hasn't heard about her latest great grandchildren."

Woody sat next to Madge inside and prepared her for each ensuing round of visitors. Now her son was coming, and with some good news on her birthday. Woody went outside to allow his longtime friend some privacy with his mother. When Milt entered the room his mother's eyes lit up as they always did. No matter how old he was (and he was by then almost 73 years old), he was always Madge's little boy in her eyes, the years and the greatness evaporated, and he was still the mischievous little tyke who squealed at passing trains.

"Milt!" she cried, trying unsuccessfully to rise out of her chair but succeeding at giving him a wet peck on the cheek as he leaned down, "how you doin', boy?"

Alexandra and her two-year-old son and nine-month-old daughter sat on the musty faded green sofa across from the lady of honor, while Milt cupped his hands around his mouth and yelled in Madge's ear:

"MAMA, THIS IS MY DAUGHTER ALEXANDRA AND THESE ARE YOUR TWO YOUNGEST GREAT GRANDCHILDREN."

"Sure enough!" cried Madge, craning her neck upward like a chicken to peer at the youngsters through her glasses. Her eyes were soon filled with tears and she lifted a handkerchief to her nose and blew. While the two children were positioned in their great grandmother's lap, Alexandra snapped a picture of them. More tears began raining from the old lady's eyes.

"I never thought I'd live to see you have grandchildren, Milt," she said. "You got such a late start sure enough."

After all of her kinfolk had visited her in small groupings, Madge was helped outside in the beautiful autumn sunshine and placed at the head of a large picnic table which several Woodvaleans had assembled for the occasion. There she had lunch and cake with the 24 people for whose existence she was directly responsible, and their spouses. Everything seemed to be going perfectly; she sighed with satisfaction at all the beautiful young people around her and felt comfortable about the course of the future. Because of her deafness, all conversation during the party was no more than a meaningless outpouring of noise to her. But when it came time to cut her cake she caught everyone totally off guard.

"For my birthday present, y'all," she said, "I want to ride in an aeroplane with my son. *I never rode in an aeroplane yet.*"

There was widespread laughter at the absurdity of the request, but Margaret Harrison insisted that she be taken seriously and burst into tears. For awhile the good cheer of the occasion was subdued until Kid, looking at his son-in-law, said: "We'll take her on one of your turnarounds to Birmingham, thirty minutes in the air there and back."

WITH GREAT FANFARE FROM the press and television media, who had unfortunately been informed of the event by Alexandra, Milton Jr. wheeled his mother to a remote corner of the Atlanta Airport the next week, where his son-in-law, a flight engineer on the Boeing 727, was to help take Madge up into the air for the first time in her 100 years. When she was seated at the terminal gate, being catered to by Milt and some of the other brass at Coastal, she breathed a deep sigh. It was nowhere near so treacherous as she had expected. Why, she should have been doing this for years.

"Milt," she said, proud of herself, "*are we flyin' yet?*"

She heard none of the uproarious laughter among the reporters and officials around her, although she did notice that her son suddenly broke into a mighty big smile.

"NO, MAMA, NOT YET. WE'RE STILL NOT ON THE PLANE YET. YOU'LL KNOW WHEN WE'RE FLYIN' 'CAUSE I'LL LET YOU SIT BY THE WINDOW AND YOU'LL BE ABLE TO SEE THE GROUND FROM ABOVE."

"Sure enough," said Madge.

Milt had purchased two first class seats in the left bulkhead row of the 727 for the round trip to Birmingham, barely a half hour's flight time away. The plane's captain and first officer, along with Dean, the flight engineer, stood by the door to the loading bridge and welcomed their elderly passenger as her son rolled her down to the plane in a wheelchair. She kept saying "Real nice", and when Milt lifted her from her chair and helped her with her walking cane to her seat, she sighed as if she had boarded a chariot bound for heaven.

She pressed her nose and thick glasses to the pane of the window to her left, clasped her frail right hand around her son's, and kept her eyes riveted on the astounding spectacle of the great machine's taxi over the apron, charge across the runway and thrust into the air. She squeezed her son's hand tightly and nervously as she watched the landscape of the world shrink underneath her. He never needed to tell her they were flying. She knew now. So this was flying. When the jet made its landing at its destination and then returned to Atlanta she repeated the words that had been coming from her almost continuously since she first got to the plane. "*Real nice.*"

As Kid was rolling her back out of the airport in her wheelchair later that afternoon she had him stop for a moment so she could share her latest thoughts with him.

"Son, that's the best birthday present I ever got. I didn't tell you this before, not one time, but I was wrong. I'm proud you stuck with aeroplanes—*that's the smartest thing you ever did."*

He leaned down to his doddering mother, whose eyes had started leaking tears again in their usual way, and he cupped his hands around one of her ears and yelled:

"THANKS, MAMA."

IT WAS TO BE HIS MOTHER'S last outing of any consequence. Within a year her frailty required her family to place her in a nursing home, and six months after that she died peacefully in her sleep at 101 years of age. In the next few years most of Milt's old friends would pass away: Cy, Britt, Chet, Bobby, Shnook, George Grantland. Ruth lasted five more years, then died suddenly of a stroke. Britt succumbed to the same malady at his Jekyll Island hideaway.

When Kid saw George for the last time, the former mayor had tried to talk him into allowing Candler Field to be renamed Kid Harrison Field, knowing full well what the old ace's response would be.

"You name any goddamn things of any kind after me, Georgie, and if I'm alive I'll come shoot you—and if I'm dead I'll order my next of survivors to come shoot you, and if they don't I'll put it in my will they'll be disinherited."

So Kid Harrison Field continued to be an imaginary place while its namesake became more and more a distant historical fossil. Every death seemed to leave the old ace more alone, more out of step with the times. And other nettlesome trends were beyond his understanding. In 1974 Juliette informed him that Alexandra and Dean were getting a divorce.

"A *what?"* he asked. "What's the reason for that?"

"No good reason," spoke Mrs. Harrison somberly, sensing a return of the dreaded depression she had been fighting since her son's death. "She said something about there not being any growth."

"What? What the hell does that mean?"

He would say roughly the same thing several years later when Melissa, his other daughter, got a divorce as well. The retired general retreated ever further into the mechanical magic of his workshop, frequently talking aloud to himself, criticizing the folly of the contemporary world. He had poured large sums of money into obtaining the tools by which he was manually building an old airplane: two giant lathes, a band saw, a rotary sander, a milling machine, hundreds of specialized wrenches and clamps, two arc-welding tanks, a large anvil, three steel tables, and a large electric wood saw.

He had never welded before, but rather than receive formal technical instruction he taught himself how to do it, drawing on his long-ago training as a blacksmith's apprentice. By his 78th birthday the wooden frame of a reincarnated relic of his youth stood in his workshop, suspended from the rafters by clamps and wires. The well-thumbed blueprints he had obtained from the Smithsonian were sprawled out on his corner desk in the shop. The fuselage, the landing gear, and the tail were nearly finished; he had precisely cut and bent spruce wood into the spars of the plane's wings; and the only significant item that remained for his acquisition was the Liberty engine. Where he might find one of those was beyond his guess.

He was lucky to have a young helper from time to time to overhear his soliloquies. His little grandson, six-year-old Tim, spent a great deal of time with his grandparents, since his mother was now working and his father had remarried and moved to California. Sometimes Teresa, the four-year-old granddaughter, would wander over to visit her grandfather, but Tim was there almost constantly when not in school.

"Grandpa, will you build me an airplane?" the little boy asked the ancient one after school one day.

"Sure, I'll build you one," answered Kid. "What kind you want?"

"Red, 'cause that's my favorite color."

"A red plane? Shoot, I seen lots of red planes before."

Though he had been intently working on his big airplane, Milt stopped what he was doing, took Tim to the local hardware store in a green 1949 Ford pickup truck which he had bought from Shnook Adams's estate, and obtained several sheets of plywood, screws, brackets, a toy wagon, and some red, white and black spray paint. They then went back to the garage behind the tree-shrouded mansion and the old man started his project to make sure his grandson had a plane of his own.

For the next three weeks little Tim was in a trance of fascination as he watched what his grandfather did. First he sketched out several patterns on the pieces of plywood, cut them into shapes on his band saw, and sanded them smooth. He made two wings, each about four feet long, along with another flat piece which was shaped like a fuselage with a tail. He added two smaller pieces for the tail wings and two flat rectangular pieces just large enough to be a seat and a backrest for a six year-old. Then he cut the wheels off the toy wagon, put one underneath each wing and one in the back, and put two short aluminum pipes on the top to resemble machine guns.

"Now, boy," he told Tim, "that's lookin' excellent."

He painted the entire plane red except for the seat, which he painted black. On each side of the top wing he painted a black Maltese cross in the middle of a white band, and he did the same on the tail. His little grandson now had his own plane of sorts, a toy tricycle which he could pedal about the driveway with its own machine guns for taking out imaginary villains.

Three weeks of continuous work by his grandfather had resulted in the custom-made toy.

"You can be the Rittmeister," Kid told the child. "That's what we used to call the best fighter from the other side. Or at least we did before I shot him down."

"You won't shoot me down, will you, Grandpa?"

"You kiddin'? I'm too old for that now. Once you get to be an old grandpa like me, your shooting days are over."

THE PROBLEM OF WHERE to find a suitable vintage engine for his big plane was a seemingly insoluble one for the man from Woodvale. He would have sought advice from some of his old friends if they hadn't already been dead. Of the old-timers who were still alive, the one most likely to know where to get such an old engine was Garrett Hawkins, who was living as a recluse in a castle on the cliffs above Malibu, California.

Hawkins referred him to a motion picture producer in Los Angeles named Gordon Waverly, who had an original Liberty engine for a DH-4 which was being used to generate wind on a back lot in Culver City. Milt flew out to meet with Mr. Waverly and eventually bought the engine from him for $1500. Hawkins had also given Milt the nursing home address of Arky Lattimore and requested that he meet with his fellow ace and former stunt performer before going home. Lattimore had had four childless marriages with beautiful Hollywood bimbos, had grown overly fond of the bottle, and had drifted into and out of sanitariums with Hawkins's monetary support and the aid of his own veteran's pension.

Kid was disappointed to find that Lattimore had grown so senile he didn’t even recognize him. It seemed a fit way for the aviator to close another chapter of his life, saying good-bye to an old colleague and rival who didn't remember him and couldn't function on his own any more, though he had once been a professional mocker of death. Los Angeles had grown staggeringly large since those Halcyon days of the Roaring ‘20’s. The city that he had known in the early years of the movie business no longer existed.

When the engine was delivered to Milt's home address by a trucking delivery service he was finally able to see an end for his project. After twelve years of painstaking work in his spare time all he needed to do was mount the engine, cover the fuselage and wings with fabric, and take the machine somewhere and fly it. Or was that feasible? He was almost eighty years old. Did he still have it in him to risk his life flying an airplane? Woody had told him he needed to do it for his son, but by "it" did he mean dying? As an elderly man he was having recurring trepidations which had never even crossed his mind in his youth. What was the point of throwing his life to the winds at this stage?

"If you think I'll ever let you try to fly that plane at your age," Juliette scolded him at the dinner table one night, "you're out of your mind. I wish you'd just let people remember you the way you were."

"Darlin'," said Kid, "the way I *was* hasn't ever mattered at all to me. It's always been *the way I am right now* that concerned me. I never lived one day in the past, and I'm not about to start now."

LATER THAT YEAR, WHEN Juliette thought she had finally succeeded in talking Milt into being a thoroughly dutiful husband who acted his age and took no foolish chances and made no foolish gestures, tragedy struck again.

The Harrison streak of wildness that had been leaving its imprint on the world for the better part of the last century had infected little Tim to the core. On the afternoon of his fourth day of second grade in August of 1975, Tim hopped on the bicycle he had only recently learned to ride without training wheels, a birthday gift which had supplanted the outgrown Rittmeister tricyle as his vehicle of choice. While his mother was at work, his grandfather sulked inside trying to act the way his grandmother thought an old man should act, and his sister played with dolls. Tim was thinking he could ride the bike all the way down to the bottom of the driveway through the woods, fetch the afternoon newspaper, cross the road, and gather enough momentum in recrossing it to ride the bike back up the hill to the house.

The driveway joined the street in a blind spot at the top of a steep hill. When Tim crossed the road and turned to come back, a speeding car seemingly from out of nowhere smashed the bike, shattered his bones, hurled him through the air, and left him curled up motionlessly in a pool of blood on the baking hot asphalt. He was mangled nearly beyond recognition.

CHAPTER 38

Miracles Come from Inside

HAVING THROWN A BLANKET over the inanimate body, the motorist who had struck the boy on the bicycle ran up the hilly driveway to ring the doorbell of the Harrison house.

"Your boy is hurt!" he cried out when the child's grandfather opened the door.

"Where?"

Milt anxiously followed the man down to the street where lay the mutilated child, his body sheathed in a stained blanket but just enough of his head visible as it rested on the pavement to resemble a bloody ball. The elderly man was shocked and, for a time, speechless. He wished the car had hit him and had killed him so he wouldn't have had to endure this. Why was this life so cruel to its most defenseless creatures?

He thought of his own son immediately, of the sight of his boy's lifeless body in the county morgue, and before he made it down to examine this latest fallen child he nearly had to stop, turn away, and fight against a nervous breakdown. A white stretch Lincoln Continental with its hazard lights flashing was parked between the body and the middle of the street; the bicycle was crushed and smashed to pieces; and the man was saying something about being a real estate agent. Mr. Stan Hughes, he said his name was, apparently a neighbor they had never met from a few houses away. Milt didn't ask if Tim was still alive. His shock was quickly replaced by the instinctive force of steel-willed determination that had guided him throughout his lifetime.

"I'm gonna save that boy," said Kid, pushing Hughes aside. "I don't care what anybody else says. I won't stand for any more children of mine to die before their time."

The boy's grandfather quickly fell to his knee, lifted the blanket off the unconscious child, and saw that his legs were disfigured, a purple welt was on the side of his face, and blood was smeared all over his body. His skimpy summer attire of a tank top and shorts and bare feet had left him with nothing to cushion the impact of the car and the pavement, and especially vulnerable to chafing and lacerations. He was breathing slowly and shaking spasmodically because of internal hemorrhaging. Kid told Hughes to run up to the house and call for an ambulance.

"I'm not leavin' this boy's side till he's better," said the man from Woodvale. "*He may be hurt, but he's not dead yet.*"

The child's fresh red blood soaked Milt's shirt and trousers as he hugged the boy, leaned over him to protect him from light, air and harm, and kissed his throbbing forehead. Juliette came down, bringing Teresa, who screamed when she saw her helpless brother on the asphalt. Juliette was so overwhelmed by the sight that she nearly collapsed. They wept and shook until the sultry air was pierced by the shrill sound of a distant siren, which closed in on them until it was practically shattering their eardrums. "Not again!" Mrs. Harrison cried tormentedly. "I CAN'T GO THROUGH THIS AGAIN!"

"Hush up!" said Milt. "That attitude won't help a bit. I'm saving this boy."

Two paramedics came from the ambulance, and with Milt's help they gently lifted the boy with the shattered legs while he screamed in blood-curdling delirium.

"Get that truck off my legs!" he was yelling. "The whole world's on top of my legs, smashing my legs!"

His grandfather sat beside him in the ambulance while it rushed them to the nearest hospital twenty minutes away. Tim screamed furiously all the way there, before he was straitjacketed in the emergency room and sedated with morphine. The major bones in both of his legs had been shattered: the femur, the tibia and fibula just above and below the kneecaps. Also, he had sustained a concussion, a broken pelvic bone and a fracture on the left side of his skull behind his ear.

Two steel pins were driven into both legs just above the knee, perpendicular to the bone and left sticking out several inches. Plaster of Paris casts were placed on the two legs. The boy was catheterized, and his legs were elevated in a hospital bed by pulleys, ropes and weights. He stayed in a coma for days in the hospital with his grandfather sleeping in the room with him and rarely leaving his side. "I've seen terrible things before," he would tell nurses, "and I just know this boy will come out of this thing."

When Alexandra came and began throwing an emotional tantrum, Milt chided her and told her she was only making the situation worse. In fact, it seemed to him that everybody was making everything worse: the doctors, the nurses, his wife and daughters, the speeding fool who had hit the boy in the first place—even the boy's father, who refused to leave his second wife in distant California to come attend to his own child who was in a coma. A fine specimen of fatherhood he had turned out to be, Kid was thinking sourly to himself. And what gratitude he had shown the man who had trained him, nurtured him and secured for him what was soon to be a six-figure-salary job. Just like all these fine, fine young people in the world of today.

Alexandra tried to order her father out of the room with her boy, thinking his obsessiveness would do no good at all and only drag him into his grave in its wake. But like a Brahma bull the man from Woodvale refused to budge.

"Dammit, I ain't leaving this goddamn place until this boy does—and he's leaving all good and well too, I don't give two hoots in hell what all these people say."

He was subsisting on a few hour-long catnaps each night, eating abominably bland hospital food, and sleeping on a long divan a few steps from where the comatose child lay in traction. He was putting a bedpan under the boy, touching his forehead to make sure he still had a pulse, and examining the toes which stuck out from beyond the casts to see that they had not turned purple from a lack of circulation.

Occasionally he would deliver long soliloquies over the child's mute form, little concerned whether Tim could understand them or not, half expecting some supernatural transfusion to deliver them to the boy's deadened brain. When the doctors mentioned the possibility of a permanent coma or permanent paralysis, Kid scoffed and told them they underestimated the stuff of this particular boy. Why, Kid had seen people recover from bad injuries before. He had broken a femur himself one time, then only a few months later was sloshing through mud puddles at Ft. Benning and revolting the digestive systems of officers at the Rhinebeck Aerodrome. The doctors couldn't wait to get rid of this crazy old goat.

Milt kept up his pep talks forcefully until one day little Tim opened his eyes, though without talking. Then his grandfather clasped hold of his hand, as if to squeeze life into him and urge him to talk. In the meantime he would continue his one-man orations about life and history and airplanes and whatever else happened to come to mind. For several more days the boy would open his eyes for longer and longer stretches, seeming to listen, though without talking.

Nine days after the accident, the child showed cognizance of where he was and what had happened to him. In looking at the apparatus of ropes and weights that elevated his own mangled legs, and the steel pins sticking out of them, and the bloodstains that had seeped through the white plaster, he evidently began feeling sorry for himself. He closed his eyes, winced, and began crying. His grandfather continued to encourage him.

"Don't worry, boy," said Kid. "You'll get better. Even if you think things will never be like they were and you'll never get out of trouble, you can escape and live. Just be patient and keep your head level, and it'll happen, boy."

The child seemed to improve in outlook somewhat, but Milt noticed that a painful sense of discouragement never seemed very far from him. At this point the elderly man decided to start telling stories about far-off places and adventures. There was the one about the flyer who shot down another flyer named the Riding Master just as he was about to attack a beautiful far-away city called Paris. And the one about the little boy who taught his daddy how to drive a flivver, who flew a plane through a snowstorm and won an air race, roamed around the countryside on a motorcycle and slept in grass and scared people because he drove so fast. And there were stories about circuses in far away places, flying alone across oceans and over mountains, going completely around the world and meeting emperors and sheiks and Sphinxes. And then there were stories about California and beaches and dream girls and explosions and swimming pools and parties with a hundred different kinds of foods.

Milt was surprised a young person would care anything at all about what his parent's parent had done fifty or sixty years ago, but the boy seemed to pay close attention to everything. The star-crossed Mitt had made his father self-conscious about discussing anything that had happened longer ago than last month. There was always the danger of being irrelevant.

"What does that mean, Grandpa?" Tim asked him when Kid finally let his reservations out.

"It means what I say doesn't apply to people nowadays. I've lasted so long in this world that my past has no meaning to anyone any more."

Tim was completely lucid for the first time since his accident, and he seemed to speak with wisdom beyond his years. It was as though he had ascended his own little version of Mt. Sinai and had read occult revelations on stone tablets. He took a deep breath before coming out with his next question.

"Grandpa, you think I'll ever walk again? Would that be like a miracle?"

"Miracles come from inside," said Kid. "If you want one to happen, it'll happen just like you plan, no matter what anybody says."

"Well, Grandpa, let's make a deal. If I walk again, will you take me up in that airplane you been workin' on? Mama and Grandma say you're too old, but an old man flyin' a plane is like a miracle, and if you really want to do it you can do it, can't you?"

Milt again grabbed the eight year-old's hand and squeezed it affectionately. He flashed out a grin which would have befitted the long-ago N.B. Excitement himself in sheer mischievousness.

"It's a deal," said Kid. "I'm finishing that plane right quick, and just as soon as you walk, we're going up in that plane, just you and me. And I'm flyin' it just like I used to when I was young—not like an old coot with gray hair and wrinkles, but just like a durn stud, man. I don't care what your grandmamma says or how old people say I am. It'll be just like I told you."

DR. PHILIP CLIBURN, the orthopedic surgeon who had been treating the Wellesley boy, had faced one of the hardest challenges of his professional career with equanimity. Years later, after he had retired to a quiet suburban life by a lake on a large wooded tract in Fayette County, Cliburn was to recall that, in a quarter century of medical practice, Tim had been the most seriously injured of any of his patients who had survived.

He had been in a complete coma with two floating knees, clean breaks of all three leg bones just above and below each knee, and had remained hospitalized for two months. When the traction ropes were lowered and the casts were cut off by a small circular saw, the boy was horrified to see that both legs had atrophied completely down to the bone and were covered with a thick mane of shaggy hair. The feet were turned completely to the side, the left one to the left and the right one to the right; with no muscular control of them, the child was unable to move them upright. He was fitted into a gauze covering from the arms down, and a hard body cast was plastered over him in stages, with only a small opening between his legs for his private functions and a steel bar wedged between his two feet to stabilize his legs.

Milt rented a van in which to carry the mummy-like boy home with his mother and sister and a wheeled stretcher for carefully maneuvering him into the house. There the ambitious grandfather became a regular guest. He turned a deaf ear to Juliette's protests that he was only getting in their daughter's way and was ill-adapted to be the child's nursemaid. How dare anyone question his usefulness! This was yet another chance for him to prove that if a difference needed to be made in the world he was capable of making it himself.

Poor Dr. Cliburn, despite having been repeatedly chewed up and spat out by the crusty old ace, had developed an admiration for him. He realized now just how it was that those crazy people of yore had done what they did—with what determination and ferocity they had gone about their struggles. There did not seem to be any room in them for failure, to such lengths did they go to strangle its possibility.

"I'm sorry I barked at you so much," Kid had told the orthopedic surgeon just before Tim was checked out of the hospital. "It's just what I thought had to be done."

"That's okay, General," Dr. Cliburn answered him. "I wouldn't have expected somebody like you to be a milquetoast."

AFTER TWO MORE MONTHS of bedridden frustration, Tim was cut out of his body cast, and many months of hot packs and whirlpools and physical therapy and surgery awaited him before the blessed day when he walked again a year and a half after his accident. He was tutored at home by a roving teacher to stay current in his schooling. To pass the idle hours the child had become an avid reader, striving for mental adventures as a substitute for the physical adventures he was prevented from having. It was to become his habit from then on. His family's longstanding tendency for action over reflection had been stopped dead in its tracks. A boy who had been disposed from birth like his uncle, grandfather and great grandfather to chase after windmills had now decided he preferred to imagine the windmills rather than go out looking for them.

"Now it's your turn, Grandpa," he said to Kid on the day he had thrown down his crutches and Alexandra had brought him back to see the old folks. "Remember that deal we made?"

"What deal?" Juliette wondered. "I don't like the sound of that, Milton. What did you promise this child?"

"I said if he ever walked again I'd finish the DH in my workshop."

"And what else did you tell him?"

"Ain't that enough to tell him? What more can I do than that? Gosh, I'm 82 years old."

Of course, Juliette, Alexandra, Melissa and all the other kinfolks didn't believe the old man would stop at just finishing the plane. They were mortally afraid the frisky octogenarian, who still had the initiative and sense of invincibility of a normal man of thirty-five, would try to steal away their miraculously-healed little boy, pretend he was on a new world-shaking mission of some kind, and attempt to show off for the child by piloting his homemade experiment with Tim in the extra seat. It was a terrifying prospect.

The vintage biplane which had taken shape in Milton's workshop was finally finished two summers later. The cloth covering had been attached to the wings and fuselage, brushed with a doping compound, and had shrunk to a tight fit; and the old man had painted the relic green, red, white and blue with a spray gun hooked to his air compressor.

It was the largest plane any person had ever built entirely by himself, nearly seventeen years in the making. All it needed for the stroke of life was to be towed to the out-of-the-way landing strip at Robin Field, there to have its wings mounted, its tank and radiator filled, and its mastermind positioned behind its joystick.

"First we'll tow the thing out to the field," Kid told Tim in the lazy summer of '79, when school was out of session. "But we won't fly it. We'll let it sit there awhile so your mama and grandmamma stay off our tails. Then a few weeks later we'll sneak off one day when they ain't around and have our little air show."

His bright green eyes glistened like marbles as he revealed this devious scheme to his grandson, and for a few uneasy weeks after that little Tim was not entirely sure he hadn't descended from a madman. In the early part of June of that year Milt oversaw the transfer of the completed plane, with its wings unattached, by flatbed truck from his home workshop to the hangar he rented at Robin Field, half an hour away by interstate highway. There it would rest next to the old Cessna 150 in which he had taught the Wellesley boy's father how to fly. To preserve her own peace of mind, Juliette had insisted on riding with Milt and Tim in their new diesel Oldsmobile as it followed the truck to the airstrip.

All day she suffered in the muggy heat as her husband, the truck driver and another young workman maneuvered the DeHavilland off the flatbed and mounted its wings to the fuselage. It was only when the hangar door was shut that she felt safe in assuming her Methuselah had no intention at his advanced age of trying to fly the machine, though he never would promise that he didn't. She wasn't exactly a green stripling herself and Kid's antics were beginning to take a toll on her. At 57, she was tired of the strain of being married to an adolescent in an 82-year-old body.

"Sure wish I was just a little bit younger and I could actually go up in this thing," Kid said dutifully to his wife, winking at Tim just as soon as he had helped her into the passenger seat of the Olds and shut the door behind her. "Wouldn't that be nice?"

KID WAS WAITING FOR a phone call from Woodvale which would provide him with a legitimate reason to go there. He had known for some time that Rev. Woodrow Wilson, 76 years old, had not been feeling well. The expected call came in mid July from Bertram Johnson, his nephew, the eldest son of Kate, one of his two late sisters. Woody had been diagnosed with terminal leukemia and had no more than a month to live.

It had been Woody's idea that Milt embark on the seemingly impossible mission to rebuild a replica of the World War I model plane for which the two of them had a special nostalgia. This was the very type plane in which a stubborn young bootlegger had smuggled a young Bahamian boy into America. It was only appropriate that the same pilot should now usher the same man out of America and into the next New World where all people must one day go.

Milt told his wife that he would spend all day reliving old times with Rev. Wilson, then return home that night. He wanted Tim, his 12-year-old grandson, to go along as well so that the child might know the ways of old Woodvale. Of course the youngster realized that his grandfather was planning to do far more than he had admitted to his grandmother: to bring the old black man back with him to Robin Field, to take him perilously up in an untried airplane with him, then to land it and ask his grandson to fly in it next.

It never crossed Tim's mind that this might be unwise or dangerous or that his grandfather might not be capable of accomplishing every single thing he set out to do. He had come to the humbling and sometimes bewildering conclusion that many of that century's most notable figures had also reached: that just when you thought the man from Woodvale had pushed you to the absolute limits of your amazement, he turned around and did something even more astonishing the very next moment.

The large metal sign on the outskirts of the country village had become so caked with the flying sand and mud of passing trucks that the words on it were now growing difficult to read. Tim had found the two and a half hour drive boring, had dozed off twice in the car, and saw nothing but a slow sleepy rundown village with a big water tower perched on a hill above a white-steepled church.

In the black neighborhood in the lowlands below Oak Street was a smaller church, immaculately kept, and adjacent to it an equally neat cream-colored wooden house on whose front porch a gray and emaciated elderly black man, pencil-thin and red-eyed, was waiting for his grandfather in a rocking chair.

"Enby," he said, "it's time for you to take me home."

Rev. Wilson's family all came out quietly and waved to Milt as he escorted the man back to his car. All the black community of Woodvale came out of their homes, gathered about the street, and in an eerily silent vigil watched as the pastor was seated and the door closed beside him.

"We'll be back tonight, y'all," Kid said. "The reverend needs to go on a special ride with me before I get too old to give rides."

Silence prevailed in the car as it returned to the metropolis. Both Milt and Woody were reminiscing pleasantly to themselves, not needing to talk, looking forward to their last great adventure together. At Robin Field the minister perked up when he saw his dream brought to life before him, the hangar door raised, and the gleaming handiwork of the self-taught mechanical genius revealed.

"You did it, Enby!" he said with all the energy he had left in him. "Just like I knew you would, man. I never knew anybody that did everything he ever wanted, except you. And maybe me, too, after I met you."

Woody had said few words to little Tim except by way of small talk, but he turned to the youngster and said:

"Some day, boy, when you get old, you won't believe what happened today. So you better watch real close, 'cause people who don't watch Mr. Excitement careful enough say later on, 'Man, no way he did that! I'm *sure* I didn't remember that right!'"

The only modifications to the original model of plane in which Milt had smuggled rum and carried mail were in the installation of a starter switch and the addition of brakes—two innovations without which even the ancient ace would have considered the attempt to fly the plane foolhardy. The boy and the two old men were all by themselves on the landing strip that day. Tim sat on the hood of the car and watched as Woody, with great effort, climbed into the front compartment and his grandfather climbed into the rear. They both put on old-fashioned leather helmets and goggles and scarves, just like the ones they had donned in the springtime of their journeys through the world.

"You never told me what your real name was back when I found you," Milt mentioned to him after they climbed aboard. "I know it wasn't Woodrow Wilson."

"It was close," said Woody. "Woodrow was actually my given name, but my surname was Hampton. Woodrow Hampton. When I told you people called me Woody all the time, I wasn't lyin', though you always thought I was."

"Mr. Hampton," said Kid, extending his hand to the front seat to be shaken, "I'm pleased to meet you after all these years."

Milt turned the key switch, the propellor whirled around, and the home-built machine forged ahead. Neither the pilot, his passenger nor the lone spectator on the ground had the slightest doubt whatsoever about whether the plane would fly. It soared aloft smoothly, and then its pilot put it into a loop, after which both of the men in the plane laughed and cried at the same time. They were both thinking it was a ridiculous joke that the boyish virtuosity of long ago continued in a man already well past normal retirement age, and a pathetic shame that nothing great could last forever. As the plane soared upside down in limbo neither would have felt particularly sorry to crash and expire at that moment. There would have been no better way to go.

When the plane came down and landed safely the emotion of the moment had not been lost on the boy. His heart was throbbing in anticipation of being the next to fly. The dying man was helped from the plane in tears, and he and his best friend hugged each other.

"You know what would make this thing just perfect, Woody?" Kid asked.

"What, Enby?"

"If I had three or four hot young 22-year-old girls in two piece bathing suits ready to jump all over me right now. Wouldn't that be great?"

"You think you could still handle 'em?" Woody laughed.

"The question is, could they handle me?"

The irreverent dreamer then turned to his young grandson and, with a nod to his past, asked him:

"Well, what'll it be, boy? The Kid Special or the Tour for Grandmas?"

"Shoot," said Tim, "you kiddin'? I want the Kid Special. I'm not scared one bit."

The Kid Special had grown considerably milder than its earlier versions above the bovine-flecked fields of dusty Hapeville, but it still involved spins and twirls and it put to shame any roller coaster ride any other suburban boy could get at any amusement park in the summer of '79. The man from Woodvale had come kicking and fighting into the world and he was aiming to show his grandson he had no intention of leaving it ducking and kneeling.

Though there were no loops in the flight as the old man decided that, unlike his previous passenger, this one had a full life ahead of him and needed to be protected; still there were enough turns and swerves to convince the boy that if indeed a Hun or a kamikaze had been trailing them, or if Adolf Hitler himself had been shooting at them from the ground, they would not only have escaped harm, but would have been able to lean out over the fuselage into the rushing breeze and thumb their noses at their would-be predators.

Now the boy had firsthand knowledge of the rush of the wind against the goggles, the roar of the engine in the open air, the majesty of the firmament above, the vast green world below, the tiny dots of humanity scurrying over the numberless little anthills they had built on the surface of the earth.

The noble DH-4 was landed after another 15-minute ride, taxied to the hangar, and pushed mostly by Tim back into its resting place. Only an hour and a half had been spent at Robin Field, but the outing was over. The car drive back to Woodvale was more pensive than the earlier trip had been. The Bahamian minister considered himself introduced to heaven now. He had seen the sky and he wanted more of it, for all eternity. He was not afraid of death.

"Thank you, Mister Excitement," Reverend Wilson hugged his lifelong friend one last time in Woodvale. The respectful neighbors had again converged late that afternoon to witness the parting. "Thank you for everything you've done for all of us."

CHAPTER 39

One Last Hurrah

WHEN SIX WEEKS LATER Woody passed away and was buried, leaving Kid with no one still alive from the early period of his youth, his previously limitless energy and exuberance began to wane.

He was almost 83, and he was having fears that were paralyzing to him: of not being able to discover something new every day; of never again facing a challenge of great difficulty, peril and importance. His grandson had turned into his best friend. Living only a short distance away from Kid's riverside home, Tim came to see his grandpa regularly. Milton was almost a surrogate father for the boy, as Dean was trapped on the opposite coast weathering the fury of what was soon to be his second ex-wife.

With the DH-4 completed, the restless old-timer decided that he and Tim would embark on another project, the construction of a Travel Air Mystery Ship, a vintage racing plane from the 1920's. Alexandra and Juliette flew with them to Wichita, Kansas, where the curator of an air museum had blueprints for the old racing plane. Just as he had done seventeen years earlier, Milt began cutting and shaping spruce wood and welding steel, rummaging through catalogs for aircraft parts to find tires and instruments, a fuel tank and an engine. The teenage boy helped the weakening man with the heavy lifting and the physically demanding chores of his project whenever he visited. And Juliette would say, "It's good for him to stay active—it stimulates his mind and keeps him busy."

But the man who had finished everything he ever started and done everything he had ever wanted to do never completed his Travel Air. Tasks which in his earlier days he might have done in a few hours were now taking weeks and even months to accomplish. Juliette's worries about her husband intensified. Age was obviously wearing him relentlessly down. How much longer would it be before Father Time completely defeated him? Or, perhaps more to the point, what sort of spectacular exit from the world would he invent?

When Tim went off to college in Virginia to study journalism his grandfather was left in a treacherous daily predicament in his workshop: ALONE. Juliette never doubted for a moment that her husband had at least one more trick up his sleeve. Though she had never heard about his clandestine flight with Tim and Woody at Robin Field, the question for her was not *whether* her 19th century heirloom of a husband would try to fly a plane again, but *when.*

Herbert Dawes, son of the late Chester Dawes and a current Boeing 747 captain for Coastal, was one of the general's most ardent admirers. It was he who planted a seditious seed in the nonagenarian's mind in the early part of 1987. Coastal was looking to restore an old DC3 for display in one of its maintenance hangars at the Atlanta Airport. Might Kid know where one was to be found?

"I'll find one, Herbie," said the gray-headed Kid, still limber, mobile, and, though a little hard of hearing, attentive and engaging in conversation. "And, god dammit, I'm gonna fly it once I find it."

He already had subscriptions to every known aviation magazine, and, with spectacles on nose, he pored laboriously over current and back issues of them all. Eventually, he discovered an article about an entrepreneur in Puerto Rico who was using an old DC3 to transport perishable produce from that island's interior to the docks at San Juan. Obviously, every man had his price. What would be his? The gears inside the venerable aviator's head, though blunted considerably by age, still spun around faster than in most younger minds.

Juliette wanted to go with Herb and Kid on their expedition to Puerto Rico. After her bullheaded spouse turned down that idea, she enlisted Tim, who was studying Spanish in college and might be of some service in translating. The college sophomore came home from Virginia one Friday in October, for a preliminary briefing with his mother and grandmother.

"I want you to keep a close eye on your grandpa," Juliette advised him. "Remember: he's ninety-one years old. Most men who were born when he was died a long time ago."

"You're old enough to take responsibility over the situation," added his mother, Alexandra. "I'm depending on you to make sure he doesn't overextend himself."

Of course Tim, who had never regained full motion in his legs from his injury though he could walk adequately, secretly wondered whether his grandfather might not be able to do more things at age 91 than he was at age 19. He certainly had no intention of trying to rein in the madman who was his direct ancestor. That would have been like trying to trap a weasel in a shoebox. Capt. Dawes, who was 56 years old himself and near mandatory retirement from the airlines, was equally indisposed to try to control the old general. He had involved Kid in this scheme for just the opposite reason: to give Mr. Excitement one last stage on which to perform a valedictory.

On the Coastal flight to San Juan, in a DC10, Milton briefly left his first class seat next to Tim and, at Herb's bidding, went to knock on the cockpit door. The captain of the flight had summoned him. Tim leaned out into the aisle and saw a flash of light as the front partition opened, the bright light of the cockpit windows shined through momentarily, and his grandfather disappeared behind the door. Half an hour later Kid came limping back to his seat.

"I'd 'a' still been up there watching from the jump seat," Milt said ruefully, "but when I wanted us to keep going straight ahead and penetrate the thunderstorm I saw right in front of us, the captain decided he'd had enough of me."

Tim knew from that point on that he would have his hands full. In Puerto Rico he thought he was on a lion-hunting safari. His grandfather's salty and occasionally profane utterances in American English he dutifully moderated in his translations for the Puerto Ricans. At the rental car agency in San Juan the female clerk behind the counter was jaw-droppingly beautiful, and Kid stared at her adoringly. She was so amused by it that she almost had to hold her mouth shut with her hands to avoid laughing.

"Gosh," said the man from Woodvale, unfortunately in a place where most of the people actually did understand English, "if I wasn't so damn old and so damn married I'd give you two guys the slip and go elope to a deserted beach with that gal. Hell, if all else failed I'd tell her I was loaded."

With Capt. Dawes in the driver's seat the trio bobbed and weaved their way through lush tropical foliage in a rental van up to the village of Barranquita in the highlands south of San Juan. Like top secret investigators they parked in some brush by a landing strip and within an hour witnessed a clunky and rusty DC3 as it made an approach and landed. Tim went out to the pilot, asked him where the owner of the plane was, and was given a village address which the three wayfarers spent the next two hours trying to find.

Mr. Jose Medellin, entrepreneur and landowner, was finally tracked down in a cramped office above a crowded street in the town center of Barranquita. Negotiations proceeded swiftly, with Kid doing all the talking in English, Tim doing the translating, and Herbert doing the listening.

"Tell him we'll swap a DC9 from the boneyard out in Tucson," said Kid, "plus give him $50,000 in cash for his trouble."

The retired and perhaps inoperable DC9 was of no concern to Medellin and he never expected to get it, but when he saw the old man pull out a black briefcase full of $100 bills his eyes grew wide and he put an end to his haggling. General Harrison was using his own money to buy the plane and donate it to the archives of Coastal.

"It's a deal!" Medellin cried disbelievingly in English, half afraid he was perpetrating an act of larceny. There were handshakes and laughs in the cramped office, and Medellin pulled out a box of fine Cuban cigars and offered them to his American visitors, who politely declined. The identity of the famous man who was buying his clunker of an airplane was never made known to him; and, since the transaction was entirely in cash, it never needed to be.

The Americans said that two of them were pilots and they would fly the plane back today, and Medellin assured them he would return their van to the rental car agency in San Juan himself. When he rode out to the landing strip with them to see them off, he was somewhat nonplussed to find that the older man was the one who sat down in the captain's seat. With ever-widening eyes he watched as the ancient one seized the wheel and held it tight. He had gotten his money already, so it was really none of his business, but if it had been up to him . . .

The DC3 was started, unchocked, and, under the ancient navigator's touch, it roared off into the sky. Medellin's chief pilot, noticing that the old man was still the one seeming to guide the plane as it left the ground, turned to him and said:

"*Qué pasa?*"

Medellin shrugged, lit up another of his fine cigars, chomped down on it and smiled.

Tim and Herb watched in dumbfounded admiration as the aged general, the long ago boy wonder of the biplane, maneuvered the controls of the dilapidated DC3, flew it smoothly over the waters of the West Indies which he remembered almost perfectly from his rum-running days, and landed it at Miami three hours later. Capt. Dawes, though never having flown a DC3, had been prepared to pilot the plane back under Kid's instruction, but Kid was the one who insisted on sitting in the captain's seat and he balked whenever his friend tried to help him from the opposite set of controls. Mr. Excitement was determined that his last flight as a pilot, if this was to be it, would be just as much of a one-man job as his first one had been seventy-two years earlier.

After such a long time at the controls, the old man's hands shook as he was landing the plane in Miami and Herb nearly had to reach in and steady them. But Kid waved him off and with one last defiant burst of energy he landed the piece of metallic junk as smoothly as if he had dropped a feather on a pillow.

"There she goes, men," said Milt when he turned off the switches. "I've taken the aeroplane about as far as I can take her. Now it's y'all's turn to see what y'all can do."

Everything had been done craftily outside the surveillance of reporters and news organizations up to now, but while the old plane was parked in

Miami, where it remained several days, the brass at Coastal announced that General Harrison had acquired a DC3 and was donating money for its restoration. When a pair of younger pilots were dispatched to bring the plane to Atlanta the news media were represented in large numbers to cover its eventual arrival there. But by then Kid was safely at home and out of the eye of publicity, just as he preferred to be.

CHAPTER 40

Remembering a Hundred Years

JULIETTE AND HER TWO daughters were assured (falsely) that the nonagenarian had behaved himself during his Puerto Rican safari, but after he returned home Kid himself soon realized he would never be able to go on any such missions again. He was unable even to drive a car safely any more. The Travel Air Mystery Ship, half completed in his workshop, would remain that way. Nowadays the old warhorse was confined to an easy chair, where he read newspapers and magazines voraciously and was frequently overheard making wisecracks to himself about what he was reading.

The elderly man and his next of kin proudly attended the commencement ceremonies of the Wellesley boy in Virginia, and in ensuing years those of granddaughters Teresa, Autumn and Candace. All of Milton's grandchildren became college graduates. There was no question, in his mind, that they were all vastly superior intellectually to him when he had been their age. When Tim decided to take a job as a cub reporter for an obscure newspaper in the west Georgia town of LaGrange, living alone miles from anyone in a small cabin out in the country, Kid's heart ached because he knew he would seldom see the boy any longer, but he bristled when Juliette and Alexandra suggested Tim was frittering away his talents and was destined for pennilessness in a dead-end position.

"Leave him alone," said Kid. "He's going his own way, just the way I did, when everybody said I was a fool."

When Teresa went to Los Angeles to try to become an actress, her 94-year-old grandfather at least paid lip service to her ambitions, but his loud soliloquies, overheard by his wife at all hours of the day and night, soon convinced Juliette that the prospect of the Thespian life was not entirely rosy in the mind of her Methuselah. She kept hearing him say: "In that line of work you're only as good as the words somebody else writes for you!"

On holidays and special occasions Kid, growing ever more enfeebled and raspy of voice though still keen of mind, would sit in his big chair and hold court while his grandchildren listened. He had started to remind himself of his own mother in his daily habits and sedentary posture and raisin-like skin, except he could hear a little better and rather than growing more sappy as time went on he was growing more witty. On Thanksgiving Day once, after the grandchildren had all begun to establish adult lives of their own, Autumn was asking him how he wanted his life to be commemorated.

"Grandpa," she was saying, "there needs to be a monument of some kind to you and things named after you like there are for other people. What do you want us to do for you?"

"Nothing!" he shot back immediately. "So help me, if y'all carry on about me after I pass away I'll come back to life and wring y'all's necks. I don't want a damn funeral or memorial of any kind. Cremate me and put my ashes wherever you like, and then be done with me."

"Come on," said Autumn, "we can't treat you like that—that's inhuman."

"Treat me like what? I'll be dead anyway, so what difference does it make? When you're dead you're dead, that's it, your feelings are just as dead as the rest of you. What matters in the world is how people treat other living people. Treat 'em right, and that'll be the same as treating me right; treat 'em wrong, and you'll have to look at yourself in the mirror every day and explain why to yourself."

"Oh, Grandpa," said Teresa, clasping ahold of one of his withering hands, "quit teasing. You're one of the greatest people of all time—there's *got* to be something to represent you in the future."

"He's not teasing," said Tim. "He's serious. That's how he wants it, and that's how it'll be. I'll make sure it's just that way when you're not here to explain youself to the rest of the world, Grandpa."

"Good," said Kid. "I'll have enough problems down there in Hell without survivors trying to remind people up here of what I did to get sent there."

Mrs. Harrison began to take extra care of her steadily diminishing husband. He no longer decided what he wanted to eat, which clothes to wear, when to sleep, when to awaken and when to bathe. She took over all the activities he had formerly reserved for himself, paid all the bills, conducted all business dealings, acted as his spokesman whenever members of the press asked for interviews and comments from him about current developments. She virtually became his mother and his nursemaid, all the while steadily denying to others that anything in particular was wrong with him.

Of course something *was* wrong with him, and it was that he was 97, 98 and then 99 years old. She read the thought constantly in his tired eyes, unspoken but still unmistakable: *"I know this must happen to everybody, but I still HATE going through this!"*

"Next weekend Tim's coming to visit," Juliette told her emaciated husband a few days after he turned 99. "And I want you to help him with that project I told you about."

Ah, yes, the project. Realizing that her husband's memory might be in its last stages of alertness though he was still able to recall events of 80 and 90 years earlier with almost pinpoint accuracy, she had suggested that Milt submit to a tape-recorded interview with his grandson about the events of his life.

By then Tim was in his late twenties, living a thoroughly average life, only now with a wife and young daughter to support. The life of a small town newspaper reporter had grown tedious to him, and he had taken a sabbatical from it to join a humanitarian organization before returning back to his old position. For a few years he had taught English in poor villages throughout Latin America, used his skills at carpentry which his granddad had taught him to help rebuild houses in earthquake and hurricane-ravaged areas, and had met and secretly married a beautiful but poor girl named Kayla Vizquel from San Jose, Costa Rica.

To the uproar which this caused throughout the family Kid had turned a deaf ear. "Hush up now, this'll work out just fine!" he had told all the others. "He's just doing things his way, and I'm sure his way will be the right way." When Milt saw his grandson for the first time after the news of his marriage he asked: "Was this your wife's second or third marriage?" On hearing that it was her first he added, with a mock tone of surprise: "See there, now where can you find a gal like that over in this country these days?"

WHEN THE BRIGHT MORNING dawned, October 1, 1996, the centenary of his birth, old animosities disappeared and all the members of his immediate family, as well as his long-estranged former sons-in-law, Dean Wellesley and Mike Lemington, came to shower him with love and respect. Wellesley was noticeably moved, especially when he saw the guest of honor clutching at Tim's hand for dear life.

"I'm worried," Kid said, trembling like a man scared of tumbling over a cliff, "I'm worried about a lot of things."

Elsewhere inside the house Tim's six-year-old daughter, Maria, was asking a steady stream of off-color questions in that persistent way of children. Her favorite hobby, like that of Matthew Adams long ago, was drawing crayon pictures of her great grandfather flying airplanes.

"If Old Grandpa dies, where will he go?" "When people are dead, do they feel anything?" "Will I ever see Old Grandpa again if he dies?" "Can we have a birthday party for Old Grandpa every year, even if he's dead?"

Her father did his best to answer his little girl's awkward questions without scaring her or causing her to break down and cry. Finally, he decided to change the subject by showing Maria an old newspaper photograph of her ancestor from the yellowed pages of the *Atlanta Georgian* in November of 1918. On the front page was a young and handsome man in uniform, the Great Ace of the Great War, his lapel resplendent with the fruit salad of myriad military honors, beneath a headline: CITY GIVES MAJOR HARRISON TRIUMPHANT WELCOME HOME. Tim read the headline for his daughter and he let her hold the newspaper.

"This is how your great-grandpa looked once upon a time." She stared goggle-eyed at the faded photograph, then looked into the next room where she knew the same man now sat.

"Let's go show this picture to Old Grandpa," said little Maria.

The family all gathered around the favorite easy chair of the guest of honor in the next room, and little Maria sat on one of the armrests beside him and held his hand. Teresa put her four-year-old girl Joy on the other armrest, telling her to sit still, while Juliette pulled up a chair next to her husband and her two little great granddaughters. Autumn, Candace and Teresa, three beautiful women in their twenties, sat at the patriarch's feet, thrilling him with their looks of pure adoration. He still had a pulse, the old man did.

"Doing OK today, Granddad?" Candace asked loudly, as had become necessary of late with Kid's declining hearing. He spoke in a slow rasp, rattling all the while he did it, trying to muster enough energy to get the words out and hoping against hope they would be coherent if he succeeded.

"About as well as I can, darling, for someone 100 years old."

"How does it feel to be a century old, General Kid?" asked Mike Lemington, Melissa's ex-husband.

"I guess it's better than being dead, my friend. But I don't know that—yet."

He laughed gently, pulled a handkerchief from his pocket, and coughed into it. Tim gave the old newspaper clipping to him and let him examine it. He held it in his rattling hand and stared at the sepia-toned photograph and the fading type, reading the article's description of the long-dead martial enthusiasm of the public which attended his return home from Europe in 1918. His eyes began to grow cloudy. True to his earlier fears, he had indeed begun to fall into the tendencies of his late mother Madge in her extreme old age, and in the last few months his emotional state had weakened to the fragility of tissue paper. He wiped his eyes with his handkerchief, took a long deep breath and composed himself.

"Yes, there I am. Young and brash. I sure was a stuck up little varmint, wasn't I?"

"You deserved to be proud," said his wife. "It was amazing you weren't killed in that horrible war, and here you are, all these years later, still with us."

He rubbed his handkerchief all over his face and forehead.

"But not for much longer, I reckon."

"I bet you had women chasing after you left and right," said Autumn, trying to cheer up the century-old man. Kid smiled and put his handkerchief back in his front shirt pocket. A sparkle of mischief, as fleeting as the glow of a firefly in the night, returned to his eyes and he winked at her.

"I can't say that I didn't, child. I wonder where they all are now."

The dying man's spirits seemed to be temporarily lifted, and another firefly sparkle lit up both of his eyes.

"Y'all, in the last week or so I've been thinking lots about what I did in this world. What I want for my birthday is to go back to the place one last time. That's what I want today. That's all I want, and I'll go out a happy man."

"What's he talking about?" Autumn asked her grandmother, in a voice too low for Milt to hear.

"He wants to go see Kid Harrison Field," said Juliette.

"Where's that?"

"Let's all go there together and you'll find out. Once my husband gets an idea in his head, even if he is 100 years old, there's no talking him out of it. So we have to go."

Just now little Maria noticed a ragged old hatchet up on the mantelpiece. Juliette had pulled it from the attic with the intention of giving it to Tim and explaining its significance. It was the same little ax Kid had used to chop up Tom Larson's barn long ago. Juliette removed it from the shelf, asked her grandson to come close to Milt's chair, and gave a brief history of the heirloom. Then she let her husband do the rest.

"I know it seems all old and beaten up and useless," said Kid, "but maybe it can be a kind of good luck charm for you, boy, as you go through life." And then he handed the hatchet to Timothy.

THE FAMILY ALL WENT out into their various cars, and, as a vehicular caravan of four, they began the trek southward to the hallowed ground the patriarch wanted to see for one last time. Tim drove the car with Milton at his side in the front seat. The century-old man was in a confused and rambling state of mind, his mouth hanging open as if all his sap had been tapped out of him. In the back were Juliette, little Maria, and Tim's wife, Kayla, who was eight months with her second child. The other members of the family and the former sons-in-law followed in other cars.

The traffic was bad on that perfect autumn day, even along the woodsy splendor of Riverside Drive, which was now a byway linking one affluent suburban neighborhood to another. The ancient wanderer stared dispassionately ahead at the fast cars on the superhighway leading to the south. He paid no attention to the concrete and tall buildings of this now vast and wealthy metropolis; nor to his grandson in the driver's seat and his wife and other kinfolks behind him; nor to the fact that a century ago, on this very day, he had been born. He only thought ahead to what would be his life's last great moment.

The caravan of cars bearing the four generations of the Harrison family stopped at last in a parking lot behind a new hotel a few minutes south of the city. It was late afternoon now and the sun was settling into the western sky. Milton's two daughters came and helped him to his feet and escorted him to a spot a few steps away in the grass. His four grandchildren came and, leaning down, plucked the accumulation of weeds away from a small worn plaque and brushed it clean. Then they all stepped quietly away at some distance to give the elderly man the privacy they knew he needed at that moment.

Though the inscription on the plaque was fading after years of weathering, it was still legible, even to the weary eyes of the centenarian. The message was the same as it had been seemingly forever, and as it would always remain until the end of time.

HERE ON THE SITE OF THE OLD CANDLER
RACETRACK GENERAL MILTON 'KID' HARRISON
BEGAN OFFERING AIRPLANE RIDES TO THE PUBLIC
IN APRIL OF 1923.

The plaque's still-living subject looked out at the field as it was now. For almost as far as he could see, there were enormous jet airplanes in a stationary line waiting to take off, and in the heavens no fewer than two dozen jets were in various stages of descent for landing. It was true, what his long-ago friend had said. Fifty good aeroplanes could almost land out there at once.

For eighteen full hours each day the hubbub went on unabated out here: runways crammed with airplanes taking off, landing or taxiing on them. The first jet in queue now revved its turbine engines, gathered momentum, raced thunderously across the concrete runway and launched itself gracefully up into the hazy atmosphere.

In his imagination, he was seeing not a massive machine capable of flying across oceans and continents, but a flimsy little biplane silhouetted against a bright afternoon sky.

EPILOGUE

A YEAR AND A HALF later, shortly after a spring thunderstorm had swept across northeast Georgia, an 18-wheel rig, carrying two massive steel construction girders, roared too quickly through the serenity of Woodvale and slid off the slick concrete of Highway 17. It capsized into a field, plowing up a large mound of mud and grass.

The driver was unhurt and his rig and his steel girders were eventually towed upright and salvaged. But one permanent casualty of the accident was that a small sign at the roadside, one that had existed in that very spot in one form or another for 105 years, was uplifted from its moorings and crushed and mutilated beyond recognition.

The state highway department, naturally, had a record of what the sign had previously said in its barely-legible condition. Even prior to being flattened by the 18-wheeler, the sign, like an aged stallion, had grown much too long in the tooth. After nearly forty years in its current incarnation, constantly bespattered by the mud and grime of passing traffic, assailed by the natural elements, and marred by the potshots and bullet holes of teenage vandals, the marker had deteriorated into an eyesore.

Its message remained the same, but the older it got, the more it had seemed to lose its resonance with passers-by: WELCOME TO WOODVALE/HOME TO GEN. R.M. 'KID' HARRISON, JR./WORLD WAR I AND II FLYING ACE/AND PIONEER AVIATOR. Young people in particular had very little regard for it. So what if he had flown planes and fought in a couple of wars a long time ago—what was so great about that?

A municipal road commissioner was insistent that a new sign bearing the exact same words be erected to replace the old one: metallic, with bold lettering so that it might be read from afar and at a high speed, and with floodlights at its bottom. There was no resistance to the commissioner until a small-town journalist, the grandson of the subject of the sign, heard about what had happened and telephoned his late grandfather's nephew, Bertram Johnson, who still lived in Woodvale. The words on the sign had to change, he told Bert. The old man had always sworn he would come back from the dead and torment the living if any monument mentioning his name were to be erected after his decease.

His family had closely adhered to the old rogue's wishes after his death. His remains had been dispatched to a nearby crematorium the day after his life ended, and his ashes placed in an urn which rested on the mantelpiece in Juliette's main sitting room, awaiting a fit time and a place for their final scattering. In this regard he had left no specific instructions, considering his ashes to be of so little importance that he had never discussed the subject. And as to any funeral or tombstone or monument or roadway or airport or office building named in his honor or public commemoration of him in any way—on these points the family had served his wishes well, for there had been none of any kind.

No obituary for him had ever been placed in any newspaper. Encyclopedias and reference books concerning the late great Kid's life for awhile had a curious question mark in the spot where his death date should have been. It was a full year after his decease when persistent researchers unearthed his death certificate in the county archives and the missing date in all the literature about him was finally filled in. The news was certainly not gleaned from any proclamations by any of his surviving relatives. He had so thoroughly warned them about coming back from the hereafter and haunting them if they made a spectacle of his death that they were afraid even to mention it to others.

"You will *not* put my grandpa's name back up there on that sign," Tim Wellesley told the Woodvale-area bureaucrats who were inclined to do just that. "There's a better way of reminding people about him. We'll think of something else."

That a commemoration of some kind needed to be placed in the vacant spot was self-evident. Too much of the modest little village's identity, bound up in the news about the greatest person it had ever produced, would perish forever if no token of his existence whatsoever had been allowed to stand. Woodvale needed the sign.

For weeks Tim struggled with the predicament: how to put up a sign honoring his grandfather by not in any way mentioning his grandfather at all. He sought help in the matter from his colleagues at the newspaper, his friends, his sisters, his mother, his grandmother, even from his father, who had retreated back to his hiding place in California. His efforts were in vain. It was apparent that the words would be entirely of his choosing and that he would make the final decision himself.

If the dead really do speak at times to those who are left on earth, then perhaps Kid was stirred to respond to his living descendant's request. For out of the blue, as Tim was pushing his daughter on a swing in his backyard about a month after he began his quest, a few simple words came into his head. They were the perfect solution.

In the early part of June the four grandchildren and their families all converged in Woodvale. They devoted a whole Saturday to building a little enclosure of rocks bound together by mortar underneath the newly-minted sign, which still awaited its grand unveiling on the following day and was draped by a blanket. They filled the enclosure with topsoil, planted a garden of climbing red roses and creeping Jennie, dusted off their hands and called it a day. Tomorrow would bring visitors, the descendants of late friends, most of the current villagers, and the late great flying man's widow and extended family.

On the unveiling day the road commissioner also put in an appearance, and a local television news crew was on hand to cover the event. Juliette had brought the urn containing her late husband's ashes from her mantelpiece, and prior to the unveiling she scattered its contents in the little garden beneath the sign. When she cut the ribbon and the cover was pulled off, all the people were hushed and a few became misty-eyed. Before them was a large dark gray rectangle of cast iron, gleaming with gold lettering and capable of withstanding shots and nicks for all of the foreseeable future.

The sign on the outskirts of the tiny settlement had never been so sturdy, beautiful of appearance, or easy to read. At once it was pronounced a monument that might last for as long as there would be eyes to read it. On top was a simple biplane and beneath it the words, all in gold:

WELCOME TO WOODVALE
One of us
Was all of us.

www.ingramcontent.com/pod-product-compliance
Lightning Source LLC
LaVergne TN
LVHW040825090826
845145LV00001BA/149

* 9 7 8 1 4 1 1 6 9 8 0 9 3 *